Danc Firebirds

— A novel of Africa —

JEROLD RICHERT

JLR Publising

Dance of the Firebirds
2012 Second Edition
by Jerold Richert

Cover design copyright 2012
Published by JLR Publishing

ISBN: This edition : 978-0-9871622-1-2 (paperback)
ISBN: 978-0-9871622-0-5 (eBook)

This book is for my wife, Lorna Rose
with all my love

Prologue

River Saba, Sasos - 869 BC

Comes this to Lord Khamisu of Sasos

by the hand of Ahinadab, emissary of Solomon, king of kings.

Lord,

Upon me it has befallen the unpleasing burden to report the loss of the gold tally to the king. The wine vessel in which it was held safe against the perils of the voyage was taken by a Wak slave in escape when but three days upon the river. For what purpose is unknown but it be for the carrying of water in the dry land. A new tally must now come in haste to Sofala lest the ships be delayed on the south wind.

Part One

The Lowveld - 1967

No colour flagged the coming of spring to the Lowveld. The rains were late, and from the Limpopo to the Sabi River and beyond into Mozambique, the mopani forests were leafless and grey and the wide rivers dry and white under the scorching sun.

On a private game sanctuary bordering the great wildlife reserve of Gona re zhou – place of the elephants – a battered, green jeep careered its way through the bush, trailing a plume of white dust and leaning precariously as it swerved to avoid the piles of elephant dung and broken branches that littered the track. The elderly African passenger used both hands to grip the frame of his seat, throwing quick glances of disapproval at the young driver.

Chris Ryan ignored him. He was in no mood for caution. He crashed through the gears as the vehicle lurched down a bank into the bed of a dry stream; the engine grinding as the wheels churned through the sand, then surging as they skipped and skidded up the hard gravely bank on the opposite side. He changed gear at the top, then suddenly swung off the track into the trees, and the old Shangaan, who had removed a hand to adjust the rifle clamped between his bony knees, grabbed quickly at the seat again to avoid being thrown out.

'Eh! Eh!'

'Well, hold on, for God's sake, Fuli.'

Fulamani clicked his tongue and shook his head, but otherwise remained silent as they swerved around the trees towards a thin line of reeds and stopped with a jerk on the eroded bank of the river. With a sigh of relief, he climbed out to follow his angry young companion down onto the hot white sand.

The waterhole lay in a bend of the dry river, a dark pool stagnating in the shade of a wild fig that stood on the bank. Fresh game spoor dimpled the sand around the pool, but few animals had gone into the water; turned away by the sweet heavy smell and rainbow sheen of the diesel fuel that covered the surface. Shrunken fragments of hide and the bones of those unable to resist their thirst lay scattered about on the sand.

'Bastards!' Chris prodded angrily with his foot at the bloated carcass of a young zebra.

'Someone's going to pay for this.'

Fulamani clicked his tongue in sympathy, although the sight of dead or dying animals did not disturb him as it did his young master. As a former poacher he was used to such things, but those days were past. The Nkosi Wally and his son had taken over the responsibility of feeding his family, so by African tradition were now a part of it. If this business angered them, then it angered him also.

'It is a bad thing, Nkosi,' he said, scowling.

It was the third poisoned waterhole they had found that morning. The first had been less than five miles from Gara Pasi, close to the boundary and, ironically, would more than likely have gone unnoticed had it not been for the sudden increase in animals at the game sanctuary's own waterholes.

Scouting the river for the reason, they had discovered the waterholes had not all dried up as they had first suspected, but had been poisoned - the stink of diesel almost strong enough to overpower the stench of the rotting carcasses.

'It has to be the new game rancher next door,' Wally Ryan had told Chris, his face tight with anger. 'Take Fuli with you and check downriver. I'll get some help and burn this lot. If you find the next hole poisoned, come straight back. Don't do anything stupid.' Wally Ryan had little faith in his son's firebrand style of diplomacy.

Chris's anger increased as he strode back to the jeep. Shooting game at a waterhole after poisoning the other waterholes around it was illegal, and Gara Pasi was their livelihood. The survival of the sanctuary depended on the survival of the wildlife. It was bad enough with the drought. They did not need a greedy game-cropper to make things worse.

Sitting in the idling jeep, Chris tapped thoughtfully on the steering wheel. 'How far to the next water, Fuli?'

The old man hesitated, then reluctantly held up three

9

gnarled fingers. 'Maybe two, three mile. But Nkosi Wally say...'

Fulamani's caution was cut short as the jeep lurched forward, and he clutched hastily once more at the frame of his seat.

The game-cropper's hides were built high on the bank overlooking the waterhole. Two narrow pole shelters with thatched tops, the front walls ending at a comfortable height for resting a rifle on while sitting down. Drapes of green mosquito netting hung from the pole eves above the walls as a screen.

The African cleaner responsible for the hide replaced the canvas folding chairs and fold-up camping tables neatly in position after he had swept the floors, picked up the brass bullet casings, and collected the empty beer bottles. He put the casings into the old paraffin tins by the doorway, then stacked the beer crates outside under a tree, ready for when the truck came with a fresh supply.

His orders had been to keep the place clean and tidy for the visitors. He was not allowed to make a fire, cook food, or wash in the waterhole, but this didn't bother him. Even though it was women's work, it was an easy job, and he was able to play his new wireless all day - as loud as he liked.

By mid-afternoon he had finished his chores. He drank the rest of the warm coke and ate the bun with the sticky, pink icing he had saved from the morning, then he flicked the switch on the wireless to short wave. Using the big chrome knob, he tuned into several foreign stations. He enjoyed going from one strange place to another by only the smallest turn of the knob. Many of the stations he recognized. Radio Mozambique, Radio Zaire, and the South African Broadcasting Service. The Portuguese station was mostly talking. He could not speak Portuguese, but recognized the sound of the language and the name, Samora Machel, which seemed to be every second word. He had no idea who Samora Machel was, and didn't care, he just wished he would stop talking. He taught him a lesson by cutting him off in mid-sentence with a small turn of the knob and tuned into a birthday request program from Salisbury.

He sat in the first hide where it was cool, dozing with his head on the table, the radio sitting on his jacket outside where the reception was good. The music was loud, so he did not hear the jeep arrive. All he heard was the crunching sound as the radio went dead. Then he heard the sound of an engine. That too stopped, and then silence.

He jerked up in alarm, trying to remember if the boss had said he was coming early. Then he remembered the wireless. He rushed out to see two men, one white and one black, sitting in a vehicle with no roof. He gaped at them in surprise, then looked for his wireless. It was squashed flat under the front wheel; a mess of splintered plastic and buckled chrome strips spread over his jacket. The shiny chrome knob had rolled away, leaving a smooth track like that of a centipede in the freshly swept dust. It flashed at him in the sunlight, and he stared at it in disbelief, too shocked to speak, or even to be afraid.

The young white man jumped out of the vehicle and pushed past him into the hide to kick aside the chairs and overturn the table, and the cleaner suddenly forgot about his wireless. He turned to see the black man coming around the truck towards him, a frown on his face, and a gun in his hands, and his fear increased. He started to move away, but the old man stopped him.

'You! Where are you going?'

He glanced nervously at the gun and heard himself speaking, although it sounded like a stranger.

'My wireless is broken!'

'What?' The old man reached out and caught him by the collar, jerking him forward.

'The truck, Baba... it stood on my wireless. It is broken!'

'Do not speak to me about your wireless, and I am not your father. What are you doing here?' The man prompted an answer with a shake.

'Nothing, Bab... sir.'

'Are you the one who put the gasoline in the water?'

'Eh?' He looked at the waterhole in confusion.

The old man shook him. 'Not this one. Do not be stupid with me!'

The angry white man appeared. 'Leave him, Fuli. Get the rope and tie it to those poles.'

The cleaner watched in dismay as they used a rope fastened to the jeep to pull down the hides. It did not take long.

'You! Come and move all this rubbish.'

He helped drag the poles and thatching into a heap and the white man threw the chairs and tables on top. A can of petrol was brought from the vehicle and splashed over the pile, then it was set alight. The two men climbed into the jeep and backed it into the stack of beer crates, sending it crashing over. Chris was about to switch off the engine and look around to see what else he could destroy when Fuli tapped him urgently on the arm and pointed above the trees. The dust cloud was close. Chris slammed his foot on the accelerator and the ancient jeep spluttered, almost stalling, before lurching forward, picking up speed slowly.

He looked for another way out, but the riverine scrub was thick. The turn-off from the dirt road onto the bush track was only a few hundred yards away, close to a bend, and he raced towards it. Few vehicles could go where the small jeep could in the bush. If he could get there first, he knew he would get away.

They were almost there when a three-ton Bedford came around the bend, blocking the road. Chris stood on the brake pedal, using his grip on the steering wheel to lift himself off the seat for leverage, and they skidded into a broadside, stopping within feet of the truck's radiator. Both vehicles were immediately obscured in a dense cloud of dust. The jeep stalled.

Chris pushed hard on the button and held his foot flat on the accelerator, but the hot engine refused to start. Excited voices came from above, a door slammed, then a blurred figure appeared. A powerful hand took hold of his shirt and jerked him out of the seat.

'You stupid little bastard! What the hell do you think you're doing? You nearly hit us!'

Blinking against the clearing dust, Chris saw a big man glaring down at him. Behind him a truck full of Africans, laughing and exclaiming loudly over the dramatically narrow escape. Some of them jumped off to examine the jeep, clicking tongues and seeming disappointed to find it still in one piece. Others were looking down the road at the smoke from the burning hides.

'I'm talking to you! Why are you...' The man broke off to bellow at the Africans: 'What the hell are you bastards shouting for?'

Several voices answered. 'Moto, Baas! Fire!'

The man left Chris and ran a short way down the road. The cleaner was running towards him, waving his arms and shouting.

Chris saw his opportunity and edged back into the seat. Fuli was sitting rigidly upright in his, clutching the rifle between his knees. The engine turned, but refused to start.

The man came rushing back, and once again Chris was pulled out and thrown to the ground. The man's strength was frightening.

'Jesus! it's you what done it. You burned the hides.'

Chris stood up slowly. No point in trying to deny it. No point in saying anything.

'Ja, man! That's what you done, isn't it?' The man's eyes narrowed and he moved a step closer. 'You know what? I'm going to give you a bloody good hiding.'

Chris stood his ground. I won't move, he told himself. The Afrikaner's going to kill me for sure, but I won't move. If he hits me, I'm going to hit him back. He stiffened in anticipation of what was coming. He knew it had to come.

'Get stuffed,' he muttered. 'Poisoning waterholes is illegal.'

The Afrikaner's eyes widened in astonishment, then he smiled contemptuously. 'Jesus, man...' He began turning away, shaking his head, as if disappointed by such a feeble response, then he suddenly swung a vicious backhand.

The blow knocked Chris off his feet. He lay stunned, shocked by the suddenness and power of the blow.

'So... It's to get stuffed am I?'

Chris rolled over and tried to get up. Another blow to the side of his head knocked him down again. He lay with his face in the dust, choking on it as he gasped for breath.

'Ja, man. A bloody good hiding is what you need!'

Chris lifted himself groggily to his hands and knees, spreading his arms to stop from falling over, spitting blood and dust. From under his arm he saw the blurred image of two large boots standing close alongside. One of them lifted out of sight, and he let himself drop. The boot glanced off his ribs, but with still enough power to make him cry out in pain.

'Ja, you little bastard! That's it Have a good cry.'

Chris pulled his legs up to his stomach and covered his

15

head with his arms. His mind screamed at him, He's going to kill you!

The next kick struck him on the thigh, then another crashed into his protecting arms, smashing them against his nose. It was like being kicked by a buffalo. He tried to guess where the next kick would land, tensing himself to receive it, but the kick did not come. Instead, a rifle shot.

A shocked silence followed the explosion. Even the truck full of laborers fell silent as the echo hammered away through the trees. Then the surprised voice of the Afrikaans game-cropper. 'Hey…what do you think you're doing, Kaffir? Put down that bloody gun.'

Then Fuli's voice, apologetic. 'Sorry, sir, but is not good for you to be kicking the nkosi.'

'You give me that gun. Now!'

'Sorry, sir, but is belong to the nkosi.'

'Jesus Christ…!"'

Holding his ribs, Chris sat up slowly. One eye was already half closed, and blood dripped from his nose. He smeared it away on his arm. His ear felt as if it had been ripped off.

'You had better tell that kaffir of yours to give me the rifle before I stick it up his arse.'

Through one watery eye, Chris focused on the blurred form of the cropper. He had moved back and was standing in front of the silent group of Africans, who seemed anxious to give him as much room as possible. Chris turned to squint at Fuli. The old man's face bore a look of stubborn disapproval.

A look Chris knew only too well. The rifle was pointed, unwavering, at the game-cropper's large paunch.

Chris smiled crookedly through his swollen lips. It hurt like hell. 'Maybe,' he said thickly, 'he's going to stick it up yours.'

'You sniveling little bastard. I'm going to have you and your kaffir arrested, you understand? I know who you are. You're from the place next door.'

Chris limped to the jeep and climbed in, and Fuli moved hesitantly to join him, the rifle pointed at the cropper.

Still the jeep wouldn't start. The sound of its reluctant grinding filled the silence, and Chris thumped the steering wheel in frustration. Then a murmur of speculation passed through the group at the sound of another engine approaching. A Mercedes came around the bend and shuddered to a halt behind the truck. Three men got out. One of them was a balding man with a solemn, horsey face that Chris thought he had seen before, and it was this man who spoke to the Afrikaner.

'Anything the matter, Hennie? We saw the smoke and came to see if we could help.' He nodded towards Chris's bloody face and the angle of the jeep. 'Has there been an accident?'

The cropper was standing with his arms folded, a smug smile on his face. 'No accident, your worship, but it's a good thing you are here. You are witnessing a very serious crime. This hooligan burned the hides at the waterhole, and his kaffir took a shot at me with the rifle. He came bloody close to hitting me. I'm going to call the police as soon as I get back to the office.'

'Good God!' The man stared at Chris. 'Is this true?' His expression changed to one of puzzlement. 'Haven't we met somewhere before?'

Chris looked down and shook his head, remembering now who the man was, and suddenly glad of his damaged face. He willed the engine to start. It refused.

The magistrate continued to frown thoughtfully, and Chris turned helplessly to Fuli. The old man put down the rifle and climbed out to push, and there was an immediate rush of enthusiastic Africans to help. Fuli's daring use of the rifle had won him some admirers. The vehicle jerked, backfired, and finally spluttered into life, and Chris drove sedately past the watching group with his head turned away.

'Don't think you're going to get away with it,' the cropper bellowed after him. 'I'm going now to call the police!'

Chris stopped a few miles down the track and Fuli poured water from the canvas cooler bag into his hands so he could wash away the blood. The old man's lined face was still impassive, the sharp, almost Arabic features of his Shangaan heritage showing no sympathy.

Chris was guiltily aware that what Fuli had done had taken a lot of courage. Threatening someone with a rifle was bad enough if you were white. Fuli was in big trouble. They were both in big trouble.

'It is a brave man who takes food from the mouth of the

hyena,' Chris joked, hoping to lighten the mood.

But the lines in the old man's face only deepened into a frown and he remained silent.

'You what?' Wally Ryan was aghast. 'For God's sake, Chris! What the hell did you do that for? I told you not to do anything stupid. Why do you always have to be so bloody otherwise?

'Well somebody had to do it, Dad, poisoning waterholes is against the law.'

'So is burning down other people's property. We could have put in a complaint to the proper authorities.'

'Yeah... sure, just like we complained about the ranchers overshooting their quotas. Nothing happened.' He had been hoping for a bit more sympathy and understanding from his father.

He was sitting on his bed, sipping morosely from a cold bottle of beer held tentatively to the corner of his bruised mouth. If his father was this upset about the burning down of a couple of hides, how was he going to react when he heard the rest of the bad news? He took a deep breath.

'You haven't heard the best part yet.'

Wally Ryan absorbed the news of Fuli's intervention with an expression of disbelief. 'The old bugger did that?' He shook his head in wonder, his anger momentarily overshadowed by surprise. Fuli had never fired a gun in his life Then his expression became serious again. 'Of course, you know they're going to arrest him and throw him in jail, don't you?'

'You haven't heard all of it yet,' Chris murmured.

Wally Ryan sat down with a sigh of resignation. 'I don't know if I can take all this. What now, for God's sake?'

Chris took a long sip at his beer before answering. 'You remember the magistrate who fined me fifty quid for riding a bike on the roof of the hotel?' He didn't wait for an answer. 'Well, he was there with a few of his friends to do some shooting over the weekend. How's that for upholding the law?'

'You mean the same magistrate to whom you gave a two-fingered salute outside the court in front of the whole town?' Wally closed his eyes and took another deep breath. 'Hell, Son. You've really done it this time.'

Chris shrugged. 'I don't think he recognized me.' He grinned lopsidedly, pointing to the closed and swollen eye. 'Because of the disguise.'

'Don't be an idiot. He'll know as soon as he hears your name. Damn! This is much worse than I thought. The police will probably be here tomorrow.'

Chris picked despondently at a smear of dried blood on his arm as Wally sat silently in thought.

Finally, Wally went outside and bellowed for Fuli. He came back to scowl down at his son. 'You've put me in one hell of a spot, do you know that? I need Fuli around here, but now I'm going to have to send him away to his village until I can sort this thing out, and God knows how long that will take. Then Wally smiled. 'You crazy bugger. You really got stuffed up, didn't you?'

Chris forced a weak smile.

'Fancy a little spell in prison?'

He remained silent, the smile fading.

'That's what I thought. Now go clean yourself up while I talk to Fuli. Put something on that eye. Then you had better get some sleep. I have a feeling tomorrow is going to be a long day.'

Wally Ryan had built the stone bungalow where it would have a view of the bend in the river, and the animals that came there to drink. After Chris had gone to bed, he sat on the verandah steps, looking out. It was a still night, with the leaves of the mahogany trees shimmering like tinsel under a three-quarter moon. Dark shadows rolled from beneath the trees; a herd of Zebra crossing the sand to the water.

A perfect night for an ambush, Wally thought bitterly, which is what would be happening this very moment on the Tshingwezi if Chris had not burned the hides. He smiled as he imagined him taking on the game cropper. Tail up and teeth bared, like a grumpy badger with a buffalo.

Despite the problems he would now have to face, Wally felt a strong sense of pride in his headstrong son. He may have acted rashly, but he had acted with courage and for what he believed in, and no man could do better than that. And perhaps it was all for the best. Gara Pasi was his own dream, and as much as he hated to admit it, the time had come for his son to move on and find a life of his own. Hopefully he would return, but for now, Gara Pasi was struggling to survive the drought and money was running short. It would be the perfect opportunity for himself to take the job with National Parks, and for Chris to leave the country for a while. He could not see him go to prison for something like this, not even for a day.

Wally Ryan woke Chris at daybreak.

'Pack your bags, Boyo,' he said cheerily, placing a mug of coffee on the floor beside the bed. 'You're off to Australia. It's where they send all the criminals like you. Don't forget to write.'

The ancient Piper Taylorcraft of 'Aero Clube de Chimoio' trundled heavily through the long grass of the airstrip, its tail swinging as it lifted, and Chris gave a touch of right rudder to hold it straight. At fifty knots he pulled gently back on the stick and the plane skipped lightly into the air. He held it down low, skimming the grass and building up speed before pulling the stick firmly back.

The small red two-seater shot jauntily into a steep turn around the clubhouse; close enough to bring Francesco, the young African watchman, fuel attendant, and sometime-mechanic, running from the hanger.

Chris circled low over the small Portuguese town of Vila Pery, searching the gravel road to the school for the green bus, but it was parked safely under the trees at the gate. He buzzed the school instead, bringing a soccer match to a halt and excited children tumbling from classrooms. He waggled the wings at them in farewell, then followed the main road leading to the coastal city of Beira, a hundred nautical miles to the east.

Beside him on the passenger seat was a bag containing his clothes, passport, and letter of credit for five hundred pounds; enough for a one-way ticket to Fremantle, with a bit left over for expenses.

Wally had driven him as far as the Mozambique border at Vila Salazar, and he had hitched a ride from there with a chicken farmer to Vila Pery where, on and off for the past two years he had done most of the flying for his private license.

Carlos Ferreira, his Portuguese instructor, had been more than helpful, agreeing not only to allow Chris to fly the plane to Beira, but also arranging a lift from there to Lourenco Marques, where he would do odd jobs around the airport until he could catch a boat to Australia.

Carlos had admired his black eye, listened to his story, then flatly refused his request to sleep in the clubhouse until Wally sent the money for his ticket. Carlos had taken him to his home, and the family had overwhelmed him with continental hospitality; filling him with his favorite meal of peri-peri chicken until he was sure he was about to sprout feathers.

The only cloud was not knowing what was happening at Gara Pasi. In the rush to get away there had been no time to reflect, but waiting for the money to arrive, and for his father to phone with news, he had more time than he knew what to do with, and had spent most of it brooding.

The prospect of going to Australia and working on an outback cattle station did not appeal to him all that much. Cattle, sheep and kangaroos were poor substitutes for lion, rhino and elephant, and were it not for the aerial mustering Vince had promised he would be doing, he would rather have stayed and taken his chances with prison. And Vince had made the promise a long time ago when he had first started flying. Circumstances may have changed, and there had been no time to contact him.

He was also worried about Fuli, and felt guilty that his stupidity was going to make it difficult for his father. It rankled that he should be the one in trouble when the game-cropper and his influential city friends were the ones acting illegally, and he still hoped his father's influence in the community would prevail and he would be allowed to return.

It was a foolish hope.

'They went over Gary Singleton's head and sent an inspector from Fort Vic,' his father informed him when he finally called. 'He came yesterday with a warrant for yours and Fuli's arrest. I told him you were already in Australia, and that I had no idea where Fuli had gone. He wasn't too amused, I can tell you.' His father had laughed. 'Did you get the money?'

Chris had been forced to swallow hard before answering. 'I got it, Dad... thanks. What about the poisoned water.. can't you do anything?'

'I'm taking it up with National Parks, but the consortium who own the ranch have truckloads of money and more pull than a herd of elephants. They'll pay the fine and put the blame on the Dutchman to keep their license. In a few days I suppose the hides will be replaced and it will be business as usual. I spoke to a few of the ranchers in the pub about it and we're going to form a committee and start putting on some pressure of our own. That sort of thing has to stop or we'll all be out of business.'

'Maybe I should come back and help,' Chris had suggested hopefully.

'No, son, there's nothing you can do, and I phoned Vince. He's expecting you. Just don't do anything crazy in his airplane.'

Carlos saw him off at the airstrip, brushing aside his fumbling attempts at gratitude with an expressive shrug and an impatient wave, then giving some last minute advice.

'Do not forget there is no radio in Bravo Zulu, so you must fly over the tower at Beira and get a green light before landing. Also, you should follow the road. She is no longer a young airplane. Maybe she will become tired and want a little rest.'

Chris stayed low and on course until he was out of sight of Vila Pery, then he turned south. A few minutes later he turned again, heading back towards the Rhodesian border.

It had begun with wishful thinking as he was brooding over what had happened, and had only became a firm plan after speaking to his father. He could do nothing to stop the weekend slaughter, but at least he could give the animals a bit of a break.

But As Bravo Zulu thumped her way above the inhospitable terrain, Chris began to have second thoughts. He was risking a lot by pulling such a dangerous stunt, maybe even his life, and he did not like the idea of betraying the trust put in him by Carlos and his father. If he had any sense he would turn back to Beira. But neither did he like the idea of leaving with his tail between his legs. If he had to go, then at least it should be for a good reason. To quell his uncertainty, he thought instead about the beating he had taken, and the animals he would be helping, and his resolve strengthened. The Dutchman could not be allowed to get away with it.

The Chimanimani Mountains appeared on the starboard wing, marking the edge of the escarpment and the international border between Mozambique and Rhodesia. Rising crisp and clear above the ground haze, it was the perfect landmark and, not long after, the glint of corrugated iron signaled the approach of Espungabera village.

Chris adjusted course to fly over the airstrip. No planes were parked on the strip and it had no buildings, only a fenced enclosure housing a tin shed and a stack of red fuel drums. He hoped they were not empty. An African in blue overalls appeared from a grass hut nearby and stared up, shielding his eyes from the sun. Chris waggled his wings then reduced power and circled for a landing.

He refueled the plane, then used the last of his escudos

to fill the several glass demijohns he had pilfered from the club canteen and hidden behind the seats. With more than enough to finish the job and still get to Beira, he took off, but landed again a short while later in the middle of a clay pan close to the Sabi river. Relieved, and well pleased with the perfect three-point landing, he spent the next half hour adding the final touches to his upcoming operation.

Hennie Joubert was in the open, halfway between the transportable cold-room and the office bungalow, when he heard the sound of a plane and looked up, and what he saw caused him to stop and gape in astonishment. An aircraft was falling sideways out of the sky. An old fashioned one, small and red, with the wings on top and its wheels sticking out like it was going to land. The engine was making only a soft spluttering sound and, as he stared, the plane disappeared behind the top of the baobab tree that stood in the centre of the building complex.

Hennie started to run for cover, convinced the plane was going to crash, but had taken only a few steps when the engine suddenly roared and the plane skimmed low over the top of the tree. Hennie ducked instinctively as it passed over his head. He spun around to watch it climbing steeply away, then shouts from behind made him turn back.

A dense cloud of smoke was coming from the green thatch of one of the four guest bungalows, and even as he stared in bewilderment, the one next to it began to burn.

He started to run. 'Get water!' he screamed at the

laborers. 'Get the buckets. Quickly! Quickly'

He was too late. The laborers were already running, but not for the line of red fire buckets. They were running towards the safety of the bush.

'Jesus Christ...!' In a fury, Hennie searched the ground for something to throw at them. The sound of the plane passing low overhead interrupted his search, and he looked up once more.

For some reason, Hennie had not associated the plane with the fire. He had taken them as two equally alarming but quite separate incidents, but this time the plane was not screened by the branches of the baobab tree. As it straightened from its odd, crab-like descent, he saw an object fall from it and burst with a dull thud against the side of the cold-room. Within seconds, it was in flames. Another object clattered through the branches of the tree and rolled towards him, and Hennie stared at it in confusion. It looked like a bottle of Portuguese wine, but where the cork should have been was a piece of charred rag.

It took a few moments for it to register, then he ran.

Hennie was no coward. He knew how to take care of himself, and had never backed down from a fight. He enjoyed fighting. He roared in defiance at the climbing aircraft as he raced for the office where he kept his weapons.

The roof of the main bungalow was now beginning to burn. Wisps of smoke puffed down from the thatching, and Hennie screwed up his eyes against the stinging as he scrabbled in the desk drawer for the keys to the gun cabinet, cursing as he tried to remember where he had put them. He wrenched out the drawer and kicked it across the floor.

He was momentarily distracted by a loud explosion from outside that rattled the windows, but he did not stop to look. Getting a weapon into his hands was more important.

He found the keys on the desk and rushed to the grey steel cabinet to fumble with the lock, cursing at the stupid regulations that forced him to keep the cabinet locked. He jerked the door open and snatched the first weapon he saw, a double-barrel shotgun. The boxes of shells were on a shelf above, and he raked them out, scattering them over the floor in his haste. He ripped open a box and stuffed a handful of shells into his pocket, then ran outside, loading as he went, searching the sky for the enemy.

The baobab tree was visible only as a ghostly shadow in the thick screen of smoke that covered the compound. All the bungalows were now blazing fiercely, the moisture finally sapped from the thatch. Even the ground around them was burning. The fuel tank on its high steel frame had exploded, and the Bedford truck standing below was awash with flame and boiling black smoke. As he watched, smoke also began pouring from the tin shed housing the tractor and his private car.

'Magtag!' Hennie began shaking with fury. 'You bastard!' he screamed. 'You bloody pommie bastard!' He ran about, searching the sky, listening for the sound of the engine above the roaring of the fire and the hollow thumping of exploding bottles and cans in the demolished kitchen.

'Kom, you bastard!' he yelled.

He waited with the gun at his shoulder, his finger on the trigger, his face red and sweating and streaked with black. He heard the sound of the engine and ran towards it, searching the sky, his hands shaking with urgency and slippery with sweat. He raised the gun and fired both barrels in the direction of the sound, then threw the gun on the ground in frustration. It was no use. The plane was too far away, the sound of its engine fading rapidly.

Her name was Julia, a leggy blonde, and Chris knew from the first moment he saw her that she was for him. She was an art student. A friend of Vince's wife, Gabriella, and he had been working at the cattle station for a bit over two years when she arrived for a visit. She came with her fiancé, a geologist with a geophysical company prospecting in the area for nickel, but Chris discounted him immediately as unworthy, and set out to win her with all the charm he could muster.

'You are the most beautiful girl I have ever met,' he told her bluntly in front of the geologist when Gabriella introduced them.

For a moment, Chris thought either she had not heard, or that he had overstepped the boundary, for she retrieved her hand firmly and returned his unsmiling gaze with one equally as serious, then a smile twitched at her lips. 'Thank you,' she said softly,' And from that moment on, Chris was hopelessly in love.

He launched his attack from all sides, engaging her in any area he thought she may be interested, but was careful not to fawn. He sensed she would not respond to too many compliments, even if sincere, so he chose his weapons judiciously, picking at her defenses with ones that were not so sharp that she would think him a wise-guy, and not so blunt she would think him a dolt. Shamelessly, he used Gabriella and Vince as his informants, enquiring about her past, her ambitions, and all her likes and dislikes.

When he discovered she had once contemplated becoming a veterinary surgeon, it seemed like a gift from above. He told her about Gara Pasi sanctuary, and how they intended to build pens there for the endangered black rhino shipped from areas where they were being poached, and he was rewarded by her close and sympathetic attention for a full hour. He also talked to her about her art, admitting his ignorance, and he listened avidly to everything she said, studying every expression on her face, enraptured by every gesture, and his interest was genuine. He wanted to be a part of her world.

And although he would cheerfully have sunk a geologist's rock pick into her fiancé's skull, he did not make the tactical error of being rude to him. Rather, he went out of his way to be polite, even helpful, offering to take him as a spotter so he could experience mustering first hand, then feigning only mild consternation at the sarcastic refusal. Neither did he respond to the glares and barbed comments, which the geologist dispensed equally to both himself and Julia.

But Julia did, and Chris watched the rift developing with glee.

Fortunately, the geologist's work kept him away most days, and at night he slept on a spare mattress on the veranda, so Chris did not have to suffer the agony of wondering what went on behind closed doors.

But he did suffer an agony that was almost as consuming, and that was the thought of her leaving. They were there for only six days, and after three of them, the geologist announced at dinner that he had to return to Perth immediately, and that they would be leaving first thing in the morning.

'But I can't leave now!' Julia responded, dismayed. 'I'm right in the middle of my project. We are supposed to be here until Sunday. That's when our return flight is booked for.'

'I'm sorry, darling, but I've had to change it. Unfortunately, work must come before pleasure.'

'Yes, you're right, Barry, it does, and my work isn't finished yet, so if you leave me the ticket, I'll change it back again. You should have consulted me first.'

The geologist shrugged apologetically. 'I suppose I should have, Jules, I'm sorry, but it may be a bit difficult now. They said they won't change bookings at short notice. They only did it for me because it was for the weekend and they had a waiting list. It may be all right if you wait until Tuesday though...'

'You know I have to be back on Monday.' She glared at him, and Chris expected an argument to follow, but Julia simply apologized to Gabriella and Vince for the unexpected change in plan, finished her dinner in silence, then retired to her room to pack.

Chris had been looking directly at the geologist as he spoke, and had intercepted the smug glance cast in his direction. He returned to his meal as though unconcerned, but his thoughts were in turmoil. It was impossible for her to leave. His whole campaign was based on her being there until Sunday. If she left now the battle would be lost.

He helped Gabby clear the table and followed her through to the kitchen, then he took her to the back door where they wouldn't be overheard. 'She can't go, Gabby,' he whispered urgently. 'You have to persuade her to stay.'

'So, I was right, eh? You like her. I knew it.' Gabriella Ridolfo was plump and vivacious, and in her veins flowed the hot romantic blood of her Sicilian ancestors. She smiled knowingly at him, showing the dimples that Chris was always teasing her about.

'I should have known I couldn't hide it from you, Gabby. I'm crazy about her.' He grinned, relieved at being able to talk openly about Julia to someone who knew them both.

'Hide? You think I am blind or something? Of course I know. Everyone knows, except maybe Julia, and I think it is because... well, never mind. Tomorrow she must leave, but don't worry, I have her address, so you can write and tell her of your amore. I think she will lose her boyfriend, eh?'

'No, Gabby, I can't take the chance. I'm going to phone and change her booking. All I want you to do is persuade her to stay if I can. Will you talk to her?'

'There is no need. She will stay, believe me, I know, so make your phone call, but first there is something I must say, Chris.' Gabby folded her arms and adopted a serious expression. 'You are like family to me and Vince, but Julia is like my sister. It was her Papa who gave Vincenzo his first work in Australia, even when he could not speak any English, so if it is just her pants you want me to help take off...' Gabby waved an admonishing finger. 'No way, Jose. It is better she should go.'

'Don't worry, Gabby, you may not believe it, but this is love, not sex. Before she leaves I'm going to ask her to marry me. I have it all planned.'

'Ho, Mama!' Gabby's dark eyes opened wide in surprise. 'So soon? You have known her only three days!'

'I knew the moment I saw her that she was meant for me.'

'Ho! The big amore, eh?' She took a handful of his hair and shook his head playfully. 'You know nothing. You men are so stupido. It is impossible in three days, but go... make your call. I do not want her to go either, and I do not like her choice of man. I will tell Julia to...' She paused, frowning in thought. 'No, that is not the right way. Make the call from the outside office, then you must tell her.' She smiled mischievously. 'And even if you cannot change the booking, you must tell her that you have. It will only be a small lie, and for the big amore it is permissible.'

When Chris returned ten minutes later, Julia was no longer in her room. She was in the lounge with Vince and the geologist, reading. He would have preferred to speak to her alone, but it couldn't be helped. The sooner she knew, the better.

From the kitchen doorway he caught Gabby's eye and winked, and Gabby smiled. She threw down her tea towel to pick up a loaded tray. 'Coffee time!' she sang out cheerily, bustling out of the kitchen. As Chris relieved her of the heavy tray, she whispered to him. 'Two birds…one stone, eh?'

Chris put the tray on the coffee table and waited until Gabby was pouring the coffee before he broke the news.

'Julia, I hope you don't mind, but I just spoke on the phone to a friend of mine at the airport. If you want to change your flight back to Sunday, there will be no problem.'

Gabby was quick to support him. 'Bravo!' she cried, clapping her hands. 'Of course she doesn't mind, do you, Julia? We have so much yet to talk about. Well done, Chris.'

After her initial surprise, Julia laughed uncertainly, glancing at her scowling boyfriend. 'No, of course not, that is good news… thank you… Chris.'

'How did you manage that?' the geologist jibed. 'Bribery?'

'No, I'm a pilot,' Chris answered mildly, but giving him a look that told he would not take any more. 'Let's just say I have friends in high places.'

Chris sat at the dining table with his coffee, to fill in his log book, but his mind was elsewhere. A clear field, crumbling defenses, and a strong ally in his camp. The campaign was going better than expected.

From the kitchen came Gabby's rich contralto raised in song: 'Birds will sing, tra, la, la, la, la, bells will ring, ding-a-ling-a-ling, that's amore...'

Smiling, Chris looked up to see Julia, elbows on knees and mug clasped in both hands, looking back at him from over the rim. She looked down quickly, but not quick enough to hide the trace of a smile, and Chris's heart skipped several beats. It was going much better than expected.

Then, inexplicably, with the battle going well, Chris's courage failed. With the fiancé out of the way it should have been smooth running, but with only two days left, every step was vital, and he became so afraid of putting a foot wrong that he began to stumble. He needed more time, but there was none to be had, and failure, rather than success, began to occupy his thoughts.

And he saw her only in the evenings. Mustering began early, usually at first light so they could beat the worst of the heat, and when he returned to the homestead after servicing and refueling the plane, she was either still out sketching, or painting on the screened verandah in the company of Gabby, and he could no longer find the courage to intrude. His awe of her, and the seeming futility of his plan, suddenly took control.

While Julia remained bright and cheerful, his own

conversation became banal and interspersed with awkward silences, during which, he racked his sluggish brain for something worthwhile to say.

It became so obvious that Gabby spoke to him about it. 'What's the matter, you having second thoughts now?'

'No, Gabby, of course not. I guess it's just that I'm afraid to ask in case she says no.'

'Mama mia! Must I tell you everything? You aim too high, cara mia. How can you speak of marriage when you have not even told her you like her? Forget about marriage, it is too soon. It will only frighten her. if it's right, it will come. But look at the stars, is it not a beautiful evening? So why do you not ask her to go for a walk, eh? When the time is right, tell her you like her very much and want to see her again. Hold her hand and kiss her maybe, just a little. She will not bite you, believe me.'

But the opportunity to go for a walk did not arise. When Chris went back to the living room, Julia had brought in her painting of a gecko - which Chris had already commented on favorably several times already - and was busily involved with the finishing touches. Vince was working on the roster for the next day's muster, and called Chris over.

'Tomorrow is going to be a busy day, my friend. The contractors have put on an extra vehicle for the big paddock and all the jackaroos will be needed for branding. You will have to take old Jack as a spotter.'

'It'll be a waste of time Vince. He can't see that well anymore, and he gets sick. I'll only have to drop him off somewhere. I'll do the spotting myself.'

'I don't know, my friend, the scrub is very thick down there, it may not be so easy.'

'I'll do it,' Julia offered.

They both looked at her in surprise. Vince laughed. 'You? No, Julia, it is not a good idea.'

'Why not? Because I'm a woman?'

'No, of course not,' Chris answered quickly. The exciting prospect of having her with him all day was quickly outweighed by the thought of her being sick. 'It's hot and uncomfortable. I don't think you would enjoy it.'

'Also dangerous,' Vince added. 'And most spotters get sick.'

Julia dabbed studiously at a spot in the corner. 'You asked Barry though,' she said, not looking up. 'Didn't you mind if he got sick?'

Chris glanced at Vince and coughed to hide his discomfort. She hadn't missed his little ploy. 'I didn't think of it... but look, if you're willing, and it's okay with Vince, it's fine with me... I'd enjoy your company.'

She looked expectantly at Vince, who held up his hands and shrugged. 'Hey, who am I to interfere, but don't say you weren't warned. Me? I get sick all the time.'

'I had better get an early night then.' She began packing up her paints. 'Don't worry, I promise not to be sick in your plane.'

Vince guffawed. 'Haw! That's what they all...'

'She said she wouldn't be sick, Vincenzo,' Gabby

interrupted, glaring at him. 'What do you want, a written guarantee maybe?'

The Santa Gertrudas bull snorted with alarm and broke from the cover of the thick scrub. He lumbered into the open then stopped to paw the ground, turning and searching for the enemy that buzzed overhead. The noise came again, from behind, and he spun to face it, his great dewlap swinging, but all he could have seen was a swiftly moving shadow skipping towards him over the spinifex. When the shadow was almost upon him it screeched loudly at him, and he ran from it in terror.

Chris switched off the klaxon and pulled the Maule Rocket into a steep, gut-sinking climb that dropped the speed off rapidly. He held it there pointing straight up, until it was hanging motionless in the sky, then he kicked on the rudder and the plane slipped sideways, the nose dropping sharply. The horizon turned vertical, then gave way to a sickening swirl of blue and brown as they started into a spin. He increased the power and pushed on the opposite rudder to stop the spin, and they turned in a slow circle directly above the running bull.

Chris glanced across at Julia to see how she had handled the stall turn, and was not surprised to see her looking unconcernedly out of the side window, her hands folded comfortably between her knees.

He smiled in silent admiration. In the hot, almost airless cabin, the steep dives and pull-ups, which usually had even inexperienced spotters reaching for the sick-bags, seemed not to affect her in the slightest. And with an artist's eye she had an uncanny ability to spot cattle in the thick scrub that he was sure he would have missed himself.

Chris picked up the two-way and informed the contract crew where they had found the bull, then he guided them in while he circled above to keep it in sight.

The two converted four-wheel-drive bull-catchers raced across the open ground, bucking and lurching as they plunged through the shallow gullies without slowing. They formed up on either side of the running bull. One of them cut in close behind and nudged it gently on the rump with the bull-bar, and it stumbled and fell in a swirl of dust. Before it could rise, the bull-catcher pinned it down with the oversize bumper, and within seconds, the two men had jumped from the vehicle and tied the bull's legs. It was a performance any rodeo cowboy would have been proud of.

Chris waited until the men had finished and were back in the vehicle before picking up the handset. 'Clap... clap... clap...' he intoned sarcastically into the microphone.

His answer came through a hiss of static. 'Stop yappin' and call up the flatbed.'

Chris called up the driver of the truck on which the bull was to be loaded, then called back to the catcher. 'What now... want some more? I'm going to need a top-up soon.'

'Give us a bloody break. Come on down, we're going to have smoko.'

'Don't forget I've got a lady on board, so you will have

to mind your manners.'

A lip-smacking, kissing sound came over the speakers, and Chris grinned. He had been joshing them all morning about what a good spotter he had.

'They think I'm having them on.' Chris said, raising his voice above the engine noise. 'I'm sorry, but they can be a bit crude at times. I hope you have a broad mind.'

She leaned closer to avoid having to speak up, and he got another heady whiff of her perfume. 'Are we going to land?'

'Chris nodded. 'Smoko time, and we need fuel.'

'Where?'

'There, next to the catchers.'

She lifted up on her hands to look forward. 'But there's no airstrip there!'

She sat back and he noticed her hands were no longer resting calmly between her knees. They were gripping firmly to the seat, and her body was rigid with tension, her feet pressed firmly against the firewall.

'Don't worry,' he reassured her. 'Tighten your belt and relax. This thing can land on a cricket pitch.'

He made one slow pass over the area he had picked out, then brought the Maule in steep. He picked a clear spot between the clumps of spinifex, cut the power, and flared out, pulling the nose higher as the plane sank. When the tail wheel rumbled on the ground he dumped the flaps to prevent ballooning and stood on the heel brakes. Before they stopped, he released one brake to ground loop spectacularly in a cloud of dust and face back the way they had come. He taxied up to the vehicles and cut the engine.

'Sorry about that. The ground ahead was a bit rougher than I thought.'

'Wow!' She giggled and held up her shaking fingers, and it was the perfect opportunity. He took both her hands and held them tightly together in his. 'I didn't mean to scare you.'

She smiled, her face flushed with excitement, her eyes bright.

He released one hand and leaned across to unlatch her door, and it was an even better opportunity. Her face was close, her lips only inches away, and it was too much to resist. He kissed them softly, as nervous as a teenager, and the feeling of relief that swamped him when she responded by clenching his hand and parting her lips made him quiver with happiness. He wanted more, much more, but now was not the time. Reluctantly he let her go.

She took a deep breath, 'Wow again!'

Chris laughed. 'You took the words right out of my mouth.'

The ground crew were lounging against their trucks, mugs in hand, and they put them down when he climbed out, to return his slow clap. Julia was still out of view, hidden by the high nose of the plane, and one of the men jumped onto the bonnet of his truck to lower his shorts and give Chris a brown eye in recognition of his performance. His first glimpse of Julia was from between his legs, and he stumbled off the truck amidst howls of laughter. Chris scowled at him.

The laughter of the men faded to an awed silence as Julia approached in red shirt and denim shorts; wisps of blonde hair showing from under her floppy engine-driver's cap.

Chris introduced her proudly, holding her possessively by the hand and still grinning happily. 'Julia is a friend of the boss.'

'We thought you was joking.'

'Who me? Julia is the best spotter in Australia. Eyes like a hawk and a stomach of iron.' He paused to pick up a mug and pass it to her. 'Not like some women I know.'

'You need plenty of guts to fly with a crazy bastard like you,' the head catcher muttered, not taking his eyes off Julia's spectacular legs. 'Congratulations, Miss, none of us is game enough to go up with him.'

'Thank you, but I was really scared silly. Chris is a wonderful pilot though, don't you think?'

The catcher's awed expression changed to a wicked smirk, and Chris groaned.

The smoko was an unusually sedate affair, and Chris's plans to use Julia to settle a few friendly scores with his normally boisterous work-mates fell flat. He had come to like and respect them immensely in the time he had been flying for Vince, and it had taken him a long time to understand their humor and play their games, but he finally had to admit defeat. It was impossible to compete against Julia's presence. He left them to ogle while he refueled the plane from the drum on the flatbed, then took his revenge by flying her away.

They mustered until midday, when it became too hot and they called it a day. Chris was not sorry. his new call sign of "Mister wonderful" was wearing a bit thin.

He climbed to a thousand feet where it was cooler and smoother, and set a course for the homestead. Julia was lying back with her eyes closed, the air nozzle adjusted so the cool air blew on her face. It took a few minutes for him to pluck up his courage, then he reached across and took her hand.

'I'm glad you came. you were a great help. Thanks.'

'No, I loved it.' She did not remove her hand.

The airstrip was two miles from the homestead. After grading a runway, Vince had used a bulldozer to mound a great pile of earth over a steel structure to make an underground hanger. Cyclones were not all that common, but planes were expensive. Chris refueled again from the drums stacked outside the entrance, then Julia helped him push the plane inside.

With six feet of earth overhead and the smooth cement floor below, it was also a good ten degrees cooler than outside. But with the temperature close to forty degrees centigrade, it was still stifling hot. When the plane was secure, Chris filled a bucket with water from one of the two forty-four gallon drums stored in the corner. Julia was standing nearby, waiting, looking out towards the opening, and Chris moved silently up behind to empty the bucket of water over her head.

She screeched and spun around to stare at him in stunned surprise, then she looked down at her saturated clothes and gasped. Chris grinned at her.

'You...! She lunged for the bucket but he held her off and refilled it.

'Allow me.' He poured it over his own head, then refilled it again and, standing close, poured it over them both.

Then suddenly they were clinging wetly to each other. She slipped her arms around his neck, lifting her face, and the bucket clattered noisily on the cement floor.

Chris flew Julia alone to Port Headland to catch her flight on the Sunday afternoon. Although the Maule was a four-seater, Gabby had refused to accompany them to see her friend off. 'You think I have nothing better to do than watch you two smooching? Mama! I have seen enough already. When you come at Easter, Julia, maybe I will see some more, eh?'

Chris and Julia stood holding each other in the terminal as the passengers were boarding, reluctant to part.

'I'll phone every day,' Chris promised. 'To tell you how much I miss you, and how much I love you.'

'If you don't, I'll never forgive you. Now let me go, I'll miss the plane.'

'Just one more...'

The loudspeaker in the terminal called a late passenger. 'Will Mrs. Julia Ryan report to gate one for boarding. Mrs. Julia Ryan... to gate one please.'

Julia pulled away to look at Chris in bewilderment, and Chris nodded, grinning foolishly. 'Yes, it's you. Sorry. I couldn't resist arranging it. I had to hear how it sounded. What do you think?'

She placed a hand on his cheek, letting it linger as she searched his face seriously for long, anxious moments. Then finally she smiled. 'Yes,' she said softly. 'I think I could get used to the sound of that.'

Julia and Chris were married on the homestead verandah – the same place where they had met four months earlier. It was a modest ceremony, with only a few close friends and Julia's widowed mother, who had travelled with her from Perth.

They honeymooned for ten days at a resort in Broome, and returned flushed with happiness and sunburn to begin their married life in a borrowed caravan parked in the garden. Chris wanted their first home to be at Gara Pasi, and they planned to leave at the end of the next muster, after Chris had trained a new pilot.

Lengthy telephone calls and discreet enquiries had established that no arrest warrants were outstanding, and Fuli had long since returned to the sanctuary. It was commonly suspected in the Lowveld community that Chris had been responsible for the petrol-bombing, but no one had noticed the Portuguese registration of the plane, and he was not short of supporters. The consortium's license had since been revoked.

Looking forward to returning and showing off his new bride to his father, Chris could not have been happier.

Then a long telegram arrived from the Department of National Parks and Wildlife. His father had been accidentally killed by a ricocheting bullet during a culling operation in the Zambezi valley.

Idling slowly in second gear along the last stretch of grassy track leading to Gara Pasi, Chris took in the changes that had been made in his absence and felt suddenly inadequate; unworthy of continuing his father's dream. An owner with no sense of ownership.

Three guest huts had been added to the complex, the thatching still fresh, and a barbecue area built on the bank of the river, overlooking the pool in the bend.

A lanky figure detached itself from the shade of a sausage tree and Chris turned towards it, switching off the engine. The changes had not extended to Fuli. He wore the same greasy hat with the hole in the crown that Chris had put there himself with an arrow when he was still going to school, the same multi-patched khaki shirt, and the same serious expression.

'You have come, Nkosi,' Fuli greeted.

'I am here, Old Father. 'It is a sad time for us, but I am happy to see you are well.'

'Yes, but now you are here, and it is told you have found

a wife.' Fuli's expression softened, as if preparing for a smile, but it was not the time. 'She will come here to Gara Pasi?'

'I came alone to bury my father. As soon as we have made the place ready, she will follow. It will be our home.'

'Ah, yes. That will be a good thing.'

'Eighty thousand escudos is as high as I can go,' Chris stated.

Seeming not to have heard, the Portuguese called to the African barmen for another dish of olives, waiting for them to arrive before answering. 'I pay the club a hundred and fifty only one year ago, senor.'

'She had an airworthy certificate then,' Chris said.

The businessman shrugged. 'It is a simple matter. I have a temporary permit until the engineer comes next week from Beira.'

Chris knew he was lying. Bravo Zulu had not been flown in six months. A new Cessna-150 had taken her place in the hangar, and the old Taylorcraft was gathering dust in a far corner along with empty oil drums and a pile of sacks that smelled suspiciously as if they had once contained dried fish. Unfortunately, Carlos had since returned to Portugal, but Francesco, the attendant, had supplied him with all the information he needed, and Chris was confident in his bargaining.

'Of course,' he said in an off-hand manner, 'I can pay in Rhodesian pounds, if you wish.'

The businessman suddenly lost interest in his olives.

Mozambique was experiencing the first ominous gusts from the winds of change, and foreign currency had a strong black-market component in the exchange rate for escudos. 'Cash?'

Chris patted the bulge in his shirt pocket - part of his father's insurance payout - and the man signaled the barmen for two more beers.

'You expect me to fly in that?' Julia inspected the small aircraft with trepidation.

'What's the matter with it?' Chris asked defensively. 'I've just had her all done up.'

'I can see that, darling, and you've done a marvelous job, really. She's lovely.'

'But?'

'I was expecting something a little bigger, that's all. Don't look so put out. I'm sure it's quite safe.'

'Bravo Zulu won't let you down, I promise, and she's perfect for game-spotting. I'll know exactly where to take the visitors.'

'Sorry, my love, I'm sure you're right, but I hope you won't be relying on me to do any of that.'

'Oh?' Chris frowned with disappointment. 'It didn't bother you before. I thought you enjoyed it.'

'I did, but now I have a strong feeling my stomach won't agree. Your child has a vindictive streak in him... just like his father.'

They named their son Timothy Walter Ryan, after both

their fathers'.

Gabriella Ridolfo flew out from Australia to be with Julia at the birth and took immediate possession of Timmy, allowing Chris to hold his son only when sitting down, and after promising not to breathe on him.

'You will make him drunk from the fumes,' she admonished, 'and cigar smoke is bad for babies. I have booked a call to Vince. Why don't you wait by the desk until it comes through...'

As Bravo Zulu had only two seats, Chris flew Julia and Gabby home from the hospital in relays; Julia first, so she could prepare the special surprise she had refused to tell him about, then a nervous and unusually silent Gabby, holding the baby.

Julia was waiting for them at the sanctuary's new airstrip, along with their small group of African employees and their families, including Fuli, his second wife, Lydia, and their four children. When Bravo Zulu came to a halt in front of her new pole enclosure - a necessary precaution against inquisitive elephants - Julia brought the group forward to inspect the new child and greet the visitor from far away.

Julia took Timmy from Gabby and, looking self-conscious, placed him in Chris's arms. She stepped back, dipping a knee in African women tradition, and recited haltingly, but in almost perfect Shangaan, 'I give you the gift of your son, my husband. I pray he will grow to be as his father.'

'Hai!' exclaimed the assembled group, and they began to

sing. First, the clear sweet voices of the women and children, then joined by the deep bass voices of the men in harmony.

'Ho, mama…' Gabby murmured. It was her first visit to Africa. 'They sing like angels. What did you say, Julia?'

Julia gave a brief translation of what she had said, and Gabby could only manage a choked ' Oh, Julia…'

'They are singing a song of welcome,' Julia continued. 'It was Lydia's idea.'

Although he had never heard the song before, Chris could have explained that it welcomed a future chief, but Julia's speech had made talking impossible. Lydia had also included a verse welcoming the visitor as the child's second mother. A sort of godmother, Chris explained later, after he had managed to control his emotions, and Gabby could only smile happily through her tears.

They put Gabby in the Zebra suite, one of the new self contained guest huts Julia had recently finished decorating in a strong African theme, with a zebra skin mat, and Julia's own paintings of zebras on the white-washed walls.

Gabby was ecstatic 'It's wonderful, Julia! And your paintings are better than you ever done. You are happy, I can tell.'

About the sanctuary itself Gabby was less enthusiastic. 'Uh, uh, no way,' she responded to Chris's offer to drive her around and show her the animals. 'I can see plenty from here, thank you. They are very beautiful, but I prefer animals that don't eat people or squash them.'

Gabby stayed for a month and departed with a promise

to return every two years to check on the progress of her godchild, and Julia also promised to visit as soon as Timmy was old enough, as her mother was too frail to travel.

They were sad to see Gabby leave, but with the impending visit of their first paying guests - a group of German tourists - there was still much to do, and Timmy had no shortage of attention with Lydia and her children.

Julia set about completing the furnishing of the other huts, while Chris and his laborers constructed a thatched dining area and bar with open sides so the guests could relax in comfort. A competent African cook with a flair for Portuguese cuisine was hired to take charge of it.

No electricity reached Gara Pasi. An ancient Lister pumped water from the river into a tank, and powered a small generator for emergency use only. The noisy thumping of the diesel engine was not compatible with the peaceful bush environment, and Chris wanted everything to be as close to nature as possible. Hurricane lamps or candles provided light, and the two paraffin refrigerators provided the cold beer and kept the food fresh. A fire under two steel drums provided hot water to the open-roofed shower.

Chris flew to Mount Hampden Airfield near the capitol and completed a conversion onto twin-engine aircraft, with the idea of being able to rent one, when needed, to fly his guests to Gara Pasi in comfort and safety. From a safari company, he bought a second-hand game viewing vehicle.

Finally, they invited a large group of local rancher friends, tour operators and park rangers to a roof wetting.

Gara Pasi Game Sanctuary was ready for business.

Then two weeks before the first group was due to arrive, a farm in the north was attacked by terrorists and the visitors cancelled.

It was a bitter disappointment.

'Well, at least we have their deposit, darling,' Julia consoled. 'Don't worry, something will come up, I'm sure.'

But Chris was worried. The unilateral declaration of independence and consequent UN sanctions had already cut off much of the overseas market. Increased terrorist activity and exaggerated news reports would soon take care of the rest, and he doubted they would get enough visitors from the local and South African market alone to make the sanctuary viable.

But it remained peaceful in the remote Lowveld, and for the next two years Gara Pasi made slow but steady progress. Currency restrictions made it difficult for Rhodesians to visit abroad, so they took their holidays at home, and an agreement with national parks allowed him the full use of the adjoining four hundred thousand hectares of Gona Re Zhou - Place of the Elephants - which was the largest and wildest game reserve in the country.

Then with the handing over of Mozambique by the Portuguese, terrorist incursions from across the border increased, compulsory national service was introduced, and even the local market dried up. Julia and Timmy were often left on their own with only the African women and children, and were completely defenseless.

'You should at least try a bit of target practice, Julia. It's not that hard, and I'd feel a lot better knowing you could protect yourself.'

'You know how I hate guns, Chris, and I'd only be wasting your bullets. If anything happened I'd be better off trying to talk my way out of it.'

'We're dealing with terrorists here, not bloody diplomats. And they're mostly cowards. A few shots in their general direction and they'll take off. Maybe I should teach Timmy. I'm sure he'd be keen to have a go.'

Julia gave him one of her looks and Chris gave up, changing the subject. 'I've been thinking about accepting John's offer of a job until things improve.'

'It seems such a shame after all the hard work. Don't you think we can hold on? This political nonsense can't go on for much longer.'

'No, I don't like the way it's going. We'll put everything in storage in Fort Vic and Fuli can keep an eye on the place until things improve. We'll be back before you know it.'

'Of course we will, darling. I'm sure the government will come to their senses eventually.'

But they never did.

Because of its remote location and abandonment, Gara Pasi remained largely unaffected by the bush war. It was away from the regular routes used by the terrorists, and those who did come through the area found the local tribes uncooperative. The Shangaans were skillful and fearless poachers, traditional hunters descended from the Nguni warriors who had defied even the Zulu king, Tshaka. Inspired and imaginative oratory by political commissars left them strangely unmoved. They attended the compulsory meetings, sang the compulsory chimurenga rebellion war songs, listened with open mouths to the glowing promises of free houses, money and cars, then went about the trying business of staying alive as usual.

The terrorists departed for more fertile areas, disdainfully refusing a headman's suggestion they leave behind their landmines, which had proved so effective in killing elephants on the road.

Chris flew to the sanctuary whenever he could. Fuli had refused his suggestion that he move his family into the house, preferring his traditional huts, but when a few of the locals began pilfering the buildings for their materials, Fuli came up with his own solution to the problem.

He approached Chris in the company of a smartly dressed African wearing a tie, and introduced him as a very important witch doctor.

It was only Fuli's solemn expression and unusually deferential manner that prevented Chris from laughing out loud. He forced his smile of amusement into one of greeting. 'A witch doctor, hey?'

'Yes, sir,' he said in English. Mister Fulamani told me you would like to protect your house from thieves.'

'I do... yes,' Chris replied, his surprise increasing. 'What do you suggest?'

'Very easy, sir. I can place a powerful dead chicken spell for only fifty dollars.

Chris smiled. He knew there had to be a catch. 'That's a lot of money. Does it come with a guarantee?'

'Exactly, sir. All my spells are guaranteed to work for as long as the chicken.'

'Mmm…I see. Well, I don't know, but seeing as you come with Fuli's recommendation…'

'No need to pay first. Mister Fulamani says you are an honest man. You can pay only if satisfied.'

'No, that's all right, I'll pay now. Mister…?'

'Jesus, sir. Jesus Mkonoweshuru.

Part Two

Sabi River, Mozambique - 1976

It was the strong smell of tinned sardines in the fresh morning air that gave them away. Lieutenant Chris Ryan was about to sit down for a well-earned rest when the smell hit him, and he turned to glare at his African companion, who usually carried a few tins in his pack, but Sergeant Mafiko was already on his knees, reaching into a gap between two boulders. He lifted out the flat tin with its rolled-back lid, dipped a finger in the oily residue remaining and cautiously tasted. He looked up and nodded. Still fresh.

They moved stealthily away from the base of the small rocky hill, retracing their steps for some fifty meters before circling the hill, searching for tracks leading in. It was a laborious process. The dull grey light of dawn left no shadow to etch the sharp imprints left by boots or shoes, and being close to the river the ground was sandy and the riverine scrub thorny and thick. There were also many narrow game-trails, used by animals coming and going to water, and they stayed on these wherever possible, carefully pushing aside the brittle spiky branches that had a tendency to screech alarmingly against the denim of their overalls.

Chris was fairly certain that whoever had eaten the sardines was part of the same terrorist group they had been sent to intercept, and that they had set up an overnight camp on the hill. He had no real evidence to support the belief. The sardine tin had the stamp mark of the Democratic Republic of East Germany, a gift to the terrorist movement, but that alone was not conclusive. They were freely available on the black market, even Oscar carried them, and he had eaten several tins himself. It was more an educated guess and his experience that supported his belief. The small koppie with their large boulders and caves were good defensive positions, and with the added advantage of height, reasonable observation points. And this one was close to the river and the heavily travelled paths that were favorite routes for terrorists crossing the border into Rhodesia on raids, or in this case, returning from one. The sardines had been consumed during the night, and more than likely in the last three or four hours. Had it been in the day the tin would have been swarming with ants. It was also standard practice on both sides to eat, and keep watch a short distance away from sleeping positions before moving into them.

They found what they were looking for a half hour later, when Chris was beginning to be seriously concerned about the growing light and the need for concealment; a smudging of footprints on one of the sandy game paths, and among them, the size twelve print with the herringbone pattern that every tracker in the army and police had been briefed to look out for since the Elim mission massacre.

The sergeant did a spoor count, drawing two lines across the path the distance of a single short pace apart, then counting the sharper edges of the heel marks between the lines. There were six, the same number as reported on the pack-radio the evening before, and going in one direction only – towards the hill. They continued searching, completing the circle in case the group had left, but found nothing more, confirming they were still there.

Chris raised his eyebrows at the sergeant and pulled a sour face, and Sergeant Mafiko shrugged in reluctant agreement. The satisfaction of being responsible for the elimination of Rhodesia's most wanted terrorist was a privilege they would have to forego. Having taken much longer than anticipated to reach their position, it was too late now to set-up a proper ambush, and too close to the terrorist transit camp at Massangena – less than five miles away - to risk a daylight assault with only the two of them against six Cuban trained terrorists, even with the element of surprise. And Tongara was sure to have posted a sentry. They discussed it quietly behind the sheltering trunk of a baobab tree that could easily have sheltered two bull elephants, and agreed there were only two options. Either they would have to get the hell out now, before their own tracks were discovered in the increasing light, or call in the yellow submarine.

Comrade Blessing awoke with a start. For several moments he lay rigid, gathering his senses, trying to think what it was that had awakened him. But other than the soft natural sounds of the bush and the faint snores of his five companions from the surrounding boulders the dawn remained silent.

Blessing sat up in alarm, suddenly remembering that he was supposed to be on sentry duty. He peered around guiltily, and was relieved to see that Comrade Tongara was still asleep, his blanket pulled over his head.

Blessing crawled from his uncomfortable sleeping place amongst the rocks and hobbled several paces away to urinate. His feet had swollen during the night, the blisters popped and stinging, and every muscle aching from all the running they had done the day before, even those in his buttocks. He prodded them experimentally and winced at the result

Standing unsteadily, yawning and looking out on the mist shrouded Sabi river below, he made patterns on the bark of a tree with his steaming urine, and thought again about the previous day, and how lucky they were to have escaped. The running had started in the morning and continued for most of the day, with the helicopters and soldiers always close behind. Even now he could still hear the pounding of his feet in his head. It was a day he would not soon forget. With the weight of their packs it seemed impossible they had been able to keep going, but with Tongara pushing from behind, jabbing with his rifle and threatening to shoot anyone who stopped or dropped his pack, what choice had there been?

Even vomiting had been no excuse; Tongara shoving him forward as he doubled over, prodding with the barrel and calling him a woman. Yet only Tongara had eaten, finishing the last of the sardines. No one else had any food, and barely the strength to crawl up the hill to sleep.

Comrade Blessing shrugged off the thought of food. Soon they would be at the camp and have as much as they wanted. He yawned again, long and shuddering, his whole body given over to the ecstasy of it, squinting against the rising sun that was now shining silver and gold on the treetops. In the far distance above the trees something else caught and reflected a flash of light, and Blessing rubbed the grit from his eyes and fixed on it with a twinge of alarm. It flashed again, at the same time as a faint pulsing sounded in his ears. A helicopter.

Blessing felt the familiar tight gnawing of the rats in his stomach. It was impossible! The security forces could not still be on their tracks. The helicopter was less than half a mile away, moving parallel to the river on the far side, its yellow body also catching the sun, and its ominous clatter, at first barely audible, becoming steadily louder, fluttering in his ears like a small insect had been trapped there.

Blessing opened his mouth to shout a warning, but nothing came out except a wheeze. It was like a bad dream. He turned to run, then stopped, suddenly remembering.. He must not panic. They were safely across the border, not far from the base camp, and he remembered now that the Mozambique railway patrol had such a helicopter, painted yellow to distinguish it from the camouflaged ones of the Rhodesian security forces, and the railway line was across the river, below where the helicopter was flying.

Blessing relaxed, feeling weak. It was not easy being a new recruit. He felt proud that he had not panicked and woken the others. You did not want to attract the scorn of your comrades. Especially Tongara. Reassured, Blessing watched the helicopter as it continued its flight down the river. When it was almost directly across the river from where he stood, he became aware that the early morning mist veiling the trees below the hill he was standing on was tinged with red. He stared at it, uncomprehending. It looked very red and very bright, and he suddenly remembered hearing about such a thing from one of the lectures given at camp. It was red smoke. A signal. He looked again at the helicopter. It had turned and was now coming directly towards the hill he was standing on.

Comrade Blessing blinked several times, as if to clear his disbelieving eyes. Why was it coming towards him? Had they seen him standing there? It could not be. Something was wrong. He hesitated for a few moments, unsure, then stumbled over the rocks to his sleeping comrades. *'Vuka! Vuka!* Wake up! The railway helicopter is coming... wake up!'

He could no longer see it, although the sound was loud and getting louder; a thumping and shrieking that beat deep into his ears, and even though he knew it was only the railway patrol, and even though he knew they were safely across the border, still the sound filled him with terror.

Then he saw the helicopter again. It rose above the boulders that had been shielding it, so close it seemed he could reach across and touch it.

Time slowed down for Comrade Blessing. The great yellow monster hanging under the blur of its spinning blades glared at him with its single shining eye, its terrifying clatter becoming muffled in his head, as if his ears were already filled and could absorb no more.

The whistling of it was like the screams of devils, the thumping a distant beating of drums that kept pace with his pounding chest. He felt the monsters hot breath on his face, saw the angry swirling of dust and shaking leaves on the trees and, as it slowly turned, he saw the open side and protruding guns, and behind the guns, the camouflaged faces of white soldiers.

Blessing launched himself towards his pack and the rifle beside it, floating slowly through the air, and even as he floated, the sound of the helicopter, the alarmed shouts of his comrades, even his own thin scream of terror, was lost in the thunder of cannon fire.

The hill shook and seemed to explode. Trees and boulders disintegrated around him. Bullets, bark and granite chips cracked like whips and hummed like bees about his head, plucking at his body, and something stung him on the cheek. The clattering of the helicopter, the explosions and crackling of automatic fire, and the swirling haze of dust and stench of cordite filled all of his senses to overflowing.

Through the haze of smoke and dust he saw one of his comrades- he could not tell who-crawling frantically on one leg, the other leg was gone, the ragged end of his denims black and smoldering above the knee. Another comrade, still wrapped in his blanket, was lifted in a plume of earth and flung into a bush, the bundle jerking and shredding as the shells ripped into it.

Comrade Tongara, mouth gaping and eyes staring large and white, dived past him and rolled over the edge of a rock shelf, and seeing him, Blessing was snapped out of his dream-like state and galvanized into panic. He threw himself over the same ledge and fell into a tangle of bushes and thorny vines. The vines clawed at him, dragging and ripping at his clothes; hooking and tearing at his flesh as he fought his way through and away from the place of death. He came up against a large boulder. An animal had burrowed underneath, making a dank hollow, and he rolled into it, wedging himself between the damp ground and cool hard rock, gulping for breath and shaking uncontrollably as he listened to the thumping of the helicopter. It was now circling the hill. He saw no sign of Tongara.

The firing had stopped. Only the regular clatter of the machine, then a hand grenade exploded above the ledge, shaking the ground. The noise of the helicopter changed. It was no longer circling the hill. It seemed to be moving away, and Blessing tried to quieten his breathing so he could listen, but he could not stop the panting and gulping, and he could not even dare to hope.

When he was sure the helicopter had gone, he eased himself from the hole and stood listening to the fading sound of it; feeling the silence closing in around him like a comforting blanket. A dead silence. He listened for a sound to tell him if any of his comrades were alive, but all was quiet on the hill, not even the chirp of a bird or cricket. He wanted desperately to call out, but he could not, and he stood undecided, absent-mindedly touching the gash on his cheek with trembling fingers, feeling them warm and sticky. He stared distractedly at the blood on his hand. He could feel no pain.

Then through the silence he heard another sound. A brief, harsh, sinister noise that brought the blood rushing back to pound furiously once more at his head and chest. A sound even more terrifying than that of the helicopter. The unmistakable hiss of radio static.

Blessing wanted to run. Every instinct was telling him to run as fast as he could, but his legs felt too weak, and it was too late to run. He scrambled back into the hole and lay huddled in the shadow against the cold damp earth. The Cuban instructor had warned them. 'If you are caught by security forces you will be tortured and killed. It is better to lie on one of your own grenades and die like a hero.'

It was something Blessing did not want to think about. He could never find the courage to do such a thing. He did not want to be a hero. And he did not have a grenade to lie on anyway, or even a rifle, which was still at the top with his pack and blanket. He recalled the earlier hollow sound of the explosion above and wondered if one of his comrades had found the courage to lie on a grenade. Father McBride had preached that to take one's own life was a sin. The priest was a *mabunu*. All whites were *mabunus'*, but for the first time since leaving the mission, Blessing wished he was back there with them. He pulled his legs up to his stomach to make a tight ball and covered his head with his arms. There was a chance they may not find him there, squeezed into the back of the shallow cave, and if they did perhaps they would think he was already dead and leave him alone. In any event, he preferred the comforting darkness and did not want to see when they found him.

Chris Ryan and sergeant Mafiko watched the brutally efficient attack on the kopje from the cover of the baobab tree some two hundred yards away. Even at that distance, the great branches above, some as thick as the body of a full grown hippo, trembled with the explosions, showering them with the morning dew and a few leaves and twigs. Chris felt a stab of sympathy for the sleeping terrorists. It would have been a very rude awakening.

He was not sorry their reconnaissance mission had been compromised. The past twelve hours had been a killer. Parachuting from the Canberra bomber at ten thousand feet, followed by a ten mile hike through dense bush on a dark night, all in enemy territory, was not exactly a picnic. He could do with some sleep himself. With luck, in a few hours he would be home with Julia and Timmy and the war, at least as far as he was concerned, would be on hold for a few weeks.

The attack on the hill was over quickly. Only minutes after releasing the red smoke canister and talking to the pilot of the yellow K-Car as he guided him in, the pilot was talking to him again.

'Tango One, we have four Charlie's visual, all history. Two got away. Want us to stick around? Can't be too long though. It's hotting up down at the camp.'

'Negative,' Chris answered. 'Thanks, but we can take it from here. That was quite a show.'

'All part of the service. Stay on this frequency. We'll watch your back and keep them busy at the camp until you've cleared the hill. Uplift you on the way back.'

Chris double clicked on the transmit button to acknowledge, then dropped the handset back in its pouch.

With the departure of the helicopter an ominous silence now filled the dawn, the awakening birds and wildlife shocked into a state of nervous awareness and silence by the explosions. They waited only a few minutes before approaching cautiously, stopping once they reached the base of the hill to listen again. Chris jumped nervously when the radio suddenly hissed, and he cursed his carelessness. It was the sort of mistake that cost lives. He switched it off and signaled to the sergeant he was moving up.

The top of the hill looked as if it had been worked over

by a bulldozer. The flat-topped acacia trees that had once shaded the area had been uprooted and the slender trunks shredded, the jagged white ends of snapped branches protruding like fractured bones. The smooth grey boulders, like a tumbled heap of dead elephants, were scarred and strewn with branches and leaves. A fine haze of dust still lingered in the still air, and the stench of burned explosive had replaced the freshness of the morning.

The smell of fear and death was there too. An indefinable smell that Chris had come to associate with the scene of a contact. A rancid fish-oil smell, combined with the acrid musk of urine. Four bodies lay within a short distance of each other, limbs twisted grotesquely, and littered with debris kicked up from exploding shells. As usual, there was surprisingly little blood. Most had already begun congealing in clothing, or had soaked into the dry grass and earth.

The sight of the mangled bodies evoked no revulsion or satisfaction in Chris, only a vague uneasiness and sadness. He had seen too many to feel anything now, and too many of their mutilated victims to feel much sympathy. These were not the same Africans he had grown up with; whose food he had shared and whose language he could speak before his own. They may have come from the same tribes, but these were strangers whose brains had been saturated in the swill of propaganda. As usual, he could not bring himself to look too closely at their faces. Unfortunately, Silas Tongara's body was not among them.

They could account for only five weapons, so either

Tongara or the other escaped guerrilla was armed. Not that it bothered Chris much. From experience he suspected both would be long gone, but it paid to be cautious, nonetheless. One of them could be too seriously wounded to run and may be holed up somewhere with the weapon and ready to put up a fight. It had happened before.

While Sergeant Mafiko went through the abandoned packs looking for useful intelligence, Chris called with the bad news of Tongara's escape. He also wanted confirmation of an uplift as soon as possible. It was no place to be waiting around.

He left the radio on and they bundled together the weapons and packs that were still in one piece. Some of the equipment or clothing may be useful in future pseudo operations.

He saw the small cave as he was giving the area a final check. A twenty millimeter cannon shell had blasted aside a boulder to expose the opening, and a symmetrical shape inside caught his attention. He reached in and lifted out a clay jar about the size of a large thermos flask. The surface was splotched with grey and green fungus, as though flicked with a brush, and the opening was sealed. A piece of rock or shell fragment had broken away a section of the base and he could see there was something inside. It looked like a rolled up piece of bark or hide. He stuffed the jar into one of the packs and they started down the hill, taking a different route to that coming up. It was obviously the same route taken by the fleeing terrorists, for the bushes and thorny vines below the rock ledge were freshly trampled.

'Watch out for jackals,' Chris called softly to the sergeant in Shona. They used no other language in the bush. 'Remember, a weapon is missing. We do not want any nasty surprises.'

He had no sooner spoken the words when he stopped, his skin crawling with premonition. He dropped to the ground immediately, not knowing what had alerted him, but something had. He whistled a warning to the sergeant, the trilling chirr of a honey-eater, and searched the trampled bushes for a clue. A smear of blood on leaves less than a foot from his nose caught his eye and he traced the line of disturbed vegetation to a large boulder a short distance away.

'I see the blood of a wounded jackal,' he called to the sergeant. 'I think he is behind the big rock, can you see it?'

'I see it, sir. I also hear the whining of the jackal.' The sergeant raised his voice. 'Come out, jackal! There is no danger. We wish only to kill you.' Sergeant Mafiko laughed at his joke and, despite the precarious situation, Chris shook his head and grinned. Oscar could intimidate a tank into submission.

From the direction of the boulder came a muffled reply. 'Please, *Changamiri's,* friends... I have no gun. I am here only by mistake. Do not kill me... I beg you.'

'Come out of your hole, jackal. Stand up and put your hands on your head.'

'Will you kill me?'

Sergeant Mafiko clicked his tongue in feigned

exasperation. 'Of course, but only if you do not come quickly.'

Following some urgent scuffling, a young African emerged from beneath the boulder, stumbling and almost falling as he hurried to raise both hands high in the air.

Chris and Oscar stood and walked towards him, converging, with their rifles held ready, and the youth looked from one to the other in abject terror, especially at Chris, with his blackened face and beard.

But it was Oscar who placed the point of his barrel against the side of the youth's head. 'Kiss your ass good-bye, punk,' he said in English. Clint Eastwood was his hero. He glared at the youth in such a menacing manner that the boy's knees suddenly folded and he collapsed onto them.

'Please, I beg you sirs! It is a mistake I am here!'

Oscar laughed. 'You don't say.'

'I was abducted, sirs. They came to steal me away from the mission. I did not wish to come, but they forced me.'

'Who forced you?' Chris asked.

'The comrades, sir. Comrade Tongara. He forced me. I did not wish to be with them.'

Sergeant Mafiko rapped the youth sharply on the head with the rifle barrel. 'You lie, *gundanga*, terrorist. We heard about you on the wireless. You were in a contact. Who did you kill? The children?'

'No one, sir. I swear it by Jesus! We were only chased by the soldiers and the helicopters. I do not know why, I beg you to believe me, sir.'

'Okay, Sergeant, let's leave the interrogation to Special Branch. He's scared shitless. Take him down the hill.'

Oscar took the youth by the collar of his denim jacket and yanked him to his feet. He searched him quickly then shoved him down the hill. 'Move, *gundanga.*'

Chris retrieved the bundle of weapons and bags, and followed. He heard the Alouette approaching as they neared the bottom. A few moments later the radio crackled. 'Tango one, do you read?'

Chris dumped his load and fumbled for the transceiver. 'Go ahead.'

'Ready for uplift?'

'Roger. There's a good spot on the river... near the baobab. We have a capture with us.'

The pilot answered after a short pause. 'Sorry, Tango One, we're about two deep in here already. Is your friend a priority?'

Chris looked at the quivering youth. Hardly an important capture. The wound on his cheek was bleeding quite badly, and he looked about ready to wet himself. 'Negative, only a recruit. We'll dump him.' Chris picked up his load. 'You copy that, Sergeant?'

'I got it, sir. Do I take him out?'

Chris hesitated, staring at the youth. He could not have been more than seventeen, and quite likely had been abducted from one of the missions and forced to join the one of the terrorist organizations like he said he had been. This was the part of the war he hated; the killing of the defenseless, and occasionally, even the innocent. There were times when it had been necessary, such as when they had been stumbled upon by a herd boy when observing the movements of a large Frelimo camp over the border. The boy had run, and he had been forced to shoot him, using the silencer. To have let him get away would have brought the entire camp down on them, compromising the mission and probably costing them their lives.

But this was not one of those times. 'Let him go, Oscar. Killing children is for them, not us. And we had better move it or they'll leave without us.'

Chris took an emergency field dressing from his pocket and gave it to the youth, and Sergeant Mafiko pushed him away. 'Run, *umfaan*, boy. Go back to your mission and stay there. Go!' He threatened with his rifle and the youth ran in the direction he had been shoved, throwing hasty glances back in fearful anticipation, but no shots came, only a few small rocks to speed him on his way.

Comrade Blessing did not stop running until he could no longer hear any sound but his own harsh breathing. Even then, he did not stop altogether, he only stopped going fast. He was getting used to running, but never before had his chest pounded so heavily. He could hardly suck in a breath against the force of it.

Finally he did stop, in the deep shade of a sausage tree, but only to vomit, holding onto the flaking trunk and retching, but nothing came from his empty stomach except watery saliva, and from his eyes, hot tears that stung the gash on his cheek. He dabbed at it with the field dressing as he continued on, walking quickly towards the border.

He felt strangely suspended. He should be dead. Who would believe that he, Blessing, had been captured by the dreaded *Skuz'apo*, Selous Scouts, and not been tortured and killed? No one would believe it. Especially Commander Tongara would not believe it. He could hardly believe it himself. Tongara would beat him for lying. The *Skuz'apo* killed everyone they captured, Tongara had told them so. Even women, children and old people who were not comrades, cutting off their heads with the thin wire from a guitar. Yet here he was, alive. It did not seem possible, and he knew they were *Skuz'apo* because of the white man's beard. All *Skuz'apo's* had beards, and the way the man had looked at him, wondering if he should be taken out. Blessing knew what that meant. Everyone knew what that meant. Had there been any water in his body he was sure he would have wet himself. The feeling had been there, even if the water had not.

Finally, Blessing stopped to quench his thirst in the river, then he sat in the shade and cover of the tall reeds for a rest, and to think. As much as he wanted to, he knew he could not return to the mission. The comrades would brand him a runaway and a sell-out, and next time they came for recruits he would be killed as an example, beaten to death with sticks in front of the whole school, as they had done to Petrus. And he could not return to his kraal for the same reason.

Neither did he want to return to the transit camp and face Tongara. Being a freedom fighter was not at all what he had expected. But he had no choice and nowhere else to go.

Reluctantly, Blessing retraced his steps, holding the field dressing to his cheek. It would be something in his favor that he had been wounded. He would say he had been too dizzy from the bleeding to run and had hidden in the rocks. Tongara would believe that. He must remember to dispose of the field dressing as soon as the bleeding stopped. He would not mention the *Skuz'apo* at all. That would be pushing it a bit *too* far.

Chris did not get the break he had been promised. After only one night at home and a day of frenzied activity trying to catch up with work, he was called up again. As a territorial officer and not a regular, he could have refused many of the missions, but with terrorist activity increasing, refusal did not seem an option. And National Parks, for whom he worked, was a government department anyway. They could afford his absence.

Fortunately, Julia was an understanding wife. Chris telephoned whenever the opportunity arose, and it was during one of his calls that he remembered to ask her about the clay jar. With no time to spare, and not quite knowing what to do with it, he had asked her to take it to the nearby tourist museum at the Zimbabwe Ruins.

'I know it was naughty of me,' Julia answered in reply to his question, 'but my curiosity got the better of me. I had one of the men in the workshop cut an opening with a hacksaw. You'll never guess what was inside.'

'A genie who asked you to make three wishes?'

She laughed seductively. 'If there had been, we wouldn't be talking over the phone, and I'd still have two wishes left. There were three sheets of rolled up papyrus with some strange hieroglyphics on them. Egyptian... or something.'

'Are you sure?' His pulses quickened. If true, it could be a significant find.

'I think so. The sheets were very brittle and discolored, but the marks were clear. I wasn't sure, so I steamed one of the sheets flat and took a photocopy. I was going to take it to the museum but I thought you'd want to have a look first. I locked everything in the top drawer of the filing cabinet where it would be safe from sticky fingers.'

'Good. And how is the owner of the sticky fingers doing. Is Tim looking after you?'

'There are some things he can't do.'

Chris grinned into the mouth-piece. He could almost feel the warmth of her breath on his ear. 'Try using some ice. I should be home later tonight. Maybe for a bit longer this time. I'm trying to arrange transport now.'

They spoke of other things for a while, then Chris reluctantly gave the phone over to a line of impatiently waiting men and made his way to the debriefing.

The ancient stone wall surrounding the Great Enclosure of the Zimbabwe Ruins inspired a sense of awe in Chris every time he saw it, but not as much as it did now, with the jar containing its mysterious message on the passenger seat beside him. He sat looking at the ruins through the trees of the car park, strangely reluctant to continue. If the jar contained what he thought it was, then he was about to cause a stir. On the other hand, now that he was faced with the reality of it, he was not so sure.

He and Julia had spent a morning at the library doing some research, and they knew what he had found was important, but they were not experts. There could be a simple explanation and he would end up looking foolish. Certainly, the woman curator, when he called to make an appointment, had not returned his enthusiasm.

'Drop it in, if you like,' she had said in an offhand manner. 'We get quite a few odd things brought in from time to time. But I shan't be able to help you much I'm afraid. It's normally very busy on a Sunday with all the tourists. You had better come early.'

Chris carried the box containing the jar across to the annex housing the museum and went in. An elderly woman with heavy make-up, dangling earrings and blue hair, looked up from behind a glass display counter.

'Miss Grant?'

'Ah, you must be the chappie who phoned from Glenkyle.'

Chris experienced a twinge of misgiving. In the years since he last visited the ruins the museum had changed. It had never really aspired to being a museum in the real sense; more a display of a few selected relics, the bulk of which were held in the National Museum, but now the shelves were filled with miniature soapstone replicas of the Zimbabwe bird, stone chess sets, and other obscure carvings more suited to roadside hawkers than a museum. It had become a tourist trap, and the woman behind the counter looked more a salesperson than a curator.

Feeling like a child showing off a pet tortoise to teacher, Chris set the box on the counter next to a display of souvenir key-rings, and removed the jar in two pieces.

'We had to cut it,' he excused. 'The top is sealed solid.'

'Oh dear.' Miss Grant picked up the jar and examined it briefly before replacing it on the counter. 'Yes, I see.'

'We had to get these out,' Chris explained, 'and I was afraid it would make a mess if I tried to chisel that black stuff away.' He lifted out two curled, brown-stained sheets of material and laid them carefully on the counter. 'I have another two in my filing cabinet at home. They feel more brittle, so I didn't want to move them around until I knew what they were all about. These opened out all right though when I photocopied them. I think it's papyrus.'

He unrolled one carefully and held it out flat on the counter. 'If I'm not mistaken, that's Phoenician or Egyptian hieroglyphics.'

She leaned forward for a closer look. 'Hmm... and you

found this where?'

'In a cave near the Sabi River,' Chris answered evasively, wary of security.

'It's *very* interesting, I must say. Although I doubt it would be either of those. The clay pot looks quite common really, maybe it's of Zulu origin. They used to write in a form of hieroglyphics, you know.'

'Zulu?' Chris was astounded. The woman had no idea at all. He knew what Zulu hieroglyphics looked like, with its typically African stylizing, and it was nothing like this and, as far as he knew, the Zulu's never had papyrus.

'Yes, well... of course it needs to be looked at by an expert, and I'm only guessing, you understand, but I don't hold too much stock in all that romantic nonsense about King Solomon's mines and the Queen of Sheba. The ruins are of a much later period than that. We have a selection of excellent books for sale that explain it. Would you care to have a look?'

'I've read them,' Chris answered shortly. 'And I've also read a few others that tell a different story, and make a lot more sense. But I see you don't have any of those. Why is that?'

She surprised Chris by laughing. 'Oh dear, I didn't mean to disagree with you, Mister Ryan. I like to keep an open mind about these things, but the accepted theory is it was built by the Bantu, and that's the one I have to promote.'

A bus arrived in the car park with a load of tourists and she looked at her watch. 'Here they come, I'm afraid...'

Controlling his disappointment, Chris replaced the jar and papyrus in the box and turned to go.

'Oh, Mister Ryan... look, I have to go to the National Museum tomorrow. Why don't you let me take it along? The director is an expert on these sorts of things.' She smiled encouragingly. 'I'm sure he'll give you an honest opinion. I should be back on Wednesday, and can give you a call.'

Chris hesitated, thrown by her sudden change in attitude, and also a little ashamed of his outburst. And there was no way he was going to find the time to take it to the National Museum himself.

'I'll be away for a while, but my wife, Julia, will be at home. If you wouldn't mind...?'

'No trouble at all, It'll be interesting to hear what he has to say, won't it?'

Ten days later, when Chris telephoned Julia from the pretty border town of Umtali in the eastern highlands, and asked about the jar, she informed him she had not heard from the museum. He considered calling the woman himself, then decided it could wait until he arrived home.

With a few hours to spare before the convoy departed for the Lowveld, and more for something to do than anything else, Chris wandered down the jacaranda-lined avenue to the small local museum, making a solemn promise to himself on the way not to mention his discovery. He was not going to make a fool of himself a second time.

The museum had very little on the Zimbabwe Ruins.

Most of the exhibits were early pioneer, or from private collections, and he was looking at a display of Roman amour when a portly man with a shock of sandy hair and a strong smell of pipe tobacco spoke at his shoulder.

'Best damned display in the country,' he said gruffly, as if expecting disagreement. 'Collected them myself.'

'Very impressive,' Chris answered obligingly.

'Going in or coming out?'

'Pardon?'

The man indicated to Chris's camouflage fatigues. 'Army.'

'Oh... just come out.'

'Bloody politicians.' The man removed an ancient pipe from the breast pocket of his leather-elbowed tweed jacket and scratched around in the bowl with a match.

'You must be the curator,' Chris said, wanting to forestall any discussion on politics. He was becoming thoroughly sick of it.

'Bob McEwen.'

'Do you have anything here from the Zimbabwe Ruins?'

McEwen pointed the way with his pipe stem to a corner display and Chris followed him over. 'These may have come from there originally, although they were found right here, at the Umtali Ruins.' He tapped the glass in front of a flat soapstone figurine. 'The goddess Tanit. Found by a Mister Andrews. The bronze axe-head is from the belongings of a dead witch doctor.'

Chris's interest quickened. He had read about the

figurines in the library. 'Isn't that a Phoenician goddess?'

McEwen nodded. 'The axe is also Phoenician. Be interesting to know how a witch doctor came by it, don't you think?'

'Doesn't that prove the Phoenicians were here?'

'In my book it does, but it really doesn't prove a thing. They could have come from anywhere.'

Sensing he was on safe ground, Chris took the plunge. 'Who do *you* think built the Zimbabwe ruins?'

By the time McEwen had finished, Chris was left in no doubt as to what the outspoken curator thought, and also what he thought of those who could postulate such a ridiculous theory as the present one.

'I have a bit of a story you may be interested in,' Chris offered, plunging deeper.

McEwen listened with a frown of concentration, sucking on his pipe and grunting encouragement as Chris talked.

'I took the stuff to the Zimbabwe Ruins Museum. It's just across the lake from where I live.'

McEwen's frown deepened. 'Is this some kind of a joke?'

Chris returned the curator's frown. 'Of course not. Why do you say that?'

McEwen only grunted. He re-packed his pipe and lit it thoughtfully, sucking the flame deep into the bowl and puffing clouds from the corner of his mouth. He waved the flaming match in the air to extinguish it, then shook his head.

'I don't mean to be rude, young fellow, but if what you

say is true, that was about the dumbest thing you could have done.'

The response was even more unexpected, and Chris bristled at the slur. 'Why?'

'Because if what you found is authentic, it's a ruddy time bomb, that's why. It could do what I have been trying to do for the past thirty years, which is to blow the lid off this whole crock they've been trying to stuff down our throats about the ruins. You should have taken photographs and had the stuff registered with the Historical Monuments Commission, or at least had it legally notarized, then experts should have been consulted. What you *shouldn't* have done, is given it to a bloody shop assistant.'

Chris was dumbfounded. As much by the curator's unexpected anger, as by his own apparent stupidity.

'Those other two sheets... you still have them?'

'Yes. I can send them, if you wish. I didn't realize...'

'No, don't send them, they're too important, bring them yourself, and I'll go with you to Salisbury to get them verified. Meanwhile, keep it quiet.'

'I have no idea when that will be,' Chris said. 'I'll send you the photocopies in the meanwhile.'

'After a few thousand years I don't suppose another week or two will do any harm,' McEwen growled. 'But believe me, son, archaeology can be a dirty business. More back stabbing behind the scenes than you'll ever read about. A find like that could make someone famous, or ruin him, depends on what side he's on. You'll be lucky to see it again.'

Chris smiled, skeptical. 'You're not suggesting someone would steal them, are you?'

'Oh, my word, yes.' McEwen nodded several times to emphasize. 'But that's not how it would appear. They will simply say it is Zulu, like that woman did, or some other rubbish. They will tell you they have sent it to South Africa for testing. Then, months later, if you still persist, they'll say it's still there, and they'll look into it, or its gone somewhere else. In other words, you'll be given the classic run-around. It can go on for years.'

'You can't be serious.'

'I am, my boy, it's happened before, to a Rosette cylinder that could have linked Zimbabwe to the Phoenicians. It went missing from the Fitzwilliam Museum in Cambridge, and a papyrus scroll found by a Portuguese army officer in Northern Transvaal went the same way.' The curator paused to give Chris a prod with his pipe stem. 'Very similar to your own situation, that one, hey?'

Chris shrugged, not knowing what to think.

'Then again, I may be just an old cynic, so why don't we give them a call and find out?'

Feeling once again uncomfortably like a child at school, but this time one about to be punished by the headmaster for losing valuable school property, Chris followed the curator to a cluttered office at the back of the building and waited as McEwen made two lengthy telephone calls. The first was to the National Museum, during which, three different people were summoned to the phone. All were completely ignorant of any clay jar or papyrus sheets. The director was away at a conference and not expected back for another week.

The second call was to the Zimbabwe Ruins Museum, and was answered by what Chris assumed to be a confused African, for the conversation was slow and repetitive - and unproductive. The woman assistant, Cecilia Grant, had left the museum and returned to South Africa.

Bob McEwen replaced the receiver and fixed Chris with a look that needed no words, and Chris grimaced in response. 'I guess I did the wrong thing, didn't I?' he murmured apologetically.

The interior of the Fitzwilliam Museum was in darkness but for a single light in the air-conditioned repository in the basement, and it was in that sterile and temperate atmosphere that Sir Aubrey Fenton-Gower contemplated suicide.

The light came from the diffused glow of the magnifier sitting on the table, which illuminated the papyri he had been working on; throwing light on a story that had been in the dark for three thousand years. Scattered around it were the notes he had made in the deciphering.

A gaunt man in his late sixties, the glow also highlighted the strain in the hollows of Sir Aubrey's cheeks and the dark rings under his eyes as he sat in his chair. It was after midnight, and he had been there since morning.

It was not so much the knowledge he had been wrong

all these years that prompted the extreme thought of ending his life - he had suspected that after the rosette cylinder affair. Rather, it was the disgrace it would heap on his family if it were proved he had fraudulently withheld the truth. For himself, he no longer cared, but if the evidence now lying on his desk were to come into the hands of his opponents, his reputation and career would be ruined, and his family name would suffer the consequences. That was unthinkable.

Deciphering the papyri had brought both pain and pleasure to Sir Aubrey. Despite the damning evidence it contained, he was a scientist, and could appreciate the unique experience of being the first to read what had almost certainly been destined only for the eyes of King Solomon.

He had no doubts as to the authenticity of the papyri, he was a world authority on the subject. Carbon, and other dating procedures would be done as a matter of course, both to the papyrus and the jar, but it would be a formality. He had established the Phoenician origin almost as soon as he had begun deciphering, not only by the distinctive character of the hieroglyphs, but by the content. A report from a man who called himself 'Khamisu, Lord of Sasos', and it was to 'Solomon, king of kings, by the hand of Ahinadab.'

It contained a list of items required by the pilot of a river boat, including; linen, nails and tools and, towards the end of the second sheet, the beginning of what could only be a gold tally, for it began: 'to the care of Ahinadab is given two talents and a half gold from the wild Zenghi. From Sofala is also brought...' That was where the second sheet ended.

Even without any mention of gold, it was enough. It established the missing link between Mozambique and Solomon that his detractors had been looking for. 'Sasos' was the ancient name for the land area encompassing Mozambique and Rhodesia, with Sofala as the port. It was already known that Hiram supplied Solomon with ships and crew, and that they took three years to return with their cargo of gold, silver, ivory, apes and peacocks. And Ahinadab had been the name of one of Solomon's governors, also one of his many fathers-in-law. Given the times and direction of the monsoonal winds, it did not need a scientist to put the equation together, any tenth grade student could do it.

As far as his opposition was concerned, and assuming the missing section of papyri were to fall into their hands, it made no difference. His colleague in Rhodesia had told him they had been photocopied, so it would be simple enough to tie them together and blow his Bantu theory out of existence. Not only would he be discredited as an archaeologist, but his papers on Bantu migrations, which had taken years to compile, would be viewed with skepticism and probably thrown out as well.

That he had not initiated the Bantu theory was irrelevant. He had given it credence by using the findings of McIver and Thompson as the basis for all his other work, and because of his reputation in ethnology, the Bantu theory was accepted, and every encyclopedia in the world subscribed to it. He had long since realized how stupid he had been to accept their findings without checking them thoroughly, but by then it was too late. He had built his career on a foundation laid by incompetents, and it was beginning to crumble. A discrepancy of a thousand years may be forgiven, but not three. His multitude of critics would crucify him.

In the end, it was for the same reasons of family that Sir Aubrey did not put the Browning to his head and pull the trigger. If he did not do something soon, he would be exposed anyway. It may already be too late, and his death by suicide would only make it worse for his family. They would not even get the insurance money.

Before switching off the magnifier and leaving the museum, Sir Aubrey returned the Browning to the safe and locked it, then replaced the papyri in the humidifier and locked that too, taking the keys with him.

He did not return to the museum the following day, or the next, but on Friday night he met his friends at the club as usual. They had been at Trinity college together, members of a privileged group that had called themselves the 'Apostles'. A name that had fallen into disrepute after the 'Ring of Five' fiasco. With the deaths, defections and disgracing of its former members, and the relegation of Ladbroke to an obscure colonial Bishopric, the number had dwindled over the years until only a handful of the original group remained.

Sir Aubrey sat with his two friends at a corner table and told them of his dilemma. Should he circulate the evidence that had so fortuitously come into his possession, and which, he told them untruthfully, could be fake, or should he just quietly forget about it?

'But there's no question, Abby, you're one of the leading experts, so if it's a fake, why not just say so and toss it out?' The speaker was an elegantly dressed man with sleek white hair, and he emphasized his point with a raised eyebrow and an expressive twiddle of his fingers.

'Absolutely!' His companion agreed, swirling the brandy in his goblet then sniffing appreciatively. 'Tell them to go to buggery.'

It was hardly the response Sir Aubrey had anticipated. 'Well, it may not be as simple as all that, Dicky. You see, I can't be sure it is a fake, at least not until I've done a lot more testing. But either way, it doesn't matter. It will ruin my career.'

'Good Lord! You can't be serious, Abby?'

'Yes, unfortunately. My three papers on Bantu civilizations are due to be published any day now. Questions raised at this stage are bound to cause them to be postponed. It may take years to sort out and, as you know...' he paused to smile wistfully at them. 'We don't have too many of those left.'

'I'm not surprised you look tired. You must be worried sick.'

'Death warmed up, if you ask me... so let me get this straight, Abby. Are you saying you have been wrong all these years?'

Sir Aubrey's smile stiffened. 'I'm not sure that I am, Roly, but we all make mistakes, especially in this business.'

'So if you have the stuff, why not sit on it?'

'I don't have all of it, only half. The fellow who found the jar still has the other half, and I have good reason to believe he is not one of my followers. It's more than likely he only sent a sample to test the reaction and has the rest locked away. I can't take the chance. If I sit on it and more suddenly comes to light in the hands of my opposition, it will only make it worse.'

'Yes, I suppose you're right.'

'So, what do you propose to do about it?'

Sir Aubrey signaled for the steward and ordered two more brandies - his own was barely touched. 'Well, you chaps are the experts in this sort of thing, I was hoping you could tell *me*.'

They discussed the problem for a while without coming to any conclusion other than that something would have to be done.

'We can't have you being ridiculed by the Philistines at this time of life, can we? I mean, even if you've been wrong all these years, what does it matter? After all, it's only a pile of rubble in the jungle.'

Surrounded as it was by African Tribal Trust lands, and with only one storm-eroded track linking it to the nearest town fifteen miles away, Saint Luke's Mission was hardly the ideal seat for the Bishop of Victoria. Nor was it an imposing one. The mud brick walls were unpainted and daubed with political graffiti, and the bare earth surrounding the scattered buildings had been trampled hard and smooth by countless bare feet.

There had been other, less isolated locations Bishop Ladbroke could have chosen, but it was the very isolation of St. Luke's that had attracted him. Also, set away from the hubbub of classrooms and dormitories, was a small building he could use exclusively for himself, where he could have his clandestine meetings without fear of being seen or heard.

The meetings were usually unplanned and late at night. A tentative knock on the door or tapping on the window, followed by requests for food, medical supplies or information. Occasionally there were also warnings of landmines or ambushes on the road when security forces were in the area. He was also informed when students or teachers left to join the freedom fighters, so he could arrange for their records to be removed from the files.

As a man of God he sympathized with their cause and helped where he could, but sympathizers and informers were on both sides, and it was dangerous. Several times he had been questioned by the police, and was still under suspicion, but so far they had been unable to obtain sufficient evidence to deport him as they had threatened.

The meeting the Bishop had asked for after receiving the letter from his brother was the first he had arranged on his own behalf, and the reason did not rest easily on his conscience. He had all but forgotten the unpleasant affair that had led to his exile, and being reminded of it in such an oblique manner, by his own brother, was a nasty shock.

He had no illusions as to the consequences if he refused the bizarre request. He would be saying good-bye to his beloved England forever.

The Bishop retired early to his study on the night of the meeting. With a storm threatening it was oppressively hot and humid, and he knew sleep would be impossible. He poured himself a double brandy and sank into his leather armchair.

He would stress there must be no loss of life. That was imperative. It was bad enough he had been forced to live with his conscience for the past ten years. He did not think he could live with himself any longer if anyone were to be killed over this ridiculous business.

Bishop Ladbroke was asleep in his armchair when an African teacher woke him at three in the morning, shaking him gently by the shoulder. 'Right Reverend... wake up. Comrade Tongara is here...'

The telephone rang as the family was finishing dinner. Julia answered it in the kitchen. She spoke for a while, then hung up and returned to the table.

'It was John,' she informed Chris. 'He wants to know if you can drop off the game-count reports from last month. He's leaving first thing in the morning.'

'Damn! I forgot about that. And I still have to do the blasted copies.'

'I told him you would bring them after dinner. You can

stop at the office on the way.'

He gave an exaggerated sigh and squeezed her thigh as she sat down, letting his hand linger. 'It's a good thing someone's in charge around here.' After eight years of marriage he still found it difficult to keep his hands off her.

'Can I come, Daddy?'

'No, Timmy,' Julia answered for him. 'You can finish your dinner then help me wash up. And stop feeding the dog under the table!' She went to the back door and opened it. 'Come on, Chaka... Out! And take your fleas with you.'

The German Shepherd gave her a reproachful look as he slunk out.

'I'll take mine as well,' Chris said, following the dog.

'Want me to open the gates?'

'I'll do it!' Timmy shouted. He pushed away from the table and rushed through the door before anyone could object.

Chris laughed. 'Anything to get out of eating vegetables.'

'Tie the dog up first, Timmy,' Julia called, then to Chris. 'You had better hurry, darling, I think we're in for another storm.'

'I shouldn't be more than half an hour.'

The dog started barking furiously at the end of his chain as Chris waited in the Land-Rover for Timmy to open the security gates. He switched on the headlights and caught a fleeting movement in the dark bush outside the fence. A foraging hippo.

He helped Timmy close and lock the gates, muttering

under his breath as he forced them together. 'I've told you before not to swing on them, Tim.'

'Sorry Dad.'

Timmy ran back to the house, shouting at the dog to be quiet, and Chris drove away. The security gates were a nuisance. There had never been a terrorist presence in the park, but at least they kept the hippos out of the garden.

He copied the reports, then drove to the warden's house to deliver them.

John Montgomery came out to meet him. 'Sorry to call you away,' he apologized. 'Come in and meet Marge's niece from Johannesburg. When she heard you were a Selous Scout she made me promise to introduce you. Hope you don't mind.'

When he saw her, Chris didn't mind at all. She was stunning. Tall and sleek, the typical big city girl, and made up like an advertisement in a glossy magazine. Her hair was cut short in a spiky, boyish style that accentuated the size of her eyes, and her tanned legs below tight shorts put even Julia's to shame.

'John has told me so much about you,' she murmured, offering her hand. She seemed in no hurry to have it back. 'I've been dying to meet you. I hear you're one of the famous Scouts we keep hearing about in the news.'

Chris grinned. 'Notorious, is more like it.'

'An officer and a gentleman,' the warden's wife remarked, 'and happily married, Angela, in case you have any ideas.'

'Aunt Marge! How can you say such a thing?' She smiled coyly at Chris.

John Montgomery brought Chris a beer and they talked, mainly about various animals in the park and the recent game count Chris had just completed in his plane.

'You have a plane?' She untwisted her long legs and moved forward onto the edge of her seat. Chris had been acutely aware that her eyes had seldom left him, even when he hadn't been doing the talking.

'Just a beat-up old Piper Taylorcraft.'

'Chris used to do aerial mustering in Australia,' John Montgomery explained. 'If you ask him nicely, I'm sure he'll take you up and show you the park from the air.'

Marge Montgomery glanced sharply at her husband. She seemed about to say something, then changed her mind as a crack of thunder sounded. The storm was getting closer. Chris put down his empty glass and looked guiltily at his watch. He had been away over an hour. 'I must be going. I promised not to be long. If the weather is good I'll pick you up early,' he told her. 'Less bumpy then.'

'Pick me up any time you like,' she said, smiling and holding his eyes. 'I'm looking forward to it.'

Chris felt his skin prickle. She was coming on faster than a charging lioness. If she wore the shorts tomorrow, he was going to have a hard time looking where he was going. An explosion rattled the windows, making them all jump. For an instant, Chris and John Montgomery stared at each other in shock, both knowing what it was, but not wanting to believe. It was not a crack of thunder, nor was it the deep sound of an exploding landmine. It was the unmistakable double explosion of an RPG-7 rocket.

Chris charged out.

'Wait! I'll get my rifle and come with you!' the warden shouted after him.

'No!' Chris shouted back. 'Close the gates then stay inside and put out the lights. Get on the radio.'

Another explosion came as Chris flung himself into the Land-Rover. Another rocket. Then the rattle of automatic firing.

It began to rain. Mud streaked the windscreen, making it difficult to see. He stuck his head out through the side window, squinting against the stinging rain, pushing his foot flat on the pedal, and cursing the sluggishness of the vehicle that was made heavy with mine-proofing.

He also prayed. 'Oh God, no. Please God....don't let it be the house...'

His mind spun, trying to think of the alternatives. It could be they had blown up the new fish-breeding tanks. Or maybe the shed housing the tractor and pumps. They would have no reason to attack the house. It had a security fence...

But it was the house. He first saw the glow through the trees then, as he skidded around the last bend of the dirt road, he saw the flames. The entire wood-framed house was burning; the flames leaping from the casement windows and lighting up the shrubs and flowers in the garden.

Chris felt black despair, like an iron claw clutching at

his chest, and he fought against it, screaming out in defiance. 'God, no! Julia... Oh, Christ...' He charged at the gates with his foot hard against the floorboard.

He saw Timmy running across the lawn. The dog, dragging his chain with a broken piece of wood bouncing at the end of it, was running to intercept. Hope surged, swamping him in a wave of relief. Timmy and the dog were all right. Julia must be too. He searched for her in the headlights, and in the flame-lit garden, then noticed Timmy was running towards the gate. Running as fast as his short legs could carry him - directly into the path of the Land-Rover.

Chris screamed at him through the open window. 'No, Timmy! Get out of the way! Get away!' But the wind snatched at his voice, and Timmy was already at the gate. He stood there, transfixed by the headlights, staring into them, seeming uncertain as the Land-Rover raced towards him.

It was too late to try and brake the overweight vehicle. Chris swerved to the side, aiming deliberately for the drainage ditch at the edge of the road, and the Land-Rover slewed wildly. And in the same instant as he swung on the wheel, and while the lights were still on the road, Chris saw the circular muddy depression close to the gate, towards which, he was sliding, out of control.

The landmine exploded under the left front wheel. It felt as if he had slammed into a concrete wall. Bright light filled his head as it struck the cabin roof, and a whirling, spinning sensation accompanied him over the edge into darkness.

Regularly every week, Fuli walked the four miles with his family to visit a friend who owned the store where he bought his supplies, and once a month the friend would take him in his old truck to the small town of Chiredzi, where he withdrew his wages from the Post Office Savings Account Chris had opened for him.

On those occasions they usually returned late, and Fuli and his family would stay the night. It was not wise to travel through such wild country in the dark with only an axe, and with a wife and four children to protect.

It was after one of his trips, while he was outside distributing the supplies he had bought amongst Lydia and the children for carrying, that he heard on his friend's radio that another terrorist attack had occurred. He did not hear the details. The storekeeper's son switched to another station before they were announced.

Bishop Percival Ladbroke heard about the attack on the RBC as he was shaving in preparation for morning prayers, and he was unable to finish for the shaking of his hand. With head lowered, he stared at the foam in the basin, watching without comprehension as it slowly turned pink with the blood dripping from a nick on his chin. Something must have gone wrong. He had told Tongara there was to be no spilling of blood.

Gabriella Ridolfo heard the news on the Australian Broadcasting Service as she was vacuuming the lounge, and hurried to switch off the noisy machine so she could listen. No details were available, as relatives in Australia had not yet been informed, but Gabby knew.

Moving as if great weights had been tied to her limbs, and with her heart beating so savagely in her breast she could barely breathe, she went to the telephone.

She was still sitting on the floor beside it, eyes swollen, when Vince came in for lunch. 'It's Julia,' she said woodenly before he could ask. 'She was killed by terrorists, Vince. I have to go.'

Timmy was still under observation in the hospital and could not attend the service. He had suffered mild concussion, a damaged eardrum, and gravel lacerations from the explosion. He was lucky. Much of the blast had been deflected by the heavy steel plate used to mine-proof the vehicle, and there had been little shrapnel. The larger pieces, such as the right front wheel, had been caught by the security fence. The dog had escaped unharmed.

Heavy rain had washed away all tracks, so a follow-up had not been possible.

The crematorium chapel was too small to accommodate all who came to the memorial service. The handful of people Julia had known filled only the first row, but every row was filled, and mourners packed the aisles and crammed the open glass doorways. Those who could not find space inside, stood clustered in groups outside in the spring sunshine.

Many had come to the service because they had suffered the loss of their own loved ones in the war, and believed that by sharing in the pain of this new suffering it would somehow lessen their own. Others, like the two government ministers and four high ranking army officers, were there to be seen lending their support.

Chris sat in a wheelchair loaned to him by the hospital, his bandaged feet all but hidden in the mass of flowers. Gabby sat nearby, on the end of the first row, and Oscar Mafiko stood possessively behind the wheelchair.

An Army chaplain conducted the service, and John Montgomery gave the brief eulogy, for Gabby was incapable, and with each mention of Julia, Chris drifted further from acceptance. He did not sing, and he did not pray or even close his eyes. He stared throughout at the flowers and willed with all his being for her not to be dead.

When the service was over, Oscar wheeled him out through the vestry to accept condolences, and he shook hands and murmured his thanks by rote, hating the commonplace routine of it, and remembering with anguish how he had gone through much the same procedure at their wedding, only this time the smiles he received were strained and he was unable to return them.

The Montgomerys' provided tea and sandwiches on her verandah at Glenkyle for the few invited guests, and they sat drinking and nibbling politely, and Chris hated that even more.

Marge had given him a bed until other arrangements could be made, and Gabby had been accommodated in one of the vacant staff cottages next door. He was grateful that Marge's niece had returned to Johannesburg the day after the attack and was not there to make things worse. The thought that he may have saved Julia had the woman - he could not even remember her name – not been there, gnawed at his conscience. She meant nothing to him. He loved Julia. Could he really have betrayed her?

Guilt nagged him also on the question of his competence. He was supposed to be the expert. A highly trained soldier with senses tuned to survival alone in hostile enemy territory, yet in his own backyard he had ignored such obvious signs as movement in the bush and the barking of a dog, assuming it was a hippo, without checking. How could he believe in himself again? And how could he expect others, like Oscar, to put their lives in his hands if he had failed to save the one that meant more to him than any other?

So far, Gabby and Chris had said little to each other, both too absorbed in their own grief to take on a share of another's, but she was with him on the verandah and spoke after the guests had departed.

'She had a good life, Chris, and she knew she was loved. No one can ask for much more.'

He laughed scornfully. 'Can't they?'

'I will stay until Timmy is well again... about two weeks, the doctor said. I can stay longer, if you want.'

He nodded, non-committal.

'What will you do now, stay on here?'

'No, I don't want to be in this place. I'm going back to Gara Pasi for a while, and then...' he shrugged. 'I don't know.'

'Why don't you and Timmy come back with me to Australia.'

'No. I can't leave... not with Julia being here.'

'Oh, Chris... don't you think she would understand?'

Maybe, but I can't leave. It doesn't seem right. I would feel as if I were deserting her... somehow. But I think you should take Timmy with you, Gabby. I can't look after him here. I have army commitments, and there's no future for him in this country, it's on the way out. I'll pay his fare and send money."

'When will you follow?'

'I don't know Gabby, maybe I won't.'

'What... you mean not at all? You would give up your son... Julia's gift?'

'No, I don't mean that. I just need time.'

'I would be happy to take care of him, of course, but he needs a father, Chris, so you should not take too much time.'

Gabby left abruptly, and Chris knew she was upset, but he couldn't do it. He didn't want the responsibility. Timmy needed more than he could give at the moment and needed a change of environment. Julia would understand.

He did not go to look at the burned-out house. On the

day the Montgomerys' took Gabby and Tim to Salisbury to catch their flight, he sat on the verandah listening to the distant rumble and screeching of the bulldozer clearing the sight and drank his way steadily through the liquor cabinet.

Timmy had been registered as an Australian born outside the country, so there had been no problem with immigration and, much to his and Gabby's relief, Timmy had accepted his departure as a holiday, and with more equanimity than expected.

'Will I be allowed to do game-spotting in Stralia, Dad?'

'Cattle-spotting, Son, and when the doctor says it's okay, I'm sure Uncle Vince will give you a go.'

'Fuli won't be there, hey? And Mum won't be there, will she?'

'No, Son, but she'll be watching, and Aunt Gabby will take good care of you. I'll phone every week, and you must send me some of your special pictures.'

Chris had his first double brandy as the dust of their departure was still settling, and followed it with several more, but it was not enough to drown the constant grinding and clanking of the bulldozer that was destroying his life, or dull the pain that came in sudden, frightening waves like the pain from a rotten tooth. The dream had ended, and with it had gone the laughter and the loving. Now there was guilt and loneliness, and he desperately needed a place to go where he could lick at his wounds, although he knew they would never heal completely.

With the aid of one of the gardeners and a wheelbarrow,

he loaded himself, the remaining brandy, his crutches, and a few spare clothes into Bravo Zulu and, gritting his teeth against the pain of his bruised feet on the rudder pedals, took off for Gara Pasi.

Fuli drew in a sharp breath between his teeth when Chris told him of Julia's death, but said nothing. For some things, words had no meaning. They sat for a long time communicating in silence, Chris poking at the sand with a stick, the old man emitting an occasional grunt of sympathy, his eyes dark with shadows.

Finally, Chris left Fuli sitting stiff and immobile with his thoughts and swung away on his crutches, aimlessly following old game paths that had become overgrown from lack of use. He wondered why it was he could not cry – or even feel like crying. Crying was not enough. Tears could wash away some of the sorrow, but it could never wash away the stain of his guilt.

It was dusk when he returned. Fuli and his family - now extended to include Lydia's sister, brother, and a few other relatives - were waiting for him in front of the main bungalow. They stood as he approached, falling silent, then each came forward in turn to express their sorrow. The men with murmured apologies and limp hand-shakes, the women silently bobbing with eyes demurely downcast, and the children stumbling into each other as they stared up.

Chris thanked them sombrely, his jaw aching with restrained emotion, and they left silently, herding their reluctant children with sharp prods in place of words.

Lydia had laid two of her brightly patterned blankets neatly in the empty lounge, but Chris moved them to the verandah, away from the hollow echoes and purple crayon scribble on the wall that had defied all attempts at removal. Lydia also brought him a meal of thick maize-meal porridge and watery vegetable gravy, and he picked sparingly at it with his fingers, washing the food down with brandy and warm water.

The next day, and for several days thereafter, he walked in the bush, at first with the aid of the crutches, then with a stick, using the physical pain to block the mental one. He went alone, refusing Fuli's offer to accompany him, taking only his rifle, which he slung across his back, and his army water bottle filled with brandy.

He responded to all Fuli's attempts at conversation with grunts or silence, but the old man was persistent. After being snubbed for a week, he approached Chris as he sat by the river and squatted beside him. He produced a tin of tobacco and a scrap of brown paper, and rolled a cigarette, twisting the ends clumsily with his blunt fingers.

'A man must walk on the path he chooses,' he said reflectively. 'Is it not so?'

Chris grunted and took a sip from his water bottle. Since he was a child, Fuli had taught him most everything he knew of the bush and its inhabitants. In many ways, he was the wisest man he knew, but now he was in no mood for the old man's philosophizing. What he needed was not words, but brandy. He had barely enough to see him through the day, and a long night lay ahead. He took a twenty dollar note from the roll in his pocket and placed it on the sand between them.

'It will be a good idea if one of your children chooses to take the path to the store for a bottle of whatever your friend hides under his counter.'

Fuli ignored the note. 'If there is a snake on the path that bites him,' he continued undaunted, 'a wise man will not run after the snake to kill it. He will rest and suck out the poison.'

Chris snorted with derision.

'The war is a very stupid thing,' Fuli mused. 'It kills many people who are not soldiers, but few who carry the guns and make the war.' Fuli lit his cigarette and blew out the flaring end in a shower of sparks. 'The path of your wife has ended, but not so your own path, or the path of your son. If you try to kill the bad things in your head with the brandy, will it not also kill the good things?'

'What good things… old man who knows everything?'

'Your son will need a wise man to choose his path.'

'I have already chosen it,' Chris said. 'He has gone to Australia with the woman, Gabby, who will treat him as her own child. He needs a woman who can be a mother, not a man who cannot be a father.'

'Eh! So I will not see him?'

'No.'

Fuli pinched out the half smoked cigarette and tucked it behind his ear, then he picked up the note. 'It is not a good thing you have done. For myself, and also for Lydia, who still mourns the death of her mistress, it will bring more sadness. In Timi lives the kindness of his mother, and I have seen also the courage that once was his father's. It seems you cry inside for the wrong person, Nkosi. I will send my daughter to the store for your brandy, even as I know it will not kill the snakes in your head.'

Fuli walked stiffly away, and Chris scowled angrily after him. Fuli had never spoken to him so rudely before. He almost called him back to demand an apology, but he knew he would not get one. Fuli never apologized, even when he was wrong.

Chris rose at dawn, haggard from lack of sleep and sick in his stomach. There had been no brandy and the cheap gin had not worked. Sluggishly, he made his way to the river and stood naked and shivering beside the water, watching the tendrils of mist steaming from the surface.

He vomited on the sand, falling to his hands and knees to heave up the sour contents of his stomach.

He crawled into the water and scoured his body with the coarse sand, rubbing it hard on his face and in his beard.

Suddenly he stopped. Standing waist-deep, he stared down at his distorted reflection, standing as if frozen, watching his image gradually take form as the water smoothed. He began hitting at it; punching it with all his strength, thrashing at the surface in a frenzy of whirling arms and fists. A strange animal sound came from his throat. A thin wailing, and he tried to stifle it by clamping both hands to his face, but still it came.

Fuli watched silently from the bank, a rabbit-skin blanket clasped around his gaunt frame, his warm breath steaming in the chill air. He turned at the sound of singing from behind, then walked to meet his small daughter coming along the path, an empty calabash perched on her head. She stopped in surprise when she saw him.

Fuli smiled at her. 'Fetching the water so early, my child?'

'Yes, Baba. Good morning, Baba...'

Fuli lifted the calabash from her head and set it on the ground. 'Come, little mother, help me first with the fire, then you can fetch the water.'

The corporal on gate duty at Army Headquarters almost suffered a mild heart attack when he turned at the end of his casual stroll along the pole barrier and saw a long-haired hippie staring at him from the other side; less than two short paces away.

A slide-show of possibilities flashed through the corporal's mind. The first was that some sort of peace demonstration was about to commence, but a quick glance around revealed no banner-wielding supporters or flower-painted vans, only the staff cars with their usual sprinkling of red flowers from the African tulip trees under which they had parked.

The man's hair reached to his shoulders, and his beard was bushy and unkempt. A filthy green tee shirt hung over greasy blue jeans, and he wore sandals made from strips of old car tyres – the type worn by African peasants. A cloth bag - large enough to conceal a weapon - was slung over one shoulder.

The corporal's right hand moved stealthily towards the white holster on his belt. 'Yes?' he asked, frowning officiously. 'Can I help you?'

'Lieutenant Ryan. I'm here to see Major Garret.'

The corporal's attitude changed abruptly. The cross-border exploits of Chris Ryan had reached almost mythical proportions in the past year. He stiffened to attention. 'Sorry, sir, I don't recognize you. Do you have any identification?'

'No. Just call him. He'll sort it out.'

While he waited on the phone to be put through to the Major in intelligence, the corporal studied the famous Selous Scout through the window of the sentry box. He had seen plenty of scouts coming and going to HQ, but never one of the funnies. He wondered what sort of man could operate alone a hundred miles inside enemy territory. He would have to be the world's biggest nut-case.

.

Major Garret came himself to escort Chris into the building. A dapper, elderly officer with a manner as crisp and precise as his uniform, he looked at Chris's attire with obvious distaste. 'I didn't expect you to come straight from the bush,' he commented. 'You could at least have showered and changed into uniform.'

Chris had little patience with protocol, and none with recycled army majors who should have stayed in retirement. 'As soon as I've showered, I'm going to sleep, and the message said urgent.'

'Well yes, but not *that* urgent. When the brigadier sees you he'll probably flip his lid.'

'Nobody told me I was going to see the brigadier. What's this about?'

'The OCC are having their meeting here today. They wanted to see you.'

'What about?'

'I'm sure you'll find out in good time, dear boy.'

Chris was too tired to care. He studiously ignored the curious stares and whispered comments as he followed the major through the maze of linoleum covered corridors to an office cluttered with maps and old-fashioned teleprinters.

'Take a seat,' the major offered, 'I'll inform the brigadier.'

Chris remained standing. If he sat down he was likely to fall asleep. Other than the short spell in the helicopter and an hour debriefing, he had been walking and jogging almost continually for the past three days. There was no percentage in sitting on your backside when a platoon of angry Frelimo soldiers were trying to shoot it off.

He moved around the office, looking without interest at the framed certificates and photographs on the wall. Photographs of a young Major Garrett being presented to the Queen Mother, an even younger Major Garrett rowing for King's College, and Major Garrett playing cricket for Sandhurst. That was the problem with the war, Chris thought tiredly. The British were running it from both ends while suckers like him were fighting in the middle.

The major returned to escort him to the conference room – the same room in which he had once attended another officer's court-martial.

'I explained to the committee that you have only just finished debriefing and hadn't had a chance to change,' Major Garrett whispered as he ushered him through the double doors.

The committee observed him for several seconds in silence, as if he were some foreign prisoner of war brought in for questioning, and Chris's impression that he was facing an unofficial court-martial strengthened.

The five officers sat in a line at one of the long trestle tables, the brigadier in the middle, and the others alongside in descending order of importance; the Assistant Commissioner of Police, the Air Vice-Marshal, Major Garrett for army intelligence, the Deputy Director of the CIO, and a stenographer.

Nobody greeted Chris. Neither was he offered a seat.

'Your name came up this morning at the meeting of the Special Operations Committee,' the brigadier said finally, looking down at his notes. 'It is quite a reputation you've been earning for yourself.' His bland tone showed he did not subscribe to the fan club. 'We seem to think it will be a good idea if you were stood down for a while. You are still a territorial, you know, not a regular officer and, strictly speaking, you should not be on continuous call-up.'

Chris shrugged. 'Why not? I'm not complaining. We're short of reconnaissance teams, and I have nothing else to do at the moment.'

'Yes, well, that brings me to another point that came under discussion. You are not operating in a team, you're acting alone, which is highly irregular. Reconnaissance is usually carried out in teams with a minimum of three men for good reason. If one man gets injured or...'

'I know all about that, sir, and with respect, I don't happen to agree. Not in this situation, anyway. A man by himself is more careful and less likely to be compromised, and only one set of tracks doesn't arouse suspicion. I've already discussed it with the colonel, and he supports my views. I think the results speak for themselves.'

It was happening again. The same old petty rivalry and stubborn clinging to conventional methods dragged out of some dusty text book in whatever military colleges the old fuddy-duddies like the brigadier had attended. They seemed to forget they were living in Africa, and that Africa made its own rules.

The brigadier's smooth complexion darkened, his thin white moustache barely moving as he spoke. 'The committee is not interested in yours or the colonel's views on this matter, Lieutenant. There is also a diplomatic problem to consider.' He turned to the officer from CIO. 'Maybe you should explain, Angus.'

The CIO man nodded. 'We have a complaint from the UN aid administrators in Maputo. We can't have you running around shooting up Frelimo officials and stealing their vehicles. We have enough diplomatic problems on our hands already.'

'Well, sir, Frelimo officials should not be transporting terrorists around in their aid vehicles, and I didn't steal it. I gave it to the SO at Chiredzi. He didn't seem to mind a bit.'

The Assistant Commissioner made a note on his pad and took a sip of water from the glass in front of him, looking pleased. It was not every day the district police came into possession of a brand-new Toyota Land-Cruiser.

The Special Branch representative cleared his throat. 'We know you people like to interview captured terrorists for possible conversion, but I have a report from one of our operatives that you have been asking questions about the attack on your house at Glenkyle. Perhaps you would like to tell us why. Surely this sort of interrogation is not an area in which you should be concerning yourself?'

Chris looked at the representative with disdain and growing anger. 'I would think that was obvious, sir. When I find the bastards responsible for killing my wife, I'm going to take them out.'

'We sympathies with your loss, Lieutenant,' the brigadier said, 'but we can't have our men conducting their own private wars.'

'I can assure you,' the Special Branch representative

added, 'our men are as keen as you are to find the culprits, and when we do, we will take care of it in the proper manner.'

Chris laughed sardonically, but said nothing. For the first time he began to appreciate what the colonel had been complaining about all along. The country had a strong shoulder to shoulder attitude, and the quality of its security forces were as good as any in the world, but as long as they were being led by committees, they were going nowhere.

And unconventional units like the scouts - despite their phenomenal success - made the hierarchy uneasy. Their dusty manuals said nothing about using converted terrorists to fight the war, and Chris was willing to bet that not one member of the so called Overall Coordinating Committee, or the Special Operations Committee, could even speak the predominating language of the majority of its soldiers. Their attitude was that one spoke English to the natives. If they didn't understand, that was their problem.

'There is one other matter,' the CIO man said. 'We have a report that some members of the scouts are involved with elephant poaching and illicit dealing in ivory. Do you know anything about that?'

Chris laughed. 'You've got to be joking.'

'No, we're not, Lieutenant, and I would advise you to speak with respect. I am positive you yourself are not involved, but as you are a ranger and have some experience in that area, we thought you may know something.'

'No, I resigned from National Parks, but that's about the craziest thing I've ever heard. Does the colonel know about this... or about me being here? As my commanding officer, I will have to report to him.'

'Do so if you wish,' the brigadier said curtly, 'but I will be informing the colonel myself later today of this committee's decision to have you removed from active service immediately, and also that his recommendation you are to be awarded the silver cross has been approved. No doubt you will be informed in due course when the ceremony is to take place. In the meantime, I believe Major Garrett has been instructed to take care of certain other details... Major?'

'That is correct, sir.'

'Good. That will be all then, Lieutenant.'

Chris could hardly believe what he was hearing. He stared, dumbfounded, at the committee members, then turned and strode angrily from the room.

Major Garrett came hurrying after him. 'Lieutenant Ryan. Will you come into my office please? There are certain things we need to discuss.'

'You can stick the silver cross where it fits best,' Chris snarled.

'Maybe you should hear what I have to say before you go jumping to conclusions, Lieutenant. It's for your own good, believe me.' He ushered Chris into his office. 'I'm sorry about all of this. You've done a remarkable job, and should not have been treated in such a cavalier fashion, but I fear you ruffled the brigadier's feathers.'

'I'd like to pluck them out one by one and stick them

up his aristocratic arse,' Chris growled. 'How the hell are we supposed to win a war with idiots like him in charge?'

'Well, that's the way it is, I'm afraid. Can I pour you a cup of tea?'

'No, thanks. What was it you wanted to tell me?'

The major unlocked the top drawer of a steel filing cabinet and withdrew a manila folder. He removed a sheet of paper from it and handed it to Chris. It had no heading, only a list of names, and his own was third from the top. Most of the others were politicians and high ranking officers, including two generals.

'It's a hit list,' the major explained in answer to Chris's questioning look. 'It was with all those other documents you chaps recovered after the last raid. As you can see, the other side want you dead almost as much as they do the PM. That's part of what is worrying the OCC. The work you have been doing is risky. If you are caught the reputation you have made for yourself will backfire, and not only cause despondency here, in the country, it will make excellent propaganda for the terrorist movement. So you see, Lieutenant, it's really for your own good that you are being grounded.'

'Very considerate of them, I'm sure,' Chris muttered. 'And what am I supposed to do now, Major, slink away with my tail tucked between my legs?'

'I'm sure with your knowledge the colonel will want to use you in training. But there is another option. The government has approved an ex gratia payment of five thousand dollars in foreign currency for men like yourself who will be forced to leave the country because of their military actions. You can have it paid in the currency of any country which hasn't frozen our assets. Most are opting for South Africa. Let me know, and I'll arrange the details. Of course, if you decide to stay you can't be paid.'

'Thanks, Major, but I think I'll take my chances.'

'I know how you feel, Lieutenant, this is my home too, but I would advise you to think it over carefully. It won't be the same as it was, and our sources tell us we should take the threats seriously. The attack on your house should convince you. Why else would they choose such a place if it wasn't that they knew you lived there. Have you considered that?'

Chris nodded. 'Too many times.'

'There you are then. And while I have the opportunity, I would also like to offer my condolences on your wife's tragic death.'

Chris nodded his thanks

'How is your son? I believe he was injured in the attack.'

'His hearing was a bit impaired with the explosion, but it seems to be improving. They don't think he will suffer any permanent damage.'

'Well, that's good news. I believe there was also a fire, you must have lost a fair bit.''Everything. It was burned to the ground.'

'Tragic business.' The major shook his head sympathetically. 'I heard somewhere you had found some sort of archaeological stuff. I suppose that was destroyed as well.'

'Yes, except for a few things I gave to the Umtali Museum.' He had almost forgotten. It seemed a long time ago.

'Oh? What was it exactly? I wouldn't mind having a peek at it sometime. Archaeology has always been a bit of a hobby of mine. Almost took it up as a career in fact.'

Chris yawned. 'Only some hieroglyphics the curator was going to send to a friend in Edinburgh for deciphering.' He was not in the mood for idle chat. 'If there is nothing else, Major, I'd like to go and get some sleep.'

'Of course, and please let me know if you change your mind about the payment, won't you?'

Driving to the barracks, Chris resigned himself to the inevitable. His quest for Julia's killers had suffered a serious setback. He could not hope to find them now when eight months of searching with access to interrogation files had achieved nothing.

And the mood of the country was changing. They were winning all the battles but losing the war, and the tidal wave of patriotism that had swept the country with the declaration of independence was receding, leaving behind a plethora of political skeletons.

He had seen some of them today, and he remembered what the colonel had said to him a few weeks ago over a quiet beer in the officer's mess, a few hours before he was to leave on another mission. 'People are looking inward, and at each other, instead of at the enemy,' he had said, uncharacteristically depressed. He usually saw his men off with a cheery slap on the back and a few words of encouragement.

'Something is going on that I don't like,' he'd continued. 'Too many things have gone wrong, and I get the feeling we are being watched and manipulated. I wouldn't be surprised if my phone was bugged. I think some rats are trying to scuttle the ship before deserting, hoping the other side will throw them a life jacket. Don't take any unnecessary chances, Chris, and keep what you find until you get back. Don't pass position information on the radio unless you want a hot extraction, and if you want to pull out now, it will be okay with me. You've done more than enough already.'

The colonel's words had depressed Chris, but he had gone anyway. Idleness was an even worse enemy. He needed the war. It was the only thing that had kept him sane. Without it, he had no idea what he would do.

He wondered what the colonel would think of this latest development. Maybe he would use his special pull with the general and go over the OCC's head as he had so often before.

But the colonel did not go over their heads. If anything, he supported their view that he was a diplomatic liability and confined him to lecturing and training recruits fresh from the selection course. To keep his sanity he went flying as much as possible. Mount Hampden airfield was only a twenty minute drive on the road into the city and, for the price of an occasional joy flight, one of the commercial operators had agreed to house Bravo Zulu in a corner of his hangar. But he could only take so much of the classroom and, after only a few months of it, Chris knew it was time to leave.

Amanda Pritchard stepped from the bus and walked briskly through the Edinburgh drizzle to her flat, struggling to unfurl her stubborn umbrella on the way. It was still closed when she reached her door, and she hooked it over her arm to fumble in her purse for the key. She was about to insert it in the latch when the sound of her gate clanging shut made her turn to see two men walking up the path towards her. She started in surprise, dropping the key, and one of the men stooped quickly to pick it up.

'Miss Pritchard?'

She moved back against the door, unhooking the umbrella and gripping it firmly by the shaft. It had a sharp point, and things were not as they used to be in the city.

'It's all right, Miss Pritchard, we only wish to talk to you.'

'Who are you?'

'We're from Customs.' The one who had picked up the key reached past her to open the door. 'May we come in?'

'Why? I haven't travelled anywhere for ages, and I always declare everything. I'm sure you must have the wrong person.'

'We're not from that section, we do parcels. I have identification in the car if you would rather talk there.' He inclined his head towards a black Morris parked on the road.

Amanda Pritchard gave it a quick glance. She was definitely *not* getting into any car with two strange men, no matter where they were from.

'It won't take a minute, Miss Pritchard.' He smiled disarmingly. 'It is rather damp out here.'

'If you're sure it won't take long then. I'm expecting some friends along any moment now.'

She walked past them into the living room, not stopping to hang up the umbrella. She decided against offering them tea. One of the men wandered idly around her room with his hands in the pockets of his overcoat, looking at her collection of ancient pottery shards and photographs from Egypt, and Amanda frowned, irritated that he had not bothered to remove his hat.

'We're hoping you can help us with an inquiry, Miss Pritchard. You recently received a package from Rhodesia, I believe.'

The statement took her by surprise, but she was relieved it was nothing serious. 'Not recently. It was months ago. What about it? I receive packages all the time. Mostly to do with my work.'

'You do realize that sanctions have been applied to all goods from Rhodesia, don't you? Can you tell us what was in it?'

'Nothing illegal or valuable, I can assure you. Only a few notes and a gift from a friend. Why?'

He ignored her question. 'Notes?'

'I'm with the university... archaeology. My friend sent

me a few notes to do with my work. It was out of my field so I sent them to a colleague in Cairo who specializes in that sort of thing.'

'What sort of thing is that, Miss Pritchard?'

'Hieroglyphics.'

The two men exchanged glances. 'Can you give us your friend's name and address please?'

Amanda hesitated. It seemed unreasonable they should be so concerned about mail from Rhodesia.

'Nothing serious, Miss Pritchard. It's only the address we need. Simply a security inquiry we have to complete on behalf of the Post Office. We won't be contacting your friend in Cairo... or the one in Rhodesia, for that matter. A bit of a farce, all this sanctions business, and from what you have told us it is obviously all quite innocent, but you know what the bureaucrats are like.' He smiled pleasantly. 'You haven't committed an offence, or anything like that, it's simply a formality that we have to follow through. If you just give us the address we'll be on our way.'

Amanda Pritchard lay awake in her bed for a long time, wondering. She had not seen Bob McEwen since the conference in London almost two years ago, but they still corresponded regularly. Bob would not be mixed up in anything shady, she was certain. He had not said much about the photocopies, other than that he suspected the hieroglyphics were Phoenician, and that the originals had gone missing. Could that have something to do with it? The

122

sanctions story didn't sound right. Maybe if she phoned Bob he could tell her more. At the same time she could inform him that she had sent the copies to Zarena in Cairo.

Chris was in the hangar, doing some minor repairs to Bravo Zulu's tail-wheel, when a man in overalls and a Yankees cap approached him. 'Great little machine you have there, buddy. They sure as hell don't build 'em like they used to.' He offered his hand. 'Billy Steel. I seen you around here a few times. You're Chris Ryan, ain't you?'

Chris nodded, unsmiling, and shaking the hand briefly. He didn't care much for yanks.

'Could have done with some of you guys in 'Nam.' the American continued. Then he shook his head dolefully. 'Nope. Wouldn't have done no good. Biggest cock-up since Custer. I was there with Air America. That was the second biggest cock-up. What say you knock off and I buy you a beer, then, if you like, I'll show you a *real* tail-dragger.'

'What tail-dragger?'

'Does the word Spitfire mean anything to you?'

Chris looked at the American with new interest. Few people outside the flying circle had heard of the restored Spitfire. It belonged to a former Battle of Britain pilot who ran a sanctions busting operation that was one of the country's worst kept secrets. The American said he had flown with Air America. It had also been a somewhat suspect flying operation.

'Do you fly for Air Trans Africa?' he asked.

'Nope.' The American grinned and winked. 'Air Gabon Cargo. But not so loud, boy. Goddamned spies everywhere.'

Chris returned the American's grin, warming to his easy manner. 'You said something about a beer?'

Mount Hampden had been a Royal Air Force base during the Second World War. Many of the original hangars and Nissan huts were now being used by commercial operators. Billy Steel took Chris to an area of the airfield he had never visited before. Three hangars had been joined to make one large building, and were set apart from the others. No company name was advertised, but large signs warned it was a restricted area. They drove through an open security gate and parked amongst several cars in front of a prefabricated office building. Two of the cars had government license plates.'First the beer,' the American said. He led the way down a corridor of closed office doors to a canteen at the end and pointed to a refrigerator against the wall. 'Grab yourself a can, I'll see if the skipper's around.'

The refrigerator was full of imported beer. Chris chose one of the less exotic and looked around. Apparently the canteen also doubled as an operations room. A large table cluttered with books and maps took up most of the floor space and the walls were covered in aeronautical charts of Africa. A spider's web of red lines joined the major airports and navigation aids of the continent.

Billy Steel returned with a sandy-haired man, also in overalls, who he introduced simply as 'The Skipper', and Chris shook the firm hand offered to him with much the same reverence as he would that of the Pope.

'Been hearing a lot about you,' he said, fixing Chris with penetrating blue eyes.

'I could say the same about you, Wing Commander.'

'That's ancient history, son, call me Skip. Everyone does.'

Chris nodded, feeling out of his league.

'Billy tells me you were flying in Australia,' the commander said, pulling out a chair and sitting down. 'We don't go that far afield, thankfully.'

After ten minutes of talking - not about Spitfires, but mostly about his own, not so remarkable flying experience - Chris began to get the feeling his visit was not entirely unexpected, and even that he was being interviewed. He responded to a question about navigation aids with a laugh. 'It sounds like you're checking me out for a job.'

The commander gave Chris a lazy smile. 'We're always on the lookout for good pilots, especially if they have foreign licenses. Interested?'

'I haven't given it much thought, sir, but I'm not rated for the heavy stuff. I'm strictly a bush pilot.' He was surprised they didn't know. They seemed to know everything else about him.

'That's just the kind we want,' the American said. 'We already have the international stuff pretty well sorted out, and with the way things are going now politically, our operation is changing. What we need is someone with your kind of experience to take over the flying to some of the smaller bush strips around Africa. We use a Beech fifty five for the job.'

'Didn't you do a twin conversion a few years ago?'

Chris looked at his inquisitors with a raised eyebrow. 'You gentlemen seem to know an awful lot about me. Why do I get the feeling I'm being set up?'

The American laughed. 'He's way too smart for us, Skip, I guess we gotta come clean.'

'Maybe you're right, Billy.' The wing commander consulted his watch and stood up. 'But I'll have to leave it to you. I've a message coming through in a few minutes.' He offered Chris his hand. 'No pressure, son. Whatever you decide, it was a pleasure to meet you.'

When the wing commander had gone, the American went to a dispenser in the corner and made them both a coffee. 'You have some friends in high places,' he said, placing one in front of Chris.

'Oh? How high?'

'How about the Prime Minister. Is that high enough?'

Chris laughed. 'I think you've got me mixed up with someone else, Billy. I've never met him.'

'Maybe so, but he's a personal friend of the skipper. Battle of Britain and all that stuff. It seems the PM had a call from a certain colonel who is worried about you. I believe you're not too happy in your present employment.'

Chris laughed with genuine delight. 'That meddling old bastard!'

'So, can I take it that you're interested? I'm beginning

to fly up the wall with this greasy palm stuff on top of everything else.'

'Greasy palm?'

'Can't tell you too much at this stage, unfortunately, but there's not much risk involved. Just buzzing around the African states to the north of us with the odd VIP, that's all.'

'That's all? Aren't they supposed to be our enemy up there?'

'Politics and graft make snug bedfellows, pal, especially the African variety.'

'Thanks for the offer, Billy, but I've had a gutful of African politics and war. I'm heading back to Australia to join my son '

'Sure, buddy, who hasn't, but if you change your mind, let me know soon. It's getting so my feet hardly ever touch the goddamned ground anymore.'

Chris never did get to see the restored Spitfire.

'It's about time you returned my calls,' a disgruntled Bob McEwen complained when Chris telephoned him. 'I've been trying to get hold of you for the past week. Don't they allow you fellows to use the phone?'

'Sorry, Mac, I'm out of the army now. I got your message from the warden at Glenkyle. What's the problem? Have you had something back on those hieroglyphics?'

'Not exactly. Where are you?'

'Mount Hampden. You wouldn't be in the market for a

forty year old airplane, would you?'

The curator grunted. 'I have enough problems, thanks. I was hoping you were in Umtali. My office was burgled a few weeks ago.'

'Oh? Anything stolen?'

'Not that I know of. They left a hell of a mess though, and I can't find my address book. That's why I've been trying to contact you. A few strange things have happened since then. It may be nothing, but I think you should know.'

'Like what?'

'I had a call from that lady friend of mine in Edinburgh. The one I sent the photocopies to. Her address was in my book, and she had a visit from two Customs men, asking if she had received any packages from Rhodesia. They told her they were looking into sanctions violations and were checking all deliveries from here.'

'Really? I didn't realize they had gone *that* far.'

'It's a load of codswallop. It wasn't a parcel anyway, it was a large envelope. Unfortunately, she told them what was in it and admitted sending it on to a colleague at the Cairo museum.

'No one else knew you had sent it?'

'Only you, and I posted it myself.'

'It doesn't sound right, Mac. I can't see anyone going to so much trouble over a few photocopies.'

'I agree, but maybe they don't know it's only copies. It could be they think it's the real thing. Can you remember telling anyone about having the stuff in your filing cabinet at home?'

'I may have mentioned it to the woman at the Zimbabwe Museum. Why?'

The curator didn't answer for a while, apparently giving it some thought. When he eventually spoke his voice was apologetic. 'I hesitate to bring it up, son, but have you considered the possibility that your house was burned down in an attempt to destroy what you had found?'

The curator's words stirred the anger he had thought was finally subdued. His grip on the receiver tightened. If what the curator said was true, it meant Julia had died for even less reason than being married to a scout. She had given her life over a few worthless pieces of paper. It was too bizarre to even contemplate.

'I think that's bullshit, Mac. It was hit by terrorists, and no one has control over those bastards, not even their own commanders.'

'Well, you know more about that side than I do, but it's something to think about. Keep in touch, will you? Amanda promised to let me know if she hears anything more.'

Chris gave it plenty of thought, and ended up more depressed and confused than ever.

In the past week, since leaving the army, he had felt as if he were at last coming to terms with what had happened and was ready to move on, but now it was happening all over again, and he didn't know where to start or what to think.

But what he did know, was that it wasn't over.

Resigned, he searched through his wallet and removed

the blank business card on which Billy Steel had written his number, then he picked up the phone.

Part Three

North Africa - 1977

It was early evening before Zarena Bontoux was finally able to leave her desk at the Cairo museum. She hurried along the Corniche to the American University, where the meeting she had been looking forward to all week was to take place. It was too late now to hope for a seat at the front, she would have to be content with standing at the back.

Despite the restriction of the ankle-length skirt and heavy crocheted bag that bounced awkwardly on her hip, her long stride covered the ground with surprising speed, and the short man following ten paces behind was hard pressed to keep up and not lose her in the crowd. She ran up the steps of the hall and was swallowed in the throng of women at the door.

The street traffic was still heavy when the meeting ended. Zarena joined a group of chattering female students as they braved the Corniche in a safety chain of linked arms, then she left them to cross the Tahrir Bridge.

It was a long walk to her small flat on the other side, but the glistening Nile with its kaleidoscope of reflecting lights was more appealing than being jostled on the overcrowded buses, and she had that evening's speech to occupy her mind.

The doctor's courage was inspiring. Despite her book on the plight of women in Egypt being banned, and the fundamentalists accusing her of sedition, she still spoke out, and her words had stirred memories of Zarena's own confusion and suffering as a child. Questions her French mother had tried unsuccessfully to answer, and suffering she had been powerless to prevent.

Zarena was still thinking about it as she climbed the last flight of stairs to her flat on the fourth floor. The landing was in darkness, the broken lights still not repaired, even though she had complained several times to the caretaker, and she made a mental note to complain again. This time she would include a few threats.

She had almost reached her door when a hand was suddenly clamped over her mouth, she was lifted off her feet, and her bag wrenched from her shoulder. The hand stifled her cries, and she lashed out with her feet at the legs behind, but her soft sandals had no effect against her attackers heavy robe. As he carried her forward she lifted her legs to kick at her door, expecting something solid against which to push, but it swung open without resistance and she was carried inside.

The door was closed behind and the light came on. The cane bookcase had been overturned, the books strewn across the floor. Her bed had been stripped and the cupboard emptied.

She tried to bite the hand covering her mouth, and managed to clamp her teeth on bitter flesh, but her assailant quickly shifted an arm from her waist and grabbed her left breast, pinching the nipple viciously between a finger and thumb. Zarena squealed in agony. He released the pressure and hissed into her ear; a sharp, snake-like warning.

Zarena froze. From behind, she heard the clatter as a second person emptied the contents of her bag onto the cement floor. He searched impatiently through them, muttering under his breath, then whispered something unintelligible to the man holding her. His hand shifted to her back to shove her forward and she sprawled over the books, her hands skidding over them before her chin hit the floor. Her glasses flew off. The light went out, plunging her into sudden, terrifying darkness, and the door closed softly.

Whimpering in panic, Zarena scrambled over the books towards the kitchenette, her flesh cringing, anticipating further clutching of hands. Feverishly she felt along the cupboards, a small cry escaping her lips as she found the cutlery drawer and jerked it open. She fumbled for the big kitchen knife and snatched it out, spinning around and holding it thrust protectively forward.

She crouched low, pressed hard against the cupboard, peering into the dark and listening against the rasp of her breathing, then she edged slowly towards the light switch and flicked it on. She looked cautiously around the doorway into the bed-sitting room. She was alone.

Still holding the knife forward, she stepped carefully

amongst the books and papers to the front door and switched on the main light. The lock on the door was broken, a large sliver of varnished wood missing from the frame where it had been forced. She jammed a chair under the handle then sat on her bed against the wall, trying to gather her wits.

Fear still twitched spasmodically at her body. She laid the knife down beside her and clamped her trembling hands between her knees, rocking gently to calm herself. Her jaw and lips felt numb, and there was a bitter taste in her mouth from the man's skin.

When her weakness had passed she found her glasses and put them on, then went through to the bathroom. The curtains below the basin had been pushed aside, but nothing had been inside to remove. She drew them and inspected her lips in the mirror. The lower half of her face was blotchy and her lips a little swollen. She probed cautiously with her tongue at a cut on the inside. She opened her shirt to inspect the stinging nipple. The aureole was discolored and three separate red marks showed where his fingers had pressed hard against the skin.

Zarena screwed up her face in distaste, but left the shirt open to prevent further pain from rubbing. The string of wooden beads entwined in her hair had come loose, causing the dark curls to fall forward into the basin as she brushed her teeth to remove the taste. The reminder. She spat, then untwined the beads and twisted the hair into a topknot. She looked longingly at the shower, but could not bring herself to undress.

Reporting the intrusion to the police seemed the sensible thing to do, but the flat had no telephone, and walking down the dark stairs to the caretaker's apartment on the ground floor was out of the question. So too was calling on the neighbors, none of whom she knew well enough.

Zarena made a cup of coffee, then set about cleaning up the mess. Nothing seemed to be missing. She didn't have much of value anyway, not even a television, and her stereo had not been touched. But why had they not taken her purse? It was in her bag, which they had searched, surely they could not have missed it?

She wondered if it had something to do with the women's movement. It was not popular with the authorities. Maybe they had been searching for banned books or newsletters. It made more sense, for her books had been scattered, and the shoe box full of old letters and photographs emptied on to the table.

But who would know of her involvement in the movement? She was not an official, and the movement itself was not banned, and she had never spoken of her interest at the museum for fear of offending some of the male members of the staff.

Still puzzling over what had happened, she braved a quick shower, then went to bed, but it was a long time before she was able to sleep.

When she arrived at her basement office next morning, Zarena was irritated to discover that someone had rearranged all the papers on her desk and work table. Where before they had been spread around in seeming disarray, now they were stacked into neat piles, totally disrupting the system she had devised for cross cataloguing the characters she had been working on.

She subdued the temptation to speak to Assistant Director Fahmy about it, and angrily set about putting things back the way they were. She retrieved her ancient scripts from the fireproof vault and started work, trying to push the events of the previous night from her mind.

Amongst the pile she brought from the safe was the package from her friend, Amanda, and she felt a moment of guilt. She stuffed it into her bag to read at home. Her work was already far behind schedule.

Zarena worked through her lunch break, only taking time off to go to the cafeteria to fetch a drink. When she returned, she saw one of the junior clerks searching through the vault papers on her desk. She stopped in the doorway of her cubicle in surprise.

'Are you looking for something, Mahfoud?'

He started guiltily. 'No, nothing. That is, I was looking to see if you had the newspaper.'

'I never get the paper,' she said, frowning with annoyance. 'Was it you who rearranged all the papers on my desk?'

'No, not me.' He left hurriedly, and Zarena sipped thoughtfully at her drink. Mahfoud had never been particularly friendly, why would she think he could help himself to anything of hers? She would have to be more careful with what she left lying around.

Late in the afternoon she was called to the administration office to take a phone call, and she took her bag with her. It was Amanda Pritchard.

'Thank God!' Amanda said in greeting. 'I've been trying to get through for ages. When is Sadat going to fix the telephones?'

Zarena laughed. 'I was thinking of you only this morning.'

'Did you get my package?'

'I haven't had a chance to read it yet, Amanda. I'm sorry. We've been very busy here, but I'll try to work on it at home.'

'Can you talk?'

Zarena glanced at the assistant director sitting only a few feet away, close enough to hear everything she said. 'Not really.'

'Well listen then.' Amanda spoke for a full minute, and Zarena listened carefully over the scratching and fading line, gradually becoming aware that her ear was pressed so hard against the receiver it was beginning to ache. When Amanda told her she had been visited by two men she pressed even harder.

'I'll phone you as soon as I know anything,' Zarena promised after Amanda had finished. She replaced the receiver and rubbed at her ear. Was it just a coincidence?

When she returned to her cubicle, Zarena removed the package from her bag and examined the two sheets with a thoughtful frown. She made another set of copies and placed them in an envelope marked for cataloguing, then she filed it with her other papers in the vault.

After work, she walked to the American University and asked a student friend if she could stay with her for a few days while her own flat was being repaired. It was not altogether untruthful, and she had stayed with Rosemary on several occasions in the past, usually after working late, but now she wanted to stay away from her own flat until she knew what was going on and the door was repaired.

She returned there before dark to pack her clothes and make a point of telling the sloppy caretaker that her flat had been burgled and she was going to the police if he didn't fix the security lights.

She worked on the photocopies over the weekend, but with only moderate success. It would have helped if the papyri had been correctly prepared before copying. Photographic enhancement and enlarging might help, but she did not have access to the equipment without questions being asked. She could slip parts of it in with her other work, but it was going to take weeks.

The hieroglyphs were undoubtedly Phoenician. Two sets of characters clearly depicted a reference to both Hiram and Solomon, which fixed the date as between the end of the second millennium BC to the middle of the first. There was mention of black boats laden with ivory and gold, and she knew these to be the sea boats of the Phoenicians; so named for the pitch that covered the deck.

From what she was able to glean from the legible sections, Zarena concluded it was a report, carried by an emissary, and probably meant for either King Hiram of Tyre, or King Solomon. She also concluded that if an original existed – and if the copies were not some elaborate hoax – it would be of immense value, and the initial excitement she experienced with the deciphering was soon swamped by a growing unease.

It increased when, on several occasions during the following week, she noticed the assistant clerk, Mahfoud, lurking in the vicinity of her cubicle. She never had much to do with him. He delivered mail and ran messages, which was about all he was capable of doing, and she seldom saw him, but now he seemed to be constantly underfoot.

At first, she thought she was being paranoid, and that it was simply his clumsy way of making advances towards her. Making passes at unattached women, particularly those who wore western clothes, was a national pastime for Arab men, but she was positive he had been searching through her papers. She had deliberately placed them in a certain order, and each time she returned the order was changed.

She decided to further test her suspicions. Taking copies of some unimportant hieroglyphics from one of her books, she placed them in the envelope she had received from Amanda and left it conspicuously open on her desk when she went to the canteen for lunch. When she returned, the package was gone - and so was Mahfoud.

Alarmed, Zarena decided to do some quick research.

The reading room of the museum had nothing on the Southern African ruins, but searching through files produced several references to papers on African civilizations. Nothing related to the copies she had been working on, but she did find in one book some embittered comments about another book written on the subject by an eminent archaeologist.

Differences of opinion were common in the world of archaeology, but Zarena did not have to read more than a few chapters to discover the controversy had been raging for a hundred years. Archaeologists on both sides, some now dead, had been severely taken to task by their colleagues.

The more she read, the more Zarena realized that the message contained in the hieroglyphics was not only important historically, but also academically. What she had already deciphered clearly supported the pre-Moslem Arabs for the origin of the central African ruins, as opposed to the Bantu. Reputations would suffer if the original papyri was proved authentic.

But that was only a part of it. Of perhaps even greater significance was the mention of gold and Solomon. The source of the famous king's gold and the location of Ophir had baffled mankind for thousands of years. Could what she have been working on be the key to one of the world's oldest mysteries?

Her situation was more serious than she had thought. She was now an unwilling participant in the war. She had tricked Mahfoud into stealing false copies, and the holder of the originals would know what she had done - and why.

Not only was she in the war, she was in the front line.

'Fakes?' Mahfoud stared at the state official in astonishment. 'But I don't understand...'

'You have made me look a fool!' the official ranted. 'It is obvious you clumsily allowed the woman to suspect you, so she provided you with fake ones to steal and you stupidly fell into the trap.'

Mahfoud opened his mouth to offer a defense, but could think of nothing that would not provoke the official further.

'You have been paid good money but have failed to produce anything of value,' the official continued. 'First you risk the involvement of the police by hiring a fool to help and attacking the woman in her flat, when you could easily have stolen the bag in the street, then you fail to discover where she is now living, even though you follow her every day from work.'

'But it is not possible to follow. She goes into...'

'And then...' the official persisted, raising his voice to drown Mahfoud's protests, 'you allow yourself to fall under suspicion and make it impossible for you to return to the museum.'

Abruptly, the official turned away and glared out the window, and Mahfoud shifted uneasily. 'But what of the employment file? It was not easy to get it. I have taken great risks.'

The official waved his hand in contemptuous dismissal

without bothering to turn around. 'Nothing we did not already know. It is fortunate we do not have to rely on you for our information.'

'What do you want me to do?'

After an uncomfortable silence, the official turned to face Mahfoud. Incredibly, he was smiling.

'Are you aware that Bontoux is not her name?'

Mahfoud frowned, uncomprehending.

'No, of course not. Her real name is el Kholi. We have discovered some interesting information about her, and we have also located her father. As you will not be able to return to the museum...' he paused to look disdainfully at Mahfoud, 'I am giving you another chance to earn the money you have been paid. You are going to Qena to see her father.'

'But why me... what can I do? And my job... I will be sacked if I do not return.'

'Stop complaining and listen!' the official snapped. 'I will tell you what has to be done - and you had better not fail this time.' He glared at Mahfoud. 'It is very simple, even for you. First you must confirm that he is her father by showing him the photographs and other information we have obtained. But on no account, must you tell him where you received the information. That is most important. He is a true believer of the faith and may not cooperate if he knows the true reasons. He is only required to know that someone of influence is aware of his daughter's whereabouts, and that she is part of a group plotting against the teachings of Islam.' The state official smiled knowingly at Mahfoud. 'Do you understand?'

Chris was finding it difficult to stay awake. The monotonous drone of the Baron's engines in the still air had a pleasant, lulling effect that was proving hard to resist. He squinted at his watch. The hands seemed hardly to have moved since the last time he looked at it. He sat up and disengaged the auto-pilot. With the massive bulk of the Ethiopian mountains looming ahead, it was no time to be falling asleep.

This was a new kind of flying for Chris, and still a novelty that he had to admit he was enjoying. The plane was a dream to fly, and having two perfectly tuned engines was a reassuring bonus. Like most of the aircraft in the fleet, the Baron was old, but the skipper did not skimp when it came to maintenance and safety.

In a month of intensive study, training, and flight checks, Chris had upgraded his instrument rating, and accumulated an impressive number of hours covering much of the central African continent. Sleep had become so precious he had taken to sleeping in the plane between flights, rather than waste sack time looking for a hotel; most of which were grubby and lice infected.

The collapsible canvas stretcher had been designed to fit above two of the rear seats and could be erected in a matter of minutes. When it was too hot, which was nearly always, he set the stretcher on four wooden blocks under the wing and hung a mosquito net from the flap hinge.

Extra sleep was not the only advantage to camping in or under the plane. It improved security at the airports where thieving was rife and spare parts non-existent, and it also made communication with the Kenyan base easier. He could simply call them on the HF radio or, if asleep, bribe one of the air traffic controllers with a carton of American cigarettes to take a message.

Mama Tembo - another of Billy Steel's pseudonymous titles for the large and jovial radio operator - was so impressed with the efficiency of his scheme, and the ease with which she was able to contact him in places she had previously considered impossible, that she had taken to calling him darling - a title she reserved only for her favorites.

Billy Steel had spent the first week with him, showing him the operation, and introducing him to many of the black officials with whom he would regularly come in contact. So many, in fact, he had been forced to make notes, which Billy had promptly burned.

'In this part of the world,' Billy explained, 'the less you know, or rather, the less *they* know you know, the better. You don't answer questions, ask them, or talk politics. As far as your passengers are concerned, you are just the dumb driver.'

Billy had also shown him the Baron's hidden secrets.

'Always use the headphones when you have passengers,' he advised. 'It not only prevents them from talking to you, it encourages them to talk amongst themselves because they think you can't hear. You would be surprised how often they

speak in English because they don't understand each other.'
Billy had paused to grin craftily. 'There's a tape recorder built into the radio. You operate it by pressing the red button next to your transmit button on the control column. Press it once to operate the microphones in the cabin speakers, twice to turn on the tape if anyone is giving away state secrets, and three times to switch off. Works a treat. Even above the noise of the engines, you can hear them whispering.'

The greasy palm operation was nothing less than sophisticated bribery. Favors were dispensed to African politicians and officials - even British diplomats - for the sole purpose of receiving favors in return.

In the largely bankrupt and corrupt Central African states, reliable air transport had proved to be the best means of dispensing these favors. It was considered fair exchange to provide the official in charge of airport customs with a free shopping trip for himself and his wife - or girlfriend, as was often the case - to one of the larger capitals in return for his signature on the manifest of the DC3 concerning its unmarked cargo.

Or, as was now the case, a free ride for three minor government ministers, two from Gabon, and one from Zaire, to yet another urgent meeting of the Organization of African Unity, and for no other reason than for whatever favors they may be able to return in the future. And, of course, for any interesting intelligence they might impart to the tape recorder on the way.

Chris found the irony of a Rhodesian pilot taking African

ministers to a meeting aimed at bringing about Rhodesia's downfall highly amusing. In many ways, it was similar to his lone reconnaissance missions in Mozambique, and he had no illusions about what would be the result if he was caught. His Australian license and passport were more valuable than a bullet-proof vest.

He had little knowledge of the rest of the sanctions busting operation, and didn't ask. He knew that several other pilots were involved, but had met only two of them, one an Italian, the other a Frenchman, and both operated out of another base in Libreville. He had not seen much of the skipper, who seemed to spend most of his time in the air or overseas, and he received his orders through Mama Tembo, who had been a news-reader with Radio Zaire. She had almost married a leading politician, but the day before the happy event was to take place, the combination of inside information and the ability to broadcast it throughout Africa had proved too tempting, and she had been fortunate to have been only jilted and not shot.

As a joke, Billy had bought her the record of *Mama Tembo's Wedding* from the hit musical in South Africa, and the name had stuck.

A shining silver thread appeared off the Baron's nose; the early sun reflecting from the White Nile, and Chris picked out the splatter of buildings that made up Juba. He adjusted his course to fly over the top, relieved he had got it right. It was as much good luck as good judgment flying in these parts. Navigation aids and meteorological data was scarce and unreliable. Dead reckoning, optimism, and a cast-iron stomach was the only way.

He began a slow descent thirty minutes out of Addis and woke his passengers. He had not activated the tape recorder. It would have recorded nothing more than a trio of snores.

He was looking forward to spending a few days doing some of his own snoring before having to return with the same passengers, but it was not to be. When he called Mama Tembo after landing, she told him he was to fly to Khartoum, where he was to pick up two members of the British Embassy and their wives, and fly them to Aswan. He managed a forty minute nap while the Baron was waiting to be refueled, and another thirty while waiting for the embassy people at Khartoum.

Aswan would be the farthest north he had been, and Chris realized this was the opportunity he had been waiting for. Since moving to Kenya, he had been trying to find the time to take a commercial flight to Cairo, to see the woman at the museum that Bob McEwen had told him about, but Billy had not been joking when he said their feet wouldn't be touching the ground.

Aswan was only about an hour from Cairo in the Baron. If he could persuade the diplomats to stay in Aswan for an extra day, he could easily fly to Cairo and see the woman, retrieve the photocopy if she still had it, and maybe learn more about what was going on.

Persuading the British diplomats was easy, and Chris accomplished it as they flew over the Aswan dam when there was nothing but water and crocodiles below.

While his passengers were occupied looking out through the windows at the pleasant view, he surreptitiously eased one of the pitch controls forward a fraction to unsynchronized the propellers. The tone of the aircraft changed from a regular, unnoticeable hum, to a resonating, uneven surging. With a worried frown, he sat up and tapped several times on the glass of the oil pressure gauge. The response was gratifyingly prompt.

'Something the matter, Captain?' The embassy official sitting next to him was a thin rake of a man with a pencil thin moustache and a nervous tic below his right eye. Chris deliberately delayed his answer, by which time the moustache was in continuous motion.

'I'm not... quite... sure,' he answered hesitantly. 'Been playing up a bit lately, but not quite so...' he broke off to tap again at the gauge, then sat back. 'I'm sure it's nothing to worry about. If it's not going to take too long, I might get it seen to when we land. I don't want to hold you up though.' He smiled apologetically. 'You know how it is with these out of the way places. It could take days. Maybe I'll just wait until we get back. It should be all right.'

The others had lost interest in the lake and were paying close attention to what he was saying, and their response was immediate and unanimous. 'No, we're not in a hurry, really… take as long as you like.'

He phoned Mama Tembo from the airport. He had no need to lie to her. It was no common charter company he was flying for, and in case of emergency, she needed to know where he was. And Mama Tembo was no fool. She knew everything that went on, and sooner or later would find out and stop calling him darling. He simply told her he was spending the time there, instead of Addis, and he would be flying to Cairo.

'I suppose you'll be going there to see the belly dancers,' she said..

'I won't have the time, Mama T, I have business at the museum.'

'Never mind, Mister Christopher, darling, I'll do one for you when you get back.' She giggled.

'I'll look forward to that,' Chris replied, grinning at the thought of Mama Tembo's large belly in rapid gyration.

Egypt was one of the few African countries the company did not operate in regularly, and it took a few hours to clear customs and immigration, complete the complicated array of forms, find fuel and fill in another flight-plan, so it was late afternoon by the time he landed in Cairo and found a place to park the plane.

He fumed impatiently as the cab idled along in the heavy Friday traffic, realizing he may be too late, and chiding himself for not telephoning the woman to tell her he was coming. If the museum was closed and he missed her, or if she was not there for some reason, he would have little chance of finding her in a place like Cairo.

He made it with fifteen minutes to spare, and it took ten of those to find the administration block. An Arab clerk looked suspiciously at the scrap of paper on which he had scribbled her name, then asked him to wait. He disappeared, leaving Chris to the puzzled looks and giggles of the female staff who were preparing to leave. The clerk returned to say he couldn't find her, and also that he must leave because the museum was closing.

Disappointed and angry with himself, Chris joined a group of office workers on their way out through the galleries. He asked several of them if they knew where he could find Zarena Bontoux, but none could help.

He was standing in the entrance hall, wondering what to do next, when one of the girls he had spoken to earlier touched his arm.

'Sir? The woman you ask for. She is there.' She pointed towards a group walking out of the main entrance. 'The one with the glasses and beads in her hair. She is Zarena.'

Chris flashed her a grateful smile and ran down the steps. He caught up with her at the bottom. 'Miss Bontoux?'

She turned to give him a quick, startled look, but did not stop, and Chris hesitated, wondering if he had been mistaken. He had expected a much older woman. He hurried after her.

'Excuse me…. are you Zarena Bontoux?'

Ignoring him, she quickened her pace, then turned sharply to mingle with a group of tourists and staff heading for the main gates.

Puzzled by her actions, and still not sure if he had the right person, Chris followed. She was his last chance. He lost her in the crush at the gates, then saw her again, striding quickly along the busy sidewalk ahead of another group of people. He ran to catch up with her, pushing his way roughly through the crowd, and reached her as she was about to cross the road. This time he caught her by the arm and moved in front to block her. The time for niceties was over.

'Wait! I have to talk to you. Are you Zarena Bontoux?'

She jerked away and tried to push past, but he stayed his ground. 'Please... it's important!'

'Leave me alone. I'll call the police.' She looked anxiously around, as if searching for one.

'What the hell for? I'm not trying to harm you, I just want to talk to you.'

'Leave me alone. I have nothing to say. Please... I must go.' She looked desperate enough to start screaming, so he stepped aside.

'All right, but I'm coming with you. I didn't come all this way for nothing, and I'm here to help you. Why don't you let me buy you a coffee or something and I'll explain. It's about a copy of some hieroglyphics that was sent to you... from Amanda, in Scotland.'

'Who are you?'

'My name is Chris Ryan. I found the papyri. I was told you were trying to decipher it.'

She stopped outside the entrance to a large hotel. 'I'm sorry. Your uniform... I thought you were someone else. There is a cafeteria here... in the lobby. It will be all right to talk, but only for a short while. I have to attend a meeting.'

She spoke with only a trace of an accent. Chris thought

it was French, but he couldn't be sure.

They found a vacant table in the crowded terrace cafeteria. She seemed uncomfortable, her eyes constantly searching the crowded terrace, as if looking for someone.

'I didn't expect you to be English,' Chris said, trying to open the conversation.

'My mother was French. My father an Arab. What did you want to ask me? There is not much I can tell you.'

'Did you hear about your friend in Scotland getting a visit from two men?'

'Yes, I did too. My flat was searched, also my desk at work.'

Chris was surprised. 'You didn't call the police?'

She shook her head. 'They could do nothing. No crime was committed.'

'Searching your flat is not a crime?'

'I did not report it. I did not want to make trouble.'

'Do you know who was responsible?'

'No.'

Chris waited for her to elaborate, to perhaps give him something to go on, but she was obviously not interested, and remained disconcertingly inattentive, her eyes constantly searching the crowd and, finally, Chris could stand it no longer. 'Are you looking for someone?'

She stared at him so intently that for a moment he thought she was angry, then she nodded. 'Someone has been following me. That is why I ran. I thought you were one of them.'

Chris searched the terrace with suddenly sharpened interest. The crowd was a mix of many nationalities, including Arabs. It was impossible to tell. The only ones who did not look suspicious were the Japanese. 'How do you know someone is following you?'

'They are wasting their time,' she said. 'I do not have what they want. I destroyed the copies. They were impossible to decipher. I have already told Amanda.'

'I don't give a damn about the hieroglyphics,' Chris said. 'I only want to know who was responsible for killing my wife.'

She stared at him. 'Your wife was killed... because of this?'

Chris told her briefly what had happened, and also what Bob McEwen had theorized was the reason, and she listened without interruption, a frown creasing her brow above the bridge of her glasses. The lenses made her green eyes large. 'I'm still not convinced that was the reason though,' Chris said. 'I can't see anyone going to such lengths over a few sheets of papyrus. That's part of the reason I'm here... to find out more. The other was to tell you to destroy the copy or make it public. It isn't worth the trouble.'

'I am very sorry about your wife,' she said quietly. 'Such a terrible thing. Also for you and your son. How old is he?'

'Seven.'

She sat silently looking down, rubbing pensively at a smudge of black ink on her finger.

'Would you like something to drink...tea or coffee?'

he asked.

'No, thank you.'

'Is there nothing you can tell me about who may be responsible? It must be someone very important, don't you think?'

She took a long time to answer, seeming hesitant, then she took a deep breath and shifted in her chair, as if reaching a decision. 'It is not only a matter of history,' she said. 'It is also a matter of reputation. There may be some people who do not want to have the truth exposed. It will prove their theories have been wrong ... do you understand?'

'Yes, Bob McEwen said much the same thing.'

She nodded. 'Then you understand.'

'Not really,' Chris answered. 'What truth wouldn't they want exposed?'

Chris had been studying her as she spoke, intrigued by the expressive manner in which her features changed with her mood, and words 'face like an open book' crossed his mind. She could be attractive if she tried a bit harder and wore the right glasses. Her cheeks showed a hint of dimples, and an innocence showed in the self-conscious manner with which she avoided his eyes. She had a graceful way of walking, and he caught himself wondering if she also had nice legs hidden beneath the ugly clothes. He frowned at the thought. He had more important things to think about, and she was not his type.

'You haven't answered my question,' he said. 'What truth?'

'I mean, if what was on the copy didn't agree with their theories, then they wouldn't want it exposed.'

'And does it?'

'Does it what?'

'Come on, Miss Bontoux... surely after what has happened, you can't expect me to believe you weren't interested enough to decipher the copy to find out the reason.'

She gathered herself, as if preparing to leave. 'I told you. It was impossible.'

Chris knew she was lying. Not only did her expression give her away, but he had seen the copies and they were not that bad. 'Sorry, Miss Bontoux, but I find that hard to believe. I've seen them, and for an expert like yourself, I would have thought you would be able to decipher enough to give you a clue, or at least tell if it was Egyptian or Phoenician.'

She glared at him and stood up. 'I don't care what you believe. I am sorry about your wife, but you are right to think it has nothing to do with what you found, and you are also very rude.' She slung her shoulder bag and hurried away between the tables.

Chris swore at himself for allowing his frustration to get to him. It was not her fault. He waited until she was a good distance ahead before going after her. He could not allow her to simply walk away. He knew nothing more than he had before meeting her.

Why she did not want to confide in him made no sense. She was clearly afraid, and probably with good reason, but he thought he had made it obvious he was there to help.

Whatever the reason, it soon became apparent by her actions that she had been telling the truth about her fear she was being followed. She had put some creative thought into hiding her trail.

She did not go out the way they had come in, but walked quickly through a residents only area, then into a narrow passage for staff only. He waited behind a clump of potted palms until she disappeared, then ran after her, and found himself in a kitchen service area full of bustling staff. 'Did you see a woman come in here?' he asked a surprised waiter.

'Sir?'

'Never mind,' Chris said, pushing past him.

He made for an open door. Through it he could see bright daylight, and he spotted her crossing an open service courtyard littered with cartons. She stopped for a moment by the entrance to allow a truck to enter, and turned to look behind, but she did not see him in the doorway, partly shielded by the truck, and neither did she see the man who ducked behind a pile of crates, but Chris did.

He wasn't sure the man was following until she started across a busy street towards the entrance to a large department store, and the man ran after her, furtively dodging behind parked vehicles in such an amateurish manner it was blatantly obvious.

Running to intercept, Chris caught the man by the collar of his jacket as he was about to step off the curb. 'Why are you following that woman?' he demanded, jerking him back.

The man, a young Arab, squealed and tried to pull

away, cringing behind his arms as if afraid of being struck. Chris hauled him back to the relative isolation of the service entrance, intending to do just that if the Arab didn't come up with some quick answers.

But he didn't get that far. An Arab woman launched herself at his back, screaming abuse and pummeling him with her fists and, while Chris was trying to push her away, the man wriggled out of his jacket and escaped, and the woman ran after him.

Chris tossed the jacket aside and let them go. The surprise attack of the woman, perhaps a wife, had all but convinced him he had made a mistake in suspecting the man. Maybe he had merely been trying to hide from his wife.

He looked across the street to where he had last seen Zarena Bontoux. She was standing in the doorway of the department store, looking back at him, but before he could signal her to wait, she disappeared inside.

Muttering to himself at her stubbornness, Chris dodged through the traffic and ran in after her, but although his height gave him an advantage, she was nowhere in sight.

He was striding angrily through the aisles, looking, when she spoke from behind. 'I'm here, Mister Ryan.'

'Trailing behind people seems to be an epidemic around here,' he muttered.

'I saw you with Mahfoud. How did you know?'

'So, I was right. He was after you.'

'I told you someone was. But why are *you* following me? I also told you I didn't know anything. I want you to leave me alone, Mister Ryan.'

'That man I caught wasn't going to leave you alone. He was obviously on to your little ruse of trying to hide your trail. It's just as well I *was* following you.'

'I am not worried about Mahfoud. He's a clerk at the museum, and I already suspected it was him. I was going to report him to the director. Maybe also to the police now.'

'He must be after you for a reason, Miss Bontoux.'

'I think he's trying to find out where I've moved to.'

'I would say that is obvious,' Chris said, trying not to sound impatient. These bookworms were all the same. All brains and no common sense, except in her case, he doubted she had any brains either. 'And why do you think he wants to find out where you live?' He felt as if he was questioning a child.

'I don't think he means me any harm, if that is what you are getting at. If he did, he would have plenty of opportunity. People are attacked in the street all the time in Cairo.'

'He's not working for himself, Miss Bontoux. He's doing it for someone else. They still want the copy, and they believe you still have it, and with your expertise, you are the one person who could do them harm. They are the same people who wanted what I had so badly they were prepared to sacrifice my wife to destroy it. They'll do the same to you if you get in the way.'

Now, he had her attention. Her determined expression changed to one of resignation, and she moved from the aisle to a quiet area behind.'But I have only one photocopy, Mister

Ryan, not an original. Anyone can fake a copy.'

'Maybe they don't know that or don't believe you.' Chris paused, suddenly remembering what she had said. 'I thought you had destroyed the copies.'

She shrugged. 'I took some more at different intensities to see if it made the characters more readable.'

'Where are they?'

'At my friend's flat, where I'm staying.'

'Right.' Chris said firmly. 'This is what we are going to do. I'm coming with you to the flat and you can give me the copies, then tomorrow, we'll both go to the director of the museum and I'll explain the whole thing. I'll give him the copies, and he can do what he likes with them, but it's important we let this character who has been following you know what we have done. We can even give him a copy to take to his masters. That should get them off your back. There's no point in taking any risks.'

Chris had been expecting some sort of disagreement. It seemed to be in her nature, but after a pause, she nodded. 'Yes, perhaps that would be best, but it will have to wait for Monday. The director will be in Luxor this weekend for a conference.'

'No, we have to see him before then,' Chris said. 'I have to be in Aswan on Sunday. Is there no one else?'

'No, I only trust the director, and he will know what to do about Mahfoud.'

Chris observed her thoughtfully. 'Why don't you come with me to Luxor now? We can see the director and,' Chris studied his watch as he calculated, 'allowing an hour or so with him, we can be back in five or six hours.'

She gave him a surprised look. 'I don't think you realize how far it is to Luxor. It takes all night by train to get there.'

Chris grinned at her. 'Who said anything about a train? I have a plane at the airport.'

'Oh,' she said, but she still seemed uncertain, and the frown remained fixed in place. 'I will have to phone the director first, and also tell Rosemary, the girl I am staying with '

Conversation on the streets was impossible, and after passing through several noisy bazaars, Chris gave up trying to memories the route and allowed himself to enjoy the unusual sights of the city. They finally entered a Lebanese restaurant, whose owner let them out of a side door into a passage and stairs to the apartment on the third floor.

Rosemary was a cheerful girl with an infectious grin, which she bestowed on Chris with obvious approval as they shook hands. 'About time Zarena found herself a fella. I'm crazy jealous. Why don't you fetch the man a beer, Zar, while I try to steal him away.'

Chris laughed, but Zarena looked uncomfortable and was quick to put her friend straight. 'Mister Ryan is here on business, Rosemary.' She gave a brief explanation and the American girl sighed. 'Is that all? And here I was thinking my life was about to improve.' She winked mischievously at Chris.

They ordered take-away food from the Lebanese

restaurant below, and Zarena made several calls to the director's hotel in Luxor, but received no reply from his extension, and she finally gave up.

'We'll go anyway?' Chris said. 'If we leave early enough we can catch him before he leaves the hotel in the morning. Or we can leave now. The plane has a comfortable stretcher you can sleep on, and I'm used to sleeping on the ground.'

'You seem to like ordering people around,' Zarena said testily.

'Sorry. Too long in the army, I guess.'

'Anyway, it's a lot of fuss about nothing. I'll see him when he gets back.'

'You should go, Zarena,' Rosemary intervened. 'It's a good opportunity to get away. You never go anywhere.'

Zarena gave a shrug of indifference. 'I still think it's unnecessary, but I'd rather sleep on my own bed, if you don't mind, and leave in the morning. I can get the train back, or return with the director.'

'Whatever you say, but I don't mind flying you back.'

'No. Thank you, but I'd rather go on the train... and now, if you don't mind, I'm going to bed.'

Rosemary smiled apologetically at Chris after Zarena had left. 'Don't worry, she's not usually so cranky. I'll make sure she goes. It will do her good, and I don't want her moping around here this weekend, I have a date. Where are you staying?'

'I usually sleep in the plane.'

'It's too far. You can stay here, if you don't mind the

couch.'

They took an early cab to the airport to avoid the congestion, travelling mostly in an uncomfortable silence, and were in the air as the sun was still glowing red through the haze of the Arabian Desert.

M ahfoud was pleased with himself. So pleased in fact, that he treated himself to an expensive English breakfast at the airport snack bar before phoning the official at his home. He was particularly pleased, and also rather surprised, at how easy it had been to persuade the man at the flight briefing office to supply him, not only with the destination of the plane, but also the exact time of arrival at Luxor. All it required was the registration number, which had been clearly visible on the tail, and a quickly fabricated story about an unpaid hotel bill. The man had even offered to contact the tourist police at the Luxor airport on his behalf.

Getting his sister to follow the couple had been a touch of genius. She was able to stay much closer and pass through areas unchallenged, whereas before he had received many suspicious looks and two threats of arrest. Once they had found the Lebanese restaurant the rest was easy. For a small bribe, the kitchen *sufragi* who delivered the take-away had been able to give him the number of the apartment and who was there.

Mahfoud reluctantly drained the last of his tea then sauntered across to one of the public phones.

'What do you mean she has flown away?' The official demanded irritably. The call had come at a most inconvenient time.

'I am sorry to disturb you so early,' Mahfoud lied, 'and to be causing you to run to the telephone.'

'Never mind that. What have you found?'

Taking his time, and ignoring the impatient grunts on the other end, Mahfoud explained his movements over the past few days, including the vicious attack upon his person by the stranger, but omitted the part played by his sister in coming to the rescue. He saved the best part for last.

'Did you not say, sir, that the bint's father is living in Qena?'

'So?'

'It is but a short distance from Luxor.'

After a long pause, interrupted only by heavy breathing and whispering in the background, during which, Mahfoud waited anxiously, the official answered.

'You have done well for a change, Mahfoud. Call me back in half an hour and I will give you further instructions. I have a few other calls to make first.'

Smiling with satisfaction, Mahfoud replaced the receiver and sauntered back to the snack bar. Half an hour was ample time for another breakfast. Maybe this time he would order the American one.

'Rameses the second,' Zarena explained, pointing to a large statue in the court of the Temple of Luxor. 'He ruled in the nineteenth dynasty.'

'Fascinating,' Chris responded. Ancient history was not one of his strengths, and he had seen enough statues and temples to last a millennium, but for the first time she was showing some enthusiasm so he tried to reciprocate.

Because of an early schedule, the director had been unavailable until the following morning, when he had agreed to meet them over breakfast, so they were forced to fill in the day by sightseeing. They had spent an hour at a cafe table, drinking sweet mint tea - which Chris thought would go better with roast lamb - and making notes on all the important points they needed to discuss with the director.

After leaving the temple, and to escape the heat and crowds, Chris suggested a sail on the river, and she entered into negotiations with the owner of a small felucca being loaded with bundles of sugar cane. The owner seemed reluctant until Chris waved an American ten dollar note above Zarena's head where she couldn't see it, and a gap-toothed smile signaled the end of the bargaining.

The happy owner sat them on a bundle of cane, with a stick each to chew, and they sailed aimlessly around in the light breeze, trailing their hands in the brown water of the Nile. When the owner's smile began to fade, Chris restored it with another note.

'You are spoiling him,' Zarena criticized. 'I don't think you are much good at bargaining.'

'I'll pay a lot more to keep away from the tourists.'

She seemed reluctant to talk about herself or her work, and sat primly on her bundle, her eyes concealed behind old-fashioned sunglasses and her hair covered by a white head cloth, reminding him of photographs he had once seen of Rita Hayworth after she had married the Aga Khan.

She had other similarities to the film star. She was tall and walked with the supple grace that only a slender and shapely figure could produce, and which the long skirt seemed somehow to accentuate, rather than conceal. Perhaps it was because she was not at work, but she looked different and more attractive than she had the day before.

Chris tried to encourage her by recounting parts of his own life he thought would be interesting or amusing, and she listened with polite attention, but said nothing about herself. All he had been able to get out of her was that she had gone to university in Edinburgh to study archaeology. Then he remembered her mother was French.

'Were you born in France, Miss Bontoux?' She had not suggested he use her first name so he kept it formal, and she did the same.

For a moment he thought she was not going to answer. 'In Qena,' she answered finally. 'It is not far from here. Twenty miles, or so.' She did not elaborate, and her tone suggested she found the subject boring, so he changed tack.

'Have you seen much of Africa?'

'Only Egypt. One day... perhaps.'

In the evening they joined a group from the hotel and

shared a horse drawn carriage to the Temple of Karnak, and Chris found himself virtually excluded when the group discovered they had an expert among them. Zarena was in her element, laughing and joking, and showing none of her previous reserve. She explained the drawings on the walls and recounted the history of the Pharaohs' to her appreciative audience until his mind bulged and he wandered off on his own for some peace and quiet.

The carriage was crowded on the return and he was squeezed close to her, feeling the softness of her thigh, and it disturbed him more than he was prepared to admit. He was not sorry when they arrived back at the hotel and Zarena excused herself to have an early night. He bid her a cool goodnight and retired to the bar.

It seemed as if his head had barely touched the pillow before he was being rudely shaken awake. Drugged with sleep and alcohol, he squinted against the light at the hotel manager.

'What?' he mumbled.

'Sir... wake up please.'

'I'm awake. What is it?'

Another voice, more authoritative, spoke from behind the manager. 'Get up, please. We must ask you some questions.'

Chris sat up and blinked at the sight of two men in the dazzling white uniforms of the tourist police. 'What?'

'We wish to ask some questions about your aircraft.'

'What about it?' Chris demanded, suddenly alert. 'Has something happened to it?'

The policeman looked nonplussed. 'Nothing has happened to it. If you will come with us please, it will be explained at the police station.' The tone of his voice suggested it was not a request. To further emphasize the demand, the policeman pushed the manager aside and looked down officiously at Chris. 'Your passport?'

'In the safe,' Chris muttered, 'ask the manager.' He swung his legs over the bed and looked at his watch. He had been asleep for less than two hours. He had probably parked in the wrong place and they wanted the plane moved. 'I hope this won't take long.'

Nine hours later, and thoroughly frustrated, he was still shivering in a detention cell at the police station. A bored and much distracted police officer had taken his statement and made several calls to try and verify his story, apparently without success.

It seemed a complaint had been made by some unnamed official that he had violated some regulations, including not paying landing fees, and that he was also a suspected smuggler. From the hotel, they had been taken him to the airport and the plane had been searched. They had been unable to find his passengers, whose names he could not remember, and who had not told him where they were staying. Telephone calls to Khartoum and Addis to check on his movements had produced nothing but more confusion, which was not surprising considering it was after midnight.

His request to phone the hotel and inform Zarena Bontoux of his predicament was refused, as was his request to call the director when the time for the meeting had arrived. Then, a few hours later, he was released without explanation and informed he was not to leave Luxor for the next twenty four hours. His passport was confiscated, and he was ordered to report to the police station every four hours. In the meantime, the plane would remain impounded.

Chris rushed back to the hotel to find Zarena gone. He checked her room and discovered her bag was also gone and the bed had been made up.

'When did she leave?' Chris demanded of the clerk behind the desk.

The clerk looked at him blankly and shrugged his shoulders. 'I have not seen her.''Fetch the manager,' Chris ordered.

'But sir, the manager is sleeping.'

'Then wake him up,' Chris said tightly, 'or I'll do it myself.'

The clerk hurried away and returned with the sleepy manager.

'But I have not seen her either,' he protested. 'None of the staff has seen the lady since yesterday, and her account has not been paid. I must insist that you...'

'Ask them again. *Someone* must have seen her!'

'*Ma arafish!*' The manager raised both hands and looked up. 'I do not know, sir. Maybe she left in the night... by the fire exit perhaps, after you were arrested.'

Chris glared at him, resisting the urge to take him by the throat. 'No, we had an important meeting this morning. She would not have left. Something has happened. Are you sure there was no message?'

The Manager sighed with exasperation. 'I am sure, sir.'

Under the concerned eyes of the manager and clerk, Chris prowled the hotel lobby. Something was wrong with the whole set-up. She would not leave without telling him, of that he was convinced, even if he had been less than polite to her. And the strange business over the plane...

The manager coughed. 'Sir, the ladies account, will you pay?'

'Never mind that!' Chris snapped. 'I will pay it with mine.' He suddenly had a thought. 'My flying bag. Do you still have it in the safe?'

'Of course, sir.'

'Get it please.'

The clerk placed it on the counter and Chris carried it up to his room, hoping the police had not searched it. He flipped the latch and looked in, then breathed a sigh of relief. The nine-millimetre pistol he had taken from the plane was still there. He stuck it into the waist band of his jeans and went back to search Zarena Bontoux's room, looking for something that would explain her departure, but he found nothing. Were it not for a few long strands of her dark hair on the floor near the mirror and the faint smell of honey and almonds, she may well have been a figment of his imagination.

From somewhere distant a dog barked, then the silence returned. A dark silence. She opened her eyes, but saw only more darkness. A strong, nauseating smell lingered about her. A smell that she knew but could not place.

She tried to move, to roll over, but her body felt numb and detached, and only her head would turn. Bile burned in her throat, filled her mouth, trickled warmly over her cheek, and she groaned.

She felt pain in her arms and tried to move them, but they were too heavy. So were her legs. She wondered if she was still in a dream. Nothing appeared in her mind to explain what was happening, although her memory struggled with images of sailing in a felucca, laser lights at the temple lake, a strange bed, then... nothing.

With sudden, chilling awareness, she realized that her hands were tied behind her back, and questions came in a rush. Where was she... why were her hands tied?

Her legs were also tied. The floor beneath her was cold and hard. If only she could see...

From outside of the darkness came a steady rumbling, growing louder, then it stopped. A door banged and she jerked with fright. Muffled voices came closer. Another door opened. Light and shadowy figures appeared; the light floating above her.

'So, Zarena el Kholi returns.'

He spoke softly in Arabic. The tone of a cultured man. A man she should know.

'She has grown to look like her whore of a mother.'

Another man with an emotionless voice. One she had prayed never to hear again. Her father.

With the shock of recognition came the knowledge of his softly spoken companion.

After a long pause her father spoke again. 'What will be your decision?'

Sheikh Ghaffer did not reply immediately. The lantern changed hands and moved close to her face, and she twisted her head away, closing her eyes.

'She has been sick. You should have her cleaned.' There was a note of censure in his tone.

'Yes. Would you have me call in the women?'

'In a while, perhaps.'

The lantern moved slowly down her body.

'Do you wish her clothes to be removed?'

Her night-dress was pulled up and she lifted her knees, turning them away, but they were forced down again and held firm. In a voice that croaked with dryness, she tried to cry out, but no intelligible words came, and she began to wail in despair.

'Silence!' The outline of her father loomed close and suddenly her head flashed to a stinging slap on her cheek, and her thin wail ended abruptly in a gasp.

Irritation showed in her father's voice when he spoke again. 'Well, what will you decide?'

'Patience is a godly virtue, Azim. Her body and skin is good, but she will be the oldest. Ten years ago maybe, when we had the arrangement, but now? I do not know…'

'She has been to university. She could be a valuable asset.'

'Perhaps, but it is not important. If I take her it will be for her color. I will extend no further generosity.'

'I expect none. The reason I called you is because you have already shown it and did not receive the benefit. Like her mother, she has brought dishonor on my family. If you do not want her, she will pay with her life. I will arrange it myself.'

'That is a harsh judgement for you to make, Azim.'

'The judgment is not mine. She has spoken against Islam.'

'At her age it is too much to expect she is still a virgin, but I must be satisfied she is clean.'

'She was done as a child, but of course, you must be satisfied for yourself. I will call in the *daya* and the other women.'

'And more light.'

'Please…' Zarena croaked, 'you can't do this to me.'

They ignored her and she resumed her soft wailing, unable to restrain her fear.

Her father returned with another lantern and four women. One of them was her aunt Hebba. The others were strangers. At an impatient signal from her father, her aunt picked up a wad of cloth from the floor and held it over Zarena's mouth, and she gagged at the remembered smell of ether, but it was not enough to put her under.

Hebba straddled her at the waist to stop her from rolling while the others removed the cloth strips binding her ankles.

Zarena looked up into her aunt's face, appealing desperately with her eyes, but her aunt remained unmoved. Her hard face, now burdened with age, held the same fixed expression of sullen reproach it had always shown. Nothing had changed.

The women forced Zarena's legs apart and the *daya* knelt between them.

'Perhaps, Azim, as you are her father you should leave,' the Sheikh suggested.

'I have no daughter,' he replied, but he turned to face the wall.

The *daya's* knowing fingers probed deep and Zarena arched her back, trying to resist, but her struggles were futile against Hebba's weight. She felt a sudden sharp pain. The *daya* removed her hand.

'Well?' the Sheikh asked.

'There is blood.' The *daya* answered.

A brief silence followed, as if it had not been what they expected.

'Is she clean?'

'To the first degree only.'

Sheikh Ghaffer spoke to her father. 'All my girls have been done to the third degree. It must be completed if I am to take her.'

'Can you do it?' her father asked of the *daya*.

'Yes, but…'

'Then do it now.'

Zarena heard the words with disbelief and horror. The pain and humiliation she had suffered as a child would be nothing compared to the agonizing butchery they were planning. She could do nothing to resist. The combined weight of the three women held her fast, and the cloth on her mouth silenced her pleas. She prayed they would use the ether.

'There is some danger,' the *daya* said, sounding reluctant. 'You must know that if I fail it will not be my fault.'

'If she dies,' her father replied, 'it will be the will of Allah.

Part Four

Egypt - 1951

It was a sunny room, filled with colorful picture books, and a window looking down on a street filled with noisy people. It was also a happy room, with a big table where her mother sat and wrote things from the books, and where she also sat drawing pictures of donkeys and pyramids. Her mother would hang the pictures on the wall and her father would admire them when he came home from work, then he'd take her for a walk along the busy street. They never went out unless her father came too. He would lift her up on his shoulders and she would hold on to his hair and look down on the people and laugh.

They left the sunny room when she was six, and went to live in a dark, crowded house with her father's family, and with the bright, happy room, went also the books, the drawing and the laughter, and in their place came the shouting, the slapping and the tears.

Zarena was seven the night she and her mother ran away.

While her father and her aunt Hebba were visiting friends in Qena, they stuffed some clothes into a plastic bag and hurried across rough fields in the dark to catch the train to Cairo. From there, her mother used the last of the money for tickets to Alexandria.

They stayed with an old Greek man and his wife that her mother had known before she was married, and they did not venture out of the house for five days - not until the day of the market.

Papa Zoupo said they shouldn't go, but her mother said they needed to get out and that it would be all right. The market was only across the square, and if they wore their head cloths pulled across their faces, it would hide their fair skins.

It was so good to be out in the sunshine again she felt like skipping. A strange city too, with exciting new things to see, and she loved the name Alexandria. It was a girl's name. Not like Qena, which sounded like a camel's name.

They were never going back there, her mother promised, and as soon as her family sent the money they were going to live in France. She liked that name too, but it was a boy's name. Alexandria was better.

Her mother held her hand so tight as they crossed the square that it hurt her fingers. She tried wriggling them free, so she could run and skip, but her mother tugged impatiently, pulling her close and walking fast.

They crossed a road full of yellow taxis and carts piled high with vegetables and fruit, then they were in the market.

It was very noisy. Tea-sellers beat on their shiny urns as if they were gongs, and merchants sitting by their goods called out and held up brightly colored scarves or long, thin fish that were all dried and smelly.

With so much to see she would have stopped more often, but the urgent tugging on her hand kept her moving.

In her free hand, Zarena held the cloth bag into which her mother put the things they bought for Mama Zoupo, shielding it from the crowd with her body so they wouldn't get squashed; raisins and olives and dates, and especially the sweet cakes with the sticky brown tops that she knew Papa Zoupo would use to tease her.

'I keep forgetting I have no children left to eat them,' he told her the first time he brought the cakes home. 'Now Mama will be angry with me for buying them. But they taste so good, little Zarena, and I cannot throw them away. You must do it. But quickly, before Mama sees them... and be careful not to leave any crumbs.'

Papa Zoupo was funny, and Mama Zoupo cried a lot, but mostly they were happy tears. She was crying the first time she saw her, the day she and her mother arrived at the house after leaving the train, and was still crying when she and Papa Zoupo returned from their walk to the sea a whole hour later.

With the bag nearly full, they were about to leave the market, walking past a jumble of empty carts, and she was looking at the donkeys standing together with their heads down like they were sleepy, when her hand was suddenly pulled free of her mother's and the bag was jolted from her hand, spilling all the good things on the ground. An arm caught her around the middle and lifted her, squeezing the breath from her so her cries were jerky as she was carried quickly out of sight behind the carts.

'Zarena!'

She heard her mother's cry and managed to twist far enough around to see her. The head cloth had gone, freeing the long hair, and a man was pulling her by it. She stumbled and fell, but still he dragged her, jerking her head from side to side, shouting and leaning over to slap at her face; slaps that bloodied her mouth and cheeks.

'*Khawaga*!' French whore!'

The man was her father.

Her mother's broken cries, the sharp slaps, the harsh voice repeating the same thing over and over, were all but smothered by the noise and shouting from the market, but Zarena heard them as if no other sound existed.

Kicking and struggling, she found her breath and began to scream, and her father stopped to stare at her. His eyes were red, and his face was swollen and ugly. He spoke sharply to the person holding her and a hand with a big silver ring on one finger was placed over her mouth. The hand and ring of her Aunt Hebba.

Her mother was kneeling with her head on the ground, almost as if she were praying. Her father lifted her face, his hand raised and waiting to slap it, and Zarena caught a glimpse of her mother's bloodied face looking out from behind a veil of hair. Her mother began to crawl forward, calling her name, but her father pushed her over with his foot and began kicking her. Kicking at the arms that covered her face and head, kicking at her body, his voice rising until he was again shouting with every kick:

'French whore! French whore!'

Several people ran amongst the wagons, and somewhere a woman started screaming: '*Bolees! Bolees!*'

A man in a white jellaba pulled at her father's arm, shouting something at him, and her father shouted back. 'French whore! I will kill her!'

Other men pulled at him, surrounding him and pushing him away and, in the confusion, Zarena was carried, struggling, around the carts and on to the street.

Her father followed a few moments later, breathing heavily, his face still strange and ugly. He jerked open the back door of a yellow taxi and pushed her in.

She kicked out, screaming, and her father leaned across the seat and raised his hand, holding it poised like the snake with the flat head she had seen standing up from its pot in the market, swaying and waiting for the right moment, and she stopped screaming to stare at it. The open palm was smeared with blood.

The blow struck her on the side of her face and mouth, knocking her off the seat to the floor.

She stayed there, huddled down with her eyes screwed tight as humming sounds filled her head, but even with her eyes closed she could see her mother's face looking at her through the hair, and she could see the hand open and waiting, and she knew whose blood it was she tasted.

The sound of her mother's frightened voice calling out her name stayed with her, and she clung to it, pushing aside everything else, and it was still uppermost in her mind a long time after they had driven away.

Zarena did not see her mother again, and no word of her was spoken. She had no way of knowing what it was her mother had done, or even if she was alive or dead. The speaking of her name was forbidden.

For a long, long time she prayed secretly that her mother would come with Papa Zoupo and take her away, but in her heart she always knew they would not.

Neither her father, nor her aunt Hebba, spoke to her on the long return journey to Qena. Orders were given in short, brittle words, and usually accompanied by a push or sharp prod, as if she were a dumb animal. Twice, her father slapped her. Once for mentioning her mother, and another time for staring at him; looking into his eyes. That too, she came to learn, was now forbidden, and she soon became stiff and awkward under the constant fear of doing something wrong,

Eight people, including herself, lived in the small house. Aunt Hebba, her father's widowed sister, and Fatma, married to her uncle. There were three other children. Two boys a little older than herself, and a four-year-old girl who wet the bed every night.

Her father was seldom there, but his absence made little

difference to the way she was treated, and Zarena wondered why she had been brought back when it was so obvious she was not wanted.

The bed she had slept in with her mother had gone and she was made to share a bed with her small cousin, and to wash the soiled sheet each morning.

All her mother's belongings; her clothes, books, photographs and jewellery had vanished. When she asked her eldest cousin about the books, he told her they had been burned because they told lies and were evil.

She cried that night, and many other nights, with the smelly sheet pulled over her head.

They came for her when she was asleep. A hand was clamped over her mouth and other hands held her legs and arms. She was unable to move or cry out. They carried her through to the bathroom where a candle was burning, but a towel was placed over her face so she could not see.

They lifted her night vest to her chin laid her naked body on the cold floor with her head clamped firmly between two knees from behind. A hand held her under her chin, pulling her head back and pressing against her nose so she could scarcely breathe.

They talked in harsh whispers, about things she did not understand, and she was rigid with fear, convinced she was about to have her throat cut. It was what happened to bad girls, she had been told.

Rough hands gripped her legs and forced them apart,

spreading them wide, and her arms were held at the wrist and elbow and pressed hard against the floor. She stopped breathing, her body trembling violently as she imagined the knife coming towards her throat. She felt the pressure of hands and fingers around her private place, then a searing pain.

The unexpected shock of it made her body jump against the hands holding her, and she screamed into the one clamped over her mouth. It felt as if she had been touched inside with a hot coal. The burning spread like a flame upwards into her belly and licked hot on her thighs. A wad of cloth was pushed up between her legs.

No one spoke as they carried her back to the bed. Her cousin had been taken away and she was left alone in the darkness with her confusion and pain.

For two days she was unable to walk or relieve herself, and she thought she was going to burst. On the third day she had no choice but to put up with the pain or wet the bed like her young cousin. She cried and bit on her lip until it swelled, and for more than two weeks after that first time she drank nothing, taking only small sips of water when she could no longer bear her thirsts and, gradually, it became easier.

She was given no explanation for what had occurred other than it was something all girls had to have done to make them clean. She was put to work preparing food and washing clothes, and that was to be her duty for the next three years. She was not permitted to attend the school with her cousins, although, thanks to her mother, she could read and write better than any of them, and even speak a little French. She was a girl, and the rules were strict. Running or raising her voice was forbidden, and she had to keep her legs together at all times. Her eyes were to be downcast whenever she spoke to any male, even her cousins, and she was not to speak unless spoken to first. If food was short, it was she who went hungry, and if she complained or broke any of the rules, even though it was not her fault, the punishment was swift.

She saw less and less of her father, and when he came she kept out of the way. He had work in one of the towns, but she never knew where it was or what he did. She was kept in ignorance of everything that her aunt Hebba thought didn't concern her. What they did tell her though, and often, was that it was because of her mother that her father had lost his good government job. Her mother was a foreign whore, Hebba told her, and should have been stoned, and if she were not careful to keep pure thoughts and a pure body, it is what would happen to her.

It was unfortunate that she had her mother's looks and fair complexion and, as she grew older, it became more noticeable. She was tall and slender, with her mother's green eyes, but her hair was dark and curly. She was a foreigner in their midst, and it was not long before they started calling her *khawaga*. It was a name also given to tourists and Jews – and her mother.

As she grew, the male members of the family began to look at her strangely, at times even kindly, and this was not lost on Hebba and Fatma. She had to wear her *galabia* more carefully and to hide her feet, and she was made to wear a head cloth more often.

It was the attention of the males that frightened her more than anything, particularly her uncle, the brother of Hebba's dead husband. He was a mean, thin faced old man with flickering eyes that followed her, and Zarena knew he was thinking bad things and tried to keep out of his way, but it was not always possible.

He worked in a neighbor's field behind the house, and she had to take food to him during the day. When she arrived, he would sit in the shade of the well and eat while she waited. Mostly he was with others, when she was ignored, but sometimes he was alone and watched her while he ate, and when this happened, she was careful to keep her distance and avert her eyes.

On the day before her eleventh birthday - which always fell on the same day as the festival holiday of *Sham en Nessim,* the celebration of Spring - she took his food as usual. The bread she carried in a basket, but the bowl of mashed eggs and olive oil she held in her hand to prevent it from spilling.

She was only a few steps from where he sat waiting, when a stick became tangled in the hem of her robe and she tripped. The bowl slipped from her hand and landed at his feet, splattering him with the food. With a cry of dismay, she bent quickly to pick it up, but he caught hold of her.

'Stupid bint! What do you think you are doing wasting food?'

'I'm sorry, Bek! It was an accident.'

He shook her, so hard that she lost her balance and fell against him.

'An accident so you say. Well then, I say you must be taught a lesson.'

He spun her around and threw her face down across his lap. Holding her down with one hand, he pulled up her robe to expose her bare legs and underpants.

Expecting to be slapped, Zarena struggled and cried out in protest. 'I am sorry, Bek! It was an accident. I am sorry!'

'Be quiet. You must take punishment in silence.'

The expected slapping never came. Instead, she felt his coarse hand forcing its way between her legs. A finger pushed painfully into her, wriggling like a giant scaly worm towards the place still protected by its membrane of honor; a membrane that only the finger of a husband or *daya* could pierce. To have it broken, she had been warned, was the worst thing that could happen to a girl. It could even cost her life,.

Zarena squealed in alarm and twisted her legs tightly together, but he was strong. His breathing had changed, and the hand holding her down began to slacken its grip. She twisted her head and tried to bite him on the leg, but the cloth of his robe filled her mouth and she was unable to clench her teeth on flesh.

In desperation, Zarena reached forward and scooped handfuls of the sandy soil over her shoulder, in the direction of his head.

He grunted in surprise and pulled his hand away to rub at his eyes, and she rolled off, scrambling to her feet. She started to run, then stopped to pick up the basket and bowl. To return without it would only mean being sent back to fetch it.

Her uncle was on his feet, still brushing at his eyes. Afraid he would follow, she ran for a short distance before slowing to a walk, not wanting to draw attention, but when she was close to the house she saw her aunt standing rigid in the doorway, looking out.

With a sinking feeling, Zarena realized she must have seen what happened, but she had no choice but to continue on with legs that felt at the same time both stiff and weak.

Her aunt said nothing as she walked past, did not even look at her, and Zarena went directly to the bathroom and stood against the closed door, her chest pounding, listening for the scuff of footsteps, but none came.

She lowered her underpants and examined them, and was relieved to see only the stains from her uncle's dirty hands. The soft skin of her thighs was scratched and blotchy, and she felt sore inside, but she was sure no damage had been done. She took a deep breath, picked up the basket, and went through to the kitchen.

Hebba and Fatma were there, talking. They fell silent as she came in and remained silent as she washed the bowl. She put it away, then picked up a basket of washing from the floor and hurried out.

For the remainder of the afternoon she kept out of the

way as much as possible, doing the washing and dreading her uncle's return.

He came at the usual time and followed the normal routine, bathing himself then sitting alone to say his prayers, running the yellow prayer beads through his fingers as if nothing had happened. But there was tension in the house. Zarena could feel it, and even her male cousins must have felt it, for they were unusually quiet and well mannered.

The crowded house had little privacy. Her uncle and aunt Fatma had to pass her bed to go to their own, so when she heard them coming she pulled the sheet over her head. She was still awake when her young cousin climbed in and curled up beside her, and for once Zarena was glad of her company. She could not believe the incident with her uncle had ended, and began to wonder if, despite the silence and tension, she had been wrong and her aunt had seen nothing.

She was jolted from sleep by a stifled scream. It was followed by several slaps and the angry voice of her uncle. 'Get out! You are nothing! Out! Out!'

Zarena sat up in alarm before realizing what she was doing.

The door of her uncle's room crashed open and her aunt stumbled out, sobbing and holding her face, and she saw Zarena sitting in the bed, staring at her. *'Khawaga whore!'* she hissed, and Zarena ducked quickly back under the sheet.

She lay hardly daring to breathe, expecting at any moment to hear the door open and her uncle come out. Her body felt cold and shivery, yet also warm and damp, as if she had a fever, and she had a sick feeling in her belly. She needed desperately to relieve herself, but did not have the courage to go.

At dawn she was still awake, her mind in turmoil. Desperate for relief, she eased out of bed and threw her robe loosely around, then padded quickly to the bathroom. She closed the door quietly and covered the gap below it with her robe before striking a match and lighting the candle.

She had already removed her underpants before she saw the bloodstain. She stared at it in horror. Looking down at herself, she saw the smears of blood.

Zarena walked slowly towards the basin, her heart thudding. She saw her image in the spotty mirror and looked away quickly, not wanting to see herself. She picked up her pants and used them to wipe her legs, hoping for a moment it was only the scratches that were bleeding, but they were not. It was coming from inside, and worse still, it had not stopped. Her stomach squirmed and she leaned over the basin, but nothing came. Holding a hand to her mouth, she stifled a sob and fought the tears.

She tried not to cry for her mother, or for her fear and loneliness; for the life she hated and for the pain in her belly she did not understand. She tried not to cry because she was a girl, or because of the blood, or because she was no longer a virgin. And she tried not to cry because she was afraid of dying.

Zarena had cried many times, but never had she tried so hard not to, and when she succeeded, she felt stronger. What she had feared had happened, and there was nothing she could do about it. Her life was as good as over, but what was left of it was not going to be wasted in tears or waiting for something to happen. She would leave, and if they caught her and killed her, it didn't matter, she no longer cared.

She washed her underpants and put them back on before emptying the basin into the hole in the floor. The bleeding appeared to have stopped. She extinguished the light and put on her robe. The house was still dark and silent.

Back at the bed, she pulled the damp sheet gently from under her sleeping cousin and quietly left the house. In the grey light of dawn she could see only one small bloodstain. She left the sheet in a bucket to soak, then hid in the chicken house with the hens. If they found her, she would say she was collecting the eggs.

It was only when she saw her uncle leave the house later than usual, accompanied by her two cousins, that she remembered it was a holiday. For a while, she considered abandoning her plan, then realized it could be an advantage. The routine would be changed, giving her a better chance to get away without being missed.

Hebba peered out from the door several times, obviously looking for her, then she left with her small cousin, going down the road towards the house of a friend, and Zarena guessed it was where her other aunt, Fatma, had spent the night. It was the perfect opportunity. No one would miss her for a long time, and with the holiday, the road to Qena would be busier than usual. She would not be noticed.

She left the chickens and went to the empty house. She knew exactly where to look for the money she needed. She removed the flat tin box from under her uncle's clothes and opened it. Inside were a few pound notes, several fifty piaster notes, and some coins. She stuffed the notes into the inside pocket of her robe and returned the box to its place.

She was guiltily aware that what she was doing was terribly wrong. Thieving was one of the worst crimes. If caught, she may have her hand chopped off. She hesitated. It was not too late. She could simply get on with her work and say she had felt ill and gone for a walk. Surely that would be acceptable? And if she left, what would she do? At the most she would have only a few hours before they missed her. How far could she go in such a short time? When they caught her they would bring her back and maybe chop off her hand, then cut her throat and leave her body lying in the field for the dogs to eat.

Zarena felt she was going to be sick. She went through to the bathroom and leaned over the basin, but nothing came. She checked to see if the bleeding had stopped. It hadn't. There was not as much, but it was still there. She saw a pale, hollow eyed stranger's face looking at her from the mirror. She stared at it, her resolve weakening further. The plan was hopeless, she would return the money.

She started towards her uncle's room when suddenly her name was called from behind. 'Zarena!'

She stumbled with fright. It was her father!

'Put on a clean robe... your best one. I am taking you to

see someone important. Be quick.'

'Yes, Father,' she answered without turning.

Her mind in a whirl, Zarena took a clean robe from the box under the bed and returned to the bathroom to change. After an agonizing few moments of indecision, she transferred the money to the new robe, then covered her hair and part of her face with a blue head cloth.

She stood nervously looking at the floor as her father gave her a brief inspection, then followed him to where a car was waiting on the road. It belonged to a friend of his from the city and, to her dismay, she saw her uncle and cousins were waiting inside it with the driver. Her father opened the back door and she squeezed in beside her cousins.

They drove away, following the bumpy road to Qena, which made her stomach ache even more.

No one spoke to her, or explained where they were going, but from the excited chatter of her cousins she gathered that it was to a football match. But females did not attend football matches.

They stopped at a large, two storey house in Qena and her father ordered her out. She followed him through an iron gate and along a stone path that led around a fountain with a statue of a lion in the centre.

A plump, shiny-faced man in crisp white trousers and a silver and gold embroidered waistcoat was standing beside the open front door. He studied her as he returned her father's deferential greeting, smiling and beckoning them politely inside.

Red and blue rugs were scattered over the white tiled floor, and she took care to avoid them. The tiles felt smooth and cool against her bare feet. The man clapped his hands and a few moments later a delicate, sad-eyed girl a few years older than herself appeared and indicated Zarena was to go with her. The girl led her into the largest kitchen she had ever seen.

Two old women were preparing food, and another girl, as black and shiny as an ebony statue, and about the same age as the first, was sitting at a table repairing a silver bracelet with wire. She gave Zarena a sullen stare before returning to her work. A chair was pushed towards her and Zarena sat down tentatively.

After an awkward silence, the girl repairing the bracelet spoke. 'Are you the new girl?'

Zarena frowned at her, puzzled.

Both girls stared back, waiting expectantly for her answer. Somewhere outside, she heard the voices of other women talking.

'I don't know what you mean...'

'We heard there was to be a new girl.'

'I am with my father. He is visiting,' Zarena explained.

The two girls exchanged glances.

'Do you... live here?' Zarena asked hesitantly, making conversation.

The black girl looked down at her work and smiled.

The other girl had busied herself with arranging two small cups of minted tea on a tray and did not reply. She left the kitchen with the tray and returned a short while later empty-handed.

'Your father wishes to see you,' she said.

Zarena left the kitchen and walked towards the sound of voices. They were sitting beside a low table sipping at the tea, and she stopped at a respectful distance to wait.

The owner of the house motioned her forward. 'Come closer, my child. Do not be afraid.'

Her father replaced his cup carefully on the tray and stood. 'Sheikh Ghaffar wishes to see you, Zarena.' He sounded unusually happy.

Zarena flinched as he raised his hand to push back her head cloth and uncover her hair. He placed a finger under her chin and raised it. Zarena kept her eyes fixed on the silver tray.

After a short silence, during which her father turned her head slowly from side to side, the Sheikh spoke. 'Yes, you are right, Azim. I believe she is all you say, but a little pale. I trust she is not sickly?'

Her father laughed. 'No, Sheikh. It is only that she has never met anyone of your station before.'

'Very well, if she is willing, I believe we can arrive at a suitable arrangement. She will have a room of her own, and new clothes. Everything she needs will be provided, although I must warn you,' the Sheikh's voice took on a sharp edge. 'I will not tolerate disobedience or laziness'

I assure you, Sheikh, she is neither of those. She will do whatever you ask.'

'On those terms, I agree.'

'When will be a suitable beginning?'

The Sheikh thought for a moment. 'I have guests arriving in a few hours. One in particular, who will be of special interest to you, Azim. A government minister of very high rank. If your daughter, Zarena... a pleasing name... were to be present, it could make our task easier...'

Her father turned to her. 'Sheikh Ghaffar has kindly offered you service in his house, Zarena. You will begin immediately.'

Zarena's feelings of uncertainty and dread became one of almost overwhelming relief. Being a servant in a place such as this, and for a man who was rich and seemed kind, was the answer to all her prayers. She would not have to face her uncle and the misery she had endured in his house, and there would be the companionship of girls her own age. Best of all, she would have a room of her own. An unheard of luxury. It was not an opportunity to miss. 'Yes, Father,' she answered positively. 'I would be very much honored.'

Her father and the Sheikh smiled at her.

She waited in the large kitchen while they continued their talk, watching the Nubian girl in silence as she painstakingly bound the broken bracelet. Then the sad-eyed girl reappeared.

'Come with me,' she said. 'Sheikh Ghaffar has asked that I show you your room and inform you of your duties.'

Zarena followed her up the stairs and along a passage with several doors along one side, each door decorated with a different, beautifully painted picture of a bird on it.

'How many people live here?' Zarena whispered.

The girl did not answer, instead, she opened a door with a painting of a white swan. 'The bathroom.' she explained. She pulled on a cord hanging from the ceiling and a startling blaze of light flooded the room, revealing a white bath large enough to lie in, and a shower above it with gleaming taps. Below a mirror that occupied most of the wall were two basins and a shelf filled with fancy bottles of soaps and perfumes.

'Use any you like,' the girl said. 'We all share.' She explained which bottles held what, then showed her confused and dumbfounded student how to operate the shower and gleaming white bowl she had first taken to be a toilet without a seat, but which turned out to have a completely different function. Zarena eyed it apprehensively as they left.

She was given the flamingo room. It was second from the end, and had a picture of a pink flamingo on the door. The room was small but luxurious, with a soft looking bed and fluffy pillows. Another of the red and blue patterned rugs covered the floor. Zarena smiled as she looked from the window and over the town.

The girl spoke from behind. 'So you *are* the new girl.'

'Yes,' Zarena replied, turning to face her, still smiling. 'Are you the Sheikh's daughter? If so, you must give me orders. I will do anything you wish.'

'You think I am his daughter?' The girl looked at her in astonishment, then laughed. 'No I am not a daughter. I suppose I am a servant too. We are all servants. There are no wives or daughters.'

'Who will give me orders then?' Zarena asked, surprised.

'Sheikh Ghaffar will give orders.' She pointed to a large wooden chest beside the bed. 'Inside you will find clothes, some are new, some are old. You can try them if you wish. When you are ready, come to the kitchen. The guests will be arriving soon.'

'I will be as quick as I can. What must I call you? I am Zarena.'

'Nirjis.' the girl replied. She moved to the door then hesitated, as if about to say more, then she quickened her step and walked out.

Zarena closed the door and swooped on the wooden box. The unpleasant events of the morning were forgotten. Not even the thought of the bleeding or stolen money could dampen her spirits. If she was accused, she would simply deny it, and who could say she was the culprit? It could as easily have been one of her cousins. And who was there to find out about her broken membrane of honor? She was much closer to the station now, and she already had the money for a ticket. If she did not like the work she could run away whenever she wanted to.

The wooden box was a treasure chest of clothing. Everything was there, in a confusing variety of colors and styles, and the quality of the materials was of the very finest. No coarse calico, as her own robe was made of, but fine cottons, silks and satins, even night clothes of sheer silk, some so fine that when she held them to the light she could see all the way through them.

She resisted the temptation to try on all the clothes, unable to believe they could really be for her. She left out a long dress with pretty pink flowers similar to the one Nirjis had been wearing, then she replaced the others neatly in the box.

She took a shower in the glittering bathroom and washed her hair, which had become dusty from the ride in the car, then she brushed her teeth with the special paste provided. Perhaps one of the girls could tell her about the bleeding, which had eased but not stopped. It was a good feeling to know she would have someone her own age to confide in. Making friends with them, she decided, would be her first task.

Not used to perfumes, Zarena left them alone and returned to her room to dress.

Music and laughter from below told her the Sheikh's guests had arrived, and Zarena bounced gaily down the stairs and started briskly towards the kitchen, determined to make a good impression.

The Sheikh and another man were talking together at the front door, and the Sheikh snapped his fingers when he saw her and beckoned her over.

'Excellency, I introduce to you my new girl, Zarena.'

The man came forward and took her hand. He lifted it to his lips and smiled. He was a large man, with a bald head and pointed beard, dressed in a white coat and grey trousers.

'Ah, Medhat, you have done it again. Where do you find such beautiful flowers? A white lotus... I congratulate you.'

Sheikh Ghaffar inclined his head. 'Thank you, Excellency. Shall we join the others?'

Zarena was not used to such attention. She followed awkwardly as the Sheikh led the way to an open courtyard filled with plants and flowers. The air was heavy with the scent of jasmine. Cushions had been scattered on the tiled floor, forming a rough semicircle, and amongst them lounged two other men. Each had a small glass table before him that held a silver plate of snacks and a jug of tej. Nirjis was kneeling before one of the men, giggling as she fed him delicacies from the plate with her fingers. The other man sat alone. They both stood hastily to greet the new arrival, bowing respectfully and smiling, and he returned their greetings politely before settling himself beside a table. He patted a cushion beside him. 'Sit here, my child.'

Sheikh Ghaffar left and a few moments later the music was changed to a tune with a livelier beat. The man sitting alone began to clap in time with the music, and the others joined in enthusiastically.

From behind a cluster of palms, the Nubian girl suddenly appeared and the clapping stopped in anticipation.

She stood before them in a pose of supplication, head back and eyes closed, arms outstretched and legs parted. With her ebony body glistening with oil, she basked in the bright sun flooding the courtyard. A short skirt of colored beads covered her loins, and another her small breasts. A band of silver coins circled her head, and strings of beads hung from it like a veil. Silver bracelets flashed from her arms and ankles.

She appeared motionless, yet the beads and coins quivered against the restraint of the rhythm deep within her. As the tempo of the music quickened, so did the vibrating of the coins, and the bracelets began to jingle. Then, as if unable to contain the rhythm any longer, her hips began to move, sensuously and slowly, and her outstretched arms began to tremble, increasing the volume of the jingling. Her head moved from side to side, swinging the bead veil, and the movement of her hips followed in time, lengthening and thrusting primitively, until her entire body was one sinuous, erotic motion.

She sank slowly to her knees and fell back between her feet, the motion continuing, becoming faster and more abandoned, the bead skirt bouncing high to reveal flashes of scarlet silk. As the throbbing drums reached a crescendo, she stiffened into spasms of ecstasy, then collapsed to lie with her arms outstretched; the breathless heaving of her abdomen the only movement.

The short silence, thick with promise, ended in polite applause from the three men and she sat up slowly. The man who had been alone jumped to his feet and moved towards her.

Zarena sat stunned and silent, her mouth dry. Never had she seen another woman's body so exposed. That she had seen one displayed so erotically, and in the company of men, left her pale with shock and embarrassment. She had been warned by her aunt Hebba never to reveal any part of her body to men, that to do so was a terrible sin, and that women who did were whores and could expect to be punished by Allah.

It was a warning Zarena had been careful to observe. She knew about sex, and knew what effect a woman's body had on men. Her own cousins, who were not yet men, had taught her. She had seen their shadows by the window, trying to look in while she was washing, and several times they had tried to catch her alone as she was feeding the chickens. They knew she would not have the courage to inform her aunt, and had deliberately exposed themselves, taunting her by holding their rigid things between their fingers and waggling them in front of her. She had seen the expression on their faces, even though her body was covered, and without looking, she knew the guest sitting beside her would have the same expression. She could tell by the way he breathed.

'Do you dance, Little Lotus?' he whispered in her ear.

Zarena shook her head, keeping her eyes lowered. 'No, Excellency,' she murmured.

'I shall arrange for you to have lessons.' He drank deeply from the jug of tej, which had remained untouched during the performance, then licked his lips. 'Feed me,' he ordered.

Startled, Zarena looked at the plate with its confusing array of delicacies. They were all strange to her.

'The honeyed meatballs look particularly tempting.'

With trembling fingers she picked up one of the sticky round balls and moved it hesitantly towards his lips. He took her wrist and held it steady while he opened his mouth and took the meatball between his teeth. Still holding her, he swallowed the meatball, then licked and sucked at her fingers, gripping tighter and forcing them deeper into his mouth as she tried to resist.

Zarena watched with revulsion. He had a big mouth with soft rubbery lips that reminded her of a camel. He withdrew her stiffened fingers slowly then, without releasing her wrist, pulled her around so she was sitting between his legs, with her back to him.

'Do not be afraid, ' he breathed in her ear. 'I will not bruise such a delicate young flower.'

He began to lick her ear, putting his wet tongue deep inside and groaning softly, containing her struggles easily by holding her hard against him with an arm firm around her waist.

Terrified and unable to move, Zarena looked around helplessly, hoping the Sheikh would see what was happening and come to her aid, but he was nowhere to be seen. Neither was the Nubian girl and the man she was with.

Nirjis and the other man were almost out of sight behind a planter. All she could see were a protruding pair of hairy legs and the bared knees of Nirjis above the flowers.

Zarena squirmed ineffectually. The man was becoming more demanding, his breathing quick and shallow as he snuffled in her ear. She could feel his thing pressing against her, poking against her buttocks like a stick. The hand that had held her around the waist moved to cover her flat breast, while the other worked her robe up over her knees.

He rubbed his hand up the inside of her legs, forcing them apart, pushing higher, and she stared down at his hand in horror. It was coarse veined and hairy, dark against the paleness of her leg, and it crawled forward purposefully on its fingers like a giant spider, the red stone of his ring glinting like its eye.

It seemed to Zarena that her life was repeating itself. Only the day before it had been her uncle's hand forcing its way between her legs. She had been as helpless then as she was now, but she had been lucky.

Zarena reached for the jug of tej with both hands and swung it back over her head, upending it and bringing it down on the man's bald skull with a hollow thump.

He fell back with a hoarse cry, both hands leaving her to clutch at his head, and Zarena sprang free as if released from a catapult, knocking over the silver tray, which crashed noisily on the tiled floor. She did not look to see the results of her effort, but lifted her robe clear of her knees and ran.

Her unplanned flight took her automatically to the stairs, and she fled up them as another hoarse bellow echoed through the house.

Zarena did not realize her error until she was at the top of the stairs, and she turned to go back, to run out of the house and away. She started down, but it was too late. The man came into the hall with a cushion pressed to his head, making his way unsteadily to the door. Blood ran down his wet face and onto his white coat.

Sheikh Ghaffer came hurriedly into the hall behind him.

Zarena turned again and raced towards her room. Ahead in the passage, a door was flung open and, as she ran past, a naked man came out.

'*Fee eh*? What is the matter?' He put out a hand to stop her, catching her sleeve and half spinning her around before she tore free. Behind him, she caught a glimpse of the Nubian girl lying naked on the bed.

Zarena shut her door and searched for the lock, but it had none.

With a stifled cry, she leapt to the window and looked out, hoping to find a way down, but it was a sheer drop onto the stone path. She stepped back quickly when she saw the man and the Sheikh walking towards the gate. A black limousine was parked on the road and the driver climbed out and hurried to meet them.

The Sheikh was clutching at the guest's arm, as if pleading with him, but he pushed the Sheikh angrily aside, and his efforts were reinforced more forcibly by the driver, who put a hand to the Sheikh's chest and pushed him hard, sending him sprawling back into the garden. He scrambled to his feet and watched from the gate as the driver helped the important guest into the back seat then drove away.

The Sheikh stood there until the car had disappeared, then he turned and walked towards the house, his face dark and scowling, and Zarena pulled back hastily.

She could do nothing but wait. She would be beaten, of that she was certain. Either the Sheikh would do it, or he would send for her father. After that, she would be thrown out, maybe sent to prison.

Had she thought of it earlier, she may have had a chance to run down the stairs and out the back while the Sheikh was in the front, but now it was too late. It would not be the first time she had been beaten. She could only hope it would be nothing worse than that.

A full hour passed, and still he did not come, and Zarena began to hope. She had prepared herself for the inevitable, and her body ached with tension. Every sound caused her body to stiffen and her breathing to stop.

Her hair was sticky from the spilled tej, and the sweet smell of it was a constant reminder. Shuddering with revulsion, she used her own saliva on a cloth to wash away the feeling of the wet tongue in her ear, but she could do nothing about her sticky hair.

She changed back to her own clothes and knotted the money into a handkerchief, which she tied on the inside of her robe. Then she sat to wait.

She saw the Sheikh once more from the window as he escorted his remaining two guests from the house, and she thought he would come then, but he did not.

He came much later, when it was dark.

Zarena heard the footsteps in the passage and caught her breath, hoping they would stop before reaching her door, but they came on, and she sat woodenly on the bed and stared at the carpet.

The door opened and he came in, followed by the two old women she had seen earlier in the kitchen. His smooth face showed no anger as he walked past her to the window and looked out. He closed the shutters before turning to face her, flexing a thin cane.

'Hold out your hand,' he ordered.

It shook as she held it out. He laid the cane across her palm to fix his aim. It made a whistling sound as he brought it down across her fingers.

Zarena gasped and snatched her hand back against her body.

'Again... the same hand.'

A crimson welt showed across the fingers, and they twitched in pain and anticipation as he rested the cane on her palm. 'Hold it still.'

She was unable to hold back a cry as it landed.

He struck her four times on each hand before speaking again, his voice calm, almost polite. 'You have made me very angry,' he said. 'I do not tolerate disobedience. You were warned, were you not?'

'I am sorry,' Zarena cried. 'I did not mean to hit him. He was doing things...'

'I am not interested in your excuses. The minister is an important man. You were to entertain him and do whatever he wished. Now, he will cause me a great deal of trouble.'

'I didn't know!' Zarena wailed. 'I wasn't told...'

Sheikh Ghaffar turned to the two waiting women. 'Tie her to the bed.'

'No... please...'

One of the women produced strips of cloth and they set about tying her quickly, ignoring her pleas and overcoming her resistance easily and without being rough. Face down, her legs were spread and her ankles bound to the rail of the bed so her feet hung over, then each arm was outstretched and bound to the corners at the top end.

Spread-eagled, she could not turn or twist, and could not lift up more than a few inches.

'Pull the robe up and lower the pants.'

'Please... it wasn't my fault.'

Her robe was pulled to her waist and her buttocks fully exposed.

Sheikh Ghaffer laid his cane across them, then changed his mind. 'Perhaps not. I do not want her scarred. She is too expensive an investment. 'Replace the pants and leave.'

Her pants were pulled up again and the women left, closing the door.

'Yes, much too expensive,' Sheikh Ghaffar murmured. 'I was a fool.' He laid the cane gently across her covered buttocks, caressing before raising it and bringing it down with a grunt of effort.

Zarena jerked as the pain cut into her. She bit into the blanket.

Sheikh Ghaffar struck her ten times on the buttocks, then moved to the base of the bed and placed the cane carefully on the sole of her left foot.

When the pain came, it was as if she had stood on hot coals. Tears sprang into her eyes and she buried her face deeper into the blanket, clenching it between her teeth.

After a few minutes, the procedure was repeated on her right foot.

'We will have a short rest now,' Sheikh Ghaffar informed, 'then we will start again. It is necessary that you have time to think about obedience. You have been a disappointment to me, Zarena. I treat my girls very well. Everything they need, even money. I give to them only the best class of customer. Important men like the minister. All I ask is that they are obedient and make the customer happy.'

At the beginning of the fourth session, Zarena fainted.

Sheikh Ghaffar waited until she came around, then continued.

She passed out again in the middle of the sixth session, and again in the next, and each time he brought her around by wiping her face gently with a wet cloth.

'Only three more sessions to go,' he consoled her. 'It could be much worse. Sometimes I have to beat the girls so much they are no longer pretty. Then I have to send them to my big house in Cairo where the customers are not so fussy. In two days, when you are better, I have promised another very important man that you will make him happy. If you do not, that is what will happen to you.'

Zarena was not aware of when it ended. When she came

around after a faint it was dark and cold, and she was still tied to the bed. Her body burned all over, not only where she had been caned, but also from the cramps in her arms and shoulders. She lay unmoving, fighting the pain, her skin cringing in anticipation at every small sound.

After a long time of lying still the burning changed to throbbing, aching, numbness and cramp, and she could only wonder at the damage done to her body. To fight the pain she tried to think, to figure some way of escaping, but her mind refused, returning again and again to the words of Sheikh Ghaffar as he talked during the terrible waiting periods.

At first, she had been unwilling to believe that her father could sell her, but the more she thought about it, the more sense it made. She had been ignored, ridiculed and treated like a foreigner by her father's family ever since being taken away from her mother. What other reason could he have for keeping her like a prisoner except to take advantage of her good looks and sell her? Perhaps he had not intended to sell her to a brothel. Maybe he had planned to sell her to someone as a wife, but the Sheikh had probably offered more money. And what was the difference to her, anyway?

As the long night wore on and the sounds in the house and on the street quietened, her thoughts became more lurid. She tried to imagine what it was like to be a prostitute; to have different men constantly abusing her body. Mean, ugly men like her uncle. The possibility of it happening filled her with revulsion and despair.

A sound at the door made her jump and begin to quiver

all over. She lay quiet, pretending to be asleep as the door opened then closed softly. She heard the whisper of feet on the carpet, then winced as something brushed against her feet.

'Shhh!' The warning was soft but urgent.

Zarena lay still and quiet as first her feet were untied, then her hands. She caught a whiff of jasmine as the person came close, and heard the soft clink of jewellery as the knots were being undone.

With no other sound but the whisper of bare feet and the soft opening and closing of the door, her silent benefactor departed.

With agonizing slowness, Zarena eased her cramped muscles through the first excruciating movements, lifting herself until she was on her knees with her face still buried in the blanket. When the cramps finally eased, she rolled cautiously onto her back and began the painful process of first sitting, then standing.

The sting of her feet touching the rug was almost as bad as the cutting of the cane. She removed two of the flimsy silk garments from the wooden chest and wrapped them around her feet, then rolled on the bed, gathering the strips of cloth with which she had been bound, using them to hold the silk in place. She forced herself through the pain, reminding herself constantly of what would happen to her if she did not escape.

She made herself stand and shuffle around, curling her toes and holding onto the wall, and when she was able to do it on her own without falling or staggering too much, she cautiously opened the door and went out.

The wrappings on her feet kept her movements silent as she shuffled along the dark passage to the stairs. She paused at the top to catch her breath and listen. No sound came from the house and she assumed it must be well after midnight. Slowly, she began the descent.

By the time she reached the heavy front door she was almost exhausted and blinded by tears, and she had to clear them away before she could find the handle. Using both hands, she turned it, but the door would not open.

Close to panic, she pushed and pulled hard, ignoring the pain in her fingers, but the door remained firm. Feverishly, she felt around for a key or a lock, and had almost given up when she found the bolt near the floor. She jerked it up and it clattered noisily, but she was beyond caring. She opened the door and went out.

As she was going through the gate a truck came along the road and she paused to allow it to pass, turning away and shrinking back from the blaze of its lights. She looked up at what had been her window and felt the first exhilarating flush of success.

A movement in the second window along caught her eye and, in the reflected light of the truck, she could see the dark form of someone standing there, looking out, and she froze. Then, in the brief moment before the truck had passed, she saw the raised arm and a flash of silver.

Every wooden bench in the third class carriage was filled to capacity, so the surplus passengers either stood precariously or sat on the floor. The lavatory could not be used as the closet had been filled with excess baggage and the door jammed open. Neither the lights, nor the fans worked, and it was hot and airless. The broken windows allowed some air for those lucky enough to be close to them, but not sufficient to stir the blended stench of tobacco smoke, body odors and exotic food.

To Zarena, it was heaven.

For the first time she felt safe. She lay on the floor half under a bench, squeezed between the greasy bag of a camel herder and the bare feet of a man wearing two ragged jellabas - one apparently used to cover the holes of the other.

The camel herder, a dark-skinned Shilluk with a face stitched across by tribal scars, sat on his canvas tent and scowled threateningly at anyone who looked as if they may want to stretch their legs in his or Zarena's direction. None did. A plaited leather whip bandoleered his broad chest, and to each bulging bicep was strapped a short, but lethal looking dagger.

The old man with two jellabas had been given special dispensation, possibly due to the supply of halva, jam, peanuts and tamarind seeds he dispensed to the herder at regular intervals In the folds of his jellabas he also held concealed a bottle of *aragi,* on which, in defiance of Sharia law, they both sipped in turn.

The Shilluk had been walking along the rail embankment and had stopped to adjust his heavy load when he heard strange noises coming from the rusted remains of an old water tank below. Investigating, he found Zarena lying amongst the weeds, making whimpering sounds in her sleep.

'*Enta kweiss?*' he had queried, prodding her with a foot. 'Are you well?'

Startled awake, Zarena had edged farther back into her shelter.

'Why are the feets?' he demanded in heavily accented Arabic. Before she could answer, he asked a further question. ' Is you English?'

Zarena shook her head, then hesitantly tried to explain. It took a long time, for she had to speak slowly and make it up as she went, and she was not sure of his threatening presence. She told him a mad uncle had stolen her from her family in Alexandria, and when she had tried to run away he had beaten her on the feet to prevent her trying again. But she had anyway, and now she was returning home.

To further engage his sympathy, she showed him her swollen hands and, scowling, he squatted to examine them, and also her feet. Without comment, he left to climb the embankment and search through his bag. He returned with a tin of evil-smelling grease. 'Good for camel feets,' he explained.

After washing her feet and hands with water from a leather canteen, he smeared his grease on the cuts with surprising gentleness. He discarded the soiled rags and produced a heavy pair of woolen socks from his bag to take their place.

'You want train?' he asked.

She nodded, and he picked her up and slung her belly down over his shoulder, solving the additional load problem by balancing the tent on his head and carrying the bag in his spare hand.

At the station, he deposited her in the shade with his baggage and, after she had given him the money for her ticket, he stood in the queue.

Aware of her pale skin, Zarena surprised a passing woman by offering ten piasters for her black shawl, which she then used to cover her hair and face. With the socks hiding her feet and her hands tucked out of sight, she felt better.

The Shilluk spent the afternoon dozing like everyone else, leaving Zarena to fidget and squirm uncomfortably on the hard ground as she tried to ease each tortured area of her body in turn; a task made no easier by her not being able to sit.

At dusk, shortly before the train was due to arrive, two policemen sauntered through the crowd, and Zarena curled up close to her sleeping companion as though she belonged to him, pretending sleep herself, and was relieved when he didn't move and the policemen didn't stop.

The Shilluk carried her onto the train, clearing a passage by simply shoving everyone aside with his bag. He placed her on a hastily vacated bench, but she moved to the floor where she could lie down, giving her place to the man with two jellabas.

The camel herder left the train at El Minya, where he was to pick up some camels and take them across the desert to a trader at Ras Charib. She could come with him, he offered and, after he had delivered the camels, she could become his wife. Then they would find her mad uncle and cut his throat. He demonstrated how this could be done with one of his knives, and the old man nodded vigorously in agreement. He seemed very impressed with the Shilluk, and looked the more disappointed of the two when Zarena politely declined the offer, saying she had a sick mother to look after.

Her would-be suitor removed one of the socks to show the old man her foot, and gave terse instructions as to her welfare. He transferred some of the grease in his tin to an empty cigarette packet and ordered her to put more on the next day. Scowling, he hoisted his baggage and left without looking back.

The old man fed her with the bitter tamarind seeds all the way to Cairo, then helped her off the train and through the crowd to the ticket office, where she bought another third class ticket for the short journey to Alexandria.

She arrived at the coastal city early in the afternoon and, with less than a pound of her uncle's money remaining, immediately set about finding the Greek family with whom she and her mother had stayed.

But the city looked different. It had been five years, and she had been too young then to take an interest in what direction they had been going. To make it more difficult, she could not remember the name of the family, only that it was a complicated one, and that they had worked each day at a Greek café, which they owned.

By nightfall, Zarena had still not found one she recognized, and walking had become difficult. The socks had worn through and her feet were sore and swollen. From a waste bin behind a shop she found some rags to reinforce the socks, then found a place to sleep between two palm trees on the edge of a small square. Several peddlers were already camped there with their carts, but she was far enough away from them not to be accosted, yet still close enough for comfort, and she already looked like an old beggar woman with her rags and shuffling walk. If anyone spoke to her, she would cough as though sick and pretend not to understand.

Next morning she bought a pair of cheap plastic sandals from one of the peddlers and discarded the socks after bathing her feet in the sea. Although dark with bruising, they no longer bled and the swelling had receded. Another few precious piasters went on a thimble of bitter coffee and some bread, and her good spirits returned.

The seafront brought back memories of a walk with the old Greek man. He had brought her there for her first look at the sea, and she sat on the breakwater trying to remember more details. She had called him a special name. Papa something. A short, funny name, and she went through the alphabet trying to jog her memory, but the name would not come. He had a black moustache, she recalled, which he twisted in his fingers, and long, thin hair on his head, which he brushed in a strange way. He had told her the moustache was not real, but was really the wings of a dead swallow he had found on the road, and that his hair was not hair either, but a piece of fishing net he had found on the beach, and which he had glued on his head to make it look like hair.

A brass plaque caught her attention as she walked back along the breakwater. On it were the names of the builders, mostly foreign, and she recognized one as being a French name. Bontoux. She said the word aloud as she continued on. It had a nice sound, and she needed a new name. That would be it, she decided, until she could find out what her mother's name had been.

Later in the day she found the market square where she had been taken from her mother. The carts, the donkeys and the pyramids of fruit all looked the same, and the road was still full of yellow taxis.

Excited, she attempted to retrace her steps of that fateful day. It had not been a long walk. But although she examined every building carefully in every direction, none appeared familiar. She continued searching until dark, then disheartened, bought an orange and returned to her sleeping place.

When the next day also proved unsuccessful, Zarena gave up the search. She needed food, and started thinking about finding work, but to find work she would first have to wash. Her *Shamma*, day robe, was dirty and her hair sticky, with the smell of sour tej. When she saw a group of women doing laundry at a canal, she offered to help in exchange for the loan of a robe while she washed her own, and that night used more newspapers and a broken cardboard box to protect it from the dirt.

Early next morning, as the Muezzins were calling to the faithful over their crackling loudspeakers, she was already on the street. A cheap comb purchased from the same peddler she had bought the sandals brought some order to her curls, and the shawl she tied around her waist to make a skirt over the *Shamma*.

She started with the cafes, still with the hope of finding the Greek family, but did not limit herself to Greek ones only. And she also tried the large restaurants, where she thought she would have more chance of finding work in the kitchens.

At the fourth restaurant, a lavish Greek one in a modern plaza, she found the two statues. She had forgotten about them.

They stood in the entrance, either side of a doorway with imposing columns, and she recognized them instantly. They were of two black women in ancient Egyptian costume, each with one leg placed slightly in front of the other, as if walking, and each had one hand holding up a tray filled with flowers. She stared at them, her memory struggling.

'Yes?'

The question was delivered by a young waiter with a white shirt and black bow tie, and his eyebrows remained elevated in query, obviously not mistaking her for a customer.

'The statues,' Zarena said. 'I remember them.'

'What?' He looked at the statues in surprise, then returned his attention to Zarena, slowly inspecting.

'I'm looking for kitchen work,' Zarena said. 'I've done it before, and don't mind working only for food…'

He shook his head. 'We don't need anyone.'

Zarena stood for a few moments longer, coming to the conclusion the statues had either been sold to new owners, or were not the same ones she remembered.

She strolled along the glass front of the restaurant, looking in. It was still too early for customers. All the tables were empty except one, at which an old man with glasses was sitting, reading a newspaper, and Zarena stopped. His hair was grey, and so was his moustache, but it was thick and curled upwards like the wings of a bird, and his sparse hair was brushed over his bald scalp in thin strands. He looked up and saw her standing there, staring in, and nodded a greeting before returning to his paper, and Zarena gasped as the name suddenly popped into her head. Papa Zoupo.

Had her feet allowed it, she would have run.

Hobbling as fast as she could, she returned to the door and went boldly in past the surprised waiter.

He came after and caught her by the arm. 'Hey…I told you no work here!'

Zarena jerked her arm free and continued on to where the old man was sitting. He had looked up when the waiter called out, and was now watching curiously over the top of his glasses.

'She wants work,' the waiter explained. 'I already told

her no.'

The old man raised his hand to stop the waiter, not taking his eyes off Zarena, waiting for her to speak.

Zarena looked down at him. To her dismay, her entire body, even her mouth, began trembling.

The old man lowered his hand, a look of concern beginning to form on his face.

'Papa... Zoupo?'

At mention of the name the old man removed his glasses and sat forward to peer at her, frowning, then his eyes widened. '*Ohi*... surely, it cannot be...'

'I'm... do you... remember me?'

He stood up. 'I do not believe it. Zarena... little Zarena?'

She nodded, sniffing loudly.

He came around the table with a broad smile, holding out his arms. 'What's the matter, Zarena... you crying because you don't want to give Papa Zoupo a little hug and a kiss?'

The smell of him as he held her close was the sweetest she had known.

He sat her down, then gave her one of the crisp white table napkins to blow her nose on while he went to telephone Mama at home with the news.

She came a short while later in a yellow taxi.

Round-faced and buxom, she ran into the restaurant with her large bosoms bouncing and dragged Zarena into them.

When the tears had been wiped away with more napkins, she examined Zarena at arm's length.

'Look, Papa... bones... nothing but bones.' She called to the waiter. 'Nicky! Bring some food for Zarena. Cakes with cream... and coffee.' She clasped Zarena's hand tightly in both of hers and responded to her wince of pain with a cry of concern. 'Dear God, Papa.' she murmured as she turned over the hand in hers. 'Look at the girls fingers...'

She examined the other one then sat down. 'Come, my dear,' she invited. 'Tell me and Papa what has happened. We want to know everything... don't we Papa?'

Years of holding back, of having no one to confide in. Years of uncertainty and fear. It came in a flood.

So did the tears. When she had finished, Papa Zoupo was so angry he was unable to keep still. He walked to the entrance and stood there for a long time with his hands in his pockets, looking out. When he returned, he spoke with quiet resolve.

'Take her home, Mama. Take Zarena home and look after her. Call a doctor to look. She will stay with us now... for as long as she wants.'

Stern-faced, he gathered the pile of soiled napkins and went through to the kitchen.

The months that followed were a glorious, dizzy excursion into an exciting and wonderful new world. Papa and Mama Zoufianopoulis swamped her with kindness, treating her like the daughter they never had. Western clothes from expensive department stores, food she could not stop eating, beauty parlors she had never dreamed existed. But most of all, love.

Papa Zoupo refused to let her work. There was no need, he told her. They had a good business and didn't need more staff. She must go to school and learn.

He sent her to a small private school run by a Scottish professor, where most of the students were European and spoke English. She learned from Papa Zoupo that her mother had stayed with them for a few days after the beating in the market place, then returned to France, knowing it was hopeless to try and get Zarena back. He also told her that her mother's name was Paulette Menard. They had not heard from her in two years, and no longer had her address.

Still fearing discovery, Zarena decided to keep the name she had seen on the plaque.

After two years, she was the top student in her class, after three, the top in the school. At home she learned Greek, at school English and French, and in the city she spoke Arabic. Still influenced by the memories of her mother, who had been an archaeologist, she studied the same subject, specializing in hieroglyphics, which led to a scholarship at Edinburgh University and friendship with her tutor, Amanda Pritchard.

It was while she was there that Papa Zoupo died. Mama sold the restaurant and went to live with her sons in Greece, and once again Zarena was on her own, but Papa had arranged in his will for her education to be subsidized, so she was able to continue with her studies.

Her looks invited many a proposition, but men had no place in her life. She worked on her career and fought behind the scenes for the women's movement, and it was not until the Rhodesian entered her life that she felt the first stirrings of something deep inside. Stirrings that aroused a confusing array of emotions.

They had nothing in common. They had been thrown together by the mystery surrounding the papyri, and shared a common danger because of it. And even in that, she was a reluctant participant. She could not even say that she liked him. She was sorry for him. That was all.

Part Five

Qena - Egypt

The rumor there was to be an honor killing spread quickly through the village.

The coming and going of the motor car during the night, the carrying into the house of someone wrapped in a blanket, the summoning of the *daya,* and the muffled screams of a woman caused much whispered speculation.

No one knew for certain who the woman was. Some believed it was Azim's new wife, but this was dispelled when she appeared in the morning as usual. Others believed it was a birth, but no one had knowledge of a pregnant woman or heard the sound of a new-born child to support the assumption.

The rumor began when Azim el Kholi's angry voice was heard repeating the words 'Khawaga whore' several times. Had the *daya* reappeared, they would have questioned her, but she did not. At midday, she left in the car with Azim, his nephew, and the woman, whom they carried between them in a blanket.

The village women watched them leave with relief.

Other than the widow, Hebba, no one there had ever witnessed an honor killing, and her chilling account had caused a ripple of unease. If a woman was to be stoned, it was better done away from the village, where they did not have to share in her shame.

Mona Hakim also heard the rumor and fingered the charms on the new silver bracelet her husband had given her with unease. He had not said anything, but she knew he had not bought the bracelet. It was not the sort of gift he would buy, even if he had the money, and she knew he did not, and she had overheard her brother and husband talking about her cousin, Zarena, so she had a good idea who it was in the car, and whose bracelet it was she was wearing. Mona did not feel good about what was happening. It had been ten years since she had seen her, and couldn't remember much, other than that they had shared the same bed and her cousin had been kind to her. She liked the bracelet, but wearing it, which she did so as not to offend her husband, made her feel like a thief and a traitor.

M ahfoud had a terrible fear of guns. During conscription, he had done his utmost to avoid both ends of them, so when he saw the barrel of one poking into his belly, his breathing stopped and he failed to speak.

'Answer me, you slimy bastard. Where is Miss Bontoux?'

The question, spoken with quiet menace by the same

man that had caught him following the woman in Cairo, was emphasized with a further prod, and Mahfoud gulped. He glanced to the side, but no one had noticed. The man was standing too close, and the steps to the gallery were clear but for a straggle of tourists and a hopeful cluster of tour guides near the door.

'Get in the car. If you try to run or shout, I'll kill you.'

Mahfoud had not thought of doing either. He moved, not too hastily, down the steps to the car at the curb. The door was opened for him and Mahfoud scrambled into the passenger seat. The man strolled casually around to the driver's side and got in. He drove the car only a short distance before stopping again in a quiet place off the main road. The gun reappeared.

'Start talking. Where is she?'

Although the man spoke calmly, almost as if asking directions, Mahfoud had a strong feeling he was not bluffing. But things were happening too fast for him. Playing for time, he put on a puzzled expression, as if he didn't understand.

'Don't bullshit me. I know you speak English.' The gun was raised and the barrel pressed against the side of his nose. Mahfoud tried to pull back, but the gun followed, pushing his head against the window. 'If she has been harmed…'

'Please… I swear by Allah… he is my witness. I have not harmed her.'

'Where is she?'

'I don't know, sir. I was only to report where she was to her father.'

'Her father?'

Mahfoud hesitated, realizing he had made a mistake, and the barrel ground into his nostril, filling it with the detested smell of gunpowder and oil.

'Where do we find her father?'

The house was in a small village a few miles from the town of Qena, and was little more than a hovel. The rusted iron roof was patched and sagging, and the once painted walls were streaked with dirt, as if a child had tried to paint on them with mud.

Chris stopped the hire car and eyed the house dubiously. It was not the sort of place he could associate with Zarena. Two women appeared in the doorway, one peering over the shoulder of the other.

'Are you sure this is it?'

Mahfoud sat hunched and sullen in the passenger seat. 'I do not wish to be seen,' he answered.

'Too bad,' Chris told him. He climbed out to open the passenger door 'Out.'

'Please, sir...'

Chris took a handful of shirt and pulled him out. 'Speak to the women. Ask them where Miss Bontoux is, and don't do anything stupid.'

Mahfoud complied reluctantly. One of the women said something in return, then both pulled back into the house and closed the door.

'They don't know anything,' Mahfoud reported sulkily.

Chris opened the door and pushed him inside. The scuff of hurrying feet, then the banging of a door at the back told him the women had fled. It took only seconds to search through the four deserted rooms.

'I think you're lying,' he said. 'Miss Bontoux never lived here. We'll try the next house.'

It was even smaller and dirtier than the first. A girl of about fourteen, thin and heavily pregnant, opened the door. She showed no fear, but pulled her head cloth over her mouth and lowered her eyes to look at the floor as Chris gave Mahfoud a prompting nudge with the gun. 'Ask her,' he ordered. 'And this time, sound as if you mean it.'

The girl spoke quietly. No, she had not seen her, but she thought her cousin, Zarena, was at the house during the night. She had since left.

Chris looked more closely at the girl. She was small and dark, with broad features. He could not believe she was related in any way to the tall attractive one he was searching for.

'Ask if her if she knows where Zarena has gone.'

The girl seemed uncertain, but she thought her cousin had gone back to the house of Sheikh Ghaffar, in Qena.

'Gone back?' Chris was confused. He remembered Zarena telling him when they were sailing on the river that she came from a place called Qena, but she had not explained further.

'Do you know where this Sheikh, whatever his name is, lives?'

Mahfoud shook his head. He asked the girl. She did not know either.

'Let's go,' Chris said tiredly, 'we'll find it.' But he felt his strength of purpose beginning to wane as he drove moodily back to Qena. He was an outsider here, and was more uncertain than ever about what was happening. His arrest, Zarena's disappearance and the strange goings on with her father. Mahfoud's involvement and the papyri. It was all becoming too much.

It took only a few minutes to find the Sheikh's house. Everyone knew it. The odd looks and smiles they received when asking directions convinced him of the man's importance in the community. Chris wondered if the Sheikh was Zarena's father. It would account for Mahfoud's increasing nervousness.

'I will take care no one steals the car,' Mahfoud offered hopefully when they stopped behind three others parked on the roadside. 'There are many thieves in this place.'

'And you are probably the worst,' Chris remarked. 'Let's go.'

It looked a far more suitable place for Zarena to live. He slipped the automatic into his belt under his shirt then rattled the ornate door knocker.

The door was opened by an elderly, smiling Arab in an immaculate white suit. The smile faded as he saw Chris and he came out, closing the door behind and cutting off the tinny sound of eastern music.

'Sheikh Ghaffar?'

The Arab nodded. 'May I be of help?' He addressed the question directly to Chris in perfect English.

'Sorry to bother you,' Chris apologized, relieved at not having to use Mahfoud to interpret. 'I'm looking for Miss Bontoux. I was told she was here.'

'Bontoux?' He frowned in puzzlement. 'I'm sorry...'

'Zarena.' Chris added.

'Ah, I see...'

'Is she here?'

'Forgive me, but who told you this?'

'Her cousin. Is she here?'

Sheikh Ghaffer stopped smiling. 'No, there is no one here by that name. Please excuse my rudeness, I have guests waiting...' He inclined his head apologetically and reached for the door handle.

Gloomily, Chris followed the hurrying Mahfoud back through the gate. The pregnant girl had not been certain. She had said only that she *thought* Zarena was going to the Sheikh's house. Perhaps she was mistaken. The whole thing was a mistake. The sensible thing would be to sort out the problem with the plane and get the hell out.

As he was deciding what to do next, a horse-drawn cab stopped on the road and a well dressed Arab stumbled out. 'Saida!' he greeted jovially as he passed, going unsteadily towards the gate.

'Saida,' Chris replied, then on impulse. 'Do you speak English?'

'Of course! I am a businessman.' He fumbled in his

waistcoat pocket and produced a stack of business cards, dropping several to the ground. 'I have the best shop for camel hair goods.'

Chris took one of the proffered cards. 'Do you know Sheikh Ghaffer?'

'Very well, my friend.' He rolled his eyes expressively. 'Each time I pass on business, I ask him for an invitation. Do you have one?'

'What for?'

'What for?' The man laughed. 'A very good joke, my friend.' He laughed again.

'You can only see the Sheikh by invitation?' Chris asked, intrigued.

'Of course. He has only eight girls.' He closed his eyes and kissed his fingers. 'The most beautiful in Egypt. Most expensive, my friend. If you wish an invitation you must come with me and we can arrange it.'

Chris forced himself to ask the question. 'Do you know a girl called Zarena?'

The man's brow furrowed in thought, then he shook his head. 'I have not heard this name, but you must ask for Suhair. She is the one I am going now to see. A very beautiful flower of paradise. Today she will take me there.' He grinned drunkenly. 'I must go, my friend, paradise is waiting.'

Chris stared after him. A brothel? He walked thoughtfully to the car, then suddenly became aware that he was alone. Mahfoud had gone.

He sat in the car, trying to work it out. He did not think

Mahfoud would complain to the police about being taken at gunpoint. He would more than likely be too thankful at getting away. It didn't really matter anyway. What concerned him now was the confusing business of Sheikh Ghaffer - a brothel owner - and Zarena. If he was her father, it would explain her reluctance to talk about her past.

But he was still not happy with the situation. Too many questions remained unanswered. The Sheikh's reaction to seeing him, then seeming to recognize Zarena's first name but not her second, plucked at his instincts. Something was definitely amiss. And he was responsible for her being here. If the hieroglyphics business was somehow involved she may need his help.

Chris decided that he had only two choices. He could either return to the police and make up some excuse as to why he had not reported as ordered, then leave with the plane, or he could bust into the brothel and find out for himself if she was there. Going back to the village to question the cousin again would be a waste of time without Mahfoud, and even with him, he doubted he would learn anything more.

He locked the car and walked to the gate. If he was wrong, the worst they could do was throw him out.

The front door was too risky. He went around to the back and found an open door leading into a kitchen. Checking to make sure the automatic was still hidden under his shirt, he walked in.

The air was thick with the smell of food and spice. Two women were eating at a table and looked up at him in surprise. They started to rise and Chris motioned them to sit. 'Saida!' he greeted them.

They returned his greeting automatically, exchanging nervous glances. Music, and the muffled sound of male voices and laughter came from a distant part of the house. Through an archway he could see a flight of stairs and a hall. No one was in sight.

'You speak English?'

They did not answer.

'Za-re-na,' Chris said, pronouncing clearly. 'I come to see Zarena.'

One of the women looked away quickly, the other glanced in a nervous fashion towards the stairs before doing the same.

Chris went through the archway, pausing briefly to check the hall was empty before going in. He had no option but to take a chance on leaving the women. Someone else may appear at any moment to complicate things. The mezzanine floor above, away from the revelry, was the obvious place to start. If he found no answers there he would come down and crash the party.

The upper floor passage had doors on the one side only, each with a painting of a bird on it. He started at the end, opening them quietly. The first two rooms were empty. Sounds from the next one made him more cautious. He eased the door open and was met by the sight of large naked buttocks pointed directly at him.

The fourth room produced his drunken friend the camel

hair man. The excess of alcohol appeared to have taken its toll. He lay snoring on his back with his legs wide open and his key to the door of paradise hanging limp between them. A girl so young her breasts had not yet fully formed, sat naked on the bed beside him, brushing her hair. She gave Chris a wide-eyed, startled look, her arms frozen above her head, and he gave her a weak smile as he closed the door.

He waited a few moments, listening, then moved on. The next room, and the bathroom opposite, were both empty. The second last room, with a faded picture of a flamingo on the door was bolted on the outside. It was the only room he had seen with a bolt, and it looked new. He slid it aside and opened the door.

She lay asleep on the bed, wearing a blue flannel nightdress, and Chris closed the door softly before going to look down at her with a frown. Her face was unnaturally pale, with dark hollows, and her breathing was labored.

The knowledge he was intruding, and that she may not want to see him, caused him to hesitate only briefly. He laid his hand gently on her forehead. It was hot and clammy.

She twitched at his touch and her eyes opened to stare blankly at him, then she closed them tightly, as if in pain.

'Zarena... it's me... Chris. 'Why are you here... are you sick?'

When she did not answer he took her hand. It was limp and unresponsive. 'Zarena? Answer me. Why are you here? Do you want me to leave?'

She appeared to have gone back to sleep, and he

sat holding her limp hand, looking at her pale face and wondering. He had found her, but that was only one question solved and more had been added. She was ill, there was no doubt, and with a raging fever, yet only yesterday she had been healthy and energetic, so what illness could have struck in so short a time? And what the hell was she doing in this place… in a brothel?

The sound of the door being suddenly bolted made him start, and he turned quickly to look. Excited whispering came from the other side, then he heard the word 'bolees' as the voices moved away.

'I think your father is going to call the police,' Chris said, more for his own benefit than hers. More trouble with the police was the last thing he needed. 'I'll have to go.'

But when he tried to remove his hand she clutched it hard and whispered something hoarsely, slurring the words, and when he leaned closer to listen he smelled the sickly sweet stench of ether on her breath.

The grip of her hand had not slackened, and suddenly she opened her eyes. They were unnaturally bright and intense. *'Get me out!'*

Chris hesitated. Her words had been so slurred he was not sure if she had told him to get out.

Her hand began to shake with the strength of her grip. *'Please… take me with you.'*

Her words, and the desperation with which she uttered them, acted upon Chris like a shot of adrenaline. His uncertainty vanished, and he felt back in control. Other questions could wait. For now he had the freedom to act instead of having to wonder, and he acted swiftly. 'Don't worry,' he said briskly, 'we're on our way.'

He tested the door, then put his foot on the wall for leverage and jerked hard on the handle. The bolt gave way with a ripping of wood and clattered to the floor. Pulling the automatic from under his shirt he checked the passage. It was clear.

She uttered a short cry as he scooped her up and he paused, concerned, but she gave no further clue and held firmly to his collar, so he continued, walking fast along the empty passage. The music and party sounds had not stopped. Apparently the Sheikh's guests were still unaware of what was happening. So much the better.

Sheikh Ghaffer was talking on a telephone near the door. One of the women from the kitchen was with him and spoke urgently to attract his attention when she saw Chris descending the stairs with Zarena. The Sheikh dropped the receiver and hurried towards them, waving his arms in agitation.

'What are you doing? I call the police. You are not allowed here.'

'Get out of the bloody way,' Chris ordered, waving the automatic from under Zarena's back. 'Open the door.'

With a swirl of his robe, the Sheikh did an about turn and scurried to the door. While he fumbled to open it, Chris knocked the telephone from the flimsy table and kicked it across the tiled floor. He resisted the temptation to fire a few rounds to stir things up.

'Go!' the Sheikh cried, looking anxiously towards the direction of the party. 'Take her, I do not care. Go!'

Chris carried her out and the door slammed behind.

Zarena groaned as he laid her on the back seat of the car and propped her head on his bag, but she did not open her eyes and he wondered if she was unconscious.

'Damn!' he muttered. 'I have to find a doctor or something.'

But he had no idea where to look, and an influential man like the Sheikh would have the entire police force chasing after him. Already suspected of smuggling - and probably a whole list of other things - they would lock him up and lose the key.

What he needed was to get them both somewhere safe and give himself time to think, and the plane was the only way. If he could get into the air, they would have a good chance. Zarena would be comfortable on the stretcher, and the medical kit was well stocked. If he refueled at Khartoum, he could be in Addis by midnight and take her straight to the hospital. His British passengers would have to find their own way home. All he had to do was avoid the police.

The road back to Luxor was busy, but no road blocks had been set up, and only one police car passed them with its lights flashing, heading in the opposite direction. Chris watched apprehensively in the mirror to see if it turned back, but it kept going.

It was dusk by the time they reached Luxor, and dark

as he drove warily into the airport. He pulled up in the administration car park and walked confidently to where he had left the plane in the company of several other light aircraft. The spare key screwed to the inside of the cowling would get him in, and as long as no police were around, he would first get things ready then drive closer. He was not worried about Air Traffic Control. If they gave him any problems he would either bluff his way out or ignore them.

Then coming around from behind the nose of another plane, he stopped, heart plunging. Leaning against each wheel of the Baron was a red sign with the warning, *Quarantined. Keep clear*.

The warning was repeated in Arabic, but that was not all. A heavy chain was looped through the starboard undercarriage oleo and padlocked to a tie-down ring set in the concrete.

The Baron was well and truly grounded. And so was he.

When he ran from Sheikh Ghaffar's house, Mahfoud had no plan in mind other than to increase the distance between himself and the gun. The horse-drawn cab had provided the ideal opportunity. With the foreigner's attention being diverted by the drunk, he had slipped unobtrusively to the other side of the carriage as it pulled away, walking out of view alongside it.

Unfortunately, the driver had then coaxed his horse into a fast trot, which, for Mahfoud, had soon become a marathon sprint.

Both sandals had come off and he had to run barefoot until the carriage rounded the corner.

He waited there, rubbing his feet and watching the car, and when he saw the foreigner carry the girl to it and drive off, he could barely contain his disappointment. He had no choice but to report what had happened to his contact. He retrieved his broken sandals then ate a late lunch before looking for a working telephone.

The official was unsympathetic. In fact, he was so unimpressed he did not allow Mahfoud to finish before blistering his ear with sarcastic rebuke.

'I pray you are never made responsible for our pyramids, Mahfoud. Within a week, they would be missing.'

'But what was I to do?' Mahfoud protested. 'He said he would shoot off my nose if I did not tell him.'

The contact sniggered. 'That would have taken care of one of the pyramids.'

'I took very great risks to escape,' Mahfoud said. 'I knew you had to be informed as soon as possible.'

'You are bleating like a frightened goat, Mahfoud. Find out where he has taken her. If it is a hire car it should be easy, even for you.'

'But he has a gun. What if I am seen?'

'I have guns too, Mahfoud. Many guns. Perhaps you would prefer to be shot by one of my guns?'

'Very well,' Mahfoud agreed sullenly. 'If I find them, I will inform her father.'

'Yes, and *When* you find them, report also to me. Meanwhile, I will arrange a complaint. The police will be interested to know their smuggler is also an armed and dangerous abductor of women.'

Chris examined the heavy chain and padlock from every angle. Bolt cutters may have worked, or better still a cutting torch, but he ruled them out. It would be hard enough to find them at the best of times, even if he knew where to look. Under the present circumstances, pushed for time and with everything closed, it was near impossible. So was abandoning the plane. Without passports, and with the police already alerted, they had no alternative. It was either give himself up and trust the police to take care of Zarena, or free the plane.

On the drive from Qena he had considered the possibility, in view of what had happened, that someone had arranged for him to be arrested and out of the way while Zarena was taken. He could not know if the police were involved, but did not want to take the chance. And he also had the skipper to consider. He would not be amused at losing an aircraft.

The padlock was a solid brass Yale with the keyhole at the base - not the type to be easily picked, even by an expert. He considered shooting into it with the automatic after filling the keyhole with gunpowder from the bullets, but it was risky, and the explosion would alert every security guard at the airport.

He took the problem with him back to the car. Zarena

was sleeping peacefully, her breathing quiet and her skin hot but dry. She needed attention, but he did not think she was in any immediate danger from whatever illness it was she had, and it may only be the after effects of the ether they had used to keep her quiet. If he could get her to a hospital or doctor sometime tonight, she would be all right.

After considering the problem of the chain for a few minutes, Chris came to the conclusion he had no option but to take the risk and shoot into the lock. If it worked and the plane was ready to go, he could be away within seconds. If it failed, he would be arrested, but either way, Zarena would be taken care of.

He drove the car to the other side of the administration block, closer to the plane.

Passengers were embarking on an Egyptair flight outside the main terminal, but there was little other traffic to worry about. Once he had the Baron on the loose it would take more than a few planes to stop him.

After retrieving the key from the cowling, he checked to make sure no other nasty surprises awaited him, then he set up the stretcher in readiness. He slid the chain, two links at a time, through the tie-down ring, moving the lock as far from the plane as possible. Blowing a hole in the wing would not be helpful.

Using the pliers from the car tool-kit, he removed a slug from its brass casing and emptied the powder into the keyhole of the lock, shaking it to spread it around. He packed in the powder from another bullet for good measure.

He would only have one chance.

Zarena came awake as he was carrying her from the car. She looked at him dazedly and tried to talk, but her words were unintelligible. He spoke to her soothingly, and by the time he had strapped her into the stretcher, she was asleep again. He ran back to the car for the spare wheel, which he placed on top of the lock for a buffer, adjusting it so the keyhole showed through one of the stud holes of the rim. For added protection, he used the two metal quarantine signs to shield the sides.

Pushing the barrel hard against the keyhole, he moved as far to the side as he could reach, closed his eyes, and pulled the trigger.

The blast ripped the gun from his hand and hurled the tire against his chest, knocking him over. He scrambled up to look, holding his numb hand. The lock had gone, disintegrated by the blast, only the steel hoop remained intact.

Not waiting to see what effect the blast was having at the terminal building, Chris threw off the chain and quickly checked the wing and fuselage for damage. Relieved to find none, he was about to step up when a hissing sound caught his attention and he looked under the wing to the wheel. The tire had a large chunk missing and, even as he stared at it in disgust, the rubber flattened out and the hissing stopped.

He could do nothing but carry on, and had the first engine turning before he had closed the door. He switched the navigation lights on, but left the radios turned off. He had enough distractions already.

The Egyptair flight was already moving onto the taxiway as he weaved out of the parking area and onto the apron. He gunned the right engine to compensate for the drag of the flat right wheel and raced the Airbus for the lane of blue lights leading to the runway, praying the rubber wouldn't shred.

With lights flashing, a fire tender sped across the grass reserve, aiming to cut him off, and Chris moved onto the grass himself to save the rubber. Landing was going to be tricky enough as it was without the added complication of a bare rim and the danger of sparks and ground-looping.

The Baron bounced past the Airbus, its wing passing under that of the larger plane, causing the startled pilot to veer away and brake sharply.

'Sorry, mate,' Chris muttered, 'but it's me first.' He crossed the taxiway and went off the other side, cutting the corner to the runway. No time for the luxury of final checks. He increased to full power before reaching the intersection and put down some flap, skipping past the white lights onto the runway, and giving thanks that no plane was coming in to land behind him.

The pull of the punctured tire on the rudder pedal was heavy, but became easier as the speed increased and he was able to hold the wing up to reduce the weight.

The fire tender pulled onto the runway ahead, and behind it came two police cars, also with lights flashing, and Chris knew he was not going to be at flying speed before he reached them. But he was already committed and going too fast to stop in time either. He kept going.

The driver of the tender jumped out and waved his arms.

'Bloody idiot!' Chris fumed. He held the aileron hard over, feeling the vibration of the flat tire on the stick, and willing the speed to increase, which it did with agonizing slowness.

When the driver realized the plane was not going to stop he abandoned the tender and started running. One of the police cars reversed back into the other and both stopped, fully blocking the runway. The doors of both flew open and the occupants ran for the grass.

As he raced towards the vehicles, Chris flicked his eyes down to the air speed indicator. Seventy three knots – almost twenty short of flying speed. Rigid with tension, he pressed the flap toggle all the way down and pulled back on the stick.

The Baron wallowed sluggishly into the air, ballooning over the police cars with nothing to spare, then sinking down on the other side, hopping and bouncing on one wheel, limping along the runway before finally reaching speed and lifting off.

Chris left the undercarriage down, letting the damaged tire cool before retracting it, and waiting with bated breath until the soft whine and rumble had stopped and the warning lights had gone out.

His hands shook with relief as he reduced power and levelled out at three hundred feet. He took a long, deep breath, then let it out with an explosive 'Ho, Mama!'

Secure in her stretcher, Zarena groaned softly.

The silver ribbon of the Nile unwound into the darkness immediately below, and Chris followed it south towards the Sudanese border, staying low, and hopefully below the radar beam. He switched the navigation lights off. Air traffic control would be in a panic, warning other aircraft to be on the lookout and to report if they saw him, but none would be flying at his low altitude.

When the lights of Aswan appeared ahead, he dimmed the instrument panel lights until the gauges were barely visible, then turned due east, skimming low over the isolation of the Nubian Desert, towards the high dunes of the Red Sea.

He turned south again when the shadowy folds of the dunes appeared below and trimmed the Baron for a slow cruise climb to clear the first of the Ethiopian Mountains some six hundred miles ahead.

Refueling at Khartoum was now out of the question. With a blown tire, only one landing was possible, and he would rather it was at Addis, which was familiar and where the company had some influence. An added advantage was that Zarena would receive treatment sooner.

She had still not stirred, and this worried him. He had no way of diagnosing what the problem was, but with the aid of the auto-pilot and medical kit was able to establish that her temperature was too high, her pulse too weak, and her blood pressure too low. His army emergency medical training suggested shock and loss of blood, but she did not appear to have suffered any injury to cause such symptoms.

Nevertheless, knowing it would do no harm, and fearing she was also dehydrated, he found a vein in her arm with difficulty – which further indicated shock – and gave her a saline drip.

Having done what he could for her, Chris turned his attention to other problems, one of which was to coax the very best performance he could out of the engines and pray for a tailwind. Addis was at the extreme end of the Baron's range, over a thousand miles, and even with the extra tank, it was going to need all his flying skill and every last drop of fuel to reach it. And when he did, the problem then awaiting him would be the most challenging of all. Landing with no tire would be to court disaster. Even if he managed to hold the wheel off until the speed had slowed right down, which would require as much good luck as good judgment, eventually it would touch and slew the plane, the undercarriage would fail, tipping the wing into the ground and probably damaging it beyond repair. They would be lucky if the Baron did not flip onto its back.

The only safe option was to land with the wheels up, scraping in on the belly. But without the stability of an undercarriage to keep it level, the wing could still be easily be damaged, and with the wheels up the propellers would come into contact with the ground. Either way, it seemed, he was headed towards trouble.

She felt no pain now. Her body was a solid, immovable lump, attached to her in some remote way, but over which she seemed to have lost all feeling and control. And neither did she want any. It was better this way, with no sense of belonging, and no pain.

At times she thought she must be awake. Hazy images materialized into solid objects with sharp outlines, but what she saw made no sense. A plastic bag with a long tube hung suspended above her head, rocking gently and, to the side of it, a window like that of a car. Through it shone moving pinpricks of light, like stars, and although they moved they no longer pressed down on her as they had before, and the humming sound that had accompanied them, rising and falling, was a steady, monotonous drone. Someone… a man, was talking, asking questions, but no one replied.

Then suddenly the pleasant drifting ended and she was jolted back. Silence closed in around her. Somewhere a door slammed, then the sound of voices, coming closer. Lights swirled around her, flashing red on the swaying plastic bag, floating in to hang poised above her. A shadowy hand reached down towards her face and she tried to pull away, but she could not, and it touched cold and wet on her lips, cutting short her cries. Her name was spoken from a distance; a soft, cultured voice she should know.

The needles of both fuel gauges were touching on empty when Chris entered the Addis circuit at three twenty in the morning. In one aspect it was a good time, for the airport was quiet, the wind calm, and the air cold and stable, but finding enough personnel to man the two fire tenders had increased the otherwise calm controller's blood pressure by several points. But finally he had accomplished the impossible and they now waited, lights flashing, close to the emergency crosswind grass runway on which landing flares had been lit.

The problem of how he too was going to accomplish the impossible and land the plane in one piece had nagged Chris constantly. That is, when he wasn't trying to will the fuel gauges to stop moving, and he had finally reached the conclusion there was only one way he could try to do it.

With clearance to make a long, straight-in approach, he took a deep breath, switched on the landing lights, and switched off the port engine. As the Baron yawed to the left, he counteracted with right rudder and ran through the engine-out checklist, increasing full power and fine pitch to the starboard engine, putting the mixture to full rich, and feathering the dead engine to prevent it from windmilling, and turning off the fuel. He did not trim out the rudder, but held it down firmly as he adjusted his speed and rate of descent, then he turned the starter on the dead engine a little at a time, watching the propeller in the reflected glow of the landing lights until it was in a horizontal position. At least one engine might be saved.

When he was certain he could reach the threshold, Chris switched off the starboard engine and feathered it too, shutting off the fuel and applying flaps, then he went through the same procedure as before, but too hastily, spooked by the rapid descent in the eerie silence, and had to make two complete revolutions via the starter before the propeller stopped in the right place, and only a few moments before the threshold marker flashed beneath and he had to give all his attention to the flare-out and landing.

With everything shut down, including the radio, he held straight and level on the increasingly sloppy controls, the plane sinking lower than he was accustomed to, waiting with breath held and jaw clamped for the first touch of the grass.

It started as a soft shrieking, barely audible above the whining of the still spinning gyros, growing rapidly into a dull, vibrating roar before decreasing almost as rapidly into silence as they slowed and stopped, still facing straight ahead, and with only a small tilt to the right. It was almost an anti-climax.

The call finally came through at four thirty in the morning. The strident clanging of the counter phone in the Addis briefing office jerked Chris from where he had been dozing in a wicker chair close-by. He answered it on the third ring, fumbling with the receiver.

Mama Tembo's clear voice drifted cheerily over the line in reply to his mumbled greeting.. 'Did I wake you up, Mister Chris?'

'No. What news?'

'Mister Billy says it's okay for Nairobi if the substitute

wheel won't fall off before you get there.'

'Did you find a doctor? Her temperature is up. I think she may be delirious.'

'I spoke to a Doctor Shingadia in Nairobi. She can't tell without an examination, but says the drip is a good idea, and to keep her as cool as possible. If you call on descent an ambulance will meet you at the main terminal.'

'And my passengers?'

'I have told the British Embassy in Karthoum they must make other arrangements, and the same with your politicians at Addis. Mister Billy says if they don't like it they can fly United.' A hurriedly placed hand over the mouthpiece failed to hide her squeal of laughter and, despite his exhaustion, Chris laughed with her, exorcising five of the most gruelingly anxious hours of his life.

Mama Tembo was still giggling when she clicked off. And so was he.

The Indian woman doctor seemed almost angry when she strode briskly into the waiting-room some two hours after Zarena had been admitted.

'She has suffered quite severe hemorrhaging, Mister Ryan, and there is infection, which does not surprise me. Asepsis is seldom a consideration with this sort of thing. At the moment she is stable, but she is going to be in hospital for some time... at least a week, maybe longer.'

'Oh?' Chris looked at the doctor in bleary-eyed

puzzlement. 'I'm afraid you've lost me, Doc. I didn't realize…. what was the problem?'

Doctor Shingadia returned his puzzled look. 'You are not aware of what happened?'

'No, I only met her a few days ago. She seemed fine then. It's a long story, but I assumed she had malaria or something. With her high temperature, all I could think to do was put her on a drip.'

'Well, it was a good thing you did. Without it she could have been a lot worse.'

'Hell, Doctor, if I'd known… when can I see her?'

'In a few days. It will be best if you telephone first.' A beeper sounded on her breast pocket and she moved away. 'Excuse me…'

'But you haven't told me…'

'The sister will give you the number, Mister Ryan.'

Eight hours later, a smiling African in a starched green waiter's jacket woke Chris with coffee and the news that lunch would be ready in half an hour. Fresh clothes had been placed neatly over the back of a chair and his shoes polished.

A robust, elderly man with a shock of white hair was waiting for him on the wide verandah of the lodge. 'I thought you had died,' Hugh Hildebrand said in greeting.

'I thought so too. You don't know how good it feels to be back in civilization.'

'Yes, I do.' He steered Chris towards a table laid with crisp white linen and silver cutlery for one.

'Only me?' Chris glanced around at the adjoining empty tables. Hugh's lodge was usually filled with guests.

'It's two o'clock, my boy. They'll soon be back for dinner, and Mama Tembo has been on the air, asking for you.'

Chris groaned.

'Don't worry, I put her off. The plane won't be ready until tomorrow morning. Meanwhile, she has given me all the news You sure got those Arabs steamed up. Let's see now...' Hugh counted on his fingers, '...we have smuggling, abduction, armed assault, resisting arrest, using explosives, dangerous flying, and contravening air navigation safety regulations, and... what have I forgotten?'

'Damage to a rental car, forgetting to pay a hotel bill, and threatening to shoot an Arab in the nose. But don't worry, I can explain everything.'

Hugh laughed. 'You had better fill me in.'

Chris told him from the beginning. With his mild, fatherly manner and deep-timbre poet's voice, Hugh Hildebrand was the easiest man he knew to talk to about almost anything. A close friend and business associate of the skipper, Chris had already confided in him about Julia's death, and expressed feelings he could not have mentioned to anyone else, and the unburdening had helped.

'I see no reason for guilt,' Hugh had tried to reassure him. 'And from what you have told me of Julia, I do not believe she would either. It is by the verdict of his own heart that a guilty man is condemned or acquitted. You will have to come to terms with yourself, my boy, not your guilt. No man should be judged for having a lively imagination, only for how it is employed.'

About the Egyptian affair he was less poetic. 'Most of them would accuse their own mother of having a bastard for a child. We'll just do what they always do and deny everything. We'll change the Baron's registration. The company still has a few it hasn't used. And we will have to think up a story for the Australian Embassy about how your passport was stolen. I don't know about your girlfriend. If she has one, maybe she can ask someone to mail it to her and I'll arrange to get it stamped.'

'She's not my girlfriend, Hugh, I hardly know her, but I got her into this mess and have to take care of it. Can she stay here until I sort it out? I'll pay for her keep, of course.'

'Just a figure of speech, lad, and I'm sure we can squeeze her in. It sounds as if she's had a rough trot. What do you think happened?'

'I don't know, Hugh, and she won't, or can't say. It's confusing as hell, and the doctor wasn't much help either, but the way she spoke I have a feeling it was some sort of operation that went wrong.'

'A backyard abortion?'

Chris shrugged. 'It crossed my mind, but she doesn't seem the type, somehow.'

'Miss Bontoux was infibulated,' Doctor Shingadia informed Chris bluntly when he called to collect Zarena from the hospital two weeks later.

Chris stared at the top of her head as she bent to write out a prescription. 'What?'

'I shouldn't be telling you this, Mister Ryan. Zarena asked me not to, but I feel it is in her own best interests that you are aware and know what to expect if there are complications. Or in case...' she paused in her writing to fix Chris with a meaningful look, '...you are planning any sexual advances within the next few weeks.'

Stunned, both by her news, and her assumption, Chris continued to stare at the crown of the doctor's shiny black hair in confusion. 'Infibulation?'

'Yes, and a messy one.'

'Has that got something to do with circumcision?'

'It's a bit more than that, unfortunately, and far too prevalent amongst the Muslim community, even in my own country. Thankfully though, this type of Sudanese FGM... female genital mutilation... is becoming less common with the advance of social awareness programs.'

'You'll have to forgive my ignorance, Doctor.'

'Female circumcision is normal practice in some communities. Mothers, grandmothers, and girlfriends have all been circumcised. Without it they would not find husbands. They would be labelled as unclean and ostracized, even by their own family and friends.'

'But why Zarena? I know she has an Arab father, but her mother was French.'

'That I don't know, Mister Ryan, but I do know that she

was circumcised as a child.'

'But I thought you said…' Chris stopped, bewildered.

'Perhaps I had better explain,' Doctor Shingadia said patiently. 'Circumcision, as you may know, involves excising the clitoris to inhibit a woman's sexual desires.'

'Yes, but…'

'It also prevents her from experiencing pleasure during intercourse and achieving orgasm.'

'I didn't realize it was *that* bad.'

Doctor Shingadia smiled cynically. 'At times I feel as if we're still living in the dark ages, Mister Ryan. This sort of manipulation of women by ignorant men, supposedly in the name of religion, but really for their own pleasure, makes me very angry.' She glared at Chris, and he raised his hands in surrender.

'Go easy, Doc. I'm on your side.'

'I didn't mean you, of course. It may help if you tell me what happened, and in what circumstances you found Miss Bontoux. She seems reluctant to talk about it.'

'I know what you mean.'

Chris related what had happened, and Doctor Shingadia removed and polished her glasses, listening without interruption until he had finished, then she put them back on and nodded in understanding.

'Yes, that explains a lot. I believe what you did saved her life in more ways than one, Mister Ryan. Miss Bontoux was being prepared for a life of prostitution. Prostitutes are nearly always infibulated to the third degree.'

'I still have no idea what that means, Doc.'

'Very well. There are three main types of excision. In the first, which is a simple circumcision, only the hood of the clitoris is removed. In the second, the clitoris and some, if not all, of the labia minora is removed, and the third, which is infibulation, the clitoris, labia minora and labia majora are all removed and, in some cases, the vagina is stitched closed, leaving only a small fissure for menstruation, urination and, of course, once the mutilation has healed, sex.'

'Jesus.. they did that to Zarena?'

'Yes, except for the stitching. Miss Bontoux was already a virgin and they probably wanted her ready as soon as possible.'

'Jesus, Doc. It seems unbelievable they would go to such lengths.'

'Unfortunately, they do. A dangerous and painfully unpleasant experience, as you can imagine.'

'I don't think I can, Doc,' Chris murmured. 'It sounds like some sort of pagan ritual. Do they sacrifice virgins as well?'

'Almost,' the doctor replied with a wry smile. 'The scar tissue must be broken before the girl is able to perform sex, so it is also an enforced chastity device. It is broken by the man during the act. Almost like breaking virginity.'

'I can't believe these people are living on the same planet.'

'Yes, but unfortunately they are, and Miss Bontoux also had an infection. Probably caused by a dirty instrument. A razor blade, most likely. That is what they normally use, although I have had a case where a piece of glass was used. Many girls die from loss of blood or infection. Zarena was fortunate.'

'Fortunate? … Ignorant bastards…'

Doctor Shingadia tore the sheet from the pad. 'She will need to continue the antibiotics for a while. The infection is under control, but I would like to see her again in four days, and if there is any sign of bleeding, increased inflammation, or rise in temperature, I want her back here immediately. I have already told her.'

Chris took the prescription distractedly, still shaken by what he had learned, and suddenly unsure of what he was going to say, or how he was going to react when he saw Zarena.

'Please remember, Mister Ryan. I would not have broken confidence and told you any of this were I not concerned for her well-being, and because I know she is going to be recuperating in your care. She is an intelligent young woman, and has had a very traumatic experience, physically, as well as psychologically.'

'I'm glad you did, Doctor, and don't worry, we'll take good care of her.'

Zarena was sitting in a wheel chair in the lobby, waiting in the company of an African nurse. Her face was gaunt, but a hint of color showed in her cheeks and her eyes were bright. A small frown creased her brow as she saw him coming from the doctor's office.

Chris grinned and waved the prescription. 'You have to take your medicine like a good girl.'

She gave him a strained smile.

The nurse wheeled her out to the car and Chris helped her up. 'Are you sure you're going to be comfortable sitting in the front? I put a mattress in the back, in case...'

'No, I'm fine, thanks.'

Then, as they were driving away. 'Did she say anything... the doctor?'

'Only that you were to take it easy, and if there is any problem you must return immediately.'

'She told me your first-aid probably saved my life. I want to thank you for that. How did you know?'

'How did I know what?'

'What to do.'

'I didn't. I just did what I would have done in the army.'

'I'd also like to thank you for getting me out of that place and bringing me here... and for the two nightdresses, the flowers, and the chocolates.'

'I'm sorry I couldn't visit. I only got back this morning.'

'Your friend, Hugh, came a few times. A nice man. He arranged for me to phone Rosemary from the hospital. She's going to make excuses for me at work, and also send me a few things... my passport and money.'

'Good.'

'I don't remember much... about what happened. It all seems so strange, me being here... like a dream.'

Chris told her as they drove, going into more detail than

he had with the doctor, and sounding in his own ears like a recording, but with the schedule Mama Tembo had arranged for him, he may not get another opportunity to speak to her alone.

'I owe you even more than I thought,' she said when he had finished.

'You don't owe me anything. It was them or us, and if it wasn't for me, maybe none of this would have happened. But I still think you should tell me a little more than you already have, don't you?'

'Yes, I suppose I do owe you an explanation.'

'That girl I met at the village. She said she was your cousin.'

'Mona? Yes, I haven't seen her since she was a child. How did she look?'

'Very pregnant. She was wearing your bracelet.'

'Poor Mona.' Zarena sighed wistfully. 'The only one I really cared for. She doesn't have much to look forward to. I'm glad she has the bracelet. I wish I could do something more for her.'

'Did you really live there?'

'For five years, until I was eleven, when my father sold me to the Sheikh.'

'You're kidding!'

'No. He hated my mother. I don't know why, and he had become very religious. I looked like her, so he must have hated me too, and I was a foreigner. He sold me as a prostitute.'

'Jesus, Zarena...'

'I ran away the first night... before anything could happen, and I hadn't seen any of them until they found me in Luxor. The sheikh had already paid for me and my father had not returned the money, so I was sent back to him.'

'Well, that's it,' Chris said firmly. 'You can't go back to Egypt now. If he found you once, what is there to stop him finding you again? I've arranged for you to stay with Hugh until you're fully recovered, then we'll see, okay?'

She did not reply and they drove on in silence.

Zarena was unable able to view the results of the *daya's* handiwork with any semblance of clinical detachment. The first time she looked she had been horrified, so thereafter she attended to its needs and applied her medication by feel alone, leaving closer examination to Doctor Shingadia. That men could consider such an alteration an improvement was beyond her comprehension.

The pain eased once the swelling had gone, and after a week she was able to move around more freely. She spent much of her time sleeping, or sunbathing by the pool once the guests had left on their daily excursions, and her hollow cheeks gradually filled out from the lavish attention of Cedric, the cook, and developed a healthy glow. For exercise she involved herself with the coffee picking, enjoying the lively chatter of the African women, or helped the stable-boy with the grooming and feeding of the horses. Riding them though, was not high on her list of priorities.

After her last visit in to see the doctor, Hugh had taken her to an optician to be tested for a new pair of glasses, as her old ones were lost, then had taken her to a hairdresser and treated her to a new hairstyle; short and spiky. As she watched the dark curls fall around her she felt as if she was back in Alexandria with Papa Zoupo. Hugh had much the same fatherly manner, and an innate wisdom that encouraged implicit trust. He treated everyone younger than himself as if they were his offspring and, on more than one occasion, Zarena found herself on the verge of calling him Papa Hugh.

She felt as if she were suspended in a new life. None of her letters to the director of the museum, explaining she was ill and asking for an extension of leave, had been answered, but with Hugh's encouragement, she gave up worrying about it, content to simply coast along and enjoy the novel experience of living like one of the rich and famous.

She took frequent trips into Nairobi with Hugh or his daughter Madeline, borrowed books from the library, and visited the Croynden Museum, where she delved further into anthropology and the work of the famous Leaky family.

She saw little of Chris Ryan. His flying kept him away for long periods, usually more than a week at a time, and he remained an enigma, one moment charming, and the next moody and unapproachable. She kept herself at a distance, never quite sure how he would react.

She knew the death of his wife had affected him deeply. He spoke of her often, as if she were still alive, and he told her he felt guilty about his son, Timothy, being in Australia, but when she asked why he didn't send for him, he told her abruptly that he was better off where he was, then changed the subject.

He never spoke about his work, but she got the impression from hearing him discussing certain aspects of it with Hugh that it was secretive, and had something to do with politics. It was not a subject she was interested in particularly. She knew nothing of the Rhodesian struggle for independence, or the duplicity of British politicians, but the men spoke with such passion and bitterness she could not help but take a sympathetic interest.

With his heavy workload, and with her own recovery, the business of the papyri seemed to have lost significance, but she knew the idyllic lifestyle could not last indefinitely, and she began giving it some serious thought.

She was sitting by the pool, doing just that, when a shadow suddenly fell across the page of her book and she looked up to see Chris smiling down at her. Quickly, she pulled the towel over her legs.

'You don't have to hide them on my behalf,' he joked, 'they look just great. And so do your new glasses. I never did like those horn-rimmed things you had before. How are you coping?'

'Fine, thanks,' Zarena answered, irritated by her embarrassment. I didn't know you were back. Good trip?'

'I had several trips, and they were all bad. What are you reading?'

'African ethnology. I wanted to learn more about the early Bantu civilizations and their migration south.'

'Riveting stuff. How about a swim?'

She shook her head. 'I've just had one.'

She put on the straw hat to hide her dry hair and watched surreptitiously from its shadow as he swam. It was the first time she had seen his body exposed. She was surprised at its lack of fat. It was the sleek, sinewy body of an athlete, and he moved like one, cutting through the water effortlessly, with barely a splash. Not like her own floundering efforts, which seemed more like drowning than swimming.

Hugh had told her a few of Chris's army exploits, and there had been more than a hint of awe in his voice, which had also surprised her, for Hugh was not the sort of man one would expect to indulge in hero worship. If anything, she would have expected it to be the other way around. But then she only had to look at her own experience. She could think of no other person, real or imaginary, that would have gone to such lengths for something that did not involve them. He had saved her life and risked his own. Despite his often puerile behavior, Chris Ryan was obviously a very capable and resourceful man.

He pulled himself out and came to sit beside her. Close enough so she could smell the male muskiness of the heat steaming from his skin. 'Tell me what you've been up to since I've been away.'

'Did you know the Pan African Congress on prehistory is being held in Nairobi at the end of the month?'

'No, but I guess this is the right place for it. This is where it all happened. The cradle of mankind, right here in the rift valley. It should be interesting. Are you going along?'

'Yes, Hugh is taking me. He's come up with a good idea. Anthropologists and archaeologists from all over the world will be there. He suggested I make a full report on the papyri, add photocopies of the original with a deciphered transcript, and hand them around at the congress. I could also send a few to the right people overseas.'

He frowned. 'But didn't you say the copies were lost with your bag in Luxor?'

It took her by surprise. 'Oh... well, yes, but Rosemary... I spoke to her. She asked a colleague of mine at the museum to find those I had left in the vault. They arrived a few days ago.' She picked up her book, dismissing the subject.

'How long before I get to see this deciphered transcript... or is it still a secret?'

Zarena slammed her book closed and removed her glasses. 'You can see it any time you like, but I'm still working on it, and you've only just arrived back, so I haven't had much of a chance, have I?' He was doing it again, but this time she was not going to be intimidated. 'And what I said about the poor quality was true. It just so happens that the museum here is helping with making them clearer. So if you don't mind, I'd rather you kept your sarcastic remarks to yourself.'

'Oops!' He grinned at her. 'Sorry, I didn't mean to tread on your ego.'

'You didn't tread on my ego. You insulted my integrity.'

'I apologize.'

'Humph!'

'I have to take the plane to Salisbury tomorrow for a major inspection. I'll be away at least a week. There's a spare seat, if you're interested.'

'Thanks, but I have a job interview with the museum.'

'Really? That's great news, Zarena. You'll get it for sure. They'll be crazy not to take you.' He stood up. 'One more swim then it's sleep, glorious sleep.'

Zarena gathered her books and retired with them to her room, but found it difficult to concentrate. His offer to take her to Rhodesia was ludicrous. Besides the fact a war was going on there, she had no particular interest in the place, and a week or more of his moodiness was asking a bit much. And she also had a career to think about. She could not sponge off Hugh indefinitely. She needed money and independence, and traipsing around the country was not going to get her either.

She took her books and notes onto the verandah and studied doggedly through the afternoon, until the mini-bus returned with Hugh and the visitors, when she went to shower and change. Hugh generally dined with his guests, and she usually ate alone, after helping Cedric with the dinner – a task she had come to thoroughly enjoy, and which made her feel as if she were paying her way, but that night Hugh had made other arrangements.

'I don't see enough of you these days,' he said, ushering

her to his private table in the corner. 'And seeing how Chris is here for a change, I thought the three of us would have a little private celebration of our own.'

Chris was already at the table, and stood to smile a greeting and wait as Hugh pulled out her chair and settled her in, then both men sat down. 'You look great, Zarena.'

She smiled demurely. 'Thank you.'

'Wine? I know you don't normally, but how about a small glass to celebrate your recovery?'

Zarena turned her smile on the green-jacketed waiter standing expectantly at her side with bottle poised. 'Just a half, thank you, Isaac.' Their table manners were easy-going and natural, ingrained colonial, and never failed to impress her. Had Papa Zoupo not owned such an up market restaurant, she would have felt hopelessly inadequate and awkward in their company.

The suggestion she had been expecting came with the coffee.

'I think you should take Chris up on his offer, Zarena,' Hugh said. 'It will be a good opportunity to visit the Zimbabwe Ruins and see first hand what all the fuss is about.'

'What about my appointment with Richard?'

'I spoke to him this afternoon. It's not necessary. He says you can start there as soon as you get back.'

'You mean I have a job… at the Croynden?' She looked from one to the other expectantly, feeling the thrill taking hold, uplifting her.

Chris raised his glass in a toast, his eyes smiling at her

from above the sparkling amber wine. 'I told you they would be crazy not to take you,' he said.

Part Six

Great Zimbabwe Ruins

It was late afternoon when Chris and Zarena arrived, hot, sweaty and tired, at the Zimbabwe Ruins Hotel. Nevertheless, as soon as they had booked in, Zarena declared that she wanted to have a quick look, 'to get the feel of the place,' she explained, and Chris accompanied her reluctantly.

They had wasted little time after landing at Mount Hampden. An hour after relinquishing the Baron to the company engineers, they were back in the air in the Taylorcraft, bumping their way south under the summer cumulus. A hot shower and cold beer had been more on his mind than a stroll around.

The rocky slopes below the ruins were still bathed in the gold of fading sunshine, but the Great Enclosure itself, now deserted of sightseers for the day, was thrown into deep shadow by the height of its own towering walls, adding an air of menace to the mystery as they meandered slowly along the silent passageways, tramping ancient stone paths worn smooth by countless thousands of feet.

'Beautiful stone-work,' Zarena remarked, 'yet there is

something about the place… it gives me the shivers. I don't think I would be surprised to see a bearded soldier running down the path wielding a spear.'

'Yes, I know what you mean,' Chris replied. 'The Zulu have many legends about it. They say it was built at a time when the stones were still soft, and was inhabited by a tribe of long-haired men, which they called the Ma-iti, or Strange Ones, and that one of their kings had a boy for a wife and used to torture and kill a woman every night for entertainment.'

'Sounds like someone I should know,' Zarena said with quiet humor, showing no recrimination in her tone, and Chris glanced at her with a feeling of respect.

'I'll be leaving first thing in the morning for Gara Pasi,' he said. 'I should only be a few days. We'll arrange with the manager for you to get all the books you need from the council library, and don't be afraid to put anything you want on the tab.'

'Thanks, Chris. I'll pay you back as soon as I get my first check.'

'Like hell you will. You're working for me, don't forget, and don't think I'm a pushover. I expect your report to blast the Bantu theory right out of the water.'

She smiled. 'Okay, boss, I'll try to remember.'

Chris felt guilty about not contacting John Montgomery, but as Glenkyle Park was so close, John and Marge would have insisted he stay with them, which would have meant explaining Zarena's presence. Although perfectly innocent, still he would have felt uncomfortable, and he wondered at his cynicism, for he knew that if she had been less attractive he would have felt differently. He compromised by calling Bob McEwen instead when they got back to the hotel, explaining what they were doing, and promising to see him on their way back to Mount Hampden.

'I'll look forward to meeting her,' the curator said. 'Amanda will be thrilled to hear that one of her brightest students will be working for the Leaky foundation. I'll phone her right away, and also ask her to collect some names you can send the report to. Maybe we're going to get somewhere at last.'

C hris knew he was taking a big risk by leaving Bravo Zulu unattended in the bush. A curious elephant or bad tempered rhino could reduce the small aircraft to scrap in a few minutes, but he had no choice. The plane was the only transport available, and the Mozambique border on the Sabi River was too far from Gara Pasi to walk in the short time he had available.

After a day at the sanctuary with Fuli, spent mainly in reminiscing, he had become restless. He had nothing to do, and the derelict buildings with their memories depressed him. He needed some action, and the idea came to him as he was about to leave and head back to join Zarena at the ruins, where he thought he could be more useful.

The hill where he had found the jar of papyri was only about fifteen miles into Mozambique, next to the river. It was a remote area. If he could land close enough, he could cross the river, walk to the hill, and search the cave for the pieces of pottery that had broken off. He could do it in a night and a day easily, and if he found the broken shards, they could be dated and may add credence to Zarena's report.

When he mentioned the idea to Fuli, the old man was sceptical.

'I do not think you can cross the river where you plan,' he said. 'It is a very bad place for crocodiles, and the headman of the village there who has the boats is a friend of the Comrades. It will be better if we cross at the place of reeds.'

'We? You will come with me?'

'How else will you find this crossing place?' Fuli answered.

Late in the afternoon, Chris landed on a dry clay pan a few miles from the Sabi River and, assisted by a relieved Fuli - who considered flying machines the playthings of crazy people - dragged Bravo Zulu into the trees by her tail and covered her with branches.

Chris sprinkled some avgas around to discourage animals from coming too close, then they waited in cover until dark, in the unlikely event that any human animals had seen them land. It was an anxious time, for their only weapons consisted of Fuli's axe, and the replacement nine millimeter pistol Chris had brought from the Baron.

They crossed the river some five miles downstream from the village Fuli had mentioned, inside Mozambique, and where the river spread itself over half a mile of flat, swampy plain in a confusing labyrinth of waist deep sandy channels cluttered with flood debris and reeds. It was a painstaking process of wading, thrashing and, when the reeds became impenetrable, backtracking.

Once across, they stayed off the main paths where possible, walking in the bush, but when it became too thick, they had no option but to press on and hope they didn't bump into anyone unfriendly. On several occasions they disturbed Hippos browsing on the river bank, and on one occasion were forced to run for their lives as one came crashing through the reeds towards them.

Chris had been superbly fit on reconnaissance, but a few months of sitting in a plane had softened him, and Fuli set a hard pace for an old man, his tough, sinewy legs, like gnarled brown walking sticks, seemed never to tire. As usual, Fuli walked barefoot, but Chris was forced to wear a borrowed pair of Fuli's car- tire sandals, and the hard rubber straps chafed mercilessly. It was a painful but necessary precaution. Even an amateur could tell the difference between an African's footprint and that of a European.

Towards dawn a blanket of mist formed above the river, and Chris was concerned it would conceal the giant baobab tree he remembered standing behind with Sergeant Mafiko, but a short while later its grotesque form materialized, and beyond it loomed the dark mass of the rock-strewn kopje.

'We are there,' he told Fuli. 'Go carefully.'

The regenerated bush had obliterated most signs of

the attack, only a few scarred rocks and trees, and a few tarnished shell casings in the undergrowth. The small cave was overgrown with weeds, but soon cleared away, and Chris wasted no time in getting down on his hands and knees to have a closer look. It was disappointingly empty. More of a crevice than a cave, it went back only a few feet, and the floor was sprinkled with the droppings of rock rabbits and, after scraping at the dank soil underneath with a stick, he found it was only a few inches thick. He scooped out the soil in handfuls, which Fuli sorted through with his fingers, and it wasn't long before the old man grunted and pulled out a few shards of lichen covered pottery no bigger than small coins.

Nothing else was found. Chris wrapped the shards and put them in the shoulder bag, and changed the uncomfortable sandals for his veldskoens. It didn't matter if they were tracked from here, they weren't coming back. 'Let's go, Fuli.'

They crossed back over the river at dusk, following their own signs out, and fighting off the swarms of mosquitoes. Night had fallen by the time they reached the other side and started wearily on the last few miles to the plane, and it was then Fuli took the wrong path.

The track they had used on the way out was little more than a game trail, so it was perhaps understandable he should miss it in the dark, but he did not realize it until they had walked for half an hour in the wrong direction; going towards the village they were trying to avoid.

Plodding mechanically, they only became aware of the

error when the thick riverine scrub suddenly ended and they were confronted by a stretch of open cultivated ground and the dark outline of huts only a few hundred yards ahead. Fuli grunted with surprise and stopped. There was no need for explanation. He turned and they started back, only to be stopped again by the sound of a woman's giggle.

It was close. So close, Chris pulled Fuli down and swung the pistol to point in the direction it came; a patch of tall grass only a few steps from where they crouched on the path. A man's voice spoke a quiet admonishment, followed by the sound of rustling.

From the village came a sudden burst of singing, covering any further sound, and Chris and Fuli had started to edge away when the woman stood up and saw them.

Chris leaped forward to take a handful of the dress she had been in the process of removing, and pulled her behind him, where Fuli promptly clamped a hand over her mouth to stop her squeals.

The man was stumbling about, trying to pull on his denims with one hand, while searching feverishly in the grass with the other. He found his rifle too late, Chris was already standing on it, and he fell back, the whites of his eyes showing as he stared at the pistol.

'If you speak or try to run,' Chris warned. 'I will kill you both.' He picked up the rifle, an AK-47, and checked it quickly while the guerrilla lay gaping in shock. 'We'll take them with us, Fuli. Let the woman go in front.' He signaled to the man, indicating with the barrel. 'Move!'

When they could no longer hear the singing from the village, Chris made the guerrilla lie face down on the ground and searched him for other weapons.

'Please! I am not running... do not kill us, sir.'

'Shut up and keep moving.' Chris ordered.

They reached the plane an hour later. Chris tied his captive's feet and made them both sit on the ground under Fuli's guard while he removed the branches and checked the plane.

He had no choice now but to take off in the dark. To wait until dawn, as he had originally intended, would be too risky. They would be followed, he was certain. It would be slow work, but it was not so dark that their tracks could not be seen on the sandy paths by a determined tracker, and the sentry or the girl may have been missed soon after their capture.

While the prisoners watched in bewilderment, Chris and Fuli pulled Bravo Zulu from her hiding place to the edge of the pan. The dark blob of the bush was faintly visible on the far side. It was enough.

'What is your name,' Chris asked the terrorist.

'I am Comrade...'

'Not your *chimurenga*, war name. Your real name.'

'I am Lovemore,' he answered sullenly.

It meant nothing to Chris. There would have to be at least five hundred Lovemores in the country.

But it did mean something to Fuli, who had been peering closely at the young African, who, in turn, was trying just as hard to avoid Fuli's scrutiny. After a few more questions by Fuli involving villages and the names of certain headmen, Fuli grunted several times in enlightenment. 'He is the one from the poisoned water at the Tshingwezi river, *Nkosi.*'

It took a few moments before Chris understood. 'The one with the radio?'

'Yes, *Nkosi.*'

'Well, I'll be buggered!'

Lovemore, the terrorist, looked at Chris expectantly, an uncertain smile fixed on his face, as if unsure if this later development was in his favor or not, then obviously deciding it was, he grinned widely and began explaining to the girl with much excited embellishment. She obliged with exclamations of amazement and giggling, and Chris shook his head in disbelief at the incongruous situation.

With common ground established, Lovemore seemed desperate to please. He answered every question promptly, telling them he had been forced to join the guerrillas while visiting friends at St. Luke's Mission, and he had tried many times to escape. He was very pleased to meet them again and to be rescued at last, and Chris laughed sardonically. 'Yeah... I bet you are. How many women and children have you murdered, Comrade Lovemore.'

'None, sir! I swear it by my mother's grave that I have killed no one.'

'What were you doing at the village tonight?'

'It was a meeting of the people, sir, to sing the songs and get food.'

'And a few girls too, hey? I suppose you were the sentry.'

'Please, Sir, you must let us run away. If you take us to the soldiers, they will kill us.'

'You have been listening to too much propaganda, my friend. Who was responsible for the attack on my house at Glenkyle?'

Lovemore looked genuinely surprised. 'I have never been there, sir.'

Chris realized he was wasting precious time, and he had another problem on his mind. Taking off in the dark was safe enough, the air was cool and would provide adequate lift to clear the stunted trees at the edge of the pan, but landing at *Gara Pasi* in the dark was another matter, and daylight was still hours away. Buffalo Range had runway lights, but also air traffic control, and Bravo Zulu was not rated for night flying. The only alternative was to sneak into Chiredzi and hope the street lights would be enough of a guide to line him up with the runway. He could take off again at dawn and fly Fuli home.

'All right, Fuli, turn them loose, it's time to get out of here. Spin the propeller.. and don't forget to walk around it.'

Bravo Zulu spluttered into life and Fuli ran in a wide circle to clamber into his seat. Glancing from the side window as Bravo Zulu surged forward on full power, Chris was surprised to see Lovemore lift his hand in a hesitant farewell, and he shook his head again at the irony. It could only happen in Africa. That was the joy of it. And that was also the tragedy of it.

Section Commander Silas Tongara was almost beside himself with fury. Not only had Comrade Wireless failed to return after the meeting was over, but one of the villagers had reported seeing him leave with a girl. It was a strict rule that no Comrade was to take local women without special permission. They could not afford to anger the locals who they relied on for food and security, and too often a jealous husband or boy friend had turned informer simply to get his own back.

And for a sentry to take a girl with him was unforgivable. Tongara told the headman that when found, Comrade Wireless would be beaten in front of the whole village as an example.

The girl's head scarf was found near the path, and a trampled area in the long grass showed where they had been lying. Further searching with the aid of carefully screened cigarette lighters revealed their tracks on the path leading away from the village and, disturbingly, those of two others.

Assuming the worst, which was that Comrade Wireless and the girl had been captured by a security force patrol, and that they could be attacked at any moment, Tongara ordered his men to bombshell, each of the twelve going in a different direction. If an ambush was sprung, only one or two would be killed instead of the whole group. Two villagers were selected to follow the tracks and Tongara went with them, following a good distance behind.

When they met at the prearranged location some time later, it became evident there was no patrol, but why Comrade Wireless and two others, perhaps friends, had met and run off with the girl, he could not imagine, but he was determined to find out. Not that he needed him - Wireless was one of his most useless recruits - but none of his men disobeyed orders and got away with it. More than just a beating was awaiting Comrade Wireless.

The tracks were easy to follow, even in the dark, and once it was established that no attempt had been made to conceal them, they moved quickly, stopping only occasionally to confirm with a quick flash from the lighter that the signs were still there.

The sudden noise of what sounded like the revving of a heavy truck in the distance caused some consternation. Someone whispered that it could be an army truck, but the men from the village said there were no roads in the area, even for four-wheel- drive trucks, and they listened in confusion as the sound dwindled into silence.

Someone else suggested it could be a helicopter, but they knew the sound of that too well. Tongara ended the speculation by cursing everyone back onto the path and they proceeded cautiously.

The mystery deepened when they reached a clay pan and the tracks were replaced by those of a three-wheel vehicle. They disappeared halfway across the pan, and again a helicopter was suggested, but one of the villagers told them he thought it was the aero plane from Gara Pasi.

'I have never heard of this place,' Tongara said. 'How far is it?'

The two men from the village consulted at length before reporting that it was as far as half a day walking. They should be there soon after the sun had risen.

'Take us there,' Tongara ordered.

It was closer to mid-morning, and Tongara was casting threatening glances in the direction of the two villagers when a road, a broken fence, and other signs of approaching habitation prompted him to stop and find a place to rest up for the day. He had never been this far south. He sent two men to scout ahead, and to find a village where they could get food.

He was surprised when the men returned within half an hour to report a deserted house and other buildings, and a group of four huts with a Shangaan woman and three children. They had seen no sign of any vehicles.

'Show me,' Tongara ordered.

One of the children, a young girl, saw them first. She was sweeping the ground in front of the chicken hut with a bundle of dry sticks and called to her mother.

'Mai! Mai! Comrades!' She ran to one of the larger huts, reaching it as a woman came out. Two younger children crowded behind in the doorway, peering around her. The woman greeted Tongara and his men politely, even though they had not been invited to enter the kraal.

One of the men pushed her aside to look in the hut. The

others ignored her, searching the other huts and surrounds. Tongara sent men to investigate the house and other buildings while he went to look at what appeared to be an airstrip, and he exclaimed with satisfaction when he saw the same strange wheel tracks as they had found at the pan.

He returned to confront the woman. 'Where is the aero plane?'

She looked down at the children who were clinging to her legs. 'It is not here.' she answered quietly.

Without apparent effort, Tongara slapped her, sending her stumbling back to fall over the frightened children, who began screaming.

The older girl, who had been standing nearby, dropped her bundle of sticks and made a sudden dash around the hut and into the trees. One of the men ran after her, but she evaded him nimbly and disappeared in the undergrowth. He returned, grinning apologetically at Tongara's glare. From the bushes came the girl's hysterical shouting. 'Petrus, run! The Comrades are here. Run, Petrus, run!'

'Who is Petrus?' Tongara demanded of the woman.

'He is my small son... please, we have done nothing.'

'Take the children away,' Tongara ordered. 'Put them in there.' He pointed with his rifle to the chicken hut.

As the screaming children were being dragged away Tongara looked down contemptuously at the stunned woman. Blood trickled from her swelling lip. 'Shangaan bitch. You think I have no eyes? Who was in the aero plane?'

She sat up, looking anxiously towards where the two

children were being pushed into the chicken hut. 'It was only the white man who owns the house.'

Tongara put his foot on her chest and pushed her back down. 'Why was he here when the house is empty?'

'I do not know, he did not speak with me. He came two days ago and has not been back.'

'Where is your man?'

'I have not seen him.'

'You are lying. He was with the white man.' Tongara spoke to one of his men. 'Take your bayonet. If the woman does not speak the truth, cut the arm from the smallest child.'

'No! I beg you! We have done nothing!'

'Where is your man?'

'Yes, he went with the white man, but he did not tell me the place.'

'Where is the next village to here?'

After she had told him, Tongara sent half his men there, instructing them to bring everyone they could find, then he ordered the woman to cook food for his men while they rested in the shade.

When the reluctant and curious people from the neighboring village arrived, herded along the path in a tight group by his men, Tongara had them sit in a circle in front of the huts while he spoke to them. He told them they were there to see justice. A comrade had been betrayed by the woman's husband and his white racist friend. They had taken him to the police and they should all be ashamed that a member of their tribe was the cause. The man and woman they had taken to the police were heroes of the people's struggle and the bush war.

'The man of this village is a sellout,' he told them, and they shifted uneasily in the dust, for they had heard of terrible things that befell those given that label.

'We will return to catch this man, Fulamani,' he shouted at them, 'and he will be punished.'

A communal sigh arose from the villagers, for they knew Fulamani well, and none could think of him as a bad man, but none dared to speak out in his defense.

'If any of you warn him you will also be punished as a sellout,' Tongara warned, 'and you will see what happens to sellouts.'

He had his men bring the woman into the circle. Her hands were tied and she was thrown face down on the ground. Two men came forward. One with a stout stick freshly cut from a tree, the other the handle of a hoe.

'*Pasi ne sellout!*' Tongara shouted at the ring of frightened villagers. 'Say it!'

The villagers responded with a low murmur.

'Louder!' Tongara bellowed. '*Pasi ne sellout.* Down with the sellout. Shout it. Everyone must shout it.' He patrolled in front of them, glaring and forcing them to chant together, conducting them with his rifle and leading the chant himself.

The one with the handle struck first, breaking the woman's ankle with the first blow. Her scream of agony was cut short by the shock of the next blow, which shattered her knee.

The reluctant chanting of the villagers changed to a long moan of dismay. A few of the women began to wail. Tongara rapped one of them sharply on the head with his rifle butt. 'Say it!' he shouted.

The beating of the woman continued remorselessly, but she no longer screamed, and the sickening sound of the sticks striking flesh was covered by the wails and chanting of the villagers. None of them looked at the woman. They stared at the dusty ground in front of them. She had been their friend, and they could not witness her degradation.

'Do not kill her.' Tongara told the two men. 'Put her inside the hut.'

The wailing began again as the unconscious woman was dragged to the hut and bundled inside with her two screaming children. Tongara threatened the villagers with his rifle and they fell quiet.

'Go!' he shouted. 'Remember what I have said. If the Comrades come to your huts, feed them. If the police or soldiers come, say nothing. Do not come back to this place.' He picked up a burning log from the fire and held it high. *'Pamberi ne hondo*, forward with the war. *Pasi ne sellout!'*

He held the burning log to the thatch of the large sleeping hut and it began to smolder, pouring thick, greasy smoke. He did the same to the other two huts then, with a casual underarm throw, he tossed the burning log onto the grass roof of the chicken hut housing the injured woman and her children.

Zarena flipped through her completed folder of notes once more then sat back with a sigh of relief. It did not look much for three days work, but it was the best she could do with the limited reference material available. The books from the library were written for laymen, and so out of date in methodology as to be almost useless. Nevertheless, added to what she had learned in Nairobi and Cairo - and from her own wanderings around the ruins - it had been possible to compile a comprehensive list of questions she was sure could not be answered satisfactorily by the Bantu theorists. To these she had added another list of possible answers and counter questions using the opposing theory.

As she had no credibility as an archaeologist, questions would be the spearhead of her attack. That way, no one could accuse her of bias, only of scepticism. Printed in booklet form and handed out to the delegates at the convention, it was certain to raise awareness if nothing else and, hopefully, even more questions. She would call the booklet The Archaeological Myth of the Century?, posing it as a question to keep it in context with the theme. All things considered, she was rather proud of it.

With her task complete, Zarena treated herself to a dinner of roasted guinea-fowl and a glass of wine from the hotel's a la carte menu. It was topped off with several more glasses when the group of locals drinking at the cocktail bar discovered why she was there. It started a lively discussion that lasted until midnight, and she walked unsteadily back to her room, giggling happily to herself and clasping a menu, on the back of which had been written the names and addresses of her new friends to whom she had promised to write and send copies of her booklet.

Chris woke her late next morning by banging on the door.

'You've missed breakfast,' he informed her with a grin when she joined him on the terrace a half hour later.

'I was up late.'

'So I heard, but don't worry, it will soon wear off, and we can have an early lunch.' He poured her a cup of coffee then unfolded a handkerchief to reveal several small shards of pottery. 'I brought you these.'

He explained briefly where he had found them and Zarena picked up a piece to examine it. 'From the same jar as the papyri?'

'Yep.' He grinned smugly, obviously pleased with himself, and Zarena concealed her misgivings under a thoughtful expression. The shards wouldn't prove anything. The pieces could have come from anywhere. It would be only his word, and in science that counted for nothing.

'I'll see if I can get them tested in Nairobi,' she said. 'Are we leaving soon? My notes are finished.'

'As soon as you're ready. I can arrange an early lunch, if you like.'

'No, that won't be necessary, thanks all the same. I'll

go and pack.'

Bravo Zulu was ten minutes out and on course for Mount Hampden when Chris received a call from Area Control asking if he could copy a message from the police. Concerned it was about his and Fuli's activities during the night - which he had not reported because he had not wanted to explain what he was doing there - he told them to go ahead and listened anxiously.

'Special Branch want to know if you saw any suspicious activity in the area of your property this morning.'

The question was perplexing. He had not returned to *Gara Pasi* that morning. Fuli had decided to catch the bus from Chiredzi instead, so he could do his shopping at the same time. He decided to play it safe.

'Why do they ask?'

'Stand by.'

Chris waited impatiently with the microphone in his hand. The controller would be talking on the phone to Special Branch. Could they have found out about his little over the border excursion?

The radio crackled. 'Bravo Zulu, an OP has reported black smoke coming from the vicinity. They wish to know if it is worth requesting an aircraft from the police air wing to investigate.'

This time Chris didn't hesitate. 'Negative. Tell them I'll go myself. If I see anything I'll let you know.'

'Roger, Bravo Zulu. I'll revise and hold your flight plan.'

Chris turned towards the south - almost the reciprocal of his original course - and Zarena, who had been gazing at the landscape below, turned to give him an enquiring look. 'Something wrong?'

'Relax,' Chris reassured her with forced smile. 'I have to investigate some smoke coming from my property. With a bit of luck I may be able to show you a few elephant on the way.'

He tried to think what it could be. Black smoke usually meant the burning of some unnatural substance, such as vehicles or buildings, but when he saw the smoke from a distance some time later, his fears gave way to relief. The report appeared to be wrong. Smoke was coming from Gara Pasi all right, but it was not black, and there was not much. Perhaps Fuli's family had been clearing a field and burning off the maize stalks.

Then as he drew close he noticed the thatched roofs of the stone cottage and guest huts had gone. Flying low over the top he saw the pole rafters still burning inside where they had collapsed. He gave them only a glance. More smoke showed from beyond the line of trees that separated the complex from Fuli's huts, and he turned to fly over them.

All four huts had been burned down.

'Is this your place?' Zarena asked. 'What is it... what has happened?'.

Chris gave her a grim look in reply. He circled the area

slowly. Two women looked up from the clear area between the smoldering piles that had been the huts. 'Can you see anyone?'

'Yes, over there.'

He looked to where she was pointing out of her side window. Two men were standing under the *Indaba* tree. One of them moved into the clearing and waved, but although it was an old man, it was not Fuli.

Chris gained some height and searched the surrounding area, flying along the stretch of river where the children usually played and washed, but saw no one, and the alarm bells began to clamor more loudly. There should have been more people.

'I'm going to land,' he informed Zarena.

He taxied Bravo Zulu through the long grass to the end of the strip and into the trees near the burned huts, then turned her around ready for a quick departure before switching off. From under the seat he removed the AK he had taken from Lovemore.

'Insurance,' Chris explained in answer to Zarena's look of consternation.. He also retrieved the pistol and stuck it in his belt. 'Don't worry, if terrorists were here those locals wouldn't be hanging around.'

'You want me to come?'

'If you wish.'

The two men they had seen came through the trees to meet them, and Chris recognized the one who had waved as Fuli's tailor friend from the store. The other man was the storekeeper. The tailor removed his hat and gave Chris and Zarena a sombre greeting. Both men wore expressions that could have been carved from soapstone.

'We are here because Fulamani is our friend and brother,' the tailor explained, and the storekeeper nodded in agreement.

'Yebbo, it is so.'

'He is fortunate to have such friends,' Chris responded, following the ritual and hiding his impatience. 'I trust your families are well?'

'The tailor screwed nervously at the hat in his hands. 'They are well, *Nkosi,*' he replied, ill at ease.

Chris came to his aid. 'Of what do you wish to speak, Old Father?'

'We have a great sadness and do not wish to speak of it, but you are also the friend of Fulamani.'

'Then tell me,' Chris said, his patience thinning. It was the sort of ritual hedging that could go on forever. 'What has happened? Where is Fuli?'

'He was here, *Nkosi,* but we have not seen him. The Comrades were here also.'

'When?'

'In the morning when it was yet early, *Nkosi.* They brought many people from the reserve. It is from them we heard of the burning and came to be with our friend, but he was already gone.'

The storekeeper spoke. 'The sister of Fulamani's wife tells that he has gone on the spoor of the Comrades. We fear greatly for him, *Nkosi.*'

Chris stared at the old man in silence for a moment, sharing his fear. Without any weapon, Fuli would have no chance if he caught up with the terrorists, and there could only be one reason why Fuli would do such a foolish thing. 'What of Lydia and the children?'

'It is the thing we do not wish to speak of,' the tailor answered. 'But for the boy, Petrus, and his sister, they are dead. The *Nkosi* must see for himself.'

As Chris approached the burned huts a woman began wailing in mourning. He stopped under the *Indaba* tree. The same shady marula tree under which all visitors usually sat when they came to visit Fuli or his family.

'Wait here,' Chris said to Zarena.

It was Lydia's sister who was mourning. She sat on the open ground between the smoldering huts with a shawl covering her head, rocking as she wailed.

Chris stopped beside a dead chicken. Its feathers had burned to charred spikes, and its comb and legs were shriveled. Several more chickens in a similar condition lay close to where their small elevated hut had been. A new fire had been made on the ashes, and a woman he had not seen before was stacking it from a bundle of firewood she had apparently carried there, building it to a fierce blaze, and he watched her for a moment in bewilderment. The only indication she gave of his presence was a quick, nervous glance.

Looking down he noticed the ground was covered with

the varied footprints typical of a terrorist group, and one in particular caught his eye. A herringbone pattern much larger than the others. Chris's sense of foreboding deepened.

Close to where Lydia's sister mourned was a patch of dried blood, covered over ineffectually with sand. Drag marks and more bloodstained earth led to where the woman was building the fire, and Chris stared at it with dawning realization and horror. He knew what had happened. The signs were all there, but still he could not accept them. He spoke brusquely to the woman.

'What are you doing?'

Behind him, the wailing suddenly stopped, cut short by the sound of his voice. The woman tending the fire gave him another quick, startled look, then glanced towards Lydia's sister, as if she were the one to provide the answer.

'The Comrades were here,' Chris said. 'I know it, so tell me what happened.'

She continued to feed the fire in a distracted manner, not answering, and Chris did not persist further. He had become aware of the smell. A sweet, cloying smell similar to that which came from the burning of animal carcasses, and suddenly he could pretend no longer. Sick at heart, he turned away.

The woman resumed her mournful wailing, the sound knifing through him, and he stopped, feeling suddenly faint. The feeling passed and he walked slowly back to the tree. He had to go after Fuli before it was too late.

'What is it, Chris?' Zarena asked, her expression

concerned.

Chris spoke to the two old men. 'You must help the woman with the fire. Make sure nothing is left.'

He turned to Zarena. 'He burned them,' he said bleakly. 'Fuli's wife and children and all the damned chickens. That murdering bastard burned them alive.'

When times were still good at Gara Pasi, Chris had built a small two-person hide at one of the river pools frequented regularly by animals. The thatched roof had long since gone, but the timber walls still stood, and it took Chris only a few minutes to cover the top with branches.

Zarena looked at it with trepidation. 'Do I really have to wait in there? What if animals come? Why can't I wait in the plane?'

'Too risky. As long as you stay inside and keep quiet no one will find you here, and the animals won't bother you.'

'How long will you be?'

'Not long. I want to find out in what direction they are going and if Fuli is following. I can't just leave him. We'll be out of here before dark and can report the incident to the police. We've been after this swine for a long time.'

'Can't you call them on the radio?'

'I have to be in the air to reach them, and I will as soon as we leave, but right now I don't want to waste any more time.' He took the pistol from his belt and gave it to her. 'Take this, it will make you feel better.'

Zarena took it reluctantly and crawled into the hide, and Chris dragged a branch over the opening. With a clump of grass he brushed out their tracks all the way to the path. The same path taken by the gang. It was covered with prints, including those of Fuli's bare feet and the large ones of Tongara. Chris estimated there were at least a dozen men in the group, and they had made no attempt to hide their tracks. In such a remote area they would not expect to be followed.

He was not concerned about catching up with them. They had at least a four hour start, and even if they had stopped for rests, which was unlikely, they would be a long way ahead. He guessed that Fuli would be a few hours behind the gang and a few hours ahead of him, so he had little chance of catching up to him either, but at least he could find out if they were going towards the border or heading back to the village on the Sabi River. Once he knew where they were going he may even be able to follow in the plane and spot them from the air, then he could pass their position to the police.

When the tracks left the path and turned north, heading away from the border, Chris decided there was no point in going farther. Away from the river the mopani veld was open, with little cover apart from the occasional scrub covered anthill. He had established they were returning to the village and no doubt would stay there for the night, which would make it easy for the fire force to surprise them in the morning. He could do nothing for Fuli except hope the old man had cooled off enough to stay out of trouble.

He stopped in the cover of one of the anthills. A glance

at his watch showed he had been following for a little less than half an hour. He could afford to sit and listen for a few minutes before going back in case Fuli, by some miracle, came to his senses and decided to return home. At least he had not heard any gunfire. Fuli would not be taken alive, of that he was certain.

Above the trees he could see the dwindling smoke of the impromptu funeral pyre. Gara Pasi was fast disappearing. First the water, then the animals, now the people. It had become a sanctuary for ghosts.

The faint rattle of a pebble startled Chris. He listened carefully, but no further sound came. Still, he stood up slowly, his hand on the cocking lever of the rifle. In his distracted state he had forgotten to cock it.

He moved silently around the anthill. When he reached the other side he heard the sound again, but fainter, and in the direction of some low bushes too small to hide the body of a man, then again farther away still, and he relaxed; only a small animal running away.

The three men jumped on him as he turned back. He heard them and swung around, but too late. One grabbed the weapon before he could cock it, another took him around the legs, and the third clung to his back with an arm around his neck.

Chris fell backwards, hoping to crush the man behind with his weight, but only half succeeded. As he lay on the ground the one gripping the AK kicked him in the stomach.

'White pig! next I use the pig-sticker.'

Three other men suddenly appeared and joined in. They jerked the rifle from his grasp and rolled him over, forcing his arms behind his back and tying them at the wrist and elbows with strips of bark quickly ripped from a nearby sapling. Hands gripped his shirt, his hair and his arms, trying to lift him.

'Stand up, Pig.'

Chris threw himself to the side, rolling on his back and lashing out with his feet, but they did not connect. He gave them a mouthful of curses. If they were going to kill him he was not going to be humiliated first.

The men laughed. One of them was strong, with a muscular, athletic build, and it flashed through Chris's mind that it must be Tongara, but it was not.

'I am Comrade Lucky,' the guerrilla said, pulling a bayonet from a sheath tied to his belt and clipping it to the barrel of his rifle. 'Today I have a lucky day. Also, I have the pig sticker.' He prodded Chris sharply on the leg with it, drawing blood. 'Get up, Piggy.'

Chris moved to his knees, looking for an opportunity, but against six of them he had no chance.

'You are very stupid,' said one. 'We watch you for a long time.'

'More stupid even than a pig.'

'This little piggy going to market,' said another, causing laughter.

They removed his shoes and watch, then two grabbed him by the arms and hoisted him to his feet. Another struck him on the head with the barrel of a rifle and gave him a shove forward. 'Walk!'

Only three of the men escorted him along the path. The other three moved off in the opposite direction, back towards Gara Pasi, and when Chris craned around to look, the athletic one pricked him with the bayonet. 'Do not worry about them. They go to see your aero plane. Did you not think we saw it?' He laughed scornfully. 'You are a stupid little piggy. Soon you will see the smoke of it and cry for your flying machine.'

Zarena shifted uncomfortably in her cramped space. It was stifling hot and airless, and she felt as if she had been there all day, yet her lying watch told her it was only a little more than an hour. Sleeping would have helped pass the time, and she was tired enough after her late night, but it was too hot, and there were too many curious bugs and ants with no other purpose in life other than to crawl over her bare legs. Also, she badly needed to relieve herself.

She had been wanting to go all morning - the consequence of drinking too much water in a futile attempt to quench her stupid hangover - but there had been no opportunity, and she had felt too embarrassed to mention it. Then the terrible tragedy at the huts had pushed it from her mind. But now it was back, and with a vengeance.

She was reluctant to do it in the hide. It would necessitate having to rest her naked buttocks on the bug infested sand while she removed her shorts, as she was unable to stand up, and that was out of the question.

And she dare not go outside either. Not with the rustling and animal-type noises she had heard. She tried to occupy her mind with something else. She had plenty to think about. Such as why she had allowed herself to be talked into coming to this wild and dangerous place. She had never been the adventurous type. And Chris Ryan, her enigmatic companion. What a surprise it had been to see him trying to hide his tears from her.

Zarena could stand it no longer. Either she had to take a pee or wet her pants. She was being foolishly overcautious. He had told her not to worry about wild animals, and she had not actually *seen* any, only heard noises. And she had a gun. She removed the branch covering the opening and crawled out before she could change her mind.

The whole operation took less than a minute. She kicked sand over the wet patch and took her first deep breath in ages, letting it out with a sigh. It felt wonderful.

The water was close, only a dozen paces across an inviting sandy beach, and her mouth and throat was dry; a further legacy of the wine. Another look around revealed no unpleasant surprises so she crossed the sand and dipped her hands into the cool water, scooping it up into her parched mouth and over her sweaty face with both hands.

Content now to return to the hide, Zarena started back across the sand, then stopped suddenly when she heard a cough. After a moment of fleeting panic she relaxed. It came from the direction of the path that Chris had said he was going to follow and, no doubt, on which he would return.

She stood on the sand and waited for him to appear, childishly pleased with herself for having found the courage to come out. At least he would see she was not a complete coward.

Then she saw them. Three black men holding guns, and she ran.

Too late, Zarena realized that had she remained standing where she was they would probably not have seen her, but the sudden movement caught their eye and one of them shouted in alarm and sent a burst of automatic fire crackling over her head.

She scrambled backwards into the hide, dragging the covering branch over the entrance, then pushed herself in as far as she could, at the same time juggling with the pistol. She held it in both hands, pointed towards the entrance.

It was eerily quiet. Only her noisy gulping. The heavy pistol was wet and slippery and refused to keep still. She remembered the safety catch and fumbled urgently with it, her finger slipping and sliding over the metal before it finally clicked over. She prayed she would not have to use it. She had never fired any sort of weapon before, and to shoot at a person was something she was not sure she could do, no matter what the circumstances. Then the words 'burned alive' ran through her head and she firmed her grip.

The sound of a voice made her start. It came from close-by, spoken in the African language, which she could not understand, but it was obviously an order of some sort directed at her, for the tone was demanding. She did not answer and, after a while, she heard them talking to each other, arguing over something, then they stopped and she heard the rustling of the dry grass as they came closer, moving towards the sandy beach.

They would see her footprints leading directly to the hide, and she removed one hand at a time from the slippery handle to wipe them on her shirt.

They began talking again, the tone of their conversation incredulous, even jocular, as if they couldn't believe what they saw, then one of them called in English. 'Come out please, Madame. You must not be afraid. We are your friends.'

'Go away!' Zarena cried. 'I have...' She stopped. It would not be wise to warn them she had a gun. They also had guns. It may only provoke them into shooting. Better to take them by surprise. 'Leave me alone!' she finished lamely.

A stunned silence followed. They spoke to each other again, then one laughed scornfully and a few moments later two of them came into broken view through the branches, walking towards her with their rifles pointed at the hide. 'We are coming to talk. You must not be afraid to come out, because we are friends.'

His tone was so reasonable that Zarena experienced a surge of elation. Maybe he was right. She was only a visitor to the country and not involved in their war. He spoke English well. She would be able to explain.

They were close now, and the man kept talking, his tone pleasant. 'Did you come in the aero plane? We heard it coming and saw much smoke, so we came to see and to help.'

Zarena was on the point of capitulating when the branch above her head was suddenly whisked away and the third man, who had previously been out of sight, looked in.

Zarena screeched and swung the pistol to point at his head. He also gave a yell of fright and fell back. At the same instant the other two men launched themselves at the hide and tore the branch away from the entrance.

Zarena swung the pistol back and both men stared in shock as it pointed from one to the other in succession. 'Get away or I'll shoot!'

The third man suddenly loosed a blind burst of automatic fire from the bushes. Bullets crackled past her head and flying twigs and bark stung her face. Sand spurted in the bank behind her. With eyes screwed tight and ears ringing from gunfire and the shouts of the men, Zarena jerked on the trigger.

The unexpected recoil pushed the pistol high, and she fired the next shot into the air, which made it even worse. Before she could lower the automatic it was torn from her grasp. The man flung it away angrily and caught her by the arm, pulling her out, and Zarena stumbled from the hide to sprawl on the sand.

The one who had fired blindly from the bushes ran towards her and raised the butt of his rifle. Zarena covered her head.

'*Ima!* Wait!'

The man lowered his weapon and all three stood looking down at her in silence, their expressions disbelieving, then the one who had done all the talking suddenly laughed.

It was the signal for instant hilarity. They giggled and slapped at each others' hands, snorted and fell about as if they were drunk. They went through a childish pantomime of what had occurred, pretending to dodge bullets and dive for cover. One of them went in search of the pistol and returned to hold it at arm's length and stare into the barrel with a look of feigned terror, and it was cause for another round of hand slapping and cavorting.

They kept returning to stare and grin vacuously at her, as if she was just too good to be true, and Zarena sat immobile and stony faced throughout, which seemed only to add to their amusement.

Eventually they composed themselves enough to talk, and the one who had spoken earlier asked. 'Why are you here, white bitch?'

His contemptuous tone chilled Zarena, and her brain suddenly lost its numbness. 'I am a visitor to this country.' Using her initiative and thinking clearly, she realized, was probably the only way out of her predicament. 'I am a citizen of one of the Arab states who are your friends. We have been helping your cause. I should not be harmed.'

They did not look as impressed as she had hoped. The man repeated his question. 'Why are you here? Why do you shoot at us?

'I did not shoot first, and I was afraid. I am not a soldier like you. I am a scientist from Egypt. I came to inspect the Zimbabwe Ruins.'

'We should make some jig-a-jig with the white bitch,' said the youngest of them, leering at her.

The older man ignored him. 'Why do you come here in the aero plane with the *skuz'apo*?'

Zarena frowned. 'Is that his name? He was giving me a lift, but he said we must come here first. He told me to hide until he came back. Are you Robert Mugabe's men?'

'You know Robert Mugabe?'

Zarena hesitated for only a second. It was worth the risk. 'I met him in Cairo when he came to visit President Sadat. A very clever man. Like you, he speaks good English.'

She saw right away that she had hit the right note. He nodded sagely then offered his hand. 'Please get up, we must go.'

'Where are you taking me?'

'To see Comrade Tongara. He will decide if you speak the truth.'

'If you don't believe me look in the aero plane. You will find my bag with the papers about my work with Zimbabwe Ruins inside.'

'We will see. Walk, please. Do not try to run away.'

She walked in front, made acutely aware of their presence by the sour stench of their sweating bodies and the occasional brushing of them against her own. The ugly, leering one with the blue baseball cap was the most insistent, walking close so he could touch her bare legs and fondle her buttocks, complaining in a wheedling manner when ordered away by the older man. The word jig-a-jig was mentioned by him several times, and Zarena did not have to stretch her imagination too far to know what he meant.

When they came to the airstrip the leader sent the other two to scout ahead then keep watch from the bush while he took Zarena to the plane. He pulled everything out, including the bags, which he emptied on the ground before searching through the contents, paying particular attention to a pair of Chris's jeans, which he held against himself to measure the fit. As he gave the notes in her shoulder bag a cursory examination, Zarena took the opportunity to pick up her long skirt and pull it on over the shorts, and when he tossed her the bag with her notes, she hurriedly stuffed a shirt in it.

'Where is the place for putting in the petrol?' he asked.

'I don't know anything about aero planes.'

He waved her away impatiently. 'Get away to the bush and wait... over there.'

Zarena waited under a tree at the edge of the airstrip. She could see the smoke from the burned village but no sign of the two old men and the women, and hoped they had made themselves scarce after hearing the shooting. She wished fervently that she could do the same.

The guerrilla dragged a dead branch under the plane and made a fire using the aeronautical charts, manuals, and all the clothes except for the jeans, and Zarena watched in dismay as the bright red fuselage slowly darkened under thick black smoke.

The man hurried to join her. 'Go,' he ordered, pushing her ahead.

Zarena struck his hand away. 'Why are you burning the plane and my clothes? How am I supposed to get to Salisbury now?'

He glared at her. 'Be careful, bitch.' He whistled for his two companions and pushed her again. 'Go.'

'Where are you taking me?'

'It is not for me to say, but to be sure, it will not be Salisbury.'

Chris was shoved and prodded through the mopani veld to a thick grove of thorny-elm trees where the main group of guerrillas were waiting. They came out to inspect and ridicule him, jostling each other for a better view. At least half were teenagers, and they flaunted their weapons proudly, holding them up and shaking them in his face as they jeered, some grinning and some scowling ferociously. The seasoned veterans stood behind, making jokes amongst themselves and calling names.

'Hey, *Mabunu*, Boer. We kill you soon.'

'*Mabunu* Piggy.'

'Soon you squeal like a pig, *Mabunu*.'

Someone barked an order from the trees and the crowd around him parted, scrambling and pushing each other to make a passage and pass him through. Another sharp order had them dispersing rapidly back to their posts in the bushes.

Chris was shoved towards the shade of the thorn trees, where an African that made the athletic Comrade Lucky seem puny by comparison was waiting. It could only be Tongara.

Taller than Chris by a head, he came forward to glare arrogantly down at him from close range, daring him to respond, and Chris looked unblinkingly at the broad flat nose, keeping his face expressionless, holding himself in check only because he could not think of anything nasty enough to say. Had his mouth not been so dry he would have spat in Tongara's face. It wouldn't matter what he did or said. He was as good as dead anyway

'Why did you not kill the *Mabunu*?' Tongara demanded scornfully of the men. 'Were you afraid to kill the famous Selous Scout spy?' He grinned at Chris. 'Yes, I know you, *Mabunu* Ryan. Even without the hair on your face like a baboon. We came to kill you but you had run away like a woman, but now we will do it, like we did with the whore and puppies of your tame jackal, Fulamani. When we catch him we will kill him also.'

The news they had not caught Fuli gave Chris a fleeting moment of satisfaction. One bright spot in a grim day. Fuli was smart. With luck he would return to Gara Pasi and take care of Zarena.

'The only baboon around here is you, Tongara, and the only whore was your mother who rutted with the dogs in her village.'

Tongara gaped at him in astonishment. Had Chris spat in his face it would have shocked him less. His eyes became suffused with blood and thick veins stood out on his forehead. Several of the guerrillas had heard the insult, for Chris spoke clearly in the Shona tongue, and they too, stared in disbelief. No one spoke to Tongara in such a manner. One of them, perhaps from nervousness, let out a snigger, and Tongara spun around and struck the man in the face, knocking him down. He returned to glare venomously at Chris, then shot forward a hand to grip him by the throat.

The gang scattered as Tongara propelled Chris through them towards a thorn tree and slammed him against the spiky trunk. 'Tie him,' he ordered, and the men scrambled to obey while Tongara held Chris immobile by the throat, glaring at him with his blood-crazed eyes.

They tied him hard against the trunk, using webbing straps from kitbags, and Chris fought to prevent himself from showing his agony as the thorns pierced his skin all the way from the back of his calves to the back of his head. Some of the spines broke off, ripping the flesh, others grated against the bones of his shoulder blades and ribs. The entire rear of his body felt as if it was on fire. His vision blurred with Tongara's choking hold until he thought he would pass out, but he was denied the relief. Tongara released his grip and stepped back.

'Now you are going to die slowly, *Mabunu,*' he said. He snapped his fingers at one of his men. 'Bayonet!'

The man jumped forward to give him one and Tongara tested the edge with his thumb, then contemptuously tossed the rusty bayonet aside. He put his hand in his pocket and removed a clasp knife, which he opened with his teeth. The honed blade gleamed bright.

'Before you die you will see your *mboro* hanging on the thorns,' Tongara gloated.

In the expectant silence they all heard the short burst of automatic gunfire in the distance.

It caused several loud exclamations of surprise, followed by alarmed speculation.

Tongara bellowed for silence, and they all stood with heads cocked in the direction of the shots. Although his pain-racked body screamed for attention, Chris listened as hard as any of them. Another burst of firing, then two single shots with a different, flatter sound, confirmed who it was. They had found Zarena.

The group had also noticed the difference. 'Security forces!' someone exclaimed, and there was some urgent scrambling for equipment before Tongara took control, but even he could not hide his concern.

'You!' He pointed to the two men closest to him. 'Stay here with the *Mabunu* while we go to look. If we do not come in two hours, take him to the Masengena camp.' To Chris he said: 'Think of your life while you can, *Mabunu*. It will soon be finished.'

Tongara led the remainder of his men away at a run, and Chris writhed helplessly against his bonds, his heart like lead in his chest. Only two shots from the pistol he had given her, and there were three men. He could not bring himself to think any further than that.

He felt an overwhelming sense of defeat. First Julia, then Lydia and her children, and now Zarena. Depression settled on him like a shroud. He had failed miserably and deserved to die. He felt bitterly disappointed that Tongara had not already killed him. He did not want to hear them gloating about Zarena. Death would be easier. Even the pain was easier to bear than the shame, and it was excruciating.

When something struck him on the knee he did not feel it. Neither did he notice or feel the one on the chest, for it struck the webbing, but he did feel the hard brown berry that struck him in the middle of his forehead, and he looked up to see a hazy figure waving at him from behind a bush some thirty paces away.

He blinked and shook his head to clear his vision against the mopani flies that swarmed around his face and sucked the moisture from his eyes. It was like trying to peer through a dark cloud, but he was able to focus long enough to recognize the waving figure and, as if he had received a shot of morphine, the pain eased and his vision cleared.

Chris glanced towards the two men left behind to guard him. One was sprawled on the ground, dozing, the other lounged with his back against a sapling, keeping watch in the direction taken by Tongara and the others. Both men had their weapons close at hand and, although in the shade, the ground was still too open for Fuli to take them by surprise.

Their attention would have to be diverted.

'Hey!' Chris called out. 'Why are you sleeping when the soldiers are coming? You should be running for Mozambique.'

The dozing guard sat up quickly. 'What?'

'You do not believe me? Do you think I did not call them on the airplane radio when I saw what you did at the village?'

He had both their attention now and their backs were to Fuli. Chris saw him run closer and dodge behind one of the larger trees. Ten paces closer.

'You lie, *Mabunu*. And we are not afraid of your Selous Scouts. We have killed many before. Soon it will be your turn.'

Chris laughed. 'I think it is you who lie. You should be running. It was not the AK's of your comrades you heard. The trackers also have them… and pistols. Did you not hear the sound of it? Did any of your comrades have pistols?'

He had them with that one. They conferred with each other quietly, no longer looking at him but at each other, and Chris held his breath as Fuli froze in his approach several paces behind. Only stunted thorn bushes too small for cover lay between them.

'Maybe I should sing you a song,' Chris said, desperate to get their attention back and to make enough noise to cover Fuli's approach. 'Have you heard the one about the ten green bottles?' He started singing. 'Ten green bottles hanging on the wall…'

Fuli covered the intervening ground quickly. Both guards heard him at the same instant and turned, but too late. Fuli crushed the skull of one with the back of his axe, then sank the blade into the back of the other as he tried to roll away. It struck with such force that Fuli had to put his foot on the jerking body to pull it free. He wiped the blade clean on the dead man's shirt before using it to cut Chris free of the webbing.

'They should have listened,' Chris murmured. He stumbled forward, falling to his knees, and Fuli caught him by the arm. 'Jesus, Fuli…'

Fuli clicked his tongue at the state of Chris's back and pulled out some of the longer spikes. 'We must leave now, *Nkosi*. There are many thorns, but there is no time.'

'Can't feel a thing, Fuli, but first we must hide these men. When Tongara returns he will think I have been taken to Mozambique, for that is what he told them to do if he was not back soon.' He paused to swallow against a sore and dry throat. 'It will give us time, and it will soon be dark, but we must lay some spoor.'

They covered the blood and relieved both dead guerrillas of their shoes, putting them on their own feet before hiding the bodies as best they could in a thorny thicket, along with the cut webbing straps. Chris also gathered the men's weapons and packs. While Fuli kept watch, he hurriedly brushed out as many of Fuli's barefoot prints as he could find, then removed the shoes to lay a trail of his own barefoot prints going not east, as Tongara had ordered his men, but north, towards the village on the Sabi River.

Towards the east the country was flat and open, with little cover, but the track north passed many scrub covered termite mounds, any one of which would be ideal for an ambush. It was a gamble, but the odds were good that Tongara would follow anyway, not wanting to lose his prize catch. He would also, Chris assumed, be angry that his two men had disobeyed orders by not going directly to the border, and had not waited the full two hours. He would not be thinking clearly.

Chris stopped at the edge of the thicket and whistled softly for Fuli to join him.

There is black smoke coming from Gara Pasi,' Fuli reported.

'My plane.' Chris informed him. Another life he had not been able to save. He considered telling Fuli about Zarena, but decided it would keep for later. They had enough to think about already. He told Fuli of his plan to ambush Tongara and the old man accepted one of the rifles taken from the two men hesitantly, but without comment.

Chris let his hand linger on that of the old man's as he handed him the weapon. 'I grieve for Lydia and your two youngest, Old Father. It is a sad thing for us both, but it is not yet over.'

'No, *Nkosi*,' Fuli answered, his lined face rigidly impassive. 'It is not over.'

'But it is the orders from Maputo Headquarters, Comrade Tongara,' the political commissar argued. 'White hostages should first be taken to show to the people in the Mozambique camps, then sent to Maputo so pictures can be taken for the television news. It is good propaganda.' He wore Zarena's glasses, which he had commandeered from her bag when he looked at her report. He was a former teacher as well as the political commissar, he had informed her, so he could understand such things as history. An impressive array of pens lined his breast pocket and several toothpicks were stuck in his woolly hair, beneath a cap that was several sizes too small. He rolled one of the picks around his mouth as he spoke to Tongara.

'You are a fool,' Tongara said scornfully. 'I do not believe the white bitch knows Comrade Mugabe, and she will slow us down. By tomorrow morning we must be back in Mozambique.'

'I agree with you, Comrade. It would be troublesome to take her, even though it is orders, but I have seen her papers and they tell of the great city of our forefather, Monamatapa. Also, she says she is one of our Arab friends and returning her will be very good propaganda, especially if we say we saved her from being killed by the Rhodesian Security Forces.'

'She does not look like an Arab,' Tongara said, 'and I am the sector commander. Do not tell me what to do.' He reached forward and caught Zarena by the wrist. 'I do not care about your stupid propaganda. That is for politicians.' He pulled her towards a patch of long grass. 'When I have finished the men will have a chance, then you can have her for your television.'

Zarena struggled ineffectually in his powerful grip. They had been speaking in their own language, so she had no idea of what was said, but the intention was obvious, and any doubts were quickly dispelled by the suggestive actions of the one with the baseball cap, who leered and made lewd gestures with his crotch,.

Zarena's knees almost gave way under the weight of her fear. She could think of only one defense. 'Leave me alone! I work for the Cairo Museum,' she cried out in Arabic. 'I am here to do work on the Zimbabwe Ruins. I am not your enemy.'

Tongara stopped to scowl at her. 'What?'

'She speaks in Arabic,' the political commissar explained. 'I have heard the language in Tanzania.'

'Speak English,' Tongara said to Zarena.

She repeated what she had said in English, making it halted to emphasize she was a foreigner.

'Please, Comrade Tongara,' the commissar pleaded. 'It will be best to take her to Maputo. I do not question your leadership, I think only of how such good propaganda will help your position with our leaders. I have written many times in my report that you should be promoted. Even to general.'

The veiled threat and sycophantic pleading was not lost on Tongara. He glared at the commissar for several moments before finally shrugging and releasing Zarena. 'We will soon see if she speaks the truth when we get back to the *Mabunu*. She will watch me kill him, and if she tries to make trouble or goes slowly, I will kill her too, do you understand?'

'Yes, Comrade Commander. I will take full responsibility, and do it myself if you wish.'

'That will not be necessary. I wish only for you to stop barking like a jackal and start walking. We have already wasted much time.'

Chris and Fuli walked north until almost dusk before stopping at a suitably covered termite mound. It was adjacent to an open area of short tufted grass that would give a clear field of fire.

While it was still light enough to see, Fuli tried to remove as many of the thorns as he could from Chris's back. It was a painful and mainly futile exercise, for many of them had broken off and embedded, and Fuli's fingers were gnarled and blunt.

'Use your teeth,' Chris suggested, gritting his own, and Fuli complied, but it made little difference, and none at all in the region of his buttocks, which had attracted the largest collection, but where Fuli preferred to persist with his fingers.

Inspection of the two packs belonging to the dead men revealed no medical kit with needle or tweezers, but one did produce a tin of antiseptic cream, and Fuli made liberal use of it, which helped reduce the sting.

While Fuli was busy with his administrations, Chris took the opportunity to explain about Zarena; how she came to be there, and his fears of what may have happened to her, and although the old man remained silent, Chris could sense his outrage. It had been a black day for both of them.

'These snakes are too poisonous to be left on the path where they can harm others,' Chris muttered. 'We will chase and kill them all.'

'They are not snakes, *Nkosi*,' Fuli contradicted quietly. 'They are hyena.'

Chris discarded the contents of the packs, including a plastic bag of poor quality marijuana, but kept the ammunition for the two weapons and a Chinese stick grenade. He eyed it dubiously before laying it carefully on the ground beside him. They were notoriously unreliable. He checked both AK's thoroughly then instructed Fuli on what to do.

'I will wait until they are very close and try to get Tongara first,' he explained. 'Then I want you to start shooting at their legs.' In Fuli's inexperienced hands the barrel would rise when fired on automatic. 'They will be in a line, so you start at the back and move towards the middle, like this.' He showed Fuli the spraying motion he wanted and how to switch the selector to automatic. 'Hold the trigger until the gun stops, then lie flat on the ground. There will be much noise,' he warned. 'I will throw the grenade, and they will also begin shooting, but don't worry. They won't know it is us. They will think it is a Security Force ambush and be running away. Much of their shooting will be in the air.'

Fuli did not like guns. He was from the old school of poaching and preferred much quieter and less complicated machinery. Nevertheless, he followed Chris's instructions carefully, experimenting gingerly with the safety catch before setting the rifle down beside his axe.

As soon as it was dark, Chris left Fuli on the termite mound and found himself a spot twenty paces away, behind a fallen mopani tree. He wanted to be at ground level so he could see the silhouettes of the men as they passed, and did not want to miss recognizing Tongara. Being separated would also give the impression of being a larger ambush. He was not worried about being overrun. The terrorists were Chinese trained. Once Tongara was dead the rest would flee in disorder. He switched the selector to single fire, propped the spare magazine where he could reach it quickly, then settled down to wait.

Zarena stumbled once again in the dark, and once again received a shove from behind.

'I can't go any faster,' she protested.

'You must walk quickly and no talking,' the man with her glasses whispered. 'Comrade Tongara has promised to kill you if you go slowly.'

Zarena struggled on with her half limp, half run. Her sandals with their heels and thin straps were totally unsuitable for bush walking. Twigs and dry grass stalks poked and cut her feet and got caught beneath the straps. She was surprised she had not already twisted an ankle.

They had stopped shortly before dark at a grove of thorn trees, when the political commissar had made some attempt to reassure her, explaining that they were going to some big camp in Mozambique, and that they would be there in a day as it was only thirty miles. It did nothing at all for her peace of mind. She doubted if she could walk another mile, but prudently refrained from asking questions, trying to remain as inconspicuous as possible. Despite the intervention of the man with her glasses, she knew that ultimately her well-being was at the whim of the ruthless and unpredictable Tongara, and she remained in a constant state of alert fear.

He had been furious when they stopped at the grove. Something had obviously happened there that did not please him. He ranted at the men, apparently accusing them of something, then had them search outside the grove for tracks. He seemed even more incensed when they found them, and had everyone moving fast soon after.

The commissar had told her that Chris had been captured, but she had seen no sign of him, or heard anyone mention his name. They may have lied to impress or frighten her, and she hoped for Chris's sake that was the case, but even if it was, he was alone and could do nothing to help her. All she could do was rely on her wits.

Chris heard the scuff of approaching feet, and a few moments later saw the dark silhouette of the first man against the star speckled sky. The second man appeared a few yards behind the first; closer than he had hoped, and he shifted the rifle butt into his shoulder. They were moving fast.

The first man bobbed out of view, and still there was no sign of Tongara. Chris realized with a silent curse that he must be bringing up the rear. It was something he should have thought of.

After four men had passed a gap showed in the line, then the next silhouette appeared, and Chris stiffened. The shape and movement was unmistakably that of a woman.

She stumbled when directly opposite him and, as if to convince him further, let out a distinctly feminine gasp. It was followed by some urgent whispering by the man behind her, and she staggered forward as if pushed, skipping awkwardly to catch up.

Chris's relief at seeing her was quickly subdued by a new threat. If Fuli opened fire now it would be disastrous. They may well get a few, but he would then have to go after her immediately in the dark, and she could easily be killed or used as a shield, and he would have lost the advantage. Rigid with tension, he willed Fuli to hold his fire.

Tongara came into view last, as Chris had suspected, his large bulk moving easily and clearly distinguishable. A perfect target. He passed out of sight and Chris lowered the rifle.

Fuli looked even more relieved than Chris that he had not had to do any shooting. 'You saw her?' Chris asked.

'I saw her, *Nkosi*, but was afraid you would not.'

'That makes two of us, Old Father.'

'We will follow?'

'No, it is too dangerous in the dark. If they stop for a rest we will run into them. It will be better if we take another track. At least we know they have fallen for our trick and will go to the village for food, and to see if I am there before crossing the border.'

Chris could not be certain if that was what Tongara would do. The terrorist had survived by being unpredictable, but it was a gamble Chris knew he had to take. With hindsight, after having recovered from the surprise of seeing Zarena, he realized he had made a tactical error. He should have taken the chance and opened fire when Zarena had been close enough to warn. With Fuli covering the end of the line where Tongara had been, the chances were good he could have spirited Zarena away in the confusion.

But he was not to know, and now he had to think of a way to rescue her before they crossed the border, where the chance of running into more terrorists or Frelimo troops was greater. And he had to do it while it was still dark and he could use the element of surprise. In daylight it would be impossible.

D awn was breaking when they finally stopped. The air was chill and dank, with the lingering smell of wood-smoke and dried fish, and Zarena guessed they were close to a river. The political commissar indicated she could sit, and she collapsed thankfully onto the ground with every muscle protesting. She cautiously removed her battered sandals and clutched at her tortured feet, wincing at the sting of blisters and cuts. They had not suffered such abuse since the night she had run away from the Sheikh's brothel.

'Is there anything to drink?' she asked

He passed her a plastic water bottle and she gulped down a few mouthfuls of the warm, muddy-tasting liquid, then poured some on her feet while he was busy relieving himself against a tree.

'You wish to make water?' he asked.

'No. Are we at the camp now?'

'We reach there today. Maybe only twenty miles.'

'What? I can never walk that far! Look at my feet… and my shoes. I can't walk with these…'

He shrugged. 'African women are walking all the time with no shoes. You must do it or Comrade Tongara will kill you.'

Zarena clenched her jaw. There was no point in pushing her luck. 'I have a spare shirt in my bag. May I have it please?'

He tossed her the shoulder bag and she angrily ripped the shirt into strips with her teeth and bound her feet, then forced the sandals back on. They were tight and uncomfortable, but at least now gave her a bit more protection and eased the chafing.

As the light increased the reed roofs of huts became visible through the trees. Tongara appeared on the path, coming from the direction of the huts, and his mood had not improved. He stopped to glare at her. 'Get up. I walk behind you now. No more going slow.'

The sandy path ran beside the river, through dense banks of reeds, and Tongara trimmed one with his knife and used it to herd her like an animal, striking her across her back and legs when she stumbled or lagged. For the most part she was forced to jog, and she pulled the restricting skirt above her knees to make it easier, but it also exposed her naked flesh to the sharp leaves and Tongara's stinging blows. Then to make it worse, one of the straps on a sandal gave way and she fell.

'Why don't you leave me here?' she cried, hurrying to remove the other sandal as he struck repeatedly at her legs. 'I don't want to hold you up. Please…just leave me… '

Tongara dropped the cane and unslung his rifle. He pointed it at her head. 'You wish to stay?'

'I can't do you any harm. I can't run anymore.'

'Comrade Commander!' The low call, accompanied by urgent finger clicking from the man ahead, diverted Tongara's attention and he left her, hurrying ahead to investigate.

The political commissar caught Zarena by the arm and yanked her to her feet. 'You must walk,' he whispered urgently. 'Soon we will be at the camp and you can rest. In Maputo you will be on the television.' His tone suggested that should be sufficient incentive for anyone.

But it was not for Zarena. She could no more imagine

walking twenty miles than she could a thousand, and neither could she imagine them carrying her, whether she was good propaganda or not. The prospect of being shot – or worse – began to loom as a certainty.

The path began to steepen sharply, then they were out of the reeds and on the high bank. The river itself was hidden in a layer of radiation fog, but the bank was clear, and now, in the brightening dawn, Zarena could see the men in front. Tongara was with them, walking slowly, studying the path and pointing, as if to attract the attention of the others to what was there.

Zarena took advantage of the pause to adjust her bindings and examine a bleeding knuckle that had come in contact with the stick. She was sucking on it when a sudden shout from the front made her look up again. Tongara and several of his men had started running. Movement farther ahead on the path caught her eye; the hazy figure of another man. A white man. He appeared to be injured, for he was limping badly, holding onto his dragging leg with both hands. He turned to look at the men pursuing and began hopping, trying desperately to run and, as Zarena watched in dismay and sudden recognition, he stumbled and fell out of view, and she thought she heard a faint, brief cry of pain. It was Chris Ryan.

Tongara bellowed at his men and they spread out, shouting to each other in excitement as they ran, baying like hounds closing in for the kill.

The commissar pushed her from behind. 'Run!'

Zarena stumbled forward, her feet on fire, her heart in her mouth, waiting in dread for the shots she knew must soon come, and when they did, her legs gave way and she sank, sobbing, to the ground. 'You savages!'

'Get up!' The commissar prodded her with the barrel of his rifle and danced around in agitation, kicking at her legs. 'Hurry! Hurry!'

More gunfire sounded ahead. So much it seemed every one of the guerrillas must be shooting, and Zarena cowered down with her eyes shut tight and her hands over her ears. She screeched with alarm as the commissar fell heavily beside her, convulsing, and she opened her eyes to stare at him. He appeared to have been hit. His eyes rolled oddly, showing the whites, and the glasses he had taken from her were lying on the ground between them, close to her hand. One lens was splattered with blood. So was her arm. She jerked it away with a cry of horror. At the same instant another body crashed into her, bowling her over, and she tumbled down the bank into the reeds below.

Lying dazed and winded on her back in a tangle of reeds, Zarena glimpsed a wild-looking African bounding down the bank towards her. He held an axe in one hand and a rifle in the other, and she opened her mouth to scream, but no sound came, and before she could catch her breath to try again the African was upon her, clamping a hand to her mouth.

'Eh! Not to make noise.' He removed his hand and pulled on her arm, trying to get her up, beckoning urgently towards the reeds, but Zarena was too petrified to move.

He stooped to duck his head under her arm and lift her quickly onto his shoulder, then scooped up the weapons and tottered off with her into the reeds, crashing through and coming out on the same path she had been on only a short time before, going back the other way.

It took Zarena several long, uncertain moments before she could regain her breath and her senses. She struggled and he put her down, but continued to move, overcoming her hesitation by pulling roughly on her arm so she was forced to stagger after him.

'What are you...'

He scowled at her to be silent, pointing at his mouth, and Zarena complied, not really understanding what was happening, but he was an old man alone, and although his handling of her was rough, it was through urgency and held no menace. She had nothing to lose except Tongara. She followed his lead, hobbling stooped over, as he led the way off the path and back into the reeds.

She was not aware she had lost her wrap-around skirt until he stopped a short way in and signaled her to wait. He ran back to leave the skirt beside the path, hooked onto a stalk as if ripped off in passing.

He returned and they continued on into the dense grassy forest, following a maze of tracks that were little more than pushed over stems. When water began squelching underfoot he sent her ahead, crawling on hands and knees along a narrow tunnel - obviously made by some large animal - while he came behind to straighten the stalks they had trampled in passing. She did not feel the sharp leaves now against her naked flesh, or the pain in her feet. Putting distance between herself and Tongara was a powerful balm.

The firing had stopped, but not the shouting, which sounded confused and questioning, and which was dominated by the angry, demanding bellows of Tongara.

The old African stopped to listen.

'What? What's happening?' Zarena whispered.

He held up a hand to silence her, cocking his head in the direction of the shouting, then he signaled for her to sit down and be still.

Zarena complied gratefully, taking the time to study the old African. His hair was sparsely peppercorned and grey, his face deeply lined and sombre; a face that had lived too long with hardship and sadness, and suddenly she realized who he was. She reached across to touch his arm and whisper. 'Are you... Mister Fuli?'

He nodded, and Zarena felt an immense relief, but also a profound sympathy for the man who must have suffered terribly over the shocking atrocity committed on his family. She wondered if he had seen Chris on the path above. Maybe he did not realize he had been injured and was probably dead. She pushed the untenable thought from her mind. Maybe he had escaped and was hiding in the reeds as well.

The shouting came closer, filled with outrage, and Zarena guessed they had found the body of the commissar. She wondered what they would make of his death and her disappearance.

She did not have to wait long to find out. A hail of bullets cut through the reeds, crackling and snapping overhead like firecrackers, and Zarena felt an almost uncontrollable urge to run. The old man must have sensed it, for he put his hand on her arm to restrain and reassure her.

The haphazard shooting continued for a while longer then stopped, but her relief was short lived. Tongara bellowed orders, then a short time later she heard the rustling of reeds as the men entered them to search.

The crashing seemed to be coming from all around, some so close she could see the fluffy tops of the tall cane waving, and the old man brushed the mud from the rifle and held it ready.

Then a shout from the path told they had found the skirt and the search moved in that direction. Fuli laid the rifle carefully down beside his axe, but he made no move to leave.

The search continued for a long time, sometimes close, sometimes distant, then it grew quiet, but still Fuli made no move.

As the sun climbed higher, it became sweltering hot and airless. The reeds provided some streaky shade, but tiny insects and mosquitoes swarmed and stuck to her damp skin. It began to itch and sting. Fuli scooped out a trench for her to sit in and she plastered her skin with foul smelling mud for protection. She also smeared it on her face, but there was no respite from the humidity that hung about them like a hot, steaming blanket and made breathing difficult.

Had she been alone, Zarena knew she would not have been able to bear it. Not only the heat and insects, but also the constant rustling noises that went on around them, either from animals, crocodiles or snakes. She did not know which, and did not want to know, but the old man seemed unperturbed, sitting stonily indifferent, even to the insects.

Comforted by his presence, and exhausted by the heat and the long night of forced marching, Zarena gradually slipped into a fitful doze.

She awoke to a burst of gunfire and sat up in alarm, but a glance at Fuli, who was calmly listening with head cocked to the side, told her they were not under attack and she returned to her doze, only to be jerked awake again by a loud explosion. She looked again at Fuli for explanation. He was nodding and grunting as if in satisfaction, and with a look on his face that came close to a smile.

'What is it?' Zarena whispered.

'The *Nkosi*,' he answered, and Zarena frowned, not understanding, but he did not elaborate, and once again she drifted into an exhausted sleep as the relative quiet returned again.

It seemed she had barely closed her eyes when Fuli shook her arm and she opened them to discover with surprise that it was almost dark. Perhaps it was time to move. But it was not, and Fuli was acting strangely, rubbing mud over his skin and even on his head, when before he hadn't bothered, and he indicated urgently that she must do the same. To demonstrate, he took a handful and put it on her head, smearing it over her hair and on her clothes, then he suddenly beckoned to her to lie down and be still.

Alarmed by his manner, Zarena froze with her heart thumping, not understanding, then she heard the noise; a deep, mournful grunting that stiffened the hairs on her neck. The reeds behind them crackled and crunched at the approach of some heavy animal, and the sounds were very close.

She saw the hippopotamus through the flimsy curtain of stalks. Chris had told her about them, and now she wished that he hadn't. 'They kill more people in Africa than any other animal,' he had told her, and now she was so close to one she was sure she could smell it even above the sour, marshy stench of the mud. Its great bulk moved through the reeds like a huge rolling boulder, along the same tunnel through which she and Fuli had crawled earlier, and its labored grunting was accompanied by the sucking and squelching of its feet in the mud.

For a terrifying moment Zarena thought it was going to walk over them, and it was only Fuli's iron grip on her arm that prevented her from trying to run yet again. She was further alarmed to note that Fuli had not even picked up the rifle, and she sat holding her breath as the hippo passed, only letting it out once the lumbering beast was out of sight and hearing.

She was still shaking when, a short while later, and by the pale light of a quarter moon, Fuli helped her up and quietly led the way through the tangled forest of reeds.

When Chris left Fuli and went ahead to act as a decoy, he was not at all confident his plan would work, but he could think of no other way that had a chance. They had lost the advantage of darkness because Tongara had taken longer than expected to reach the village. Probably because Zarena had slowed them down. But at least that had given them an opportunity to scout the path and lay a trail.

He was acutely aware that he would have only one chance at rescuing Zarena. To do it he would have to divert Tongara's attention elsewhere, and he had to bait the trap with something he knew Tongara could not refuse.

He had left his barefoot prints on the sandy path along with the prints of the borrowed shoes worn by Fuli, knowing that Tongara would be confused at seeing only two sets of tracks instead of three and wonder what had happened to his other man. Finding the empty pack on the path would confuse him further, either slowing him down or causing him to stop to consider the implications. Either way it would distract his attention away from Zarena.

It worked even better than he had hoped. Not only did the guerrillas stop, allowing Fuli to come in close from behind, but most of them then forgot their training and crowded forward, leaving Zarena at the rear with only one man to guard her, and his attention was focused on what was going on ahead.

From his higher vantage point, Chris saw Fuli moving stealthily on the path behind the gang and, for the first time, felt confident Fuli would get Zarena away. The rest was up to him.

The wounded man routine came close to being the real thing.

The idea of holding onto his leg was to let the guerrillas see he was unarmed, and he had expected them to chase with the intention of capturing him alive so Tongara could continue his torturing. He had not foreseen they would start shooting, and the fusillade had come alarmingly close, prompting him to fall sooner than he had planned. It had been a long leopard crawl to the edge of the bank and the two captured AK's he had waiting there.

He had also expected Tongara to be in front and to run into his ambush first, but the veteran terrorist was too canny, sending two men ahead on the path and the others spread out in the mopani forest while he lagged behind, shouting for his men to hold their fire and to take Chris alive. It was unfortunate, for had he been able to kill Tongara, Chris was sure the rest of the gang would have abandoned the chase and run for the border, which was now less than a mile downriver.

The two men running close together on the path, yapping with excitement like jackals on the heels of a wounded doe, did not see Chris waiting for them below the bank until it was too late.

He killed both with the same single burst of fire, their momentum causing them to almost fall on top of him. He managed to collect only one of their weapons, the other flying clear to land in the reeds. He fired another burst down the path in Tongara's direction, prompting another wild fusillade, before running along the path himself in the opposite direction.

From then on, for the rest of the day, it became a game of cat and mouse, with Chris alternately playing the role of both, taking the initiative when the game lagged by firing haphazardly to cause confusion, trying always to lure the gang away from the reeds where he had instructed Fuli to hide with Zarena.

Heavy firing from the area soon after he had ambushed the two men caused him some concern, and he listened carefully to the pattern of it before coming to the hopeful conclusion it was too sporadic to be meaningful. He hoped the shooting would be heard by a security force observation point and reported, but it was a long shot in this remote area, and too close to the border for investigation by a fire force already hard pressed by the shortage of helicopters. If anything, it would more than likely be another group of terrorists that responded.

Early in the afternoon, after some hours of quiet during which nothing seemed to be moving in the heat, not even the birds, Chris stumbled unexpectedly on a man coming towards him with head down, looking for signs.

Both were equally surprised, but it was Chris who managed to get in the first lucky shot, wounding the man in the leg, but also giving away his position, and the ensuing chase in the heat pushed him almost to the point of exhaustion. He had been going hard for over fifty hours, and the need for sleep was making him careless. He was also thirsty, the half bottle of water he had salvaged from one of the dead terrorists long since finished, and he realized he would have to satisfy both needs soon.

He was also running short on ammunition, and knew he was going to need every round he could get. Even with a wounded man, Tongara was showing no sign of giving up.

The river, with its densely packed reeds would provide the best place to lie up and sleep, but movement in them could easily be seen, and to reach them he had to cross open ground. If they saw him going in he would have no chance of escape. To get water and rest he would have to create another diversion.

He led the chase inland, circling away from the river and moving in an erratic pattern to prevent his pursuers from guessing his direction and cutting him off. He made no attempt to hide his tracks, gambling on their fear of another ambush to keep them at a respectable distance.

Chris played them at their own game. A game he had become expert at during his time with the scouts. Guerrillas were not used to being on the receiving end of hit and run tactics. That was their own method, as dictated by Marx and Mao Zedong, and the plan would never have worked had they been properly trained and correctly disciplined, or even had they been Matabele, with that tribe's Zulu heritage. But these were Shona recruits trained in Mozambique or Tanzania by a hodgepodge of African, Chinese, or Cuban instructors, and they were led by a man who used fear to discipline rather than pride. As long as he remained out of sight, Chris was confident he could keep them guessing.

When he estimated he was about a mile from the river, he began weaving and dragging his feet, staggering as if on the point of collapse. He dropped the empty rifle, and a few yards farther on stopped in his tracks. He unslung the remaining pack taken from the dead terrorist, slipped the empty water bottle and spare magazine down the front of his shirt, then removed the Chinese stick grenade.

It had been like another thorn in his flesh all day with its unstable bulk pressing so close, and he had been tempted to get rid of it more than once, but now he was glad he had not. It made the perfect booby trap.

He removed one of his shoe laces and snapped it in half, jamming one end into the spring mechanism of an empty magazine, and tying the other end to the safety pin of the grenade. He used the second piece of shoelace to fix the grenade to the back of the bag near the carry straps. He fastened the buckles and laid the bag on the ground with the straps uppermost, as though it had fallen and, working blind, eased the safety pin until it was almost out.

When the bag was lifted the weight of the magazine would pull out the pin and the metallic sound of the spring release would be taken as something loose inside the bag. The grenade would explode before the bag could be opened - hopefully by Tongara.

Assuming the unreliable grenade went off, he reasoned it

would kill at least one man and possibly kill or wound more, which would make life easier, and maybe even persuade Tongara to give up, but it was the noise of the explosion itself that would provide the diversion.

Chris continued laying his staggering man spoor for a good hundred yards past where he had left the bag, then he ran in a wide circle back to the river, moving fast, for he wanted to reach it before they sprang the trap.

He was sure Tongara would leave at least two men at the river to keep a lookout for Zarena, probably close to the same spot she and Fuli had entered the reeds, so he angled his run to come out well away from there.

He was not quite at the river when the explosion came.

'Surprise, surprise,' he muttered with satisfaction and relief.

When he reached the path he ran along it to blend his tracks with the many that were already there, trusting in the explosion to keep any watcher's heads pointed in the other direction.

He entered the reeds where others had entered before and crawled through them to the water, listening for any shouts that would tell he had been spotted, but all remained quiet.

With his thirst quenched and the bottle filled, he moved into a dry patch of reeds and, almost instantly, fell asleep.

A soft evening breeze rustled the tops of the reeds, covering the sounds and shielding the movement of Zarena and Fuli as they moved slowly and tortuously through them, stopping every few yards to listen and, much to Zarena's consternation the first time it happened – signal; a high pitched warbling, followed by a squeaking and clicking sound that Fuli made in his mouth with a piece torn from one of the hairy leaves.

The sliver of moon was low down in the sky when they finally stopped.

Zarena thought she could detect the same stale wood smoke and dried fish smell as she had that morning, and remembering, she suddenly realized that both strips of cloth binding her feet had gone. It did not surprise her after what they had crawled through, but her feet were so numb and caked with mud it was hard to tell if she had anything at all below the knees.

Fuli signaled again, and again there was no reply, but a sudden heavy rustling close behind made her spin quickly to see Chris standing a few feet away. He grinned at her, his teeth flashing white against the black mud on his face. He moved towards her and gave her arm a reassuring squeeze. 'You look like hell,' he whispered, so low she had to strain to hear. 'But you're the best sight I've seen in a long while. Are you okay?'

Zarena could only nod, almost overcome with a sudden rush of confused emotion. She lifted her hand to return his reassuring touch, but he had already moved to grip Fuli in a bear hug, lifting the old African clear of the ground, and Zarena felt her throat suddenly tighten with emotion.

Chris replaced Fuli on the ground and whispered something to him before turning back to her. 'Come on, love, let's get the hell out of here.'

Tongara crumpled the soiled strip of cloth in his fist and threw it at the face of the man who had found it in the reeds. 'You let the *mabunus* get away while you sleep, you useless dogs! You think you are freedom fighters?' He laughed scornfully. 'No, you are children who must hang on your mother's teats. Five comrades are killed, but you want to run away and forget them. Go find the *mabunu*! Search for their signs and follow them, even to Harare if you have to.'

'The wounded men, Comrade Commander...' ventured a man tentatively. 'What must we do...?'

'You donkey! What do you think? Find them a place to wait near the village and leave them food. If the people return before us they can look after them. Or do you wish to carry them yourself to Mozambique?'

'I only wish to do what you order, Comrade Commander,' the man replied, wilting under Tongara's menacing glare.

'Then go and do what I have told you. We are wasting time with foolish talk. Leave them the morphine and tell them we will bring them the white bitch to play with. It will make the waiting easier. Go!'

With so many thorns still embedded in his flesh, sitting down was impossible for Chris. When they stopped for a rest shortly after dawn, he knelt to examine Zarena's feet, propping them on a log. 'Why didn't you tell me they were this bad?' he admonished her.

'I thought you had enough to think about, and they were numb. It wasn't so bad.'

'Well it's bad now.'

Both feet were swollen and the soles glowed scarlet, as if they had been badly sunburned, and where they were not red, they were blue with bruises or crimson with cuts and lacerations. The arches and toes were also streaked with raw flesh where the narrow straps of her sandals had rubbed away the skin, and both heels oozed clear liquid from broken blisters. Her arms and legs, and particularly her knees, were not much better.

'Not a pretty sight,' Chris remarked. He trickled some more of their precious water over them to remove the last traces of mud, then gently smeared them with antiseptic cream, and Zarena laughed quietly.

'What's the matter... ticklish?'

'No, just remembering the last time someone did that.'

'What?'

'It's not important. I'll manage if I can find some cloth to bind them.'

'We can use my shirt, it's buggered anyway, but it won't be enough. Fuli and I will take turns carrying you.'

'How far?'

Chris thought for a moment. 'As the crow flies, about forty miles. But we're not crows and we ain't flying.'

Zarena was aghast. 'You could never carry me that distance!'

'We'll do it in stages, and maybe we can give Tongara the slip, then I can go for help. We'll know more when Fuli gets back from seeing what our friends are up to, meanwhile, we'll get your feet sorted out.'

Chris removed his shirt and tore the tough khaki material into strips. He gave them to her and went to find the dead terrorist's shoes that Fuli had contemptuously discarded. Of the two pairs they were the smaller, and with Zarena's feet bound, should fit well enough to give some protection, or at least keep the dirt out of her open sores.

Behind him Zarena gasped. 'Oh, Chris! Your back... what happened?'

'If you think that's bad you should see my bum.'

Zarena's cheeks flushed and Chris smiled apologetically. 'Sorry, I keep forgetting you're an old fashioned girl.'

'I'm not old fashioned.'

'Of course you are, but that's all right. Too many women these days have forgotten what they are.'

'I didn't realize you were a chauvinist.'

'I'm not. I feel the same way about men.'

'Except for you, of course.'

'No, I'm right in there with them. What's the matter, Zarena, had a bad day?'

'You could say that. I'm sorry. It's just that I feel so

useless.'

He fitted the shoes over her bound feet and helped her up.

'How do they feel?'

She pushed his hand away and hobbled around slowly. 'It will be fine once I get going, I'm sure.'

'You're a brave girl, darling, but we need to move a lot faster than that. Give me your arm, I'll give you a lift.'

'No, don't patronize me, I'll be okay. And I wish you would stop calling me silly pet names. It's demeaning.'

Chris didn't argue. One fight at a time was as much as he could handle. He removed the magazine from the worst of the two rifles and shattered the stock against a tree before flinging it into the bush. He added the rounds to the magazine of the remaining rifle and handed the water bottle to Zarena.

'Hold on to this,' he said. Before she could resist, he caught her by the wrist, slipped an arm between her legs and hoisted her onto his shoulders in a fireman's lift.

'What are you doing? Put me down. I can walk.'

'Keep still.' He picked up the rifle and started walking.

'This is not helping your back. Put me down, I can't breathe.'

'Then stop squirming and talking.'

Chris followed game trails that stayed fairly close to the river. Ten miles ahead the Sabi River turned north after it joined with another great river coming in from the east. It wound through the rugged Sibonja Hills of Gona re Zhou National Park, which was the shortest route to Chipanda pools and a security force base.

He would have preferred taking the more remote and less rugged country to the south, along the eastern boundary of the park, but it was a long way around, and they only had one water bottle between the three of them.

Fuli caught up with them at noon, and the news he brought was not good.

'They follow, *Nkosi*. Six men.' He held up six gnarled fingers. 'I try to hide the spoor, but no time to do a good job. Maybe two hours behind.'

Chris groaned.

'What's the matter?' Zarena asked.

'I was hoping the bastard would leave us alone and take his wounded men into Mozambique. I guess I should have known better.'

'What are you going to do?'

'Well, we can't outrun him, and we can't outgun him, all we can do is try and outsmart him.'

Chris took Fuli's rifle, removed the magazine and used the point of one of the rounds to flick the others onto the ground. Only five. He replaced four of them then added the other to his own magazine, making a total of seven for himself. It was hardly what he would call firepower, especially coming from the muzzle of an AK, but it would have to do.

'We'll cross the river now,' Chris told Fuli, 'before they get any closer.'

The place where they had stopped had once been a

crossing point for wagons, with large expanses of open sand and little cover, but the bottom sand was shale washed from the hills and reasonably clear. It had several channels, but only one that came higher than chest level, and Chris made Zarena sit on his shoulders when they reached it

'I'm not a child,' she protested. 'I can swim, and I could really do with one.'

'Not here you can't,' Chris said. 'Hold the rifle clear of the water and keep your eyes peeled for anything that looks like a hungry crocodile.' Her sharp intake of breath, the sudden clenching of her thighs around his ears, and her silence, reassured him she was doing her job.

He relieved her of the rifle when they were almost across and dumped her unceremoniously into a clear pool. 'You have thirty seconds, so make the best of it. There won't be another chance.'

She disappeared below the surface in a flurry of splashes and bubbles, scrubbing furiously at herself and her muddy clothes. She reappeared to sweep the water from her face and hair, oblivious to the clinging shirt, and Chris tore his eyes away to search the far bank for signs of pursuit.

Back in the thick riverine forest, Chris put his sodden burden down and spoke to Fuli as he emptied Zarena's shoes of water and checked her bindings. He was relieved to see the swelling and livid color were both reduced. The rest and cool water had done some good.

'This is where we part company,' he explained. 'I'm going to stay and borrow us some time. Fuli can carry you over the rough bits, but you may have to do some walking on your own. Think you can handle it?'

'I'm sure I can manage without him having to carry me at all,' Zarena answered.

'Good girl. But don't overdo it. I've told Fuli to walk for two hours and then rest up. I'll try and hold them off until dark, then we'll be walking most of the night, so try to get some sleep.'

'What about you? You've been carrying me for most of the morning. Won't you need to get some rest too?'

'Don't worry about me, I'm used to this sort of thing. And don't panic if you hear any shooting. I'm going to be handing out a few surprises.'

Chris set himself up in a jumble of flood debris, close to the bank where he had a good view of the other side. It was an ideal spot for an ambush. He had the cover and protection of a solid wall of logs, and the approach was open. Tongara would see the tracks going in and be tempted to follow, as it was the easiest crossing. If he tried to cross downriver he would have to negotiate thick banks of reeds, and if he went farther upriver where it was narrower, he would have to swim through deeper water and take the risk of crocodiles.

Chris wished he had a decent rifle and his binoculars. The opposite bank was too far for an accurate shot with the AK, even if the guerrillas stood in the open, and with field glasses he could have learned a lot about their intentions from their gestures and movements.

Fuli's attempt at hiding their tracks had obviously not

fooled Tongara for long. Chris had been lying in position for less than an hour, and was still busily filing down the points of the slugs on a rock when he saw movement on the far bank.

A man emerged from the bush and followed their tracks down and across the sand to the first shallow channel before returning to the trees. A short while later the same man appeared with another and both set out across the sand at a clumsy run, parting to leave a wide gap between them. Tongara wasn't taking any chances with his own neck.

Chris slipped the flattened bullets into the magazine and cocked the weapon, pushing the selector onto single fire.

The men reached the deep channel and stopped, less than fifty yards from the bank and Chris's cover. They argued about who should cross first while the other kept watch, and Chris smiled grimly. 'It's not the bloody crocs you should be worrying about, my friends.'

He waited. It never ceased to surprise him how stupid they could be. Never underestimate the enemy, was the slogan, and Chris never did, but he often felt almost insulted when the poorly trained enemy did not return the compliment.

With the argument finally resolved, one of the men began wading across with his rifle held high, and Chris smiled sardonically when he noticed the guerrilla was wearing his large black diver's watch. It would make killing him easier.

The other man searched the water for crocodiles, not once looking up to scan the bank, and had he been feeling adventurous, Chris could easily have stood up without being seen. He wasn't though, and was surprised to see the man enter the water before his companion was all the way across. Perhaps he had been feeling lonely.

Chris waited until the first terrorist was out of the water and the other well in before, almost regretfully, holding his breath and squeezing the trigger.

He heard the solid thud of the flattened slug clearly as it struck the man in the centre of his chest with the impact of a sledgehammer, throwing him back into the water, dead before he hit it.

'And then there were five,' Chris murmured.

The second man, almost a third of the way across and already up to his armpits, ducked under, firing his weapon wildly and unseen from over his head until it was empty. Most of the bullets did not even hit the trees.

Shots came from the opposite bank where Tongara and his remaining men still waited under cover, but none came close. Chris waited for the man in the channel to surface, but when he did, it was some distance from where he had gone under and it was only to take a quick gulp before disappearing again, and apparently swimming downstream underwater, for he quickly overtook the floating body of his companion and his own blue cap.

Chris let him go and gave his attention to what was happening on the other side, but nothing could be seen, and the firing had stopped abruptly in response to a clearly heard bellow from Tongara.

Chris remained in his position. Like him, they would

be watching for a while at least, and an unseen enemy was always the most intimidating. He tried to foresee what Tongara would do next. If he still insisted on pursuit, he would have to cross the river somewhere, and the next safe crossing was at the Chitove falls, some eight miles upstream, where he had told Fuli to wait.

But Chris reasoned that if he were in Tongara's position, he would wait until dark and cross here. Only two reasonable choices of destination were available. St. Peter's Mission, to the north on the Sabi river, or Chipanda Pools, to the east on the Lundi river. Of the two, St. Peter's was the easier, but was also the more distant, so in reality there was little difference, and Tongara would not risk going sixteen miles out of his way for nothing. To be certain, he would cross here and try to pick up their tracks, following until he was sure which way to go, then he would ignore the tracks and move away from the river to circle ahead of his much slower quarry. It would be the most sensible thing to do.

Chris decided he would be wasting time by staying longer, but assuming Tongara and his men were watching, he did not want them to see him move. He had about twenty yards of open sand from where he was to the nearest cover, and was wondering how best to negotiate it unseen when he received help from an unexpected quarter.

Several quick, terrified screams erupted from the reeds a short way downriver, alongside the channel in which the fleeing terrorist had been swimming and, after his initial start of surprise, Chris wasted no time. He ran to the bushes and dived behind them.

Thunderous splashing accompanied the screams, which quickly dwindled to silence.

'And then there were four,' Chris said.

The Lundi river turned sharply towards the south east at the Chitove Falls, meandering for some twenty miles through the Sibonja Hills, and some of the most spectacular scenery in the park, before turning again towards the north east and the Chipanda pools with their herds of tourist attracting hippo.

It was close to dusk when Chris reached the falls. He found Fuli sitting at the top of the rapids, his feet in the water and his back against a boulder. Scattered around him lay the discarded crushed pips and brown skins of marula fruit.

'All is well?' Chris asked.

'It is well,' Fuli answered. He passed Chris a handful of the fruit, and another of the nuts that he had already extracted from the pip, squinting up against the smoke from one of his home-made cigarettes. 'The *Nkosikasi* walk without carrying, or even stopping too much. And the comrades?'

'Two are dead.'

'Au! With only one bullet?'

'Mister crocodile was hungry.' He was surprised that Fuli had picked his single shot against the barrage of automatic fire that had followed it, but that was Fuli. Always full of surprises.

'Eh, eh, mister crocodile.' Fuli shook his head in

understanding at that reptile's gruesome reputation, pinched out his cigarette, then tucked it securely behind his ear.

Zarena lay asleep on a sandy patch nearby. Her bindings had been removed and washed, and Chris took the opportunity of examining her feet while it was still light enough to see. They were swollen again, but not quite as bad as before, and there was no bleeding. Nevertheless, it was going to be a long and painful walk for her that night. They could not carry her all the way.

He told Fuli what he expected Tongara would do, and they discussed the problem at length, their voices hushed under the rustle of water. It was wonderfully peaceful, and the view of the river in the mild evening was beautiful. He thought of his father and the pleasant evenings they had spent only a few miles upstream from here, at the Clarendon Camp with their neatly thatched huts, watching the herds of elephants coming down to drink at the river in the evening. That was before the war and the subsequent destruction of the camp.

Listening to his father's stories about the animals he had known in the park - particularly those involving an incorrigible bull elephant called Crooked Teeth, who used to chase vehicles - watching the cliffs turn from orange to red to purple in the setting sun, and the tantalizing aroma of venison steaks grilling on the open barbecue. It had been his idea of heaven.

The elephants had been unafraid then, as if knowing they were in a sanctuary, and had come close to the unfenced camp perimeter to watch them in return, often making them laugh by the way they kept their curious calves under control, dragging them back when they wanted to investigate further. Look, but don't touch, seemed to be the message.

It was in this same area of the park that Wally had first come across Fuli.

Poaching had become a serious problem, not only poaching by the local Shangaans and tribes from Mozambique, but also from white 'weekend hunters' from the cities and mines. To Wally, who understood the philosophy of the black poachers, who had been hunting the area for the past hundred years and more, these white hunting parties were far worse. They did not decimate areas as the snares often did, but they set a bad example, and with four hundred thousand hectares of mopani forest to hide in, the possibility of being caught was remote.

When Fuli had been caught snaring and arrested by Wally, he had protested angrily. 'What of the white men who even now kill many zebra near to Chikombedzi? Do they come here to take food for their family as I do? Must I tell my children not to drink the water from the river because it now belongs to the white men who took our land? I have no gun to shoot many zebra, and no truck to carry their skins to sell in the city.'

'You have seen such white men there?' Wally had asked, somewhat taken aback by the poacher's indignant tirade.

'Many times, but I have not seen them arrested, only myself.'

'If you take me there I will arrest them,' Wally promised.

'Then I will take you,' Fuli said, and he did, resulting in prosecution of the white poachers and freedom for Fuli whose forthright manner had impressed Wally. Using the principle of setting a thief to catch a thief, he gave him a job catching poachers.

For a long time it perplexed Wally that Fuli only managed to catch white poachers or those tribesmen from Mozambique, while members of his own Shangaan tribe - amongst whom he had suddenly achieved the status akin to a chief - remained relatively untouched. When Wally mentioned this surprising fact to him, Fuli was quite honest about it.

'There are too many poachers,' Fuli had told him, 'for one man, or even one hundred men to catch, so I tell my people to take all snares of the Mozambique people and to chase them away. For themselves, I tell them only to use the small wires and not the ones for catching *chipimbiri*, rhino, or soon they will be chased by the police also, and so it is what they are now doing. Is this a stupid thing?'

Wally had reassured him it was not, and had seen his faith in the wily Shangaan and his unauthorized assistants justified by the dramatic decrease in big game poaching in the park.

Chris could not see the Clarendon Cliffs from where he and Fuli were sitting, but he knew they would be glowing red in the sunset as they had when he saw them with his father, and as they no doubt had for thousands of years. Shangaan legend told of a 'White City' on the plateau above the cliffs, which had been built at a time when the rocks of its walls were still soft, and the legend had spread. Chris had searched for it in vain, flying several times over the area soon after getting his license.

The thought suddenly struck Chris that the reason he was sitting there at that very moment was because of another ancient city not that far away to the east, and that he had found the jar with its papyrus scroll even less distance away to the west. The cliffs were almost on a direct line between the two places, and the area was wild and uninhabited, the bush thick. Stone walls would be quickly overgrown. Could the White City be more than just a legend?

The realization that he was there because of something that had happened thousands of years before seemed bizarre. It was much easier to accept he was simply in the war and fighting terrorists, as he had so often in the past. But that was not the reason, and the proof of it was lying only a few yards away. He glanced across at her sleeping form as if to convince himself.

She was there and in danger because of what he had found. Julia had died because of it, and so had others. And he still did not understand why, only that he was responsible. He wished now, with all his heart, that he had not found the jar.

'She has much strength inside,' Fuli remarked, breaking into Chris's thoughts. 'She is a woman who does not want to be shamed, I think.'

It took Chris some moments to figure out what Fuli was talking about. Then he grunted in understanding. Fuli was leading up to one of his philosophical lectures, and he knew him well enough to have a good idea as to what it was about. But he was not in the mood to discuss his private life. 'I have been thinking we should leave the river now and cut straight across the bend to Chipanda. The walking will be easier.'

'But the rain has been short. Maybe we will not find water.'

'We will have to take the chance,' Chris said. 'If we stay with the river it will take much longer and be too easy for Tongara to get ahead and ambush us in the thick bush. He may not follow us across if he thinks there will be no water.'

Two hours after dawn, when the sun was showing its strength and mouths were dry after the long walk through the night, Chris called a halt and found the water bottle was missing.

'Who the hell used it last?' he demanded angrily.

'I'm sorry, I thought someone had picked it up.' Zarena looked at Chris in dismay.

'Water not too far now,' Fuli said, coming to her aid.

Chris scowled at Fuli. It was not like the old man to forget something so important, especially as he had been carrying the bottle to begin with. 'Well, no point in stopping then, is there?' he said irritably, picking up his rifle. 'We'll just have to keep going until we bloody get there.'

It would not have been too serious had it only been himself and Fuli. It was less than twenty five miles now to Chipanda, but it was not just the two of them, and he doubted if they could make it in another two days. And they couldn't make it without water in this heat.

There was only one place Fuli knew of where they may have a chance of finding water. Known locally by those intrepid enough to venture into the area as Tusker's last stand, it was nothing more than a sharp bend in a dry river bed, and had received its name from a bull elephant that had been shot there. On the rare occasions that the river ran, which was usually only for a few hours after a storm, water collected above a clay bed several feet below the surface. Protected by the sand from evaporation, it could hold water for months.

Only man and elephants could dig far enough down to reach the cool water, the elephants probing with their tusks, then sniffing the end for the damp smell before dragging the sand out with their feet and trunks, then trampling it back in as they clambered out.

Occasionally a buffalo, if it was quick enough after the elephants had departed, could paw away enough sand to get a few sips, but if it happened to be hampered by a leg snare attached to a heavy log, which tumbled down the sand after it, that is where it died.

Chris and Fuli smelled the rotting carcass long before they reached the bend, and looked at each other in grim understanding.

The buffalo had been in the hole for about two weeks, and was lying on its back with the shredded bones of its legs collapsed out to the side. The wire loop of the snare was still embedded in the bone of one hind leg. The carcass was half covered with sand, enough to discourage most predators, but not the metallic blue flies that swarmed over the putrid remains. There would be nothing to drink that day.

'Bastards!' Chris swore, turning away. 'They don't even bother to check their snares.' Even if they dug past the mess, what water lay underneath, if indeed there was any, would be rotten.'

'It will be best if I run to Chipanda and bring some police with a truck,' Fuli volunteered.

'It's about all we can do,' Chris agreed. 'No wild fruit around here. Not even a baobab tree.'

'Only the river, *Nkosi*.'

'It's too far. The girl will never make it. She must have water soon. We must all drink soon.'

Zarena was sitting in the shade where he had left her upwind of the stench. He explained what had happened and she looked at him blankly, as if she hadn't understood. 'I'm so thirsty. Is there nothing?'

'Fuli is going ahead to get help. He should be back by morning with the cavalry, fresh orange juice and cooked breakfast of powdered eggs.'

'You must go with him, Chris. You have a son that needs you.'

'What the hell are you talking about? I'm not going

anywhere. In a few hours we'll be out of here.'

'What about the men coming after us?'

'Don't worry about them. I think they've given up.'

Chris carried her through the heavy sand of the riverbed until they were well beyond the rotting buffalo. He scooped a comfortable place for her in the bank beneath the shade of an overhanging bush, then removed her shoes and bindings, keeping his face emotionless as they snagged on dried blood.

But there was no need for his poker face. Zarena's eyes were closed. The fine lines about her mouth were deeply etched and drawn, and the soft pouches under her eyes so dark they looked bruised. He touched her cheek. It felt like parchment, and his spirits sank further. She was more dehydrated than he had thought. She had suffered a lot in the past few days, and without complaint, but she could not take much more.

'Don't worry,' he reassured her, his voice sounding hollow and unconvincing in his ears. 'I'll find you something to drink... somewhere.'

While Chris had been attending to Zarena, Fuli had gone in search of some form of nourishment. He returned with a handful of stubby roots, which he scraped clean with his axe then cut into bite-size pieces, but although not unpleasant tasting, they were old and fibrous, with little moisture. Zarena nibbled on hers lethargically for only a few moments before losing interest, and Chris took Fuli to the side.

'Before we stopped, did you see the herd of impala

resting in the shade?'

'I saw them, *Nkosi*.' Fuli looked at him expectantly, waiting for him to continue. It was not polite to ask obvious questions.

'Do you remember me telling you about the three soldiers who died of thirst in the Zambezi valley, even though they had guns and the spoor of many animals was around them?'

Fuli nodded, his face adopting a sour expression.

'I can't take the chance of waiting for you to get back with help from Chipanda,' Chris continued. 'Something may happen to delay you, and she will not last another day and night. The river is closer, but still too far, and we have nothing for carrying enough water for all of us.'

'If the comrades have followed they will hear the shooting,' Fuli warned.

'We will have to take the chance, but we will not make it too easy for them. I want you to take the AK you have and walk for about one hour towards the river. When you hear my shot, count three fingers and also fire one shot, then come back here quickly. If I have to shoot again, then you must do the same. It is only a small thing, but it will confuse them and they may split up.'

Fuli did not look all that convinced, but wasted no time in setting off with his axe, the AK and a section of root to sustain him, and Chris set about organizing his part of the plan.

He made sure Zarena was comfortable, reassuring her

he would be back soon and not to be alarmed if she heard shooting, and she responded with a vague nod. He stacked dry branches around to conceal her and brushed away the tracks leading up to her hiding place, then he continued along the riverbed until he was adjacent to where the impala were resting. Crawling up the bank, he was relieved to see they had not moved. He tested the air with a pinch of dust. It hung motionless.

It took Chris more than the full hour he had allowed Fuli before he was satisfied he had squirmed and crawled close enough for a certain shot. He would have only one chance. If he missed, the herd would run and be too skittish to approach again.

The nearest animal standing side on was a doe, but he could not afford to be sentimental. He aimed for the shoulder, giving the inaccurate weapon the largest possible target.

The doe leaped forward to fall on her knees, and Chris ran, listening for Fuli's answering shot, but could hear nothing above the clatter of the departing herd. The doe was on her chest, slender legs scrabbling ineffectually, and Chris jumped astride her before she fell and began thrashing with her sharp hooves. He gripped the muzzle and twisted savagely, pulling back until the neck snapped with a soft click and she collapsed.

He stood looking down at the sleek animal, his breath rasping painfully in his dry throat, finding no satisfaction in the kill, only immense relief. One life in exchange for another. 'Sorry, old girl,' he murmured.

With Fuli's pocket knife he cut through the soft skin between the bone and tendon of a hind leg and pushed the dainty hoof of the other through the slit, then he dragged the doe to the nearest mopani tree. He snapped off a branch above his head and, staggering under the dead weight, lifted the carcass and placed the crossed legs over the end of the branch so the doe hung with the head touching the ground. He picked up the AK and ran back to Zarena. The shot would keep predators at bay for a while, but not human ones if they were close.

She was still dozing, her breathing shallow and rapid, as if it was she who had been running. She woke as he was replacing her bindings and shoes. 'Are we walking again?' the words were thick and slurred in her dry throat.

'I'll carry you. We're going for a drink.'

Chris lifted her onto his shoulder and carried her back to where he had killed the doe. It was safer there than in the dry river where he would not be able to see anyone approaching. He set her down against a tree, and seeing the carcass hanging in front of her sparked a surprised response. 'Oh, poor thing....'

'She's about to save your life, but you're going to have to make a small sacrifice in return, I'm afraid. I need your shirt.'

'What?'

'Your tee shirt. What's left of mine is too thick.' He removed it and handed it to her. 'Fair exchange. It should be enough to cover you decently. I'll turn my back.'

'But I don't understand. *Why* do you need it?'

'You'll see in a minute, trust me.' He turned away and started on the carcass, slitting open the belly to expose the stomach and remove the entrails.

'It's too short, and I'm not wearing… anything underneath,' Zarena said. 'Can't you think of something else?'

'Not unless you want to give me your panties.'

'Are you trying to be funny? Because I don't see the joke.'

'I'm not joking, I'm serious… and I'm happy to see you still have some fight left in you. Now can I have the shirt please? Or the panties, which ever you feel most comfortable without.'

'What about your own?'

Chris turned to grin at her, and she hastily folded her arms. 'Sorry, don't have any. Wear 'em for special occasions only.'

'That's disgusting.' She removed one arm to toss the shirt to him. 'I'll have it back as soon as you've finished.'

'I don't think you'll want it… I'll also need one of your shoes.'

She removed one and tossed it to him without comment.

Chris stuffed the toe of the shoe - the smelliest part - full of leaves plucked from the tree, then he spread the shirt on the ground in front of the carcass. He slit open the stomach membrane and carefully lifted out a double handful of soggy, partly digested vegetation, which he deposited in the centre of the shirt. He folded the cloth around until he had a secure bundle.

While Zarena watched with an expression of disgusted disbelief, he held the bundle over the shoe and squeezed a trickle of sickly green, foul smelling liquid into it.

He lifted the shoe in a toast. 'Cheers,' he said with a wink, then gulped the liquid down. When the shoe was drained, he screwed up his face and shuddered violently. 'Wonderful!'.

Zarena's sympathetic shudder of revulsion was no less violent than his own, and her face, already pale, turned several shades paler. 'If you think I'm going to drink that you're mistaken.'

Chris squeezed some more of the green liquid into the shoe and took it to her. 'Sorry, but you must.'

She turned her head away, holding her nose. 'It stinks! I'd rather die of thirst.'

'No, you wouldn't, believe me. Drink. It's not that bad. Every scout and tracker in the army has to do it on a survival course, so why not you?'

'No, Chris, please, I'll be sick...'

'It doesn't matter, we have plenty, and every bit of moisture inside you will help. Now drink, or I'll have to force you. Hold your nose and imagine it's a lime milkshake.'

Zarena spewed up the first mouthful, and Chris held her steady until the retching had passed, then he refilled the shoe and made her drink again, and again she spewed it up, but on the third try she held it down with difficulty, gulping threateningly, and he ruffled her hair in congratulation. 'Well done, love. I've seen big hairy men pass out just smelling it. You've got more guts than any of them.'

She smiled weakly, eyes watering.

He managed to get two more shoe loads down her before she rebelled. 'Please, no more... oh God, it's vile! And that awful smell... It keeps repeating. I think I'm going to be sick again...'

'If you puke it up you'll only have to drink some more,' Chris warned. 'Try and hold it down and I'll give you something to take the taste away.'

'Hurry...'

Chris went to the carcass and brought back a chunk of liver, and Zarena, her face already screwed up in distaste from the effects of the liquid, could only appeal with her eyes. 'Hasn't this gone far enough?'

'Try it, what can be worse than what you've just swallowed?'

She took a reluctant nibble and shuddered. 'I don't think I can... it's slimy... and still warm... ugh!'

'Must we go through it all again? Raw liver is good for you, and you haven't eaten in days.' He popped a piece into his own mouth and chewed with gusto before swallowing. 'Mm... I feel better already.'

'Well, I don't.'

Nonetheless, she bit off a small piece and swallowed it without chewing, and Chris beamed at her. 'A star is born.'

'I hope you haven't any more nasty surprises for me.'

'Only more of the same. Keep chewing, I want you to grow up to be strong and healthy.'

'Sadist.'

Chris laughed. 'See? You're feeling better already, and you're looking better too. Now eat up like a good girl while I have some more milkshake, then we're going to get out of here before every hyena in the park arrives. They can smell this stuff from miles away.'

'I'm not surprised.'

The shots came as Chris was wrapping the fillets and what remained of the liver in the shirt, and he leapt to his feet to listen. More shots came. Automatic firing, and he kept his face turned away so she could not see his expression. The shots were clear. Less than a mile away.

'What's happening?' Zarena asked anxiously. 'And where's Fuli? I haven't…'

'Quick, on your feet, we have to move,' Chris said, snatching up the bundle of meat, the shoe and the rifle. He put his shoulder into her stomach and lifted her, then set off at a brisk walk through the trees, closing his mind to Fuli's predicament and applying it to their own. He could not take the initiative and attack, as he should. He did not have the ammunition, and it would mean leaving Zarena unprotected. All he could do was find a secure place to hide her, then lay a defensive ambush and try to reduce the odds.

He told her what he intended when he stopped to change shoulders.

'No, I want to stay with you,' she said firmly. 'I don't

want to be left alone again, without knowing what is happening. What if you don't come back?'

'I don't have time to argue with you,' Chris growled. He went to lift her up but she pushed him away.

'No. If you're going to lie in wait for them, I don't see why I can't hide with you. I don't want to be alone, Chris.'

The determined look on her face convinced him he would be wasting his breath trying to change her mind. And maybe it wouldn't be such a bad idea. It would save time and he wouldn't have to worry about leaving her unprotected. And suddenly he didn't want to be alone either.

'All right, but you will have to be quiet and do everything I tell you.'

'I will, and I promise not to get in the way.' She smiled and raised her arms, ready to be lifted. 'Going my way, Mister?'

Chris grinned. 'You're something else, Zarena.' He shook his head in genuine admiration and lifted her onto his shoulder.

Not all of his admiration was for her courage. By lifting her arms in his mutilated shirt she had unwittingly displayed two beautifully pert and shapely breasts.

Chris found what he was looking for near a termite mound. The mound itself was well covered with thorny scrub, the ideal place for an ambush, but that was only part of what attracted him to the spot. About forty yards to the side were two fallen mopani trees, one lying across the other with their branches entangled.

Termite mounds were few and far between in this area, but not mopani trees pushed over by elephants. Tongara and his men would approach the covered mound cautiously, giving it their full attention, and would not expect to be ambushed from somewhere else. One or two of them may even try to use the fallen trees as cover to approach the mound, and that would be a bonus. He would have them at point blank range with a chance of getting their weapons and ammunition.

Chris pointed the fallen trees out to Zarena. 'I'm going to put you down,' he explained. 'I want you to walk over there carefully, putting your feet down flat, and try not to stand on any of those dry tufts of grass, insects or anything else that will leave marks. The bindings on your feet will help, but keep your toes curled up.'

'Where are you going? You're not going to leave me there, are you?'

'Don't worry, I'm going to keep walking past that anthill, then come back and join you from another direction.'

Chris stood in his tracks and watched as she stepped daintily towards the fallen trees, arms outstretched for balance, holding her shoes in one hand and the bag of meat in the other. Her bare legs and the wide strip above her narrow waist that the shirt didn't cover were scarlet with sunburn. He could see the imprint of his hand on the back of one leg from where he had been holding her, and the intimate implication brought a twinge of guilt, as if he had violated her in some way without her knowing.

Stepping heavily and short, as if still carrying a load, Chris continued on until he was well past the termite mound, then he walked backwards in a wide circle to the fallen trees where Zarena waited.

He made them a comfortable place to lie, arranging the branches on all sides to give as much cover as possible, and using dry bushes and grass to block the larger gaps low down. White skin, even if it was sunburned, stood out in the bush like an albino elephant.

With not much room between the branches they were forced to lie pressed together with naked flesh touching and, by her stillness, Chris knew she was as acutely aware of their closeness as he was.

The shadows were lengthening with the late afternoon when a grey lourie alerted Chris with its distinctive call of 'go away, go away', and he rolled stealthily into position with the AK ready. Four men and five bullets. The unbalanced arithmetic stayed fixed in his mind. Every round would have to count.

He heard the clank of metal, as if two magazines had knocked together, and saw movement in the trees, a fleeting shadow moving swiftly on their tracks. Zarena must have heard it also, for she stiffened and placed a nervous hand on his bare shoulder. 'May Allah be with us,' she whispered.

Fuli did not go directly towards the river as Chris had directed. Instead, he went to the waterhole in which lay the rotting buffalo and removed the snare. He indulged himself in a few moments of professional criticism as he twisted the wire free.

No Shangaan would have attached the wire in such a way that it could move to the end of the log and be dragged. And both the wire and log were too short, allowing no room for snagging in the trees. Obviously the work of an amateur.

It was not out of any altruistic motive he removed the snare - he saw no essential difference in how an animal was killed. And neither was it because he wanted the wire to catch an animal of his own. Those days were past, and he no longer had the need. But a snare could also catch a person, and for that he did have a need.

Fuli cleaned the wire in the sand then looped it over his shoulder before climbing the bank, being careful to stay well out of sight of the impala the *Nkosi* would be hunting, and heading, not towards the river, but back on their tracks of that morning.

It was a foolish thing he had done, he realized, leaving behind the bottle of water in the belief he would find water in the dry river. And he could not be sure that the comrades would follow, or that they would find the bottle if they did, even though it would be daylight by then and only a blind person could miss it in such an obvious place as he had left it for all to see. And even if they did find the bottle as planned, maybe they would have no need to drink so soon. Maybe they would save the water for later, as he himself would have done - when the killing was over.

That the water would be drunk at sometime or other he was almost certain. It was as good as water for free, so who could resist, in this dry place. He was also sure that whoever drank it would either die or be so sick as to no longer be a threat, for the juice from the fruit of the *Kyapeni* tree was more than just a poison for fish.

If the comrades followed, Fuli was confident he could kill at least one of them, either with the gun, which he did not think likely, or with his axe or wire, so even if he himself was killed afterwards, there would only be three comrades left at the most, and maybe only two if one had drunk the fish poison. If they were stupid enough to follow after that, *Nkosi* Chris would kill them, that was also for sure.

Fuli was not afraid of the comrades. Neither was he afraid to die. He had lived all his life in this place of the elephants, and risked death many times. He had killed a lion with a wire and a stone, so why should he be afraid of the men who killed only women and children? His woman and his children.

So even if the comrades had not followed them, he would go after them and finish what he had started out to do in the beginning. He was chasing snakes on the path as he had told the *Nkosi* he should not do, but the *Nkosi* had been right for a change. A man must avenge the killing of his own flesh, no matter what the cost, or he is not a man. *Nkosi* Chris would survive, he had no doubt, and his woman also. They had no need of him now.

As he walked, Fuli stopped briefly at every suitable

young sapling to strip off its soft bark and hastily fashion a length of rope, twisting and knotting several strips together.

It did not matter that he would not be as far away as the *Nkosi* expected him to be when the time came to answer the shot. Confusing the comrades was the last thing he wanted. What he wanted was for them to stay on the tracks.

He stopped at a place where the trail passed alongside a tall mopani tree that had been pushed over against another tree, snapping off the branches. The trunk was heavy but moveable, so Fuli stripped off his shirt and went to work.

First he collected two of the broken branches that had good forks, one long and one short, and both sturdy enough to hold the weight of the trunk, and he used his hands and feet to trim them, for the sound of his axe would travel far.

Grunting with the effort, he lifted the fallen trunk near the end with his shoulder and jammed the short fork under to hold it up. He repeated the procedure, lifting with his shoulder and moving the fork forward each time until the log became too heavy, then he went back to where he had started and began lifting with the long fork, gradually decreasing the angle of the log until it rested against the trunk of the younger tree about fifteen feet above the ground.

Leaving it propped there, Fuli climbed the younger tree and used his axe to scrape the rough bark from a branch above where the propped tree rested, exposing the hard slippery core beneath. He passed the rope over the scar and attached it securely to the propped up log, then he climbed down and hid the dangling rope as best he could behind the tree where it would not be seen from the path.

Fortunately, the amateur who had owned the snare had not neglected to soften the wire in a fire. The loop had no spring to slacken it once it had closed firmly about a neck or a leg. Fuli opened it to the full width of the path and buried it in the sand, brushing the area afterwards with a branch, then sprinkling it with dry leaves before walking over it to leave his footprints. He cut his rope to the correct length so there would be no slack and attached it to the wire, then he returned to the pole that was propping up the log.

With a normal snare he would have fashioned a notched trigger and a trip-stick to spring the trap automatically, but for this occasion he wanted to release it himself, to be sure of catching the right quarry.

Fuli attached what was left of his rope to the base of the pole, then carefully sat the butt end on a long sliver of wood so it would not jam in the earth when he pulled. He concealed the rope with branches and grass, then selected a few branches that still held a quantity of the coppery, butterfly-shaped leaves to cover himself. He looked up at the sun. The entire operation had taken less than an hour.

The awaited shot came as he was covering himself over with branches, and he scrambled amongst them for the rifle, having forgotten about it, but he did not fire it as instructed. He released the catch then set it down carefully beside the axe at his side, then he settled down under his concealing branches to wait.

Sector Commander Comrade Silas Tongara had always been a man to respect and fear, even when things were going well. When they were not, it was best to keep mouths shut, do as told, and stay out of his way. And that was exactly what the three remaining men in the group intended doing.

When Tongara announced his intention to continue after the two whites and the Shangaan, they remained silent and compliant, responsive to his every whim, and taking care not to whisper amongst themselves for fear he would think they were complaining or criticizing. But it was not necessary to talk. Each had a good idea what was uppermost in the minds of the others, and the atmosphere spoke for itself.

The operation had been a disaster. Two thirds of their original group had been killed or wounded and, as if that was not bad enough, the man responsible had been in their custody. He should have been dead, but not only had he escaped, the woman had also been taken.

The men knew that Tongara had no choice but to follow. If he allowed them to get clean away he would be the laughing stock of the entire Liberation Army. And Tongara was not the most popular of commanders, even amongst his peers and superiors, many of whom considered him a threat to their own positions. They would probably demote him and charge him.

But this would only happen if they heard about the debacle, and the three remaining men had no illusions about Tongara's ruthlessness. He had killed his own men for less than what was at stake now, and the knowledge sat heavily on their already troubled minds.

And it did not improve matters when Comrade Zingai died after Tongara beat him for drinking water without permission. He must have already been sick, for the beating was not that bad it should have killed him, but Tongara said it served him right for disobeying orders. No one was allowed to carry an extra water bottle, only extra ammunition.

When Fuli saw only two men approaching, and not on the path as he had expected, but well to either side of it, he realized he had made a mistake by not remembering about combat tracking.

He had never heard of such a thing until the *Nkosi* had told him. Reading the signs of someone or something was an art that few could master. It was more than just following marks on the ground. It was necessary to know when the marks were made, how big and how fast the person or animal was that had made them, their strength or weakness, and even what they were thinking.

For these things one had to understand the bush and its inhabitants, the sounds they made and when, the time they drank or if they had no need for water, and also such things as the time different spiders built their webs and the ants their nests.

And then there was the weather and the vegetation. How long it took for a certain leaf or broken branch to dry.

All these things and many more, a good tracker must know if he was to successfully track down his quarry, and he must give the signs on the ground all his attention. He could not be looking for ambushes as well. That, the *Nkosi* had told him, was why the army sent men ahead and to the side - to protect the tracker from being ambushed, which was exactly what he was trying to do, and which Tongara was trying to prevent.

Fuli was certain the man on his side of the path must see him. He was coming directly towards his hiding place, and may even have to step around him. From where the man was he must surely see the trap, for it was only hidden from the path, and Fuli could see the fresh shine of his new rope as clearly as if it had been painted white.

He gripped the handle of his axe and tensed himself to spring. He could see the face clearly; just a boy, and he was nervous, his eyes jumping from one place to another without seeing, and he looked back almost as much as he looked forward, more concerned about being in the right place than about ambushes.

Fuli saw him glance in his direction then, incredibly, move to step around the obstructing branches. Had he looked down he would have seen the rope and, no doubt, him as well, but he saw neither. He actually stood on the rope, passing so close that Fuli was tempted to reach out and catch him by the ankle, but then he saw Tongara on the path and held still. When the youth was safely past, Fuli edged his hand from the axe to the rope.

Tongara's bellow of shocked surprise as the snare closed on his thigh and flipped him upside down rang out only a heartbeat before the heavy thud of the falling log shook the ground.

The wire loop slipped down Tongara's leg, sliding over the denim in a series of jerks until it stopped at his ankle, and Tongara bellowed again, this time in pain as the wire bit into his flesh. He bounced in the air, slamming against the tree and dropping his rifle.

Both Tongara's men stood as if frozen, gaping in astonishment at their inverted and bellowing leader, then Fuli stood up from his hiding place, shedding branches, and both men jumped in surprise, gaping, but still they did not move. Only when Fuli pointed the rifle at the man nearest him and pulled the trigger, raising two spurts of dust near his feet, did both men yell with fright and flee for cover.

Fuli tossed the empty rifle aside and picked up his axe.

Tongara was pulling himself up the tree, trying to get upright and ease the weight on his ankle, at the same time shouting for his men to come to his aid.

Keeping Tongara and the tree between himself and the two running men, Fuli used the longest of his two forked poles to push the rope away from the tree, pulling the trapped leg out almost horizontal, and Tongara shouted for his men with increasing panic, clasping firmly to the tree with both arms.

Fuli wedged the butt of the pole into the ground to keep the wire taught and away from the tree, then he lifted his axe and aimed at one of the clinging arms, and Tongara let go with a yelp to swing free and dangle helplessly above the path.

'Kill him!' Tongara screamed at his men. 'Kill the stinking Shangaan!'

The two men had joined together and moved closer, their courage apparently stirred by their leader's shouting and cursing and, no doubt, seeing only one old African armed with an axe. One of them opened fire, the bullets hitting the tree and kicking up dust dangerously close to Tongara's dangling head. He screamed at them to stop. 'Come closer, you donkeys! Charge him!'

They ran forward hesitantly, ducking and weaving, skirmishing as they had been trained, but not shooting, and Fuli picked up Tongara's fallen rifle. Making no attempt to take cover, he calmly clicked over the selector as Chris had showed him, then pointed the rifle at the charging men, poking it well forward and away from his shoulder as if it were a bow. He pulled on the trigger and released it again in surprise as the rifle shuddered upwards to point at the sky.

For a moment, Fuli thought he had killed both men, for he could see no sign of them. Then he saw the back of one crawling through a patch of dry grass towards a tree. Fuli pointed and fired again with much the same result as before, only this time he did not close his eyes, and he saw the man running bent over and jinxing like a startled hare, followed a few moments later by his companion.

'Attack him!' Tongara screamed.

'Go!' Fuli shouted. He pointed and fired again, holding the barrel down more firmly and squeezing on the trigger until the rifle stopped by itself. 'Go!' Fuli shouted again. 'Run to Mozambique and tell them Tongara is dead!'

'I am not dead!' Tongara yelled. 'He has no more bullets. Attack the Shangaan or I will kill you both!'

Fuli reversed the rifle, taking the hot barrel in both hands, then he swung it with all his strength at Tongara's legs.

Tongara screamed as the stock smashed into his knee. He continued screaming as Fuli struck him again and again with calm deliberation. Cracking first an elbow, then a hand, then the other elbow before returning to his legs and his body. He was careful not to hit him on the head. 'You will die more slowly than my woman and children,' he promised.

Tongara had courage, and he was strong. He stopped screaming and began cursing, perhaps realizing he was doomed and hoping to provoke Fuli into killing him quickly. 'Your diseased bitch and stinking children howled and squealed like puppies when we burned them. Your daughter begged my men to jig her, but they said they would rather eat dung.'

Fuli ignored his tirade and looked for the men. If they came now he would have to kill Tongara and leave, for he had no more bullets. No doubt Tongara would have some in his bag, but he did not know how to put them in the gun.

The men were still where he had last seen them, standing half behind the tree, and Fuli angrily waved them away.

'Go!' he shouted. He pointed the gun, and was gratified to see them dodge out of sight. Perhaps they did not know the gun was empty. 'Go!' Fuli repeated. 'I will not kill you if you leave now, quickly!'

Tongara shouted also, but his voice had lost its power in his bloated neck, the words running into each other.

Fuli went behind him and removed the terrorist's pack, then he sat down with his back against the tree and went through it, tossing out all the papers, clothes and empty magazines, keeping only the two full ones - which he held up and waved so the two men could see them - a medical kit, a pistol and a half bottle of water. He took a long swig from the bottle after cautiously tasting it for poison, then he fished in the breast pocket of his ragged khaki shirt for some badly needed tobacco.

From the cover of the trees, Comrade Blessing watched the beating of Tongara with a strange sense of unreality. It should be the other way around. Tongara did not take beatings, he gave them, yet there he was being beaten by an old man. And not only would he be beaten, he would be killed, for Blessing had no intention of trying to intervene. Tongara was finished, and with Tongara would go his fear.

Blessing's companion called in a whisper. 'Should we attack together?'

'No, it is another of the *mabunu's* tricks. We should leave.'

'But what of Tongara? If we do not do as he says and help him we will be in big trouble.'

Blessing allowed himself a small superior smile. No need to whisper now, with all the noise, and Tongara was as good as dead, but his companion was inexperienced and still full of fear - as he had once been, so could be forgiven. Blessing knew they could take the old man without too much trouble, but if they attacked, Tongara would probably be killed first anyway.

'Do you wish to carry him like the donkey he is always calling us?' Blessing asked. 'Did you not see the old man break his legs? If we try and save Tongara the *mabunu* will follow and we will all die, but if we leave he will not follow because of the woman. It will be better to go now and help our other comrades who are wounded and need us.'

'Yes, I think you are right, Comrade. Tongara is too big for even both of us to carry, and we should look after the others who are our friends.'

Comrade Blessing smiled again at the relief in his companion's voice. He fingered the scar on his cheek, remembering. For a long time he had wanted a proper *chimurenga*, war name, but Tongara's scorn had prevented him. Now he would have one. He would become Comrade Scarface. It was a fitting name for a veteran like himself.

Comrade Scarface slung his weapon casually over his shoulder and sauntered off through the trees, and this time no rocks or sticks came to speed him on his way as they had on that fateful day when they had been attacked on the hill by the yellow helicopter.

Fuli saw the two comrades walking away and smiled with satisfaction. 'Your men have gone,' he informed Tongara. 'Soon I will go also. Fuli sat quietly for a long time listening to Tongara's heavy wheezing and groaning, and also the sounds of the bush returning, and when he was sure the men had really gone and would not be back, he lifted the fallen tree a short way, lowering Tongara onto the ground, but with his leg still suspended far enough so he was unable to crawl to the tree. They must be able to reach everything. Nothing must remain.

He went to stand on the path next to Tongara. 'You talk much of dogs,' he said. 'That is good, for soon you will see many dogs. Can you not hear them coming? They are closer now than before, so I will go. I do not want to disturb them with their eating.'

'Please, old man, I beg you... you must kill me. In the bag is a pistol. Shoot me, or leave it with me, I beg you. I am sorry for your woman and children.'

Ignoring him, Fuli picked up the bag and his axe and walked away.

'Stinking, dung-eating Shangaan!' Tongara screamed after him.

The hyenas had already found and consumed the impala carcass by the time Fuli reached the dead buffalo waterhole.

He heard their whoops and whines as they squabbled over the bones, and saw their ugly distorted forms slinking amongst the trees before he went down the bank into the dry riverbed. Soon they would have more bones to fight over.

He left the *Nkosi's* tracks where they climbed the bank and continued on until well past the hyenas. Not that he was afraid of them. He had maimed more than one with his axe and made his escape while the pack ripped their bleeding member to pieces.

He walked quickly towards the fast setting sun, searching the ground until he found the tracks again, then he followed them at a swinging trot, anxious now to catch up and share the news. The *Nkosi* would be worried about the shooting, and Fuli could tell by the shortness and irregular pattern of his prints that he had been carrying the woman and moving fast.

The bag bounced and the two magazines clanked noisily, but they had no need for silence now, and they could have a fire this night, maybe even meat if the *Nkosi* had not left it all for the hyenas.

The passing of his wife and two youngest children still weighed heavily, but Petrus and Emily had escaped, and he had avenged their death with the blood of the killers, and that was as it should be.

A grey lourie fluttered in the trees ahead, croaking out its warning cry and, hearing it, Fuli launched into one of his own mournful songs to warn the *Nkosi* of his coming.

Zarena hobbled restlessly about the camp. It was such a bright, peaceful morning, and after three days of constant danger and hectic activity, she found it impossible to keep still.

Fuli had left at dawn for Chipanda pools, but they could not expect anyone for at least eight hours, Chris had told her. It would not be too soon. A hot shower and shampoo, clean clothes and the fresh peppermint taste of toothpaste would be bliss.

The place could hardly be called a camp. They had no shelter, only the dead trees on the ground, against which she had leaned uncomfortably to sleep, but the fire on which they had grilled their meat made it seem like a camp.

Chris lay sprawled on his stomach beside the ashes, his head pillowed in his arms and his naked chest resting on her bloodstained and stinking tee shirt. The rifle lay half hidden beneath him, his right hand resting on the stock near the trigger, as if he had just lowered it after shooting; protecting even in sleep and, looking at him, Zarena was struck once again with the fond memory of the camel driver. In many ways they were so alike. Fiercely aggressive and capable when the need arose, but also quiet and thoughtful. In his own way, Papa Zoupo had been such a man, and Hugh and the old African, Fuli. And then there were men like her father and the terrorist, Tongara. Evil men who used ideology and religion as an excuse for their weakness.

Sitting on the fallen tree beside Chris, Zarena wondered

about her own weaknesses. She had many, she knew. Her involvement in her work to the exclusion of everything else was a weakness. At university she had been labeled a lesbian because she never went on dates, and because she had been part of the women's movement. At one stage she had even wondered herself if she could be lesbian, but the thought of being intimate with a woman was even more disturbing than the thought of being intimate with a man, so she guessed she was not.

Being circumcised reduced desire. She knew that, and had accepted it because she had never experienced what many girls said they had. Some she had known spoke of how they got excited just thinking about sex, and she had been amazed and disgusted by their lurid descriptions. Now she was not. Men still frightened her, but not as much as they had, except, ironically, for Chris. She felt safe with him, but also uncomfortable and somehow threatened, for although she had not experienced what the other girls had, lately her imagination had begun venturing into some disturbing new areas.

Zarena pondered the problem analytically, as she would a tablet of script. Some signs were clear, but others she could only interpolate from what she already knew. She knew she was attracted to him in a strange sort of way, she could not deny it, and she was also sure that he found her desirable. She could tell by the way he sometimes looked at her, but she did not have the inclination to respond. There were too many unknowns, and that was another of her weakness. Her fear was not of him but of herself, for the tablet was broken and she was not a complete woman. She may never have children and could not be sexually aroused, and after the mutilation done to her by the *daya*, how could any man see her as desirable? Especially such a man as Chris.

As if she had spoken his name, he groaned and shifted uneasily. Part of his body was now in the sun, mostly his back and, not for the first time, Zarena experienced a twinge of guilt. He was still unable to sit or lie on his back. It was a mess of inflamed scratches and sores. Carrying her must have been agony, yet he had not mentioned it once. He had done so much for her and she had done nothing in return.

With his constant attention to her feet and refusing to allow her to walk, the swelling had gone again, and with the new ointment and bandages from the medical pack Fuli had brought, so had the stinging. The sunburn to the back of her legs and chafing from being on Chris's shoulder bothered her more. That and having to be constantly aware of exposing her breasts in the remains of his shirt.

'Are you awake?' Zarena asked quietly.

He lifted his head quickly. 'What is it?'

'Nothing. Sorry, I didn't mean to disturb you. Everything is fine. I just wondered if you were awake, that's all.'

He peered around sleepily, then saw her and dropped his head back with a groan. 'I feel like I've got a hangover.'

'I'm not surprised, you and Fuli were talking for most of the night.'

'How late is it?'

'It's still early, but you're lying in the sun.'

'What's for breakfast?'

'Cold charred liver.'

He grunted. 'I think I'll give it a miss and wait for the powdered eggs.'

'I was thinking. There are a few needles in the medical pack Fuli brought, and some of those thorns look ready to come out. Would you like me to try?'

'Be my guest, but be gentle. I'm a coward.'

She cleaned a needle with antiseptic cream and used the bag to kneel on.

'There are so many I don't know where to start,' she said, but Chris only mumbled incoherently, already half asleep.

She probed cautiously. The thorns lay black and bulging under the deep brown of his skin, and many of them she would have to leave for the doctor. They were too deep or too angry looking and would need anaesthetizing first. She worked only on the ones she knew would cause a minimum of pain, and her gentleness told, for he did not flinch.

His skin was surprisingly firm and smooth where it was not marred by grazes or thorns, but she could feel the hardness beneath and wondered again at the strength of him. He did not bulge with muscle, and had very little hair except for a soft downy patch near the base of his spine, which disappeared beneath the band of his shorts.

Not so the backs of his thighs, which were dark with hair. Fortunately, he had been able to remove most of the thorns there himself.

Zarena stopped when she reached the waist band, reluctant to go farther, even though the band was loose and she could glimpse thorns that would come out easily. She moved the band down a little and removed two of them, but lowering the band revealed more, showing stark against the creamy skin on the rise of his buttocks. She could see the beginning of the cleft. She dare not go farther.

She sat for a while, resting her arm. Chris's breathing was regular and soft, and Zarena realized she was being foolish.

With sudden determination, as if to make up for her timidity, she kneeled again and pulled the shorts down a good three inches, revealing half of his buttocks and the deepening cleft. It was more than she had meant to go, but it was too late now, and the thorns were begging to come out. If he woke she would brazen it out. After all, if she had been a nurse she would be doing this sort of thing - and more, all the time.

Where the skin of his back had been firm and smooth, his buttocks were soft, almost silken, but as she pressed gently on them to coax out the spikes she could feel the same firmness beneath. She pulled the shorts down lower, revealing almost all of his buttocks, and went to work with fingers that had become unaccountably clumsy.

With the worst of them removed, she mopped at the serum with a piece of gauze bandage, then gently smeared his buttocks with antiseptic cream, pressing it lightly into the wounds. Then she eased the shorts back on.

Chris sighed 'You have magic fingers, Zarena. I wish you would give Fuli a few lessons.'

Mortified, Zarena felt the blood rush into her face. She fumbled as she tried to replace the lid on the tin of cream and placed it on the log, still open. 'You should move out of the sun now,' she mumbled.

She hobbled to the edge of the small clearing to hide the shame in her cheeks and the unsteadiness of her breath, knowing it was not so much because he had been awake, that she felt that way, as it was the sudden awakening in herself.

Part Seven

Buffalo Range - Zimbabwe

'Miss Bontoux seems to have suffered no permanent damage,' the doctor at the Buffalo Range Clinic assured Chris. 'I've given her an antibiotic and told her to keep off her feet for a week or so. They should be fine. She must take better care of them though. She has scar tissue from previous damage to the soles of both feet.'

'She has plenty of guts, Doc,' Chris said. 'She went through hell and never complained once.'

'The strong silent type, hey? Not like some others I know. You're going to have a few scars of your own, I'm afraid.'

'Perhaps if you didn't use a pitchfork...' He was lying face down and naked on the examining table under a powerful light while the doctor probed. 'Are you sure you're a doctor?'

'Only part time. I'm usually the gardener. Now hold still.'

Freshly doctored, showered, fed and clothed in clean Police Reserve issue shirts, Chris, Zarena and Fuli were driven to Combined Operations Headquarters by the same police unit that had picked them up in the bush.

In the short time they had been in the clinic word had spread, and they were accorded something of a celebrity welcome when they arrived. Someone had organized a wheelchair for Zarena, and the commanding officer himself pushed her towards the officer's mess through a crowd of awed and ogling soldiers.

The debriefing was an informal affair, conducted in the mess with ice-cold beer and a bottle of champagne for Zarena. The colonel filled her glass then raised his own and proposed a toast.

'Here's to the only lady in the world to have drunk gut-juice out of a terrorist's shoe. Well done, Miss!'

'Damn right!' came a chorus of assent.

For the next hour, and with few interruptions, Chris gave his report on what had happened to an assembly of often disbelieving army and Special Branch officers.

'Let me get this straight,' said the CO in an incredulous tone. 'You and the old man here killed *ten* of the twelve terrorists?'

'No,' Chris said. 'Two were wounded and one was taken by a croc.'

'How can you be sure that Tongara is dead?' asked a major.

'I can answer that, sir,' a Special Branch officer said. 'The old man took the Police Anti-terrorist Unit to the place where he had snared him. All they found was a few shreds of clothing and a foot still in the snare. Must have been too high for the hyenas to reach. They brought back the size thirteen shoe for confirmation and we matched the herringbone pattern.'

'Jesus! What a way to go.'

'The old bugger deserves a medal,' the colonel said, shaking his head in admiration as he looked at an extremely uncomfortable Fuli sitting primly on the edge of his chair.

'We should keep him pissed for a week,' agreed the major.

'He wouldn't know what to do with a medal and he doesn't drink,' Chris said. 'But what he does need is a lift for himself and his children to his traditional kraal at Mateke. It's too risky for them to go back to Gara Pasi now.'

'No problem, we'll sneak him in with one of the patrols. What about you and Miss Bontoux?'

'First a good sleep, I think.' Chris tilted his head in the direction of Zarena. Her eyes were almost closed and she was nodding forward in her chair, the champagne barely touched. 'Then I have to make a few calls. Tomorrow I'll try and hitch us a ride in a plane to Fort Vic. I don't think my backside will take too kindly to being thumped around on the bench of a truck.'

'I'll see what I can do,' the colonel promised.

'You said that two of the group were wounded,' the Special Branch officer questioned Chris. 'Do you know how badly?'

'I don't think they were walking wounded, if that's what

you mean,' Chris answered.

'And the two chased off by the old bloke here. Can you point out the exact location?'

Chris showed him on the large operations map and the officer tapped thoughtfully on the spot for a few moments before turning to the colonel. 'We have a chopper sitting on the ground at the moment sir, it may be worth sending a few trackers down there to have a look. If the wounded gooks can't walk, we may be able to offer them a lift to prison.'

'How long?'

'If the pilot doesn't wait around he can be there and back in an hour.'

'Okay, Scottie, do it, but I want the chopper back pronto. If you find anything we can always send him back.'

'Try the huts first,' Chris suggested.

Chris and Zarena said their farewells to Fuli early next morning.

'Go well, Old Father,' Chris said, clasping his hand. 'I will arrange money for you at Nuanetsi Ranch. When the war is over we will start again.'

'Have we killed all the snakes, *Nkosi*?'

'Some we have killed, but not all,' Chris replied.

Zarena offered her hand. 'Go well, Old Father,' she said, repeating Chris's words in perfect Shangaan, and Fuli was so surprised he almost forgot to take her hand. Then he grinned widely and shook it vigorously.

'And you also, Little Mother.' Then he adopted an almost stern expression and turned to Chris, who was thinking about another time he had been surprised by a woman speaking the language.

'She is afraid,' Fuli said in Shona, 'But I have seen in her ways that she is ready and waits only for the asking. A man needs a strong woman, and a son needs a mother also.'

Chris frowned.

'What did he say?' Zarena asked.

'He said you have courage and it's been a pleasure knowing you. Now we had better get going or we'll miss our lift.'

The Lynx dropped them off at the Glenkyle airstrip and John Montgomery came to pick them up. Chris had telephoned the night before to brief him on what had happened.

John and Marge had been close friends of both himself and Julia, and he was still not comfortable with the idea of introducing them to Zarena, even though their relationship was perfectly innocent. But sooner or later they were bound to hear about her, and if they had not met it would only look as if he had something to hide.

He discovered they had already heard. 'Welcome, Heroes,' John greeted them. 'You've made the headlines.'

'Monty, this is Miss Bontoux, the hieroglyphics expert from Cairo I was telling you about. What headlines?'

'I've got a few papers at home. You and Miss Bontoux have caused quite a stir.''Please, call me Zarena.'

'She came to help unravel a mystery, and instead got

abducted by terrs,' Chris said. 'You'll have to excuse her fluffy slippers. The bastards made her walk barefoot.'

Marge Montgomery met them on the verandah with a tray of tea and cream scones, and while she served and fussed over Zarena, Chris had a look at the newspapers. He groaned as he read the first headline.

Woman Hostage Rescued by Selous Scout.
Most wanted terrorist snared.

He skimmed through the write up. As usual they had it all wrong. He turned to the next paper.

Abducted Woman Scientist Rescued.
 Ten terrorists killed in running battle with poacher and scout.

And farther down.

Woman survives by drinking water from stomach of impala.

'Makes some interesting fiction,' Chris remarked. He passed them to Zarena. 'I wonder where they got it all from. *We* sure as hell didn't talk to any reporters.'

John Montgomery laughed. 'That's what *you* think. But I happen to know that the reporter of our local paper is a police reservist. He was probably with the guys who came to pick you up in the bush.'

'Well, all I can say is that he's got a bloody good imagination.'

'Maybe so, Chris, but it's just the sort of boost the country needs right now. Things are not going so well politically. The peace talks are nothing but a sham.'

'It's just as well no one knows we're here or we'd have reporters all over the place.'

'Don't forget the TV. So tell us what *really* happened.'

Chris told them, beginning with the tragic death of Fuli's family, and Marge wept openly. Tragedy was commonplace in the bush war, but no one ever got used to it.

Zarena told her own part reluctantly. She seemed ill at ease, despite Marge's encouragement and attempts to make her feel at home, and Chris wondered if something had offended her.

'What do you plan to do now?' John asked.

'I've organized a lift to Umtali this afternoon with the police air wing I have to see the curator at the museum. Tomorrow it's back to Mount Hampden to pick up the plane, then on to Kenya. Zarena has to prepare another report for an archaeological conference in Nairobi, and I have to get back to work.'

'Before you leave you must see Julia's Garden,' Marge said. 'It's finished now.'

'I think you'll be impressed. Marge has done wonders with the flowers. We just have to figure a way of stopping the bloody hippos from eating them.'

All that remained of the original garden was the large Jacaranda tree that had shaded the back of the house. The foundations had been bulldozed out and replaced with a pond in the shape of an artist's palette; the many different colored flowers denoting the paint.

'We thought that as the plumbing was already here we may as well make use of it,' John explained to Chris. 'The fisheries section allocated the funds, so technically it's a hatching pond for Tilapia.'

A rustic bench made from a slab of raw timber stood on the section that protruded into the pond, and before it had been erected a simple white cross. A wreath of freshly cut blue and white Iris's was draped over the upright, partly concealing Julia's name, which had been burned into the crosspiece.

'It's where the kitchen used to be,' John explained. He had no need to elaborate. It was where Julia had been standing at the time of the attack.

'You've done a terrific job, Monty, thank you. Julia would have loved it.'

'It was mostly Marge's doing.' John tactfully excused himself and left to join his wife and Zarena at one of the new picnic tables overlooking the lake.

Chris sat on the bench, observing the simple cross. It seemed such an inadequate symbol for her life, yet he knew she would have approved. She had never been a pretentious person. And in reality, what difference did it make if it was a simple cross or a Cheopsian pyramid? No piece of wood or pile of stones could adequately symbolize her life. All it could do was serve as a reminder for those left behind. But he would never forget anyway.

Chris felt an overwhelming desire to talk to her. He

knew it was foolish, and he had an uneasy feeling that the desire was motivated by self pity, but there was so much he wanted her to know. And nothing he could say. He could not speak of his guilt, or of violence and tragedy. Neither seemed appropriate. But he felt so close to her there. To leave without saying anything would be like admitting he didn't love her.

'Oh, hell, Julia, you know how hopeless I am at this sort of thing…I love you…'

Walking away from the garden was one of the most difficult things Chris had ever had to do. He could not get over the feeling that he was turning his back on her. He struggled with his emotions. It was so unfair.

'I hope you'll bring young Tim next time you visit,' John Montgomery said quietly to Chris as they waited at the airstrip for the Lynx. Zarena and Marge were in a conversation of their own.

'I will,' Chris promised.

'And Zarena too... if she is still around.'

Chris looked at the warden with a sardonic smile. 'You and Fuli must be on the same wavelength. She won't be, Monty. She's here on business, and anyway, she's not my type.'

'That's a pity. She's a lovely girl.'

They sat together in the back of the Cherokee. Zarena was enthusiastic as the plane taxied to the end of the strip for take-off. 'I'm so glad you brought me here,' she said. 'Such nice people. Marge has promised to write.'

'That's nice,' Chris replied.

Zarena remained silent until they were airborne and the pilot had reduced power, allowing her to be heard without shouting. 'She told me all about Julia. I wish I had known her, Chris. You must have loved her very much.'

'More than you'll ever know,' Chris answered, and Zarena turned away quickly to stare out the window.

The ground below was already in shadow; the horizon obscured by purple haze; glowing red above. A bruised and bloodshot sky.

B ob McEwen poured more coffee for himself and Chris before turning on the television to catch the morning news. They had already gone through the morning papers. The evening television bulletin had made only brief mention of Chris and Zarena's exploits and, as with the newspapers, had not mentioned names or other details, which was normal. With the war situation, detailed information was always withheld for obvious security reasons. Nevertheless, as he was no longer in the army, and Zarena was a visitor, Chris wanted to be sure the government censor had been paying attention.

He accepted his coffee with a yawn. They had been up late, recounting their adventures to Bob and talking archaeology – or rather Zarena and Bob had. Chris had written a letter to the insurance company reporting the demise of Bravo Zulu – not that he expected compensation.

With their penchant for invoking the small print, he was sure the company would declare it an act of war. He had read the *Herald* a second time, then spent a restless night on the curator's lumpy couch in the study with its strong smell of dogs and pipe tobacco.

After meeting them at the airstrip and discussing the situation, Bob had suggested they stay with him, not only for the one night as arranged, but for a few extra days, to keep out of the way of reporters and give himself and Zarena an opportunity to replace her lost notes. Chris had accepted gratefully. It would give them both a chance to catch their breath.

As the news came on, Chris stared at the screen with sleepy disinterest, expecting to hear still more political rhetoric on the peace talks, but it was something different for a change.

'The Bishop of Victoria, the Right Reverend Percival Ladbroke, was killed late last night when the vehicle in which he was travelling struck a landmine on the road to St. Luke's Mission in the province of Victoria. Because of the late hour, no details are as yet available, but it is believed the Bishop was returning from a meeting in the capital. Two African teachers travelling with the Bishop were also killed in the explosion. A security force spokesman confirmed this was the third such incident in the area in the past month, and cautions the public again about restricting their travel between centres to main roads and escorted convoys, and to avoid travel in isolated areas after dusk, particularly on gravel roads where such incidents are more likely to occur.

'It was reported that evidence found at the scene, and in a subsequent follow-up by security forces, points to involvement by a Zanla group of terrorists who remain active in the area despite the recent death of their notorious commander, Silas Tongara, and several of his men.

'Bishop Ladbroke joined the church after graduating from Trinity College in nineteen thirty six and came to Rhodesia in nineteen sixty. His only living relative, a brother and prominent member of the British Labor Government, has been informed, but has so far refused to comment.

'In other news this morning, the minister for finance...'

'Hold on a minute...' Bob McEwen switched off the television, then quickly sorted through the stack of books and archaeological papers left on the coffee table from the previous evening. He picked up a thick tome and flipped through the pages until he found what he was looking for. He gave a grunt of satisfaction. 'I knew that struck a bell. What is it they say about running with thieves?'

'The same as they say about playing with fire, I think.'

'Quite. But in this instance it has another twist. Tell me where you've heard this before.' He recited directly from the book, using the stem of his pipe to punctuate each word. '... graduated from Trinity College in nineteen thirty six.'

'They just said it on the news. Must have used the same reference book.'

Bob McEwen held the book up with a triumphant smirk. 'This is a Who's Who of archaeology, my boy, and I was reading about our friend Sir Aubrey Fenton-Gower, director of the Fitzwilliam Museum. What would you like to bet they were as thick as thieves in university, along with the bishop's brother?'

Bob McEwen didn't wait for an answer. He strode towards the study and a few moments later was talking loudly on the telephone.

Chris yawned again and stretched. He wished Zarena would wake and take over. He was finding it hard to keep up with McEwen. He turned his attention to the Basset Hound sitting nearby, regarding him dolefully. 'I suppose I've got your chair as well,' Chris said, and the hound's droopy eyes took on an expression of reproach before it turned and flopped onto the floor with a groan. Chris echoed the groan with a smile. 'I know exactly how you feel.'

He gave up the chair and strolled along the wall of the lounge, looking at the curator's collection of pictures. He stopped in front of a team photograph. It had been taken in the entrance of a period stone building, and the caption above the list of players read: Edinburgh University Rugby Team -1944.

Looking for McEwen in the lines of boyish faces, Chris was suddenly struck by the notion he had seen a similar photograph not long before. He tried to recall where, but was distracted by Zarena coming into the room.

She had showered. Her face was shiny and glowing and her hair was turbaned in a towel. The blue dressing gown she had borrowed from McEwen was several sizes too large, showing only her fingertips and toes.

'You look like a young Ali Baba,' Chris greeted her, smiling cheerfully with the hope it would lighten the unpleasant atmosphere of the previous day. 'Sleep well?'

Her strained smile in return showed that it still lingered. 'Yes, thank you.'

'Half your luck. I had to share with Fred. The coffee is still hot. Bob's on the phone, as you can hear.'

She silently helped herself to coffee and Chris continued on the line of photographs until McEwen returned.

The curator was frustrated. 'That's the trouble with living in the boondocks. There's a five hour delay on all overseas calls.'

'Where are you calling?' Chris asked.

'Edinburgh. I'm going to ask Amanda to do some nosing around.'

'Oh? What do you want her to find out?' Zarena asked. 'I'd love to say hello.'

'Certainly, if we ever get through. Did Chris tell you about the bishop?'

'Not yet,' Chris answered for her. 'Why don't you fill her in, Bob. I'm still not sure what you're getting at.'

Zarena sat on a portion of the chair reclaimed by the Basset, coffee mug resting on her knee, and a frown of concentration on her childlike face as Bob McEwen recounted the news broadcast, and his theory about the bishop and Fenton-Gower knowing each other.

'It stands to reason they must have,' McEwen said.

'Everyone in a graduating class knows everyone else.'

Zarena glanced at Chris with a puzzled expression. 'I'm not sure I understand either.'

Bob McEwen sighed. 'And I thought you had an analytical brain. Well then, let's look at the facts and discount coincidence, shall we? Fact one. Fenton-Gower is the champion of the Bantu theory for the Zimbabwe Ruins. Fact two. Vital evidence, which could have challenged his theory mysteriously disappears while in his care. Fact three. New information found by Chris that could do the same, also disappears, but, and this is important, he doesn't have *all* the information. Fact four. The information he doesn't have is destroyed in a terrorist attack on a house that would not normally be a target. Fact Five. Fenton-Gower and the bishop were classmates. Fact six. The bishop has often been accused of aiding and abetting terrorists. Fact seven...' Bob McEwen paused. 'Do you see where I'm going with all of this?'

Zarena was skeptical. 'Are you saying that the bishop was responsible for Chris's house being blown up?'

'Indirectly. And not blown up, my dear, burned to the ground.'

Zarena looked at Chris in support of her disbelief, but his attention was elsewhere, on a line of photographs on the wall, and he appeared not to be listening.

'I can't imagine a bishop would be involved in such an atrocity,' Zarena said. 'And how would he know the evidence was in the house?'

I think I told him,' Chris said, and both Zarena and McEwen looked at him in bewilderment.'

'Isn't King's College also at Cambridge?'

'Of course, why do you ask?'.

'I know a man who was there at about the same time. An old man in army intelligence. He casually asked me where the stuff was, during a debriefing, and I told him.'

'By God!' McEwen slapped the table in excitement, rattling the crockery and giving Zarena such a start she spilled her coffee. 'Sorry dear, didn't mean to startle you... what's his name?'

'Garrett. I don't know his first name, but it opens up a whole new area. Our colonel in the scouts was convinced there was a spy somewhere high up in the army. Too many of our missions were compromised, and Garret's the top man in army intelligence.'

'I'll ask Amanda to check through university registrations or something for his name,' McEwen said. 'King's College in the thirties or early forties.'

'Just because they were all there at, or about the same time, still doesn't prove anything,' Zarena argued. 'The facts are fairly convincing, I know, but it still sounds rather far fetched to me. Bishops, terrorists, spies in high places. It's too circumstantial.'

'Even if it's true,' Chris said. 'There's not a hell of a lot we can do about it. We'd be in way over our heads. Look what they've managed to do already. And Zarena's right, it's too circumstantial. We're only assuming they knew each other, and even if they did, it *still* doesn't prove anything.'

'Don't you believe it, my boy. There's always a way.'

They sat pondering the problem in silence, the initial euphoria gone in the face of new hurdles.

Finally, Zarena looked up at Chris. 'Do you remember what you told me after we had crossed the river and I asked why you were staying behind? You said that survival depended on initiative. That you had to play the enemy at his own game and go hunting for him rather than the other way around. Surprise him and keep him guessing so that he is more worried about saving his own life than taking yours. Hit and run tactics, you called it.'

'I'm surprised you remember so well.'

Zarena smiled. 'I remember because I was frightened out of my wits.'

'Trauma learning,' McEwen mused. 'So what are you getting at, Zarena? Are you suggesting we take the initiative?'

'Yes. We do exactly what Chris does in the bush.'

'How? Where do we start?'

'Instead of calling Amanda, why don't we simply call Fenton-Gower and get the information we need from him?'

Bob McEwen raised his bushy eyebrows high in query. 'Oh? How do we do that?'

'We work on the assumption that they do all know each other,' Zarena said. 'It's likely that Fenton-Gower hasn't yet heard of the bishop's death if it only happened a few hours ago. It's the middle of the night in England. If you call him person to person using this Major Garrett's name, then inform him of the bishop's death, he is bound to react in some way, and it may give us a clue. If he doesn't respond you can hang up.'

This time McEwen only slapped his knee. 'By God, my girl, what a brilliant, sneaky little devil you are!'

Chris grinned. 'I think I'm going to recommend you for a commission in the scouts. You've already passed the selection course with weapon handling, forced marching, anti-tracking and bush survival, and we can call the assault course that part where you had to hang on my shoulder. Now you've just completed tactics. They should make you a captain at least.'

Zarena flushed under the heap of praise. 'Only a helpless woman doing her best,' she murmured, and both McEwen and Chris bellowed with laughter.

'May God protect us from helpless women.'

They worked on the details over scrambled eggs and a fresh pot of coffee.

'Only a few problems,' Chris said. 'I can't speak like a toff, I don't know Garrett's first name, and there's a five hour delay getting through. By then Fenton-Gower may have heard the news. Also, we don't know the number.'

Zarena solved them swiftly. 'Directory enquiries will get us the number. There can only be one Sir Aubrey Fenton-Gower living in Cambridge, surely, and we can tell the operator the truth. It's an urgent call to inform someone of a sudden death. They should put you through immediately. If you simply call yourself Major Garrett and sort of whisper, as if you didn't want to be overheard, it might work.'

Chris had been watching her steadily throughout, intrigued by the sparkle in her eyes and the color in her cheeks. He had never seen her looking so animated – or so attractive.

Zarena lost some of her confidence under his scrutiny and finished with an uncertain shrug. 'I think it will, anyway.'

'It will,' Chris said, giving her a winning smile. 'You're a star.'

'A superstar,' McEwen amended. 'Let's get on with it then, shall we?'

Chris recited his rehearsed sorry tale to the operator, then waited anxiously. She returned, sympathetic, to say she could do nothing. Fenton-Gower's private number was unlisted.

'You mean you don't have it?' Chris asked, putting on a plaintive voice.

'We are unable to give it out, sir.'

'But I have to speak to him, operator,' Chris pleaded. 'It will be a terrible shock if he hears about his relative's murder on the news.'

'Yes, I understand, Major Garrett. I'll see if I can persuade the British operator to call him. I will have to give your name.'

'Of course, but please tell them not to say why I am calling. I must break the news to him personally. He has a weak heart, you know.' Chris pulled a hopeful face at Zarena and McEwen, who were watching expectantly, and received nods of encouragement in return.

'You're through, Major Garrett, speak up please.'

Chris whispered hoarsely, close into the mouthpiece. 'Hello? Aubrey?'

'Clarry? Is that you? Good heavens! I haven't spoken to you for years. Is something wrong? The operator said it was urgent.' The cultured voice was so clear it could have been coming from the next room.

'Bad news, I'm afraid. Did you...'

'Can you speak louder, Clarry? I can hardly hear you.'

Chris raised his voice a little. 'Can't speak louder... may be overheard. Percy Ladbroke has been killed.'

After a short silence. 'Good Lord! Percy is dead?'

'Afraid so. Killed by a landmine only a few hours ago. Thought you should know.' Chris widened his eyes at his attentive audience and nodded in affirmation.

'Yes, thank you, Clarry. Good heavens, how terrible. Has Roly been informed?'

'It was the same gang of terrorists that Percy recruited to burn down the house and destroy the papyri.'

This time the silence was much longer, and Chris realized he had gone too far. He pulled a face of frustration at his audience. Then Fenton-Gower spoke again in a much stronger voice. 'I'm not sure I know what you mean. Is this some sort of prank?'

'No, Sir Aubrey,' Chris said in his normal voice. 'This is no joke, it's serious, and I've just proved that you *do* know all about it.'

'I don't know what you're talking about. Who is this?'

'This is Chris Ryan, *Sir* Aubrey, whose wife you had murdered to protect your rotten reputation. But it's not going to work, *Sir* Aubrey, because Julia died for nothing. I still have the papyri and a whole lot of other stuff to throw at you in Nairobi. I'm going to blow your reputation right out of existence, you slimy bastard!'

Chris almost slammed the phone down in his anger. Then he caught himself and returned the receiver to his ear in time to hear a faint 'Oh, my God, no,' before the line went static. He replaced the receiver and looked at the others. McEwen's face was impassive, but Zarena was still staring at him with her hand over her mouth.

'I forgot to tell you,' Chris said to her. 'When you have the enemy on the run, always press home the attack.' Then he grinned sheepishly at them both. 'Unfortunately, I got a bit carried away.'

Sir Aubrey replaced the receiver and sat staring at the phone for long moments, suspended in shock and disbelief. It was too much to accept that such an innocuous and familiar piece of grey plastic could, in the space of only a few heartbeats, cause such anguish. It was a betrayal. It was his own instrument, squatting complacently on its crocheted doily next to the bedside lamp. A piece of modern electronic gadgetry meant for his own convenience, yet it had become the instrument used by someone from across the world to shatter his life. It was so unreasonable.

Sir Aubrey was not a violent man, and seldom emotional. Anger rarely stirred his blood, but this was too much. He lifted the telephone in both hands and hurled it on the floor, then he buried his face in his hands. It was not meant to be like that. Not killing and bloodshed. He had made them promise there would be none of that. And Percy of all people. A man of God who had sworn to uphold the sanctity of life. It was impossible to ask that he bear the responsibility for their betrayal of his trust. He had told them, but they had taken the matter into their own hands on his behalf.

He had to talk to Dickie, but the telephone was in three pieces and no longer working. Nevertheless, Sir Aubrey assembled it as best he could and replaced it on its doily, then he dressed, switched off the bedside light and left the flat.

A security guard startled him as he was fitting his key into the service door of the museum. 'Good morning, sir, making an early start?'

'Morning? What time is it?'

'A quarter after one. No rest for the wicked, hey sir?'

Sir Aubrey nodded absent-mindedly and let himself in, locking the door again behind him. They used to have night watchmen and coal braziers. Now they had security guards and guns.

He went to his office and opened the safe, removing a key, which he then took down to the repository room to open another safe. He extracted a flat wooden box, locked the safe, then returned to his office. He made himself a cup of watery cocoa in the staff room, then set to work, starting on the pile of correspondence in his in-tray. He put off calling Dickie until he was finished. No point in both of them having a sleepless night.

Grey light was showing at the two windows by the time Sir Aubrey's tasks were completed; two neat stacks of documents to be filed and mailed, including a parcel. All that remained in the tray - which was no longer required - was the final draft of his presentation to the Pan African Congress in Nairobi.

Sir Aubrey took one of the stacks to the mail room, then switched off the light on his desk and sat in his armchair to watch the encroaching dawn. The panes were streaked and spotted with drizzle. Another miserable day by the look of it.

He thought of what he would say to Dickie when he called him, or if he would even bother to call him at all. It seemed so pointless now, and Dickie was not the person he used to be. His years in the secret service business had changed him, eaten away at the softness within to leave only the brittle shell.

But was he any different? Had he not also changed? Then he realized he hadn't. He had only become older. Another relic in the museum. Perhaps he should have been renovated like the club. Old oak and worn leather replaced by smoky glass and chrome.

Percy's body, or what was left of it, would be flown back for burial. The Archbishop would no doubt conduct the service, unknowing. He wondered what they would do for himself when his time came. Perhaps simply burn him on a pyre of his worthless papers. That would be a fitting conclusion for an ancient relic without worth, and what difference would it make in the end? God would never forgive him. And God would certainly never forgive Percy.

B ob McEwen persuaded one of his elderly lady friends to watch over the museum so he could help Zarena recompile her list of questions for the Nairobi conference. ' I haven't had so much fun in years,' he chortled happily to her.

Left to his own devices, Chris also made a list. So much had happened in such a short time that his mind seemed to be bulging at the seams, yet when he sat on the chair with Fred Bassett, a pen and blank sheet of paper folded on his knee, he could think of only two things to write; check on Baron and call colonel. He wrote neither. He relinquished his share of the cushion and went to the telephone.

He called Mount Hampden to check progress on the Baron and was informed it was ready and waiting, and that Billy Steel had called several times. He told them he would be there next day and left the phone number in case Billy wanted him urgently, then he called the operations clerk at Andre Rabie Barracks.

Corporal Barnes was one of those people no army could function without. He was the epitome of Corporal Radar O'Reilly of MASH 4077, even to his small stature. Chris sometimes wondered if Barney also slept with a teddy bear.

'Er... excuse me for asking, sir,' the corporal said hesitantly, 'but are you operational?'

'Not officially, Barney.' The corporal knew very well he wasn't operational. He was simply letting him know that he mustn't ask too much.

'Was that you they were talking about on the news, sir?'

'It depends on who's asking, Barney.'

'Wow! Great stuff, sir! The colonel suspected it was you. He was jumping up and down for a while, mainly because of the reporters. He called the bloke from the Herald a bullshit artist.'

Chris laughed. 'That sounds like the colonel. When you see him, tell him I need to speak to him urgently on a security matter.'

He gave McEwen's telephone number and was about to hang up when he suddenly had a thought. 'What do you know about Bishop Ladbroke and the landmine, Barney?'

'Only what came in on the sitrep, sir, which was the same as on the news, and a request from Repulse to check our Zanla weapons register for an AK match. They recovered one at the scene.'

'Were you able to match it?'

'Yes, sir, it came from one of Tongara's men. Slack bastards. Was he really eaten by hyenas?'

'Hyenas aren't fussy about what they eat.'

'Wow! By the way sir, do you know that Sergeant Mafiko picked up the two terrs you wounded? He called for instructions. He thinks one of them can be turned around.'

Chris was surprised. 'No, I didn't even know Oscar was in the area. What's he doing down there?'

'He's been temporarily seconded to help organize the new batch of Shangaan recruits into tracking teams.'

Chris was disappointed he had not seen him at Chiredzi when he and Zarena were there. He and Oscar had never been close friends as such. The gap in their cultures was too wide and their personal lives outside of the army too different. Their relationship had been a working one of mutual respect and trust. In the bush they had shared a special bond and, as he thought about it, Chris began to get the feeling that something was not quite right. It was more intuitive than anything, but it was strong.

'You wouldn't happen to know who did the follow-up on that landmine incident, would you Barney?'

'No, sir.'

'I wish I had known Oscar was down there, I would have made a point of seeing him. He owes me at least a dozen beers. Do you have a number you can reach him on?'

'Only the special branch number at Com-Ops Repulse, sir. That's where he called from yesterday.'

'You wouldn't like to do me a favor and call them would you? Leave a message for Oscar to phone me at this number... the one I gave you earlier.'

'No problem, if you want to hang on, I'll call them now on another line and let you know if he's there.'

As he waited, Chris wondered if he was not being

paranoid. After what he had learned from this morning about Fenton-Gower, the bishop and Garrett, he was beginning to suspect everyone. But putting things together like McEwen had, it did not seem too fanciful an idea. Oscar had found the two wounded terrorists and questioned them, or he wouldn't have mentioned the possibility of turning one around. If the man he questioned had told him that Tongara had received his orders to burn Chris's house from the bishop, it would not be unlike Oscar to do something about it. Scouts took care of each other, that was the code. It was what caused the bond. And why would Tongara's men blow up one of their most helpful allies?

Corporal Barnard returned on the line with the news Chris had half been expecting to hear. 'Sergeant Mafiko went on the landmine follow-up, sir. They lost tracks in the mission complex. Too much foot traffic.' The corporal's voice took on a contemplative tone. 'Sir? You don't think Sergeant Mafiko...'

'No, Barney, I don't, and I don't think you should either.'

'I don't get paid to think, sir.'

'Yes you do, Barney. And not enough. Now ask the colonel to call me, it's important. Tell him not to use any of the usual lines, and you be careful what you say on the phone, too, Barney.'

'Is this some sort of spy thing, Lieutenant?'

'The walls have ears, Corporal.'

'Jeeze...'

Chris replaced the receiver thoughtfully. It was still

only an educated guess, but he would be willing to bet a lot more than a dozen beers that it was Oscar who had planted the mine that had killed the bishop.

Chris said nothing to Zarena or McEwen about his suspicions. Not even after McEwen's overseas call to Amanda Pritchard came through and she told him that she had heard on the morning news that Sir Aubrey Fenton-Gower had shot himself.

'I really don't think we can do much with all of this now,' Zarena said, indicating the scattered papers and books on the table. 'We won't win any friends by trying to discredit a man who has just committed suicide. Maybe at the next conference, when things have eased off a little.'

'I can't help feeling responsible,' Chris said. 'If I hadn't called him he would probably still be alive.'

'Nonsense, my boy. It was his guilty conscience that pulled the trigger. It just proves we were right.'

'I suppose it would be too much to ask that he left a note confessing everything.'

'If he had they would have mentioned it, I'm sure, Chris.'

'There are still a few things that worry me. Fenton-Gower said he hadn't spoken to me... I mean Major Garrett, for years, and he sounded really shocked when I told him he was responsible for Julia's death. Oh, God, no, were his actual words. I somehow got the impression he was genuinely upset. Maybe there are other people involved that we don't know about. He did mention one name. He asked if Roly had been informed.'

'That'll be Roland Ladbroke, the bishop's brother,' McEwen said. He's an MP.

'Maybe he's the one who arranged it.'

Well, whoever it is, if there is anyone, it's unlikely we'll ever find out, and even if we do, there won't be much we can do about it. And the same goes for them. They know you're onto it, and if they were only trying to protect their pal, Fenton-Gower, there's nothing more to worry about. If you ask me, I think it's all over. At least as far as the papyri is concerned. Your hit and run tactics worked too well, Zarena.'

'At least we've done as much as we can and have the notes if we need them. Meanwhile, I'm starved.'

'I think you two deserve a break,' McEwen said. 'Chris, why don't you take Zarena to Leopard Rock tomorrow and show her the mountains. Take the car, I won't be needing it. I have a pile of work waiting.'

'I'm supposed to pick up the plane tomorrow.'

'Surely, after what the two of you have been through in the past week they can wait another day. A bit of R and R will do you good.'

Chris was about to refuse when the idea took hold and he changed his mind. Another day would make no difference, and it would give Zarena the opportunity of buying a few clothes and seeing a different part of the country. 'Thanks, Bob, you've got a deal, but you'll have to lend me some cash, my travelers checks went up in smoke.'

They cleared the table and ordered in fish and chips in time to watch the evening news, but heard no more about the bishop than they had already throughout the day; a litany of praise by religious leaders and mealy-mouthed politicians for the bishop's unstinting dedication, and vehement propaganda-style denials of involvement from Robert Mugabe speaking from Maputo. For once he was right, Chris thought wryly.

No mention was made of Sir Aubrey Fenton-Gower's suicide.

'All a bit of an anticlimax, don't you feel?' Bob McEwen remarked.

The colonel did not call until after nine, when they were all contemplating bed. Chris took the phone and held it away from his ear.

'What's all this cloak and dagger bullshit, Chris? I've been up to my arse in crocodiles all day and what's left of it is now getting frozen off in a bloody call box.''Sorry about that, sir, but I...'

'And what about this Errol Flynn crap you've been pulling? I've had reporters on my back all day as well. Am I supposed to be your bloody agent or something? And what the hell are you doing here anyway, you crazy bugger? You're supposed to be in Kenya.'

Chris talked solidly for the next ten minutes without interruption, and he knew the colonel would remember every word he said. He told him everything that had happened from the day he arrived at the Zimbabwe ruins with Zarena. He stopped short of mentioning his suspicions about Oscar's involvement in the landmine incident, though. The colonel did not approve of his men taking the law into their own hands. At the end, the only response he received was an emphatic, 'Jesus H Christ.' Strong words from the colonel, who did not normally blaspheme.

'Major Garrett has to be the one responsible for some of our missions being compromised, sir,' Chris said. 'No one else had all the relevant information.'

'I think you're right, Chris. I never did like the bastard, but we may be too late. He failed to turn up for a briefing this morning. He's probably been warned and has left the country.' The colonel's voice sounded tired. 'Maybe I should start thinking about doing the same.'

Should she apologies? The question plagued Zarena as they flew north above the shining length of Lake Malawi on their return journey to Kenya. It had been on her mind since the previous day in the Vumba mountains.

Chris had gone out of his way to be pleasant, taking her shopping and buying her the yellow dress she was now wearing, more underclothes than she needed, a pair of denims, and several tee shirts, one with a comical yellow hippopotamus and the words 'Rhodesia is Super' printed on the front. Then he had realized she couldn't wear it and had taken it back. 'If you flaunt that around in Kenya they'll probably arrest you as a spy,' he had joked.

They had negotiated the winding road of the green mountains while singing along to the Beatles, pausing at the top in the crisp, bracken-scented air to look out over the vast plains of Mozambique while they waited for the tired engine of the old Peugeot to cool down.

The hotel at Leopard Rock was like something out of another world. It had literally taken her breath away. A Swiss chalet against a backdrop of lush jungle-covered mountain instead of snow, with sweeping green lawns and gardens of blue hydrangeas. Even a stone castle nestled amongst the giant trees on the hill to complete the illusion of a lost fairyland.

It was so majestic and peaceful, it seemed impossible there could be a war going on, until Chris showed her the scars on the walls from bullets and mortars. It had saddened her to have her illusion shattered. It was not a peaceful fairyland after all, only a remote part of a lost empire, war-torn and forlorn.

But it was still beautiful, and they had strolled around soaking up the atmosphere and building an appetite for the delicious lunch, which was served by a jovial African waiter in a starched white uniform and green cummerbund. 'Almost as good as raw liver and gut juice served in a shoe,' Chris had joked, and they had laughed for longer than the joke was worth, purging themselves.

Then he had spoiled it.

He had surprised her by taking her hand across the

table. The romantic gesture, and the way he had smiled had, for a terrifying moment, made her think he was going to say something embarrassing.

'We've been through a lot together, haven't we?' he had said, squeezing her hand and stroking the fingers. 'More than most people go through in a lifetime.'

She had replied with something inane, distracted and more conscious of his brown hand covering hers on the starched white napkin than what she was saying. She had not known how to respond, whether to remove her hand or return his squeeze, so she did nothing, letting it lie there like a limp fish while she glanced around the dining room to see if anyone was watching. No one was.

It was so absurd. They had been in much closer physical contact than touching hands, but the implication had thrown her completely.

'Do you really think it's a good idea to go looking for your mother in France? You have no idea where she is anyway, and besides, it's hellish expensive and full of Frenchmen. And what about your new job?'

'You forget that I am half French,' she had responded, more abruptly than she had intended, but it had given her the opportunity to remove her hand.

'I didn't mean it like that, it was a joke. I was just hoping to change your mind.'

'Why?'

'I guess I've got sort of used to having you around.'

'Is this some sort of proposition?'

She had held her stern expression and the question had evidently flustered him, making him frown, then he had shrugged. 'Who knows? Anyway, I'm going to send for Tim. I'd like you to meet him.'

That was when it ended. Until then it had been so enjoyable and, so she had thought at the time, innocent. But making the assumption she had nothing to do with her life except wait for him in case he needed her, and then the realization that everything before had been only to soften her up, and that he only wanted her around to look after his son, was too much.

Perhaps she had overreacted, and maybe the anger was born of disappointment that he should take their unique friendship for granted, but whatever the reason, it was still anger.

'I'll tell you who knows, Chris. I do. If you think I am going to wait around until your need overcomes your guilt, you're mistaken. And I *do* happen to know how much you loved your wife, but I did not ask anything of you, and I expect nothing, least of all your patronage. You hurt me for no reason. If I gave you the impression I was interested, I apologies. We are friends... or at least we were. That's all. Now I think we should leave.'

She had said too much, and he had said nothing, remaining silent for all the endless drive home, and he had not spoken to her since except where absolutely necessary, and then politely.

Several times she had almost apologized, mainly for

Bob McEwen's sake, for he was uncomfortable with the atmosphere and obviously distressed by their attitude towards each other, but she had not. That morning at the airport, as Chris was checking over the plane, Bob had smothered her in a bear hug and spoken gruffly in his usual direct way.

'You are right for each other you know. Maybe you are both still too fragile to realize it yet, but you will. Give him time, my girl, and send me an invitation.'

But Bob McEwen was wrong. They were not right for each other. Or more to the point, Zarena corrected herself, she was not right for him. She had been adapting all her life - and what had been her own life did not seem all that exciting now - but she could not compete with his dead wife, either emotionally or physically.

Bob's less than subtle suggestion they get married was ludicrous. She could feign her desire to please him, as she knew many circumcised women did, but she could not hide the ugly mutilation done to her. That she would have to live with forever, as she would the shame that went with it. Shame and embarrassment that would surface every time he wanted to have sex with her. Sooner or later he would realize she was not the woman he expected and would become disillusioned. He would seek the company of other women – complete women - and she could never adapt to that.

The more Zarena considered apologizing, the less she felt inclined to. It would only lead to further misunderstanding and unpleasantness, so perhaps it was best to simply let it go. The moving finger writes, and having writ, moves on, is what Hugh would have recited. What had been written in blood could not be washed away by tears.

Saturated with phosphorous and sulphur, chlorine and soda, the water boiled and spurted from the fissures of the volcanic cauldron and ran into the depressions of the Great Rift Valley - a ten thousand kilometer scar on the face of Africa - to form the shallow lakes rich in blue green algae that only the firebirds could consume.

But not even the firebirds could drink the noxious water. That, decreed Mother Nature, they must find elsewhere, for balance must be strictly maintained. For every cause an effect, for every action a reaction. There were to be no free meals.

So every day the firebirds took to the air, leaving behind, for a few short hours, the steaming water of the hot green lakes; flying south to the cooler, less caustic lakes where they could drink, bathe and preen the soda deposits from their feathers, which was also a cause of balance, for without the sulphur and beta carotene there would be no colorful plumage to fire the imagination. From ugliness, beauty.

For the beautiful firebirds it was a life of tragedy and hardship. A life where overnight the spirolina on which they fed could froth and die, when they would have to depart in search of other, more remote lakes, leaving behind those too weak or too young, to perish.

And only the hot water would do; where predators

would not enter. Steaming lakes in which they would raise their young on small mounds of mud under the scorching sun, where there was no respite from the unrelenting heat and thirst, and no escape from the eagles. And when the young in their still drab plumage grew too large to feed, but too young to fly, they walked to the drinking water. A multitude of ethereal grey shapes materializing from the primordial steam to sustain the legend of the phoenix. And perhaps that was the worst time of all for, defenseless against the predators, thousands perished.

But for those that survived, the balance of life would turn, bringing joy and a time for courtship and mating. A time for dancing.

Hugh had left the Land-Rover for them at the airport. A message on the windscreen informed them the key was at the briefing office and he would see them back at the lodge for dinner.

They drove with an oppressive silence between them; Zarena staring out of the side window, and Chris clenching the wheel and glaring ahead, both clinging stubbornly to their pride.

Chris was becoming thoroughly fed up with it. In the plane it was not so bad, but alone with each other in the vehicle, the uncomfortable atmosphere was getting to him. On a few occasions he had been on the point of apologizing, just to break the monotony and see what would happen, but could not quite bring himself to do it. He did not feel he had done anything to apologies for. His intentions had been nothing but honorable. She, on the other hand, had taken it the wrong way and jumped all over him. He did not need any more drama in his life. She could go look for her mother in France and bloody good luck to her.

He saw the flamingos as they were passing through the foothills; a vast shadow flashing with pink in the afternoon sun, gliding down towards one of the many caustic lakes that dotted the valley floor like scattered emeralds. He glanced across at Zarena to see if she had noticed, but she was either asleep or pretending to be, her head turned away and her arms folded.

The flamingos had not been there for years, Hugh had told him. Chris had seen them on a few occasions when flying, but had never had the opportunity to observe them from close range. He acted on impulse. When he reached the broken down sign of the Magadi Soda Company, he turned onto the rough track leading to the lake.

'Where do you think you're going?' Zarena asked stiffly.

'Don't worry, I'm not going to abduct you. I want to have a look at something. You may even be interested to have a look yourself.'

She did not answer, resuming her indifferent staring out of the side window, and they bounced along in silence as far as the last small rise before the lake, when Chris switched off the engine and coasted down into a dip where the lake was still hidden from view.

'What now?'

'If you want to see you'll have to walk up the bank. It will be worth it, I promise you.'

'No thanks, I'll wait here.'

'Please yourself.'

Chris climbed the short incline and looked down. From where he stood, the lake's edge was less than a stone's throw away, yet for twice that distance at least, the green water was invisible under a giant swathe of pink; a feathery beach that followed the perimeter of the lake until it turned out of sight half a kilometer away.

Absorbed in the spectacle, he was unaware that Zarena had followed until he heard her gasp of surprise. 'Flamingos!'

'The firebirds of Africa.'

'There must be thousands of them.'

'More than a million, I'd say.'

'The colors... so beautiful...'

They had not arrived too soon. As they watched, a ripple of movement began at the far end. It spread rapidly through the flock towards them. The birds had stopped drinking and were moving, walking about in a seemingly aimless fashion.

'I hope they're not going to fly away,' Zarena murmured.

A pattern had begun to emerge from the aimless wandering. Groups of birds had formed into lines, following each other and mingling with other groups that were doing the same. As a line moved, so another moved in an opposing direction, heads dipping and twisting in a flowing, rhythmical wave of intermingling circles, as if in some gigantic and stately cotillion.

'What is it... what's happening?'

'They're dancing,' Chris answered. 'Hugh told me, but I never thought I'd ever see it.'

Zarena glanced at him, disbelieving. 'Dancing?'

'It's the mating season.'

Looking at the puzzled expression on her face - a mixture of disbelief and wonder - Chris felt he should say something to break whatever it was that was threatening their friendship. Life was too short. 'Zarena…'

'Look! Something is happening...'

The birds were starting to fly. Threads of white appeared on the surface of the lake as, necks astrain, they ran and scrambled aloft, a few at first, then in ever increasing numbers until the shallow lake was a frenzy of flapping wings and frothing water.

They rose slowly higher, turning in unison like the unfurling of a giant banner, sweeping back across the lake and turning it dark with their shadow. Again they turned, swirling and wheeling, one moment a thin dark line, the next a broad and dazzling band of pink

'It looks like they're still dancing!' Zarena exclaimed.

Four times the flock circled the lake, performing their flamboyant aerial display then, as if the music had suddenly ended, they turned away towards the north.

Zarena and Chris watched silently until the flock had disappeared and the lake was still and silent. The wonder of it holding them, both reluctant to return to where the ghosts of their argument lurked.

'I have never seen anything so beautiful.' Zarena said softly.

'I have,' Chris said, taking her hand.

'Have you? It must have been...' She saw his expression and stopped. For a moment she held his eyes, then she looked away. She tried to withdraw her hand, but he held on to it, pulling her gently towards him. He did not try to kiss her. He simply held her close, inhaling the sweet almond scent of her hair, and she returned his hug briefly, her body stiff and unyielding, as if she was in a hurry to break away and was only responding so as not to hurt his feelings and, disheartened, Chris let her go.

On the road again, and to prevent them falling back into the silence, Chris told her what he knew of the flamingos. 'They have a hard life. The nests are built on mounds of mud in the hot lake so the hyenas and jackals can't get to them. It's so hot they have to keep changing legs, and if a chick happens to fall in the water...'

'No, please... I don't want to hear any more. You're spoiling it.'

The silence returned, and Chris finally resigned himself to the fact they could only be friends... maybe not even that. 'Cheer up,' he said. 'At least we can still be friends, can't we?'

When she did not answer, he glanced at her. She was still gazing out of her open window as if she had not heard, but her fingers plucked and twisted nervously together on her lap.

'Stop the car,' she said.

'What?' Against the grinding of the engine in four-wheel drive he could not be sure he had heard correctly.

'*Please*... stop the car.'

There was no mistaking her that time. Chris brought the Land-Rover to a halt.

'Switch off the engine.'

Chris turned the key and the vehicle shuddered into silence. 'Look, I apologies if I said the wrong thing, but if you're going to give me another lecture, save your breath. I've got the message.'

'Nothing like that.' She studied his face earnestly. 'We are good friends, aren't we, Chris?'

'Yes, of course... I guess so.'

'I want you to do something for me... as a friend.'

'What is it?'

'You don't have to, if you don't want to. I won't be offended if you refuse.'

'How can I if I don't know what it is?'

'I'm really embarrassed about having to ask you, but you're the only male friend I have. I know we've had our differences and that you think I'm a cold fish, but there is something I have to know, and you're the only one I can trust to help me... as a friend.'

'Zarena...'

She took a deep breath, coming to a sudden decision. 'I want you to have sex with me.'

'You *what?*'

'You know… make love to me.' Her tone was even, her face pale and taught, and she stared straight ahead. 'That is… if you want to… of course.'

'Look, Zarena, I didn't have that in mind when…'

'No.' She turned to face him, her expression showing a hint of uncertainty. 'I'm assuming a lot, I know, and I will not be offended if you refuse. God, I hate having to do this… but I need to know.'

'Zarena, you don't have to do anything.'

'Chris please… listen to me. This is not easy. What you said at the hotel… about us going through so much together, it's true. You are probably my dearest friend, and I'm asking this only as a friend. I could never ask this of another man.'

'Jesus, Zarena.'

'There are things you don't know about me, Chris. Things I don't even know myself. I was hoping we could go through this last trial together so I could find out. I know you still love your wife. It's one of the things I admire about you, so I'll understand if you don't want to.'

Chris studied her face, smiling.

'What?'

'Your analytical brain.' He rescued one of her hands from being mauled by the other and held it secure. 'Yes, I did love her, I guess I always will, but there are also things you don't know about me. The night she was killed… well, I was visiting Marge and John Montgomery. Marge's niece was there from South Africa… I can't even remember her name, but she made it plain she was available and I stayed longer than I should have. I made plans to meet her the next day, and I know damned well I would have been unfaithful. Had I left earlier, maybe I could have saved Julia's life. So you see, I'm not all that honorable.'

'You may also have been killed. But yes, I can see how you would feel. I'm sorry.'

'I feel guilty as hell, Zarena. I loved her. We had something special, but she's gone and there's nothing I can do about it.'

'I understand. Perhaps it will be best if we just forget about the whole thing.'

'Life must go on, Zarena... for both of us. I'll do whatever you want...and as a friend if you want it that way, but I would rather it was a bit more.'

For long moments she looked thoughtfully down at their clasped hands, fidgeting nervously with his fingers. 'I'm not so sure anymore, Chris. I have never been with a man. Until I met you the thought of having sex frightened me. It still does, in a way. I had resigned myself to becoming an old maid and involving myself in my work. I don't have the same desires as other women.' She paused to take a deep breath and let it out in a long sigh. 'At least I don't think I do. I just don't know...'

'Why... what don't you know?'

'I've never thought about it much… in that way... except once. That's why I'm no longer sure.'

'Oh, when was that?'

She smiled. 'Never mind, It's not important.'

'Was it with me?'

She nodded, shy.

'Are you going to tell me, or must I guess?'

'It really doesn't matter.'

'Was it when you were removing the thorns?'

'You knew?'

'Not exactly, but I had a feeling, a good feeling, and if you had known what was happening as you were rubbing cream on backside you would have been shocked. So what did you feel?'

'Not excited or anything, if that's what you mean. I'm not physically like other women you may have known. I was not truthful with you in Qena. When I was ill and you took me away from the Sheikh I told you they had done things to me so I could not get pregnant. In a way that's true, I may not be able to have children, but they did other things as well. Terrible things that they do to women there.'

'Are you talking about your circumcision and infibulation?'

Zarena stared at him in surprise. 'You know about that?'

'The doctor told me.'

'I told her not to say anything.'

'Don't blame her, she had no choice. I had to know so I could take care of you if in case of a relapse. And she wanted me to know in case I had sex on my mind.'

'What else did she tell you?'

'Only that you would get no satisfaction, but there

429

shouldn't be any pain.'

'She said that? God. If only you knew how I was feeling right now.'

'You're not going to cry on me are you?'

'Can I have no secrets of my own?'

Chris tilted her chin and grinned at her. 'None.' He kissed her briefly on the cheek – a friendly kiss. It was too soon for more. 'If you still want to go through with it, I'll organize a nice candlelit dinner for tonight to set the mood, then we can go to my cabin. But not as a friend. It's more than that.'

She squeezed his hand. 'You make it easier, thank you. But if you don't mind, I would like it to be now, without too much planning. I don't want to think about it. I just want to do it.'

'Here?' Chris glanced around the Land-Rover. 'It's not the most comfortable place... not much room.'

.'No, not here. Back there, where we saw those wonderful flamingoes.'

Chris reversed back, at the same time digging surreptitiously in his bag on the back seat for something they could lie on.

'Don't expect too much and you won't be disappointed,' he cautioned her as they climbed the bank. 'Making love is not just a one-off, satisfaction thing, even for me. Sharing and being fulfilled is what it's all about.'

'Yes, but if I ask you to stop, will you?'

Chris laughed and rolled his eyes at her, 'That, I can't

promise.'

She stood hesitantly by as he spread a towel over the grass. 'Must I take off my dress?'

'No need for that, leave everything to me. First we must get the mood right.' He took her in his arms and held her close. 'Nervous?'

She nodded against his chest. 'Petrified.'

'Me too. He stepped back. 'Would Madame care to dance?' He took her hand and, holding it high, began swinging it and counting. 'One, two, three. One, two, three...'

She giggled uncertainly. 'What are you doing...?'

He began to hum the Blue Danube waltz, stepping in time to his humming and forcing her to step along with him, and she moved reluctantly, shy and awkward, but he held her hand firm and led her slowly.

She picked up the timing and laughed again, more openly. 'You look so serious!'

'Shush! I'm concentrating... One, two, three...' Changing hands, he turned and waltzed around her, then he pulled her close, continuing to rock to the imaginary waltz as he caressed her softly, lovingly.

Hesitantly at first, she pressed against him, feeling, then, when the tension had gone from her body and she relaxed in his arms, he kissed her, gently coaxing her lips for response and, when they finally parted and it came freely, passionately, he knew it was time.

Hugh Hilderbrand reluctantly closed his volume of the *Ruba'iyat of Omar Khayyam* and flicked the switch to respond to the radio call from Air Gabon. 'This is Kilo Base. Go ahead.'

'A message from Mister Billy, Kilo Base. Our French contacts have found the person you asked about... over.'

Hugh answered quickly, disbelieving. 'Claudia Menard? They found her?'

'She is at the Musee Oceanographique in Monaco. Mister Billy says one crate of beer will not be enough. It must be champagne.' Mama Tembo giggled. 'Over...'

'Ah, love, could thou and I with fate conspire.'

'Say again, Mister Hugh?'

'Nothing, Mama T, except a special thanks. I'll pass on the good news. Out'

Hugh switched off and sat back with closed eyes and a sigh of contentment, his cherished volume of verse forgotten for the moment, but not the words, which he mouthed silently, a satisfied smile on his moving lips.

As the Air France Boeing leveled out from its climbing turn onto a northerly heading, the cabin speakers chimed softly and the captain's voice, calm and self-assured, informed the passengers they would see Mount Kenya from the starboard windows.

The young woman in the yellow dress did not lean

forward and turn in her seat for a final glimpse of the snow-capped mountain as did the others. She looked the other way, at something no one else could have seen far below. A lake of emerald green and, along its shores, a crescent of pink. Threads of silver streaked the green; another flight taking off and heading north. Had they danced before leaving she wondered? And the thought stirred a memory of another dancer and another flamingo from another time. How strange, she thought, that the lives of the flamingos and her own life should have mingled so symbolically in both sadness and joy.

The flight attendant stopped the drink trolley next to the row where the young woman sat twisting her fingers. 'Something to drink, Mademoiselle?'

When no answer came, the attendant leaned across to touch the girl gently on the shoulder. 'Mademoiselle? would you like... oh, pardon, I did not realize... are you all right?'

But through the tears the girl was also smiling. A wistful, yet bright smile that belied the attendant's concern.

'No, everything is just wonderful, thank you.'

Printed in Great Britain
by Amazon

40156764R00249